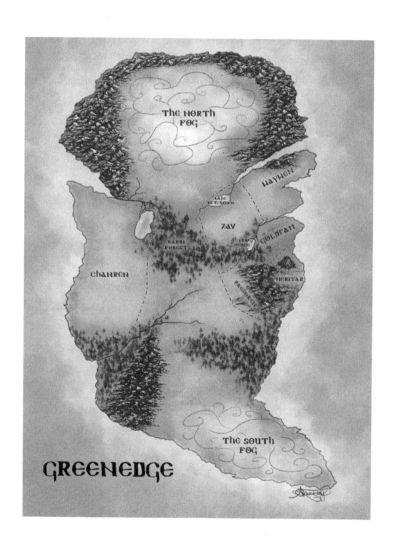

THE NORTH
FOG

HAYHEN

LAKE
OF TORRAW

ZAV

COLMAH

KARRI
FOREST

LAKE
HORM

HERITAR

CHANREN

FRIDDRICH

THE SOUTH
FOG

GREENEDGE

Prologue

There were several theories as to what could've created the Bastial crater, all of which were derived from the only two facts they knew: There was an earthquake and then an explosion.

And such an explosion it was. Shattered pieces of mountain the size of statues rained down on the Elves in Meritar and the Humans of Goldram, killing many and injuring more.

But why the explosion? What could've made a blast so great to create a crater eighty miles wide? This, they had no idea. And in the middle of the mountains as well—in the heart of the jagged peaks that separated Meritar from Goldram, secluding the Elves from the rest of the continent.

Was it the Elves performing some sort of experiment? This is what most believed, but the Elves denied it.

Whatever it was that caused the explosion, at least everyone knew the result. Somehow it had created Bastial steel, the most valuable material in the world.

Discovered and then mined in the Bastial crater formed by this explosion, the steel had been used to forge many swords in the ten years since the creation of the crater.

Unfortunately, this same steel also brought forth the Bastial Steel War, when the three territories surrounding Goldram came together to fight the Takary Army for access to the crater.

Only one man knew how it all started. He was the only one there to witness it, killed in the process, of course. But it was a glorious death, filled with fire and surges of energy powerful enough to make mountains soar like eagles.

His name was Rami, an old man who took to the mountains in his dying years. He found a cluster of intriguing plants in the heart of the peaks. What he didn't know was that they were the same plants that Krepps and Slugari came to know as eppil plants, black as ink and twisted, doubling back into the patch of hard dirt from which they grew.

Rami lived among the eppil plants for years, trying a taste only once and nearly vomiting up his lungs. Being a lover of nature, he filled many pages in his journal with notes about this undiscovered plant. Unfortunately, it was destroyed soon before the explosion, the paper incinerated just like the old man's skin.

The earthquake was alarming, causing him to crouch under a mountain ledge he knew to be sturdy. The shaking was so violent it tore the dirt open around him, and a gush of Bastial Energy escaped through the quickly widening cracks. But not all of the energy made it into the air, for the eppil plants were thirsty, drinking it in. The black and twisted plants swelled, gathering over the opening to fight for the Bastial Energy.

Rami watched in amazement as a ball of swirling red and yellow began to form. It was the size of his fist at first. A breath later, it was larger than him.

Regrettably for Rami, that was the end of his life.

He didn't get to see the burning ball double in size, and then again moments later, reaching over twenty feet tall and disintegrating the clouds above. He didn't get to witness the soil melting beneath it so that it fell deep into the world, collecting more Bastial Energy as it went. He certainly didn't get to see the explosion that ripped the world apart, leaving a hideous scar in its wake.

Rami's body and mind were gone long before then—burned to dust from the pulsing heat the powerful little sun created before it exploded and assisted in the formation of a new metal.

Rami would never know what this so-called Bastial steel would do to the world.

But if he'd had to endure the war that followed and the death of his family as they fought for Goldram, he would've been thankful for this sudden yet painless end to existence.

Chapter 1

Cleve could feel fingernails being dug into his mind. He tried to force them out, pushing against them so hard he uttered a scream. But they were too strong, immovable. They dug deeper, causing such sharp pain his vision began to blur. Now in place, they were beginning to pry him open. His mind slowly ripped apart like an orange being separated down the middle.

"Fight back!" Rek yelled. "Push me out." Through the screeching pain, Rek's voice was faint, as if it had passed through walls before reaching Cleve's ears.

Cleve managed to squeak out a question between groans of pain. "How can I fight you when I can't see you attacking?"

"You won't be able to see the attack, but you can feel the pain coming. Fight back as soon as it starts."

In their windowless cabin on the boat, it would get too hot for comfort as soon as they began training. Cleve's shirt was already off, but his skin was still burning. It felt as if his blood would start boiling any moment.

It was their second day since their exile from Kyrro, and Rek had decided Cleve was ready to start learning how to fight against the psychic spell of pain.

"Can you switch the pain to somewhere else?" Cleve asked. "My head feels cracked."

The corner of Rek's mouth folded with disappointment. "Perhaps we should stop for the day."

Cleve pushed himself up from the bed to stand. "No. Continue."

The door creaked open. Jessend Takary cautiously stepped in, her dark hair dancing from a gust of wind that rushed in behind her. She edged closer to Cleve, elegantly brushing her hair over her ear and letting out a sigh.

"More training?" she asked.

Cleve nodded, reaching for his shirt.

"That's not necessary," she told him urgently, showing a sly smile while her eyes ran down to his stomach. Before Cleve could decide if her gaze was making him feel flattered or uncomfortable, she said, "Will you come with me to the deck, Cleve? I'm sure Rek will miss you dearly," she spoke sarcastically, "but I'd like to spend some time with my betrothed and not in the same room as a psychic."

Rek stood, lowering his head in respect. "Lady Jessend, two days being unable to leave this room has been tortuous. You have my word that I will not use psyche. I will not turn this ship around, even if I had the power to convince you or your captain to do so—which I assure you I do not. Please allow me to walk about this magnificent ship of yours. My legs need to be used."

Jessend smiled forgivingly. "It's my father's ship. And yes, no man should be confined to one room...unless he's dangerous." She tilted her head, her two front teeth coming over her lower lip.

"I'm only a danger to my enemies." Rek's tone was calm. "And you are no enemy of mine."

Cleve slipped into his shirt. By the time it was in place, Jessend had approached and put her hand on his wrist. "How do I know he isn't using psyche on me right now, Cleve?"

Cleve's first thought was to shrug and tell her to ask Rek, but then he realized that would be like asking a liar to explain how to tell when he's lying. So he thought back to his recent lessons with Rek to find the answer himself.

"Confidence. Don't have doubts." It sounded simple, but he knew it wasn't easy. "Trust your instincts," he added, knowing doing so was simpler than his first suggestion. "Do you think he's using psyche right now?" Cleve decided to ask her.

Jessend let her hand slide off his wrist as she turned to Rek.

"I don't, but I'm not sure." She shifted a foot forward to lean the rest of her body back, one hand confidently on the curve of her hip. "Use psyche on me, Rek. I want to see what it feels like. Convince me to do something I wouldn't want to do—convince me to leave this room without Cleve."

"I would need a reason to make you leave here, something logical. It's just like a lie, Lady Jessend." There was substantial respect in Rek's tone as he spoke to the Princess.

Cleve would've felt disgusted if the Elf was speaking to him that way, but Jessend seemed to think nothing of it. Cleve wondered if she was so used to being addressed with deference that she might not even have noticed.

"Could you elaborate?" Jessend asked, her head now leaning forward over her petite body. "What do you mean it's like a lie?"

"Psyche won't work unless it's believable," Rek said. "If we smelled smoke, I could claim there's a fire to make you leave this room. If someone shouted your name, I could convince you that it's important you speak with them immediately. But without something like this, I have nearly the same chance of convincing you to do something with psyche as without."

Jessend shifted her weight as she pondered, seemingly having difficulty staying still, as if the discussion of psyche had made her uneasy.

"I'm always honest," Rek continued. The comment surprised Cleve, making him wonder if the psychic had picked up on something Cleve hadn't, perhaps Jessend's worry about whether or not she was hearing the truth?

Rek added shortly after, "I feel that's only fair, given I can tell when others lie."

"Alright." Jessend gave one quick nod, smiling halfheartedly. "I believe you, Rek. But please allow a moment for me to inform my guards of your exit so they aren't alarmed when they see you." She gracefully turned on her heels to Cleve, extending her small hand for him to hold.

It felt like a child's in his grasp, and even more so from the way she dragged him after her through the door, where guards had been stationed to stop Rek from leaving.

On the vast deck, Jessend bent her arm around Cleve's. They stood at the side of the ship, looking out over the Starving Ocean.

Cleve had never been on a boat before. He might've found the endless ocean calming if he wasn't leaving his uncle and his friends behind to fight the war without him—if he wasn't leaving Reela behind. Thoughts of her always seemed to tug on his heart as they crept their way past his dense worries, making him forget where he was momentarily. Jessend stretched her arm up to reach his cheek, turning his gaze down toward her.

"Two days, Cleve, and all you do is stay in the cabin with Rek. At first I wasn't sure, but now I am. Why are you avoiding me?" Her voice was deep for a woman, especially such a diminutive one. She wore an elegant blouse, open at the collar.

On their own, Cleve's eyes traveled down her golden-brown skin to her bosom. After just a blink, he lifted his gaze to her wide brown eyes and her nearly black hair whipping in the breeze. He could feel his own hair fluttering across his forehead in the same way.

Because when I steal a ship and sail back to Kyrro, we'll never see each other again. It'll hurt less if we don't know each other.

"I haven't been avoiding you," he lied.

She grinned like he'd told a bad joke. "Yes I'm sure you treat *all* women as if they have the plague," she said sarcastically, "just like you're doing with me." Suddenly, she shoved him. Her face showed playfulness, but there was surprising strength in her arms.

Cleve stumbled back while she giggled.

"You're a bad liar," Jessend said. "I'm glad." She came after him with her arms out. "But what I don't like is how easy it is to knock you off your feet." Showing her white teeth in a wide grin, she went for another shove.

His arms came up to block her, and soon their limbs were locked in a struggle. She laughed and surprised him by swinging her foot around for a trip.

"What are you doing?" Cleve easily stepped over it but found himself losing his balance when she tried for another trip, this time around his ankle.

Something slammed into his side, sending him soaring through the air long enough for him to brace himself just before colliding with the deck.

Cleve swung his head back to find two swords aimed at him—Jessend's guards.

She was already sighing. "We were just playing," she told them.

But the aggression on their faces only stiffened, their swords remained pointed. Cleve wondered if two dogs would've been easier to convince he wasn't a threat.

"Stand down," Jessend demanded.

They relaxed their weapons, though their hard glares remained.

Cleve felt himself beginning to roll as the ship turned at a drastic rate. The guards stumbled and Jessend gasped.

Was Rek lying? Did he convince Captain Mmzaza to turn the ship back to Kyrro?

By the time Cleve got to his feet, Jessend was already running to the front of the ship, her guards and Cleve close behind.

But Rek wasn't there.

"Did the Elf tell you to turn?" Jessend asked Captain Mmzaza as she glanced around frantically. "Where is he?"

"The Elf?" the old captain replied in his crude accent, confused. "No, me pretty...er, me lady. The ship-eater ahead of us is the reason for the turn."

"Ship-eater?" Jessend squeaked.

Captain Mmzaza lifted a telescope over his eye. "Aye, ships...among other things they eat." He pointed, handing the telescope to Jessend. "There. Hurry, me pretty, before it ducks back underwater."

Jessend looked through it while Captain Mmzaza took in a deep breath. "My you smell nice," he uttered.

Jessend was too busy gasping at what she saw to pay attention.

"It's a giant squid," she said, correcting him.

"Is that what you call them in The Nest?" Captain Mmzaza laughed cruelly, taking back the telescope for another look. "It ain't no squid, me pretty. Squids don't come to the surface like ship-eaters. And squids wouldn't use their tentacles to crush our vessel, devouring everyone and everything that touches water. Cousins of desmarls these are, you should know that, being from Greenedge. That's why we're going around it. Monsters have good eyesight, they do. Smart, too. Once they catch sight of a ship, they go underwater and head toward it, coming up only rarely to make sure they're on the right path."

As smooth as a cat, Jessend nestled under Cleve's arm so that it fell around her shoulder. "So it won't see us, Captain Mmzaza?" She clung tightly to Cleve, her voice worried.

"Shouldn't." The gnarled sea captain lifted the telescope to his eye again. "Unless it's already caught sight of this enormous ship—oh," he interrupted himself. "Better ready your archers. It's coming for us." His tone was so calm it took Cleve a breath before he even understood what Mmzaza was saying.

Jessend blurted it through a shriek. "The giant squid is coming for our ship?"

"Ship-eater, and yes. Hurry and ready your archers, me pretty—me lady," he quickly corrected himself. "It'll only resurface a few more times on the way here."

Jessend jumped to the two guards nearby. "How many archers do we have?"

"Three, my lady," one answered.

"That means four including me." She spoke softly, as if thinking aloud. Then her head shot up to meet the eyes of the guards in front of her. "Do we have five bows on the ship?"

"Five, my lady? Yes we have five."

"Cleve needs one as well. Bring the archers and bows to the deck and hurry."

The guards were off. Then Cleve noticed that so was the captain.

"Where are you going?" Jessend shouted after him. "Who'll steer the ship?"

Captain Mmzaza ignored her, running to the opening in the deck and dropping to his chest to sink his head within the empty space. The old man was surprisingly agile.

"Ye rowers, we got a ship-eater on our ass! Get us moving faster than a man's bedding with his first woman or we're dead."

"You heard him," some man bellowed below. "Row! Row! Row!" His voice fell into a steady pattern. Cleve felt the wind picking up as the speed of the ship increased.

Captain Mmzaza was huffing loudly by the time he returned.

Soon, the deck was filled with the rest of Jessend's retinue. There must've been at least thirty of them.

All flocked together, they created a buzz of worried murmurs. They seemed ready to burst into flight like birds anticipating a predator. But they could not fly to safety, only sink, the looks on their faces making it clear this had become apparent to each of them.

Cleve had been brought a bow and quiver and aligned himself alongside the other archers on the edge of the ship, peering out over the still and silent sea. Jessend had her own bow to his right. It looked identical to the one Cleve had shattered with an arrow in King Welson Kimard's castle.

To Cleve's left came Rek. "They say some monster comes for the ship." The Elf was smiling for some strange reason. Perhaps he was in disbelief?

"It's true," Cleve tried to convince him, keeping his eyes

steady on the dark waters, waiting for movement.

From the corner of Cleve's eye, he noticed Rek's mouth slowly straightening. "What kind of monster?"

Something jutted out of the water, maybe a hundred and fifty yards from their ship. It was too small to see clearly, but Cleve still could tell it was gigantic. The way it displaced the water was as if a boulder had risen from the depths.

With Bastial Energy at the ready, Cleve pulled back his string and fired, soon noticing he was the only one to have done so. Some of the others let out disapproving grunts.

"Don't waste the arrow," one archer said while Cleve's shot arced.

Cleve waited to see what happened before replying, his aim looking to be perfect, at least in that moment. But the beast submerged again just before the arrow struck.

"Bastial hell," the same man muttered when he saw that Cleve's arrow would've hit if he'd just released it sooner.

Each of them readied their arrows then, Jessend included. Cleve didn't see how she had the strength to shoot such a long distance. But when the creature came up again, at around a hundred yards, her arrow was the only one besides Cleve's to strike the beast. Its roar was like distant thunder, yet sharper, angrier.

The ship turned, Captain Mmzaza yelling from its front, "It won't come up again, so we'd better change direction! When it can't find us, that's when it'll show its ugly head."

"How will we know where to look for it, then?" Cleve shouted back.

"We're turning back to the west, boy. The ship-eater's coming from the north. So it'll pop up somewhere to your southeast. Spread along to the other side of the boat and the rear."

While Cleve didn't trust any other advice Captain Mmzaza had tried to give during their voyage, most of it being about women, at that moment, Cleve knew not to doubt him. Jessend ran with Cleve to the other side of the deck, the other three archers taking the rear.

Soon the crisp sound of breaking water turned Cleve's head to the back of the boat, the three archers each desperately loosing arrows. As Cleve hustled over, a tree-sized tentacle swept over the ship.

Brushing over the archers, it caused them to tumble backward as it coiled in on itself and grabbed one of them.

Cleve and Jessend each shot at the speeding tentacle, both arrows sticking into it as a toothpick would into a man's arm. Though, it was still enough for the beast to lose its grip on one of the archers before taking him into the sea.

Cleve noticed a shadow above him. Turning to his side, he found another tentacle coming over the railing. Screams from Jessend's retinue burst out, yet the Princess did not join the chorus. Like Cleve, fear had not yet made her lose control of her body. She was steady as she aimed at the beast's arm coming toward them.

They put two more arrows into it, and the tentacle snapped back into the water.

There was a shriek too deafening to be from a Human's throat. With no more tentacles coming over the railings, Cleve took the chance to run to the stern in hopes of shooting the beast in the head. But Rek was already there with his palm out. The Elf was screaming as well. It was the loudest Cleve had heard him utter, but it was nothing compared to the bellowing beast below. Cleve knew the psychic must be putting all his energy behind his spell of pain.

The ship-eater couldn't seem to handle it, no longer chasing the vessel and sinking back into the dark waters. Its screams were muffled but still shrill, quickly fading as the distance grew between it and the speeding ship.

Nearly a full minute they waited in silence, each watching for a sign of it resurfacing.

Eventually, Cleve came to realize it did not wish to follow—

the Elf's painful psychic spell was too much to bear.

"You *are* dangerous." Jessend took two steps back from Rek, tilting her head away as if he were a living flame. "My father might still like you..." She glanced behind the boat, where the ship-eater had sunk back into the sea. "Or he might fear you worse than a desmarl."

Chapter 2

When they arrived at the docks in Goldram, Cleve followed Jessend through the winding wooden walkways suspended over the water, watching as man after man stopped what he was doing to bow before the Princess. They gawked openly at Cleve. He could feel their curiosity pressing against him, heavier even than the salty humidity.

Cleve's feet went no farther when he saw what he believed to be a carriage.

"Are those horses?" he asked.

With an excited grin, Jessend gasped. "That's right, no horses in Ovira. But how did you recognize them, then?"

"We do have books and paintings," he replied snidely.

He thought to apologize immediately after, but then he noticed a grin among her pouty lips.

"And here I thought you were a simple warrior who knew more ways to kill a man than he did names of books."

The carriage to escort them to the palace was draped with a cloth embroidered with what Jessend explained to be the Takary family sigil—two blue soaring wings.

"It's a long ride to the palace," she said as they got inside and their driver somehow made the horses start galloping. "The palace is in the middle of a city called The Nest."

The name came off as strange to Cleve, but he didn't see a reason to mention it.

"Living in The Nest is supposed to represent how our citizens are treated like family." There was some embarrassment in Jessend's tone. "I didn't think of the name," she said flatly.

During the next bumps and turns of the road, Jessend slid her fingers along the knuckles of Cleve's resting hand. He felt nothing from her touch and was glad for that. His mind was set on Reela. He wanted his heart to remain that way as well.

Jessend was beautiful, so much so he'd been worried he would find himself attracted to her. But then he would think of Reela's shimmering green eyes over her sly grin, and his heart would twist, his stomach would rise, and he'd realize it was silly to worry anyone could replace her.

The Princess was a child compared to Reela, short and thin, and with small hands. Her touch did nothing. Absolutely nothing.

Soon, she stopped playing with his knuckles, letting her hand lie still underneath his like a dead fish.

That didn't last long, either. She cleared her throat and pulled her hand back to her lap.

Cleve kept his mind busy looking out the window of the carriage, desperately trying to remember the scenery and the route. He would need to return to the docks to sail back to his home continent, Ovira.

"You don't need to gag Rek when we arrive," Cleve suddenly thought to tell her. The poor Elf had endured enough. "His psyche is strong, but he can't convince anyone to do something they don't want to do already."

"King Welson Kimard of Kyrro told me you were sent to kill Rek," Jessend said. "Did the Elf change your mind with psyche when you met him?"

"No," Cleve gladly informed her. "My mind was changed when I found out the truth about which side he was on, and I never wanted to kill him anyway. He didn't need any psyche to convince me."

"You're saying that—without psyche—you came to the decision to attack your own king's castle?" It was clear by her tone that she'd always assumed his mind was twisted into that choice.

Cleve studied her face before deciding how to answer. For the first time, she seemed completely serious, worried even.

When he'd shot an arrow at her, breaking her bow in two, she'd shown him excited shock, her mouth even on the verge of grinning. But she held no amusement with this question.

"It was the only logical thing to do."

She forced a nervous smile. "If things ever get that bad again, come to me first." She slid close to him, wrapping her arm around his and leaning against his shoulder. "You and I are a team now. We'll help each other."

Guilt pushed the air out of his lungs in a sorrowful sigh. Out of pity, he twisted his neck to kiss Jessend on the top of her head.

Poor little girl, he said to himself.

She nestled against him even closer, intertwining her fingers with his.

A gate lined with guards appeared to be the only way into the front of the Takary Palace. Their driver opened the carriage door for Jessend, and Cleve crawled out through her side before he realized the same man was coming around to open his door.

"My betrothed shouldn't be crawling out of carriages." Jessend giggled. Her laugh was deep, lower than her voice even. It erupted from her stomach with a strong rhythm.

The rest of her retinue started passing through the gate, lowering for a bow or a curtsy as they went by the Princess.

"Twist me horn, look at this place!" Captain Mmzaza got down on both knees and kissed Jessend's left foot. "Thank you, me pretty. Captain Mmzaza's been to Goldram before, but never inside the Takary Palace." He clumsily rose to his feet, nearly losing his balance.

Cleve wondered how the man had gotten so drunk when Cleve hadn't seen any alcohol. *Or was he captaining the ship in that state?*

"Is me bed big, and does it come with a woman?" Captain Mmzaza let out a cackle. "Just a joke. Captain Mmzaza can find his own woman."

Jessend had a frozen smile. "Thank you for sailing my father's ship. You're welcome to walk about The Nest and stay in Goldram as long as you'd like, but I regret to tell you that I cannot offer you a room within the palace." She waved a guard over, going to her toes to whisper something in his ear.

Captain Mmzaza's head went so low, his chin nearly touched his chest.

A strong feeling of pity surprised Cleve. The old captain had been nothing short of irritating during every conversation they'd shared, but Mmzaza so desperately wanted to be in the palace that Cleve couldn't help but feel remorseful.

"This guard will make sure you're paid for your service," Jessend said. "You can follow him into the palace and take a tour."

Now, Cleve's pity was for the guard who had to spend the day with Captain Mmzaza.

"Thank you, me pretty! Captain Mmzaza's just happy he gets to see it."

Cleve decided to really look at the palace, being likely he'd be there for some time. It was quite magnificent, putting the castle in Kyrro City to shame.

The palace wasn't as tall as Welson Kimard's castle, but ten castles could fit within it if they were turned on their sides. It was mostly white, with gold decorations along the pillars and walls.

"Beautiful, isn't it?" Jessend said with a soft voice. "This is where I was going to tell you we're to be married, if you were more patient when we were leaving Kyrro."

"How big is it?" Cleve asked, unwilling to allow the topic of matrimony to continue.

"About a square mile. I'll make sure you don't get lost." Cleve looked down at Jessend to find her smiling up at him.

"So this is the famous Takary Palace." Rek came up with a hand to Cleve's shoulder. "And what am I to do here?" His tone was polite. Cleve assumed he was just happy not to be gagged or confined to a room.

"I'm sure my father or his adviser will have some idea," Jessend answered confidently. She pointed to the marble steps ahead. "That's my father's adviser right there. Micah Vail is his name."

The man's hair was black and straight, hanging down over his forehead and ears. There was an eerie contrast to the way he walked compared to his age. He seemed young, certainly no older than thirty. Yet, his carefully placed feet down each step showed a sense of purpose and duty as if he'd worked the same job for twenty years.

"He's a close friend to our family," Jessend said.

Micah Vail knelt down before Jessend when he was close. "I'm so happy to see you've returned safely, Princess."

"Micah, you're embarrassing me," Jessend said, letting out a light laugh. "Get up and hug me like usual."

He smiled and obeyed.

"And who are these two..." Micah's face showed shock when his eyes met Rek's.

Jessend laughed loudly. "I think that's the first time I've seen you surprised, Micah. Yes, I brought an Elf."

But Micah's eyes hadn't even glanced at Rek's ears yet. In fact, only after Jessend mentioned Rek's race did they sway to the side for a look. His head snapped back even farther then.

He was surprised about something else the first time, Cleve realized, now examining Rek to see if he could figure out what it was. That's when Cleve noticed the Elf's expression. His head was low, bent subtly to the side to look deep within Micah with psyche.

"Jessend?" Rek spoke in a curious tone. "Didn't you tell me you've never met a psychic before?"

"I thought you said you had a good memory," Jessend teased him. "Yes, I told you I thought they were a myth until I went to Kyrro."

Rek gestured toward Micah. "But this man—" Rek was interrupted by his own scream, dropping to a knee.

Jessend hurried over to him. "What happened? Are you alright?"

Rek had an angry glare at Micah. "It was nothing," he muttered.

"Jessend." Micah turned toward her, holding his smile the entire time. "Would you mind if I took this Elf with me into the palace? I would like to speak to him."

Jessend seemed too confused to answer.

Cleve knew what had happened, though. Yet, what he still couldn't figure out was why Micah Vail was hiding that he was a psychic. *This place might be dangerous for Rek.*

"I was hoping you would speak with Rek, anyway," Jessend admitted. "He's very powerful and can be of use to us."

"Thank you, Lady Jessend." Micah nodded and motioned for Rek to follow him.

The Elf shrugged at Cleve and hurried after the king's adviser.

"That was strange," Jessend said. "Are you ready to see your new home?"

A woman's excited scream caught Cleve's attention. "Jessend!"

It must've been her sister. They looked too much alike for it not to be. She was running to meet them at the gate.

"I'm so glad you're back. Who's this huge man?" Stopping a few steps from Cleve, the other woman intertwined her wrists and leaned forward toward him.

"This is Cleve." Jessend slapped him in the stomach and kept her hand there for a rub, making him feel like a pig being marketed on the street.

"He looks like—"

"I know," Jessend interrupted. "Cleve, this is my twin sister, Lisanda."

He extended his hand for her to shake. She took it

awkwardly, looking to Jessend with a pressed grin, her hand dead weight in his.

"He doesn't know much about nobility, does he?" Lisanda teased.

"You should've seen him crawling out of my side of the carriage."

They each giggled.

"Speaking of inappropriate behavior," Jessend said, "what happened with Jek? Did stubborn Father make him the King's Mage after all?"

Lisanda's mouth became a flat line with no trace of her recent smile. "A lot has happened. I'll tell you later." Her tone was grave. "Come inside. I'm sure Father wants to see you. He's been eager to hear how many men you've brought from Kyrro." Lisanda glanced around. "But is this the only one who came to fight for us?"

Jessend sighed. "Kyrro is at war, and a Takary no longer controls it. I was only able to bring two, but wait until you see how good Cleve is with a weapon in his hand and the power of the psychic Elf. He's with Micah right now. Father might be pleased if he's not too frightened."

Lisanda gasped. "A true psychic?"

"Yes. There are many of them in Ovira. But this one is the strongest of them all." Jessend wore a proud smile.

"And you said he's an Elf?" Lisanda seemed to be holding back a squeal.

"Yes. Let's go, beautiful." Jessend took her sister's hand, wrapping her other arm around Cleve's and pulling them both toward the palace. "There's too much to do to be standing here any longer."

After a few steps, Jessend pulled on Cleve's shoulder, forcing his head lower.

Expecting a whisper, he was shocked when she pressed her lips against his cheek for a kiss.

Didn't Jessend tell me her father might be able to send help back to Kyrro? "If I was brought here to fight, what about the mention of your father's army being sent overseas to fight for Kyrro?"

Jessend was hopping up the stairs to the palace door two at a time, stopping abruptly the moment Cleve finished his question.

"I don't know too much about my father's army," she said. "He keeps that from me. But I meant that after we win this war, they might be able to help Kyrro."

Frustration twisted within him. *She talks about war like a child would, as if it were some sort of game with a clear beginning and ending.*

Cleve thought to ask about this war but realized that question would be better for her father, or really anyone else besides her.

They finished climbing the stairs in silence. Once Jessend had her arm hooked within Cleve's, the guards politely avoided eye contact with him.

"Father's meeting with the King of Zav," Lisanda told her twin.

"Oh, I would like to meet him as well—the man's likely to be our enemy in war," Jessend added.

"I don't," Lisanda said. "But if you're going, then I'll join you."

"Cleve, promise you'll behave?" Jessend smiled to show she was teasing him. Her tone was as if they were old friends.

Cleve didn't understand the joke. "Yes," he muttered.

"You should've seen how I met Cleve," Jessend said. "He stormed into his own king's castle with thousands of rats, and then he shot at me with his bow, breaking mine in two. It was an amazing shot."

Lisanda peered around Jessend to show Cleve a skeptical look. "My sister likes to make things more dramatic than they really are. How did you two really meet?"

"It's true!" Jessend squawked.

They'd crossed the long entrance hall by then, its marble floor decorated with blue outstretched wings in the center. A group of servants met Lisanda by the base of a set of curved stairs.

"Anything we can get for you, my lady?" The servants each lowered their heads.

"Thank you, but not at this time."

Cleve hadn't had a good meal in too long, but he didn't feel right bringing it up. The sisters seemed to be in a hurry to get to this meeting, Jessend hiking up the stairs two at a time again.

"I'll tell you the whole story later," she told Lisanda. "When did the meeting begin?"

"Just now."

The floor of the entire palace seemed to be tiled in marble. With its tall walls and curved ceiling painted white, the place was a little too colorless. Though, it did bring out the garish designs on the clothing of the few people walking about who weren't guards or servants.

Jessend had brought many different garments to Kyrro, wearing something different each day on the ship. But it seemed that she'd saved the most elegant dress for this day.

It was dark blue with a light pink ribbon around her waist. A gold chain was about her neck, hanging low against her skin. The sleeves of her dress were slightly transparent, giving sight to her slender arms.

It was probably the least practical dress Cleve had ever seen. He assumed getting it caught on the corner of a table could rip it. However, he didn't imagine that happening to Jessend. The way she moved was too practiced. She seemed aware of every motion of her body, even more so than many warriors Cleve had met.

There were two guards outside the door of the meeting room. Jessend tilted her head at the one on the left. "Are you new?"

"Yes, my lady." The guard shifted nervously.

"I wish to learn your name and how you came into this position," Jessend said, her tone now commanding. "But it must be some other time. We're in a hurry." She motioned toward the door.

The new guard she was addressing put out his hand to stop her. "My lady, I don't think it's a good idea for you to go inside."

The other guard smacked him hard in the chest, his chain mail ringing like a dull chime. "It's fine," the veteran guard corrected him. "And not your place to say otherwise."

The new guard furrowed his brow. "I really would advise against it."

The one who'd smacked him sighed. "Please excuse his ignorance, my lady. You can go on in." He opened the door behind him, stepping inside to introduce the Princesses Jessend and Lisanda Takary.

Cleve entered behind them, immediately embarrassed about his drab and frayed clothing. Bright colors invaded his senses like a hurricane passing through a sea of paint.

There were two men on one side of the table. One of them had to be the King of Zav based on his crown. Beside him was a little boy, probably seven or eight years old by the look of him. Cleve didn't know who the other man was, the King of Zav's servant or adviser most likely.

On the other side of the table was Jessend's father, the King of Goldram. Cleve knew from the blue wings embroidered on his shirt and the crown on his head.

"I apologize for this interruption," the King of Goldram said.

"No troubles," the ruler of Zav answered in a tone that Cleve thought was too friendly for them to be enemies. "Are these your daughters, Danvell?"

"They are. Jessend here has just come back from a trip over the Starving Ocean." Danvell stepped toward his daughter with a relieved smile. "I'm happy to see you're home safely." They shared an embrace. The King's accent was just like Jessend and Lisanda's, rhythmic, as if the words were elegantly dancing their way through the air.

"Who's this young man?" Danvell asked, his smile fading as he looked to Cleve.

"A friend from Kyrro," Jessend answered. "Please, don't let us interrupt. I'll tell you everything later, Father."

He nodded back to her. Jessend and Lisanda made their way to the corner of the room, Cleve following them there.

The two monarchs picked up their conversation quickly, relaxation gone from their stern faces.

"You were saying that the movements of your army had nothing to do with Goldram?" Danvell Takary questioned, his tone somewhat dubious.

"That's correct," the King of Zav answered. "Our scouts noticed messengers going between Presoren and Waywen. I believe they're setting up for some sort of attack, so I positioned my men to cover all sides. I can see how those who came close to Goldram made it seem that we were preparing for an attack, but it's quite the opposite. We couldn't be sure your territory wasn't involved with Presoren and Waywen, so we were just setting up defensively."

While the King of Zav talked, the man beside him stood like a statue. His eyes were absently staring at the table, as if he wasn't even listening. Cleve thought it to be strange unless the man was a servant, but he wasn't dressed as such. Cleve was no tailor, but it was clear the man's clothes were of high quality. His face and hair were too clean, his beard groomed too neatly.

The little boy was the opposite, incapable of standing still. Cleve felt him staring but let him be. He would never blame a child for his curiosity. More than anything, Cleve wondered why a child would be present during the meeting. The whole situation was confusing him the more he thought about it.

"You're telling me you honestly believe your former allies

might attack you?" Danvell let his skepticism come out in his tone.

"Make the treaty with us an alliance instead," the King of Zav dared him. "If we're attacked, your army will defend Zav as if it were your own land, and we'll do the same for you. Now, if I'm requesting this, why would I lie?"

The little boy tugged on the King of Zav's hand as he whimpered, "Father..."

"Not now, Harwin. We'll be done soon."

"We've received information that proves Waywen and Presoren are preparing for an attack as well," Danvell said, coming around the table to stand before the King of Zav. "I would be happy to agree to an alliance with you." He extended his hand.

Both rulers smiled as they shook and then bowed.

Cleve noticed Jessend and Lisanda whispering to each other. He couldn't hear their words, but their tones were filled with excitement.

"This is a pleasant surprise," Danvell stated. Then he lowered his head solemnly. "I apologize for the incident with Harwin. After we get the contracts in order for the alliance, I would like to offer you a gift of ten Bastial steel swords."

A shocked smile came across the King of Zav's face. "I would be happy to accept your—"

"What does he mean, Father?" Harwin interrupted. "What incident with me?"

Just then, another man entered the room. With investigative eyes darting around, he cautiously walked toward the King of Zav. He seemed concerned when he saw Cleve and the Takary sisters in the corner, as if he thought they weren't supposed to be there.

Then Cleve noticed stiffness in the man's right leg. Terren, his uncle, had trained him to notice when a man concealed a knife at his ankle.

Why would he bring a weapon in here? Cleve figured it was

unwise to hold his tongue.

"Who is he?" Cleve blurted, pointing, even starting toward the man.

The King of Zav folded his arms, a scowl forming. "He's my other trusted adviser and a good friend. Who are you?"

"Ignore him." Danvell grabbed Cleve's shoulder, whispering, "Don't interrupt."

"That man has a knife hidden at his ankle," Cleve quickly whispered back.

"Are you certain?" Danvell asked, all sense of anger suddenly gone.

The King of Zav came toward them. Sensing the change in Danvell's expression, he no longer seemed annoyed. "Is there a problem?"

With practiced quickness, the man with the knife bent down. He popped back up with two knives, handing one to the other man who was no longer staring at the table. Life was in his eyes, each of their faces hard with aggression.

One leapt at the King of Zav, while the other started toward Harwin. The little boy screamed, running along the wall to escape his pursuer. Cleve jumped over the table and slammed into the man chasing the poor child, squashing him between his shoulder and the wall.

The knife dropped, the man falling as well. Cleve bent to pick it up, ready to drive it into the attacker's chest, only then noticing the blood on the man's temple. He was knocked unconscious.

Cleve heard Danvell shouting for guards as he spun around to check on the other man with a knife. He and the King of Zav were in the middle of a struggle. Jessend was on her feet, cautiously approaching with her arms up defensively.

Is she insane? The little princess would be trampled by the men fighting, likely to take the knife in her chest if she got in the middle of it.

Cleve found his opportunity when the struggle slowed as

each man had hold of the knife, the King trying to prevent his attacker from driving it into his stomach.

"Why?" the ruler of Zav screamed. "Why?"

"You and Harwin need to die!" the man yelled back, spit escaping from between his clenched teeth.

Cleve drove his knife hard into the man's belly, hearing a crash and glass shattering behind him just after the man collapsed. He took a moment to disarm the man he'd cut before turning to see what the noise was.

Just within the door was a guard of Goldram—Cleve recognized him as the new guard who didn't want the Takary sisters inside. For some reason, the guard had purposefully knocked over a towering clock. The massive structure was now strewn across the closed door, thousands of glass shards all around it.

Why would he block the exit?

Then the guard drew his sword and hastily went toward the King of Goldram—his own king.

"What are you doing?" Danvell asked, backing up into the wall.

Jessend put herself between them, bending her knees with her arms out in preparation for an attack. She looked like a little mouse in comparison to the armored man before her.

"Move, Princess," the guard threatened. "Both kings need to die, along with Harwin."

Cleve, now armed with two knives, took Jessend's place, pushing her back to make sure she was out of the way. She resisted at first, so he shoved her harder.

"Stay back," he said, brandishing both knives at the guard in front of him.

The door was being slammed into the fallen clock from other palace guards trying to get in. "Your highness, are you alright?" someone shouted from behind it.

The traitor lunged at Cleve with an overhead swing of his sword. Unable to sidestep it in fear of the Takarys behind him being struck, Cleve crossed his daggers to intercept the blow.

Cleve kicked the traitor in the stomach as he'd done thousands of times in training. Against the man's chain mail, it did nothing but send him back a step.

Guards were breaking the top of the door with their swords. Cleve knew he just needed to keep his enemy at bay and they soon would be inside the room. His attacker must've also realized this, for his aggression doubled in that moment.

He swung wildly from side to side as Cleve dodged and waited for an opportunity to strike back. But he found none. As desperate as the man was with his weapon, he still knew not to leave himself open for a counterattack. He was clearly well-trained, and he wasn't about to allow Cleve to let this go any longer than it needed to.

Unable to defend himself much longer, Cleve had to create his own opportunity to strike, not something he'd practiced with daggers against a sword.

He threatened to throw one dagger, cocking back his arm after jumping away to create distance. It halted his attacker for a heartbeat, the man turning his shoulders inward in preparation.

But Cleve knew the dagger would have to strike the man in the face for it to do any harm, and his opponent was moving too quickly to be sure it would work. Instead, Cleve took a different risk. He started toward the false guard of Goldram.

The guard thrust his weapon at Cleve's chest. Unable to deflect the blow with his daggers, Cleve had to know it was coming for his plan to work. Luckily, he did.

Moving to the side, the man's sword caught Cleve's shirt but not his flesh.

Cleve drove both daggers into the soft underbelly of the man's chin.

The guard stumbled backward and fell, gasping as his sword slipped from his hands. Cleve picked up the sword intending to drive it through the man's heart, but his protective chain mail threatened to prevent his death from being merciful. It was likely to take a few painful strikes before Cleve could pierce his heart.

So he stood over the man's face, the sword raised high. But Cleve had the thought to look around first.

He found gaping eyes and the little boy shaking with terror. His father had his arm around him.

"It'll be alright, Harwin," the King of Zav said, trying to turn the child's face away.

But the Prince wouldn't take his eyes off Cleve.

Neither would anyone else.

"Look away," he told them, the man at his feet still gasping for life. There was no use for him to be in pain, and his agony was only making the situation more traumatizing.

Everyone turned, Jessend taking the longest to do so. Then Cleve drove the man's own sword down through his forehead, sliding it out and flipping him over when he was done so the others wouldn't have to see.

The door finally cracked open. Four guards ran in, followed by more, and then some more. They circled around Cleve.

He dropped the sword to show his hands, the sign of giving in to their authority...at least in Kyrro.

"He's not the enemy," Danvell Takary said. His voice had none of the same urgency or mandate that Cleve had heard earlier. It was strained, as if his throat had been tightened by the incident. "They are." Danvell pointed to the fallen bodies.

The man who'd attacked the King of Zav was dead in a puddle of his own blood, a long wound through his stomach. Cleve was surprised to see how deep it was. He didn't realize he'd driven the dagger across the man's stomach so violently.

Cleve figured the other one wasn't dead, the one he'd slammed into the wall. He was certainly still unconscious, though.

"He should live." Cleve pointed.

"Why did they try to kill you?" Danvell asked the King of Zav.

"I'm wondering that myself." He had his arms around Harwin, kneeling down to hold the boy's head against his chest.

"They must've been spies," Danvell said.

"No, I've known them for years," the King of Zav argued. "Your guard must've been a spy."

"He certainly was, but your men were also." Danvell's voice was humbly quiet. "You must see that by now?"

"It can't be possible!" The King of Zav was in disbelief, Harwin weeping loudly against him. "There must be something that would explain their actions besides that."

Cleve caught Jessend's attention with a glance. "We should bring Rek in here to question the one who's still alive," he said.

Meanwhile, Lisanda was holding onto her father, crying. He had his arm around her shoulder, guiding her to the guards nearby. "Please make sure she gets whatever she needs, and take her to her room. Lisanda, I'll visit as soon as I can."

Lisanda kept her eyes at her feet as she wept, reaching out blindly for someone to take her hands. Two guards came to either side of her and steered her out.

"Father," Jessend said, her tone the calmest of anyone's. "Cleve is right. I brought a psychic who can get the truth out of the last survivor. He's with Micah Vail right now."

Fear struck Danvell's face. "You brought a psychic into my palace?"

"He's a close friend of Cleve's...an ally," Jessend argued. "He can help us."

"If you wouldn't mind," the King of Zav stood, "I also would like the psychic to question him." He looked to Cleve. "It is true they can tell whether a man is lying?"

"Yes," Cleve answered.

"But what else will he do?" Danvell asked worriedly. "What will he do to the rest of our minds?"

"Nothing," Cleve said as calmly as possible. "He can't—"

"I want to go home!" Harwin blurted, sobbing.

"Is there a secure place Harwin can wait?" the King of Zav asked.

"I apologize for not offering sooner," Danvell answered. "A team of guards will watch over him."

He gestured at the men in the room. One nodded and came forward. He knelt in front of Harwin.

"Come with us. We'll keep you safe, and your father will be with you soon." The guard's sweet tone made it clear that Harwin wasn't the first child he'd spoken to.

The boy reluctantly left his father behind, whimpering as half of the guards from the room followed them.

Danvell approached Cleve, his hand extended with a sad smile. "I don't know who you are, but let me offer you the warmest welcome to the Takary Palace." Suddenly his mouth went flat. "But are you certain this psychic friend of yours isn't dangerous?"

Cleve shook the King's hand, remembering Rek's answer to Jessend on the boat. "He's only a danger to his enemies." Cleve kept his tone lighthearted, only realizing then that what he was about to say aloud was the truth. "And we have no enemies in Goldram...at least none that we're aware of."

"Well, it looks like you just made some enemies in Presoren and Waywen," Danvell said.

"I can live with that." *Especially given they would've murdered a child.*

Danvell took in a slow breath, still clearly considering whether or not he wanted the psychic in his palace, let alone in the same room as him.

Finally he turned to Jessend. "I'll have someone bring Micah Vail and this psychic in here. But I want ten guards between me and him first. I hope he won't be insulted."

"He won't," Cleve guessed. "By now, he's used to being feared."

Only then did Cleve realize he had little idea what had just happened. Both kings nearly had been killed by their own men, and it was right after a discussion of alliances that somehow came as a surprise to the Takary family.

What did I just step into?

Chapter 3

When Rek and Micah entered, Danvell was cowered in the opposite corner, ten guards lined in front of him just like he'd said.

Cleve almost laughed at the idea of it, like they'd really be able to stop Rek if he wanted to harm Danvell.

"Bastial hell," Micah uttered, his hand going over his mouth. "What happened in here?"

Rek came to Cleve's side. "Are you alright?"

"I'm fine." Cleve felt numb from the whole thing and was glad for it.

"They want me to question someone?" Rek asked.

Cleve pointed at the still unconscious man. They'd put him in a chair, his slouched body held up by ropes.

"Him," Cleve said.

He could overhear Danvell speaking with Micah Vail in a low voice, but Cleve was too far away for their words to be clear.

"Is there anything you can do to bring a man back into consciousness?" Cleve asked.

"Nothing with psyche," Rek admitted, kneeling next to the man for a touch to his forehead. His hand shifted to the man's cheek, patting it roughly until his eyes popped open.

"What's your name?" Rek asked the now frightened man.

"Podd." He glanced around. With one eye squinted, he seemed dazed. Slowly, though, both eyes opened wider as they found Cleve. The man tried to stand, but the ropes prevented him from doing so.

Looking down, he noticed the restraints then, fear suddenly making his actions frantic as his head swung around the room and his hands tried to free themselves.

"Stop," Rek said, reaching his palm out. "Or I'll need to hurt you."

Podd investigated Rek. "You're an Elf!"

"And a psychic," Rek told him. "So I'll punish you if you lie."

Podd took in a loud breath, leaning as far back as he could. The chair tipped backward, slamming into the ground. He scrambled unsuccessfully to get to his feet, reminding Cleve of a beetle that had gotten flipped onto its shell.

"Get away from me!" Podd yelled as Rek came to his side.

Rek pulled the chair back upright. Placing his hand on the man's shoulder, he said, "Relax. There's no need to be afraid as long as you're honest. Can you do that?"

Podd's struggles stopped. He lowered his head and gave a subtle nod.

"Good," Rek said. "Now, tell me what happened here? Tell me everything you remember."

"They attacked me and my son!" the King of Zav yelled, gesturing aggressively. "Ask him why he did it!" Then, the King quickly stepped back, making sure to keep his distance from Rek.

"You heard his question," Rek said. "Now answer it."

"I don't know why," Podd claimed. "I was just told to do it."

"That's a lie." Rek held out his hand to pain the man with psyche.

Podd screamed and cursed the Elf. Cleve noticed frightened gasps and murmurs buzzing around the room.

This might not be a good idea, he was beginning to believe. *Are they going to throw Rek in prison after this, perhaps exile him like the King of Kyrro did?*

Rek didn't seem to be concerned, though. He was busy making demands.

"Start at the beginning," Rek said. "Why was this murder plot set up?"

Podd seemed defeated, giving out a slow breath before answering. "Waywen and Presoren want control of Goldram and the Bastial steel crater." His gaze stayed on his lap with quick glances to the King of Zav between words. "We've been planning to take over both Goldram and Zav for years."

"You bastard," the King of Zav muttered. "You would've killed my son. You made me think we were friends. Years! I could kill you right now."

Podd didn't lift his head. "We were planning to release the desmarls around The Nest and attack while the Takary Army was distracted. But there were problems with the men responsible for the desmarls. Then we found out about the kidnapping of Prince Harwin and this meeting. The plan changed to kill both kings and Harwin. Based on the rumors of war starting between Goldram and Zav, it would just look like they'd attacked each other. Especially after the kidnapping, everyone would've believed it."

"Is this really the truth?" The King of Zav was incredulous.

"It is," Rek answered.

"Chaos would then ensue," Podd continued. "Waywen and Presoren were to attack while leadership was still being decided in Zav and Danvell Takary's son and successor, Raymess, was all the way in Chanren."

"So, that's why your armies have been moving," the King of Zav realized.

"Yes. As soon as news reached Waywen and Presoren about the assassinations, they would strike."

"I'm so sorry about the kidnapping of Harwin," Danvell said, his low voice faint through the wall of guards. "I made a terrible mistake."

"All of that is behind us," the King of Zav answered.

Cleve had a question he couldn't hold any longer. "Why weren't they checked for knives?"

"They were," Danvell said. "No one in this room was allowed any weapons."

"Then how did this man come in with two of them around his ankle?" Cleve asked.

Podd answered, his voice soft from shame. "There was a guard of Goldram outside the door who was a spy for us. He hid the weapons within the palace. When I excused myself to use the bathroom, I equipped myself with them."

"There were two guards outside the door," Danvell said, addressing the guards between him and Rek. "What happened to Ken, who stood beside the traitor? I never saw him enter the room."

One guard turned to address his king. "He was killed by the traitor, your highness. We were going to tell you after. His throat was slit."

"So much death," Danvell muttered.

Cleve suddenly felt sick, disgusted even. There were speckles of blood along his hands and arms. He wiped his cheek to find more there. He'd heard enough of this conversation. Knowing he was no longer needed, he approached Jessend.

Her eyes were lost along the marred tiles of the ground.

"I would like a bath, if that's alright," Cleve said.

Life came back into her face after she looked up at him. She wrapped herself around him, squeezing almost too tightly.

"Thank you," she whispered.

He felt the urge to embrace her. She'd already ruined her elegant dress by pressing against him, blood surely staining it. But he still refrained, not wanting to give her the impression that he cared for her in that way.

"We have showers here from the aqueducts," Jessend informed him. "They are much better than a bath." She stepped back, taking his bloody right hand with both of hers but not seeming to care. "I would like to see my sister and speak with my father. I'll have someone take you to the showers and give you fresh clothing. I'm sure we'll find something that can fit."

The clothing given to Cleve made him think Jessend was playing a joke on him. But with all the recent deaths, he figured she wouldn't do that at this time.

The pants were simple enough. They were dark blue and came with a belt dyed gold. The white undershirt was easy to figure out as well.

It was the fancy coat that confused him. It looked to be a jumbled mess of sleeves, straps, and buttons.

He tried to put his arm in what he thought to be the left sleeve, but there was a puzzling amount of extra hanging fabric, making him believe he was wearing it the wrong way. Turning it around, Cleve pulled the sleeves inside out.

Then the coat made sense to him. He slipped it on.

Why would they give it to me inside out?

But then he noticed the buttons were poking into his skin. Clearly, it was wrong. Letting out a discouraged breath, he turned it in on itself again.

He tried sticking both arms in wherever they would go. But then it hung loosely from his shoulders like a torn towel. The damn thing had too many buttons, and they didn't just go down the middle of the coat. There were long straps with buttons on them as well.

After ten minutes of failing and building frustration, he jerked open the door to find two guards stationed outside.

"How do I put this stupid thing on?" Cleve asked, incapable of fighting the irritation coming out in his voice.

The guards laughed. One took a step toward him, reaching out a hand. But he seemed to see someone over Cleve's shoulder and stopped, stiffening his back.

A voice came from behind Cleve. "That *stupid thing* is only given to honored guests." Danvell Takary had a smile to show he wasn't offended.

"My king." The guards bowed their heads.

"Help him with that," the monarch told them.

One took the longest strap and brought it diagonally across Cleve's chest twice. He took the other strap around Cleve's stomach and tucked it into the first one, snapping gold buttons to keep them together.

Cleve soon figured out the rest, doing the buttons himself.

"Join us for dinner, Cleve," Danvell said. "There's much we need to discuss. Tell me what's happening in Kyrro. I've heard it from Jessend, but she's been known to exaggerate. You don't seem the type to do the same."

"Kyrro is at war with the neighboring territory, Tenred," Cleve began as he walked down the hall with Danvell. "Krepps have sided with Tenred to fight against us."

"I knew that was true," Danvell said. "I want to hear more about your attack on your own king's castle."

Oh, that.

Cleve studied the King of Goldram to get a sense of what he'd already assumed. Danvell's tone was indifferent so far, showing no signs of derision. With a flat mouth and eyes gazing ahead steadily, his face revealed no emotions, either.

Cleve just decided to tell the truth as he remembered it.

As he described his missing bow, the meeting with the King of Kyrro, and his order to kill Rek, Cleve couldn't pay attention to where he was being led. With guards close behind Danvell, they traveled through many hallways before reaching a stairway that led them to even more hallways.

It became clear to Cleve that he didn't know if he was being led deeper into the palace or farther from its center. Even if he wanted to flee, he wouldn't know which direction to go.

"So, this Elf is an enemy of Kyrro?" Danvell asked halfway through Cleve's tale.

"No, that's just a misunderstanding. He wants to fight with Kyrro against Tenred. That's why we tried to speak with King Welson, to convince him of this."

"But if he's a psychic, then he could've twisted your mind into believing he was an ally." Danvell stated it like a fact.

"There's a lot about psyche you don't know."

The King stopped, showing Cleve a malignant glare. "I have many experts in all kinds of subjects. I am the King of

Goldram. There is much I know that you do not, and it would be wise for you to remember that."

At the thought of being thrown in prison, Cleve felt his eyes bulging. "I apologize." *I'd better watch my words more carefully.* "What I meant was that there was a lot I thought I knew about psyche until I met Rek and Reela."

"Reela?"

*Reela...*Cleve hadn't meant to let out her name. He took a breath as he thought of how to describe her. "A psychic who's related to Rek. They each taught me a lot, and I'm certain Rek fights for Kyrro."

"I wouldn't trust psychics, but if you choose to do so then that's your decision. I won't try to change your mind. Right now, Rek is with Micah Vail, my top adviser. The Elf has been told not to speak with me directly or to be in the same room as me. I'll feel more comfortable about keeping him in the palace as long as these rules are followed."

Yet your top adviser is a psychic as well, Cleve dared not say. At least not then when there was no reason to.

The King continued. "So I hope you can communicate for me if we need the Elf's assistance."

"I can," Cleve said.

Two women walked by, each wearing an elegant gown embroidered with the blue soaring wings of the Takary sigil. It reminded Cleve of Jessend.

"What did Jessend tell you about me?" he asked.

"That you two are to be married," Danvell said plainly, giving no hint he wished to say more.

"I'm confused by your indifference," Cleve admitted, unsure what else to say to have the King elaborate.

"You're not the first man, not even the second. I've been through it too many times by now. Jessend desperately wants to marry someone besides the man arranged for her on her seventeenth birthday next year. She seems happy with you, and I can tell you'll protect her. You have the skill for me to make you into a noble warrior, so I'm not worried about your status at this point."

The King clasped Cleve's shoulder. "And I like you better than the rest she's invited to my palace." He took his hand off Cleve abruptly. "Though, you'll have to learn better manners. I don't know why both my daughters fall for men who know nothing of nobility. Sometimes I think it's just to defy me."

Cleve decided not to bring up wishing to leave at that point. Danvell's affection seemed genuine. The last thing he wanted to do was ruin that. But he found it disconcerting that the King didn't even seem to wonder what Cleve thought of Jessend.

They arrived at an outside garden secluded within the palace walls. It was at least twice the size of the dining hall at the Academy that Cleve attended in Kyrro, which was big enough to fit all three thousand students inside. A blood red vine decorated the stone walls surrounding them. There was just enough sun left in the sky to reach the green grass that was neatly trimmed.

Jessend was seated at a metal table. Two trees that were closer to gold than they were to brown gave her shade. A swarm of servants buzzed around, quickly setting plates and silverware at the sight of the King. Two pulled out seats for him and Cleve.

"Lisanda isn't feeling well," the King told Cleve as he was seated. "After that incident, I don't think I'll be eating much, either."

Cleve wasn't sure how to greet Jessend, so he let his gaze rest on her face until she gave him a clue. She smiled and nodded, so he did the same, though he could feel his smile was not as genuine as hers.

While the food was delicious, the tiring questions that continued to interrupt his chewing soon made him wish to leave as soon as possible. Though he didn't dare let that attitude come out, and the King didn't seem to notice it, seemingly more and more pleased with Cleve's answers as the meal went on.

Danvell claimed he liked that Cleve had continued to train with the bow even though it was outlawed in Kyrro. He thought Cleve was courageous, modest, and even told him he wished more warriors were like him.

Jessend was unusually silent, as if the presence of her father had brought out a shyness in her that Cleve didn't know existed.

After the last course was completed and Cleve was finally free to leave the table, darkness had set in, so a mage was needed to light their path back inside the palace.

"I've never seen my father take a liking to a man so quickly," Jessend said with a proud glimmer in her eyes. "But saving our lives probably has something to do with it." She locked her arm around Cleve's.

He kept worrying Jessend was going to bring up their betrothal, giving him a date it was to happen. If marriage in Goldram was anything like it was in Kyrro, then a contract was signed at the end of the ceremony—a legal document that bound the man and woman together until death. Adultery was the only way out of the contract, but the guilty party would be imprisoned for breaking the marriage oath.

Cleve wanted to know if it was the same in Goldram, but he wasn't going to ask until Jessend brought it up. *Maybe she's not in a hurry to get married.*

Cleve almost laughed aloud at the absurd idea. Jessend had a cat's confidence with the impatience of a dog. The thought of her waiting for something she wanted was harder to imagine than a child wanting to finish his chores before opening a gift.

"I want to find out what happened with my sister and Jek before I tell her about you and me," Jessend said, then quickly continued before Cleve could ask who Jek was. "He kidnapped Prince Harwin and also Lisanda just before she was to marry someone else. I don't know what happened while they were together, but she believes she loves him now, and she doesn't fall in love easily."

Like you? Cleve almost asked.

Jessend placed her other hand on Cleve's arm, leaning against him as her walk slowed. "I even trust the psychic Elf more than I do Jek. But my father was considering making him the King's Mage because his ability with Sartious Energy is the best in Goldram. I left for Kyrro before finding out what happened. I don't know if he's even in the palace or not. If my sister still thinks she loves him, and she finds out you and I are to be married, she might get excited about the idea of a double wedding and rush into it with Jek. I wouldn't want that."

Cleve felt he wouldn't have a better opportunity than he did right then. "Don't you think you're rushing into this with me?"

"But I know you." Her tone was soft, as if she was about to laugh. "I don't think she really knows Jek."

Cleve had to say it, no matter what it would do to her. "I'm not who you think I am." He unhooked his arm to take hold of her shoulders, staring down at her to make sure she understood. "You act as if I'm someone else."

"I know you're not him." Her tone was irritated, her mouth a flat line. But she didn't take her eyes away from his. "You're Cleve Polken. You stormed your own king's castle with the psychic Elf. You're a skilled archer who would shoot at a princess. You're dedicated to what you believe is right, no matter how hard it is. You choose your words carefully. You're strong and very handsome, yet I can feel your innocence. I can tell you haven't been with a woman."

Stunned, he let go of her while his head snapped back. No words came, not one.

Jessend looked ready to laugh. "Nothing to say?"

Cleve badly wished he was a better liar. He could tell her that he'd been with countless women, that he had less innocence than a prostitute. Then he could convince her she actually didn't know him as well as she thought she did. But he knew she would just laugh at his attempt to prove her wrong, probably find it cute for some strange reason. So he was silent.

"I know you're still uneasy about this," she said. "I am too, just not as much as you."

"You don't seem like it."

"I'm better at hiding things than you are." She tugged on the straps around his fancy coat. "Come on. We're going to my room for the night. We'll get to know each other better."

There was nothing seductive in her tone, but her words alone gave his stomach a twist.

Chapter 4

There were two guards outside the door to Jessend's room. One of them turned to unlock it for her.

"You can leave us," Jessend said. "With a lock on the door and Cleve beside me, I won't need your protection."

"Yes, my lady."

One guard turned as he left, studying Cleve. He seemed to approve, turning back without a word.

Entering, Cleve never would've guessed the room belonged to a princess. There were five different bows hung on a wall. She lit two lamps before closing the door and locking it. The light they gave danced along the bows, making Cleve want to touch them.

He ran his finger down the black longbow in the middle. It reminded him of his own that was somewhere in King Welson's castle in Kyrro, at least he hoped it was. For all he knew, it could've been given to a guard who was in the midst of mistreating it, leaving it out in the rain or hanging it by the string when not in use.

"It looks like yours, doesn't it?" Jessend took it down and handed it to Cleve.

He ran his thumb halfway down the wood. "But it feels completely different."

Jessend slid her fingertips down his arm, as if searching for familiarity. She let her hand drop and turned away from him.

"I'm going to rinse my face and change." Her voice was distant, like a painful memory had just struck her. She grabbed some clothes from the nearby wardrobe and went into the adjacent room. "Have some wine," she told him before closing the door.

He took off his coat. Well, he tried to. The straps seemed to be buttoned on his back as well as his front. He undid the buttons down the center and tried to twist the coat around to undo the rest, but it got stuck.

Frustrated, he decided he would have some wine first, pouring himself a glass.

He planned to tell her that he didn't want to marry her. He figured the wine would help with the process. The thought of what she might say or do made him dreadfully nervous, but he knew the sooner he got it over with the better.

Even more than being nervous, he felt pain, an ache in his heart. He imagined what it would be like to finally return to Kyrro, grab Reela, and lean down to kiss her, only for her to push away and tell him she cared for someone else.

I might not be able to do this, he realized, quickly finishing his glass of wine and pouring another.

By the time Jessend came out, he was on his fourth glass, and his feverish nervousness had finally begun to calm.

She giggled when she saw him. "Let me help you with that." His coat—somehow he'd forgotten he'd never gotten it off.

As she came over, he noticed she'd changed into some sort of nightgown. It was made of a light fabric of beige color, and it covered her completely.

"Take off your shoes," she told him when his coat was off. "Get comfortable."

"Jessend." He tried to tell her when he knelt down to untie them, but he couldn't finish the sentence aloud. *I don't want to marry you.*

"Yes?" She seemed to sense his anxiousness, her brow now furrowed.

"I..." Cleve sighed. *Why do women turn me into such a coward?*

Jessend let out a light nervous giggle. "Are you scared of me?"

With his bare feet against the rug, he stood as tall as he could and looked down at her. "I'm not."

Her giggle grew to a laugh. "How much wine did you drink? Your whole mouth is dark."

Cleve licked his lips and teeth, tasting the residue quite strongly. "Three and a half glasses."

"In just that time I was in the bathroom?"

Cleve nodded.

Her mouth twisted, her eyes squinting. "I had a suspicion you didn't drink."

"I usually don't."

That seemed to sadden her. Her gaze went to the rug. "I see."

"Jessend, there's something I need to tell you."

"You don't love me."

That was a start, at least. He felt courage knowing he just had to go from there. "No," he said.

"Did you think I loved you?" She went to the wine and poured herself a glass. "I'm not insane. I don't fall in love the moment I meet a handsome man. Of course we don't love each other yet. Is this what you're worried about, that you don't love me?"

"Not just that."

"I know you want to go back to Kyrro," she said. "You're worried about the people you left behind. But Cleve, you're needed here as well. You don't know the monster that's waiting for me if you leave. And even if you go!" She surprised him by shouting. "You won't be welcomed back by your king."

Jessend stood next to the table with the wine, shifting her eyes between Cleve and the chair before her. Without thinking, Cleve found himself walking over to pull out the chair for her, pushing it in as she sat. He joined her on the other side of the table.

"It's fine that you have worries," she told him, her tone calm once again. "I do, too. You haven't even been in Goldram one day. Just take some time before you jump to any conclusions. For now, drink with me."

She held up her glass.

He did the same.

She was right. Tonight wasn't the time to tell her. With immense relief, he sipped his wine, focusing on the taste for the first time. He didn't like it, too bitter.

Several hours later he'd lost track of both time and how many glasses of wine he'd had. He learned that Jessend knew many card games, and she was either excellent at all of them or Cleve was terrible.

When Cleve grew tired of losing, he started blatantly cheating, finding more amusement in what he could get away with than in actually winning.

He asked Jessend about a painting on the wall behind her, looking at her cards when she turned. When he was about to lose, he pretended to sneeze and mixed up his cards with the deck. To his amazement, she either pretended not to know or really didn't notice him doing it, for she said nothing.

When she went to use the chamber pot in the other room, and he switched his hand with hers, he thought surely she would say something this time. But no, she came back...and even beat him without mentioning it.

He couldn't stand it any longer. Before he knew it, he was out of his seat and shaking her by the shoulders. "How have you not noticed I'm cheating?"

She burst into laughter as if she'd been holding it in for hours. She stood as well, grabbing his hands to playfully wrestle. "Of course I noticed. I just wanted to see how far you would go."

"You're such a good actor!" Cleve couldn't believe it.

He knelt down to throw her body over his shoulder. She screamed with a giggle as he hoisted her into the air.

"But there's no way you can knock me off my feet without your guards around," Cleve said, a warmth from the wine making him want to take his shirt off and wrestle.

"Put me down and we'll see about that." Her voice had a

competitive edge to it.

He let her body slide down through his arms. Instantly, she grabbed his waist and tried to pull him over her foot. He stumbled a bit but found his balance, tightening every muscle and getting low.

She pushed his shoulders, but he barely moved. She tried to step into him to shove his chest, but he grabbed her hands and pulled them out to the side.

She stepped back and hummed in thought. In another attempt to catch him off guard, she ran and jumped at him, but he moved to the side, and she crashed onto the floor.

From the way she was laughing as she rolled along the rug, he knew not to ask if she was hurt.

"Give up yet?" Cleve asked instead.

She rose to her knees, sticking out her rear as she laughed uncontrollably. But it was another trick. With amazing agility, she spun and jumped to him, wrapping her legs and arms around his torso.

The force of her petite body still was enough to make him slip. He felt his back and head slam into the rug, and a groan of pain sputtered out of him.

Jessend gasped. "I'm sorry!"

It just took a moment for him to realize he wasn't injured. A small laugh escaped from his lips. "Don't be."

As Jessend climbed off him, he felt her hands on his bare legs. Only then did he realize he didn't have his pants on anymore. He vaguely remembered removing them during some ridiculous scheme to distract her so he could cheat.

His weariness had caught up with him by the time he was back on his feet. He looked at the bed eagerly.

"It's definitely time for me to rest," he said.

"Just stay here." She spoke indifferently, even giving a shrug. "There's plenty of room in my bed."

She guided him onto it before he could think of an excuse, not that he really wanted to come up with one. He lay down on his back, hoping if he closed his eyes he and Jessend might fall asleep without anything happening.

It was hard to ignore the rustles of the bed as she made herself comfortable beside him. Flipping onto her side, she let her arm drape over his stomach. He felt the urge to touch her as well but stopped himself from reaching for her arm.

It's possible to find comfort in a woman's touch without being attracted to her, isn't it? Or does this mean I'm starting to like her? He forced himself to think about what it would be like to kiss her, as a test.

Luckily, he felt no flutter in his heart, no tingle down his back. Then his mind went to Reela, the way she'd pushed her lips against his in the dungeons beneath Welson Kimard's castle.

That brought him out of his numb state. He could feel his blood pumping through his body. With it, his worry was relieved, so he put his arm around Jessend, knowing she couldn't make him feel the way Reela did.

She snuggled closer, propping her head on his shoulder. He was blanketed in comfort and slowly began slipping into sleep.

A kiss to his cheek brought him back. "Don't sleep just yet," she uttered into his ear.

He looked to his side to find her eyes wide and staring.

"Were you planning on never kissing me?" She spoke in an overly cute voice.

"Yes," he dumbly admitted.

Her eyes squinted in concern. She sat up. "My Bastial stars, Cleve. What's so wrong with me?" All the sweetness was gone from her tone.

He sat up as well. Feeling dizzy, it took a breath for him to gather his thoughts. The first thing that came to mind were excuses. *You're too short. You're too thin. You're too rich. Your hands feel like a child's.* They flew by like arrows, there and gone in an instant. He knew they weren't reasons why he wouldn't kiss her. There was really only one answer to that.

"I want someone else...someone back in Kyrro. Nothing is wrong with you. I like you." He was surprised to find it was the truth. "But I can't give up on this other woman."

Jessend folded her arms as if she'd abruptly gotten cold. "And she feels this way about you?"

"Yes."

"You realize that even if you go back, you'll only see her when she visits your prison cell."

Cleve didn't see that as the truth. He would find a way to prove his loyalty to Kyrro. He just needed another chance. But he wasn't about to argue against Jessend. There was no point.

"So, it's this girl that's caused you to be so distant?"

Cleve found it strange how sometimes he'd notice her accent more pronounced than usual. With her hands now on her hips as she spoke of Reela, her low voice and noble inflections were extremely prominent.

"It is." He reached out to touch her knee. "I do appreciate everything you've done for me. I feel I owe a debt to you. But I must go back to Kyrro. Rek and I must both go back."

She bit her lip, looking as if she wanted to cry as she took in a breath through her nose. "I can't just help you back to Kyrro. Even if I wanted to, that's not something I can do. I don't own a ship, nor do I command a crew. And to be honest, I don't want you to go."

She grabbed his hand. "Cleve, I like you, but you're mad. How can you possibly believe you'll be returning to Kyrro? The only way that would happen is with help from my father—a lot of help. Stay by me. Help our family. In time, you may be able to request a ship, but certainly not without something to give for it." Her shoulders slumped. "I think that's the fairest I can be, given the circumstances. But if you're leaving, you'd better wait until I find someone else. I'm not marrying Kasko Lage, that monster."

Completely surprised by her cooperation, he leaned forward and squeezed her. "That's more than fair."

"Who knows," she uttered with difficulty from his tight embrace, "maybe when that time comes, you won't want to leave anymore."

So that's her plan, he realized. *She thinks if I spend enough time with her I'll change my mind. That's why she's not so upset by this.*

Her hands came up to his face. "But you have to do something for me right now. And I'd better not have to ask for it or tell you what it is."

Cleve understood. He closed his eyes and put his mouth against hers.

They tried to move their lips once they were touching, but it was sloppy and uncoordinated.

Jessend pushed him away. With a tilted head, she looked confused.

"Let's try that again."

Cleve felt a dry swallow as he leaned in. This time their lips connected like a handshake...perhaps too much like a handshake, gripping each other tightly and then getting lost as they came loose.

She pushed him away harder this time, making a sour face. "Are you doing that on purpose?"

"Doing what?"

"I don't know," Jessend let her voice trail off. "It feels strange, but I don't know why."

"It does. But I'm not doing anything on purpose to make it that way." *That's how I kissed Reela, and it worked far better than this,* he almost said.

"Kiss me again. Kiss me like you mean it, like I'm this other girl." Her grossly obvious plan was coming out even more now. She figured with enough time he could learn to feel the same way about her that he did for Reela. She didn't even seem concerned about hiding it.

Cleve was so confident it wouldn't work, he wasn't worried.

They tried a third time, and their lips fell into a smooth

pattern. There was rhythmic smacking as they pressed their lips to each other's. But Cleve felt no urge for more of her like he did for Reela. He didn't mind the kiss, yet he didn't long for it, either.

But soon he changed his mind. The kiss was becoming strange, like how he would feel if he and Effie kissed. He felt obligated to keep his lips against hers, though.

Luckily, she pulled away. Her face said it all. "I feel like I'm kissing my brother."

"It's the same for me."

"But why?"

"Because I'm not who you want me to be," Cleve told her.

Sadness began to swell in her glistening eyes. "And I'm not either, am I?"

"No." *No girl is like Reela.*

Her gaze drifted away, and Cleve could see the deep pain on her face.

"That's how it was with the last man I was with," she said. "I thought it would go away." Tears began to roll down her cheek, though her voice didn't waver. "Ever since the first man I loved died, kissing anyone else has been like this. Why can't I feel the same way I did with him?"

Cleve could feel the same hurt squeezing his chest. "I know what it's like to lose someone like that." Tired, he decided to ease her down onto her side, wrapping his arm around her as he lay beside her.

"You loved a girl you lost?" Jessend asked, wiping her tears.

"A little different than that. My parents were killed." The familiar ache of death surged through his body. With a tight stomach, he could feel himself wanting to cry. Images of the men he'd killed earlier twirled through his mind, spinning so violently he wondered if he was going to vomit.

He sat up and got ready to jump off the bed if needed. He closed his eyes and focused on his breathing.

Soon he was meditating, pulling in Bastial Energy to feel the warmth push out his panic.

He exhaled, letting it all out and opening his eyes. Jessend's hand was on his back. He'd almost broken down, but now that he hadn't, he felt strangely strong. Especially with Jessend there—someone who knew what he was feeling.

They gazed into each other's eyes, no words exchanged. Yet, he felt he was having a conversation.

We share the same pain. Do you know how to get rid of it?

He let his body back down, and she turned away and followed. He pulled her into him, holding her small body tightly. She kissed his arm and squeezed him as well.

"Both parents?" Jessend asked.

"Yes."

"That's terrible. How old were you?"

The pain he thought was gone came back with the memories of their faces. It was starting to overwhelm him, so he took a breath and pulled Jessend into him even harder. A soft whimper escaped from her, but she didn't seem to object, pressing his arms down on her with her small hands.

"It's very difficult to talk about," he managed to utter.

She spun around to face him, burying her face against his neck and blowing. It made a flatulent sound and tickled him to the point of bursting laughter.

At first he was angry, but then she pulled away smiling, and he realized the pain was gone again.

She spun back around, nestling her back and rear against him once again.

"It's easier to forget, to leave the memories buried rather than deal with them. Isn't it?" Jessend said, her solemn tone a stark contrast to her recent playful attempt at making him laugh.

He held her close. "It is, but easier isn't always healthier. I was nine when it happened." The familiar feeling of wanting to cry came over him. But as usual, it felt like he didn't know how. It was like something was holding him, preventing him from letting out the tears, from opening himself up.

It was the barrier, he realized. It was the wall he'd been building throughout the years, the one that kept his emotions trapped where he wouldn't feel them. He could feel himself pushing against it. Deep down, his emotions were swelling, the force of them causing the wall to bend.

He worried about what would happen if it broke, but he almost wanted to see for himself.

He heard Jessend sniffle. "I miss him so much it hurts."

Turned away from him, Cleve could hear Jessend crying.

"It's painful to the point where it makes you wish you could forget your memories," Cleve said. "But then you feel ashamed at the thought of wishing to forget."

The wall was barely holding now.

Jessend sniffled again and let out a weep, taking a breath to stifle the next.

"But it seems that forgetting is the only way to get over it," she whispered.

Hearing her say what he'd always believed broke him. His barrier shattered, and tears freely flowed from his eyes.

She interlaced her fingers with his, pressing his hand against her heart.

"I know there's another way besides forgetting," Cleve said. "I just haven't figured it out yet. Forgetting is wrong."

She turned with tears streaming, throwing her arms over his chest, pressing herself against him.

"I know it's wrong." She held in a shaky gasp of a weep so she could continue. "And I hate myself for thinking it."

Tears continued to explode out of him. Yet somehow there was no pain, just sadness. He wept without shame or remorse. He wept with strength, knowing this was a way of healing. His body encouraged him to keep at it.

This was wrecking his wall, which he'd constantly worried it would, but he didn't even feel scared. He knew he would need to rebuild it, but it was just like knowing he had a long day coming with a lot of hard work. It was something he could do. It might be arduous, but there was no point in worrying because it had to happen. And if his barrier broke down again, he could rebuild it once more. He might even get better in the process.

He found comfort in the feeling of Jessend's arms holding on to him, knowing she felt the same way he did. The Princess wrapped her legs around him as well.

His weeping calmed, his tears stopping with it. But he still could feel her hot tears rolling onto his shoulder as she nestled her head into him. She didn't seem to be recovering in the same way he was.

"Don't hate yourself," he told her. "I feel the same hatred, so it must be normal."

Her sniffles came to a stop.

"We have all night," Cleve said. "You tell me everything you can remember about him, and I'll tell you everything I can remember about my parents, no matter how painful. We'll get it all out."

Finally feeling comfortable with their death, Cleve wanted to remember everything he could about them. He'd never felt this way before—wanting nothing more than to speak about his mother and father.

She kissed him on the cheek. It was hard and tender at the same time, like that from a mother or sister who'd been gone for too long and had just come home.

"I can think of nothing in the world that would be better than that right now," she said.

Cleve lost track of the hours.

It wasn't until the sun was up that they finally fell asleep cuddled close together.

His last thought was of her hands. He'd spent a lot of time touching them that night, and he couldn't help but still think of them as childlike. They were so small in his grasp, unnervingly fragile. They gave him strength when he thought of his own body compared to hers. How could someone like him be so easily broken?

But he was. Within himself, he felt the same fragility as he did about her hands. He knew it was the barrier he would need to rebuild. And he looked forward to it—after he rested.

Chapter 5

Cleve awoke from a soft knocking at the door.

A murmur came through. "Lady Jessend?"

Jessend grumbled and turned away from Cleve and the direction of the door.

The knocking continued. "Lady Jessend?" The voice was louder this time.

Cleve shook her shoulder. "Someone's at the door."

"See what they want," Jessend replied with a demanding tone.

Not a morning person, Cleve thought, pulling the sheets off him.

He noticed Jessend petulantly grabbing the sheet that slipped off her shoulder and throwing it over her head as he went for the door.

A pale servant girl had her eyes at Cleve's chest when he opened it. Startled, she looked up to find his face and her cheeks became flushed.

"Oh, I..." With wide eyes, she turned her head down in an obvious manner to look away.

Cleve was surprised by how young she was, probably thirteen, he guessed.

"I didn't know there would be a..." She scratched her neck. "A guest."

"Is there something you need from Jessend?" Cleve asked.

Jessend shouted before the poor girl could answer. "What do you want Gerace?"

"Your father asked me to dress you and bring you to him. Kasko Lage has announced he'll be visiting soon."

"Tell my father I'm sick." Jessend faked a cough.

"He said you would say that. And he told me to tell you..."

Gerace swallowed hard. "May I come in, my lady?"

"What did he tell you to tell me?" Jessend sat up, her wild hair a mess across her face and shoulders.

"I'd rather not repeat it."

Cleve thought he should put some pants on and left the doorway to do so.

Jessend jumped from the bed. "One moment." She threw the door shut and gave Cleve her eye. "Please don't leave me alone with him."

"With who?"

"Kasko. I want you to be there when I have to meet him. I need you to see what he's like."

"Why?" Cleve already was thinking of excuses.

"So you know what you're protecting me from. He's the man I'm to marry if I don't find someone else who can earn my father's approval."

Cleve was hoping he could go back to sleep. It was only a few hours ago that they'd been holding each other and speaking of painful memories. His mind felt raw, like an open wound. But he owed it to Jessend.

He nodded.

She let out a breath, showing him red eyes over a troubled smile. "I'll send someone to get you from your room."

He got a little more sleep in his own bed before knocking woke him again.

He was surprised to find that Gerace was the one Jessend had sent. "I'm to take you to the throne room," she said, easily looking him in the eye this time. "Jessend wants you to hurry."

"What do I wear?" Cleve thought to ask.

Gerace invited herself in, reaching through his wardrobe and throwing a shirt and a pair of pants onto his bed. "And please use the mirror. Your hair is unkempt."

Cleve started removing his shirt, and the redness he'd first seen in Gerace's cheeks came back with a rush. She practically ran out the door.

"Come out when you're finished," she said into the hallway, closing the door behind her.

Luckily, there were no confusing straps to the buttoned shirt chosen for him, and soon he was following Gerace through the palace and into the throne room.

Jessend looked to be hiding behind her father, peering out around his shoulder. In front of them was a man Cleve assumed to be Kasko Lage.

This is who Jessend is afraid of?

He wasn't much older than Cleve and quite short for a man. For some reason Cleve thought of Reela and how she was probably taller than Kasko, most likely even outweighing him. It could have been his nearly blond hair that made Cleve think of her. He wasn't sure.

Kasko had a cheerful smile, open-mouthed with bright teeth. Jessend waved Cleve over and wrapped both arms around his right arm as she stood beside him.

"See," Jessend said. "He's big, so you'd better stay away."

"Jessend!" Danvell Takary shouted. "You're going to spend all day in the kitchen if you don't start behaving."

Kasko laughed merrily. "It's fine, my king. Jessend and I like to joke." He turned his attention toward Cleve. "So you're my competition?" He kept his smile and held out a hand for Cleve to step forward and shake. Cleve didn't see the harm and slipped from Jessend's grasp to move toward Kasko.

Kasko grabbed Cleve's elbow with his free hand and leaned in to whisper, "Such a strong man, but your skin cuts just as easily as anyone else's."

Cleve shoved Kasko hard. The small man stumbled backward dramatically, his face filled with shock.

Two guards pointed their swords at Cleve, edging forward.

"I don't know where you get the idea you can act like that," the King of Goldram scolded Cleve. "But if you touch Kasko again, you can look forward to spending the rest of your time imprisoned."

Kasko shook his head at Cleve in disbelief. "I just told him that he should be ready for competition. I won't let Jessend go so easily."

"No," Cleve corrected. "He threatened to cut me."

Kasko gasped. "And he's a liar as well!"

Jessend stomped her foot. "He's—" She stopped her shout when her father folded his arms and glared.

The King turned to Cleve next. "Apologize to Kasko Lage and promise you won't touch him again."

"I'm sorry," Cleve muttered. "I promise I won't touch you." A mixture of embarrassment and frustration made him boil with rage.

Kasko smiled nervously, playing the scared little boy all too well. "You're forgiven. I understand some men can't help but feel threatened by competition."

Cleve bit down hard to keep himself from balling his fists.

Kasko cocked his head toward Danvell. "May I take Jessend out of the palace?" he asked sweetly. "I'd like some time alone with her."

"Of course," Danvell replied, his tone as if Kasko didn't even need to ask. "Jessend..." He took her shoulder and glanced at her with one eye, tilting his head to the side.

Apparently there was some sort of understanding between them, for Jessend meekly nodded before letting her gaze sink to the floor.

She shuffled to Kasko and latched her arm around his without a glance.

When they left, the King spoke before Cleve could go. "Jessend can be very manipulative. She likes to overdramatize, and men can be drawn to her, taking her side whether or not they believe it's right. Did she tell you to do that to Kasko?"

"No. Kasko said my skin cuts just as easily as anyone else's." When Cleve heard himself say the words, they didn't come off as threatening as they had from Kasko's mouth. The way the small man had squeezed his elbow and whispered it was menacing. Cleve had felt the man's evil like a cold wind reaching the bones beneath his skin.

"It sounds like he was just referring to a friendly duel. He did mention competition. You need to calm yourself. I greatly appreciate what you've done for this family already, but if you become aggressive with Kasko again, I'll need to punish you. His father is a brilliant man who's revolutionizing safe surgery. He's invented numerous techniques, sterilizations, and he's even working on a way to transfer blood safely from one Human body into another. He's richer than I am, with a staff of medical experts that would be a major advantage in any war."

Danvell glanced toward the doorway, lowering his voice. "Jessend may not love Kasko, but their marriage could save thousands of people in Goldram if the Lage family was on our side." The King fell into silence, making Cleve wonder what he should say.

"I can see how Kasko's family is important." *But there's something wrong with that man.*

"Yes, but Kasko has done nothing for this family yet, unlike you." Danvell showed Cleve a proud smile. "It's rare for me to like a man that Jessend has brought to the palace, but you're different than most men." He stopped to look at a timepiece from his pocket. "I would like to speak with you more about this whole situation, but I don't have the time at the moment." The King turned to leave.

Cleve decided to take his chances with a possibly dangerous question. "May I see Rek?"

"Who?"

"The psychic Elf who came with me. I'm not sure where he's staying."

"I'm keeping him far from me. I'll have a guard bring you to him."

Rek's room was adorned with many vases of flowers along

with pictures of Elves on the walls.

Cleve was confused by them. "Do you know these Elves?"

Rek laughed. "Not one of them. I don't know why they thought to litter the walls with paintings of Elves I've never met. I guess they believed it would comfort me." He shook his head. "It seems they know as little about Elves as I do."

"What happened with the King's adviser—the psychic one?"

"Micah Vail." Rek was nodding now. "He's a very cautious man, and he has good reason to be."

"So you're not going to tell anyone he's a psychic?"

"I have no reason to. He's helping me." Rek lowered his voice. "Probably because I'm cooperating."

Cleve was about to ask if Rek could be sure Micah's intentions were genuine, but then he remembered who he was talking to.

"What's he doing for you?" Cleve asked instead.

"I'm going to visit the Elves once I learn how to ride a horse."

Cleve felt his eyes go wide. "Are you coming back?"

Rek squeezed Cleve's shoulder, and he felt his worry lessen. "Of course. But I have to take this opportunity. I'm sure you understand."

Cleve did, nodding to show it.

"Micah Vail says it's better for me to leave soon," Rek continued. "He's worried that the longer I'm here and the more I prove myself useful, the harder it's going to be to convince the King to let me go...although, I'm pretty sure both of them realize there's not much they can do to contain me. Micah has learned to trust me, but he says the King probably never will, probably won't ever want to be in the same room as me."

Rek let out a bitter laugh. "I didn't think I would meet someone who was more scared of psychics than you."

"I tried to tell him there's nothing to worry about, but he doesn't want to listen to me."

"It's fine. It might even be better if he's afraid of me." Rek adjusted a nearby painting of a female Elf with blonde hair. "I like this one the best. Her eyes don't stare at me with the same judgment I feel from the other paintings."

Cleve didn't feel nearly as safe knowing Rek was leaving the palace, but he wasn't lying earlier—he did understand the need.

"What do you hope to happen when you visit the Elves?" he asked.

Rek turned to Cleve, tilting his head. "I want to learn everything I can about what happened between the Krepps and the Elves. I'm hoping I can convince them to come back and fight with us, but I know nothing of Elven culture. I'm nervous about what they'll think of me...given I can't even speak their language."

"Do you know if many of them are psychics?"

"I don't know that, and neither does anyone in Goldram, apparently."

A guard knocked. "Cleve Polken? We have a letter for you."

Cleve opened the door, and the guard handed him a sealed note. "It's from Kasko Lage," the guard said.

Cleve opened it to find a folded piece of paper with some sort of red substance dripping from it. No words were written on it. "What is this?" Cleve wondered.

Rek peered around Cleve. "It looks like blood."

Blood? Cleve maneuvered the letter to avoid the blood touching his skin.

"That's strange," the guard commented, leaning in for a closer look.

"What does it mean?" Rek asked.

The guard shrugged. "I've never seen that before."

"I think it means I have a new friend," Cleve muttered.

Chapter 6

The sun was nearly gone from the sky. The only reason Cleve noticed was because he was having trouble seeing the target that he'd been staring at for the last few hours.

Guards had set him up in the training grounds with a bow. They stayed with Cleve to shoot some arrows, only to succumb to frustration and leave when they soon found themselves far less skilled than he was.

One made Cleve promise him a duel the next day, to which Cleve gladly agreed. He'd been aching to use both a sword and bow, craving them like a fatigued body begs for sleep.

"Did you hit the target?" Jessend surprised him by asking just after he shot. She had a hand cupped over her eyes. "I can't even see it."

"Come closer and you can." He waved her toward him.

She closed the door to the palace, folding her arms with a slight shiver and walking to him. She leaned against him and squinted.

"You did hit it. Is this how far you usually shoot from?"

Cleve judged the distance to be around fifty yards. "Something like this, usually."

Jessend pushed him playfully. "You're sweaty. You need to shower before you get in my bed."

Cleve had no reply. He must've made a face, for she showed him a disappointed look.

"You don't want to stay with me like you did last night?"

"I'm very tired," Cleve admitted. "But I want to hear what happened with Kasko. As long as we don't stay up too late..."

Jessend nodded. "So I assume you got his letter?"

"Yes. Whose blood was that?"

"His own. He made me watch him cut his hand. He thought

it would scare me, but it didn't. Kasko can cut himself to pieces in front of me and I would only smile. I pretend to show fear, only because I don't know what he'll do if I don't." She shivered.

"How does your father not see that Kasko wears his sanity like a hat?"

"Because he's never taken it off in front of my father. And I'd say a wig would be closer to the truth—it's more deceiving than a hat." Jessend looked toward the door. "I'm tired as well, always am after a visit from Kasko. Get in the shower so we can go to bed. I'm going to look for my sister in the meantime. Come by my room in an hour."

"Alright," Cleve agreed.

When Cleve came by later, Jessend's door was locked, and his knocks went unanswered.

Probably found her sister, he guessed.

He sat on a velvet bench nearby, his thoughts wondering about home. It always made him nauseous to imagine a battle raging against the Academy's walls with him not there to help defend it. Thousands of Kreps storming into the school, the students and teachers outnumbered and outmatched.

Cleve's fists clenched as if he felt it was happening right then.

Why did he keep seeing Reela getting killed when he thought of her? It pained him every time, like a needle pricking his heart.

But he did manage to realize that it hardened him as well, made him remember his priorities. He swallowed a thick stream of saliva that had built up in his nausea and pinched his leg to distract himself from the worsening pain in his chest.

Cleve couldn't sit any longer. He noticed a guard coming down the hall.

"Do you know where Jessend is?" Cleve stood and asked.

The guard glanced over his shoulder. "She's in Lisanda's

room."

Cleve thanked the guard and started to leave before he realized he had no idea where her room was. "Can you tell me where it is?"

The guard grunted dismissively. "Right there." He pointed to the room next to Jessend's and went back to his route.

Cleve knocked.

"Cleve?" Jessend asked from behind the door.

"Yes."

She opened it just wide enough to slip through, closing it behind her and stepping out into the hall. Her eyes were red and her hair tangled.

"I'm sorry I wasn't there earlier, but...Lisanda..." Jessend choked down her next words. "She was finally telling me about Jek. It's really bad. I had no idea how close they really were—are, close they are," she corrected herself twice, shaking her head as she took a breath. "I'm going to spend the night with her. Tomorrow you're starting horseback training. I'll send someone to get you in the morning." Jessend turned and slipped back into the room.

Alone in his bed, Cleve missed Jessend's company more than he ever would've guessed.

He tried to remember the last time he'd felt as lonely as he did that night.

When I was in Welson's castle, after he told me I had to kill Rek, Cleve realized. *I didn't even sleep then.*

But in bed now, he did manage to drift off, awaking with the sun peeking in through his window.

Soon after he was up. Gerace was knocking and slowly opening his door without waiting for his answer.

"Cleve Polken, I'm bringing your breakfast," she announced, keeping her head low as she entered. Cautiously looking up, she seemed to let out a breath of relief when she found Cleve dressed.

She wheeled in a plate with a fancy silver lid atop it. "Eggs, bacon, cheese, bread, and juice," she told him.

"Thank you, Gerace."

She pushed her top lip toward her nose in a petulant manner. "It's Jay-riss."

Cleve could tell she was saying her name slightly different than he was, but he couldn't hear the difference. He felt himself squinting as he attempted to figure it out.

"Jay-ress?" he tried.

She rolled her eyes. "Jay-riss!"

Cleve became disinterested, not wanting to try again, but she seemed to be waiting for him to say it. He sighed.

"Jerr-iss?" Cleve knew it was wrong the moment he said it.

She scoffed, her curly dark hair bouncing with her head. She turned on her heels and left.

Cleve could hear her sit down on the bench outside. He waited, but she didn't move. So he peered out curiously.

"What?" Gerace asked, displaying her annoyance with lowered eyebrows.

"Why are you just sitting there?"

She rolled her eyes. "So I can take you to the horse range when you're done, since you still don't know your way around."

"You're just going to sit there and wait for me to eat?"

"Yes, so if you wouldn't mind starting, I have a lot to do."

Cleve went back in and started eating. The food was hot and delicious, but he couldn't enjoy it knowing Gerace was right outside waiting.

After a few bites, he got back up and said, "Will you come in here while you wait?"

"Do you need something?" Her anger had turned to curiosity.

I just don't want you sitting out here, isn't that enough? "Do you want some food?"

She shook her head. "I've already eaten." The way her eyes drifted down to his feet made it clear her meal had not been nearly as good as his.

Cleve heard someone walking down the hall. Before he turned, Gerace jumped up and bowed her head. "My lady."

Lisanda stopped to curtsy. Cleve hadn't noticed before, but she was taller than Jessend by perhaps an inch. She had the same small head, with big brown eyes, but her nose and chin were more pronounced, giving her face a slightly less round shape than Jessend's.

"Cleve, are you not hungry?" Lisanda asked, noticing his nearly full plate inside the room on the table.

"I am. I just felt awkward eating with Gerace sitting outside waiting for me."

With her hands on her hips, Lisanda turned to the pale young girl. "You're making him uncomfortable. Please make yourself busy until he's done."

"I didn't mean—" Cleve started to say.

"Yes, Lady Lisanda." Gerace ran off before Cleve could correct his mistake.

Now she's going to hate me even more.

Lisanda strolled into Cleve's room and sat at the table with his food begging to be eaten. She eyed his empty seat until he sat.

"Go ahead and eat," she said. "I just want to get to know you better while I have this chance."

Cleve hesitantly scooped some food into his mouth as he waited for her to continue.

"Are you a psychic like your Elven friend?"

"No. Why do you ask?"

"I've never seen Jessend so confused. What have you done to her?"

Cleve would've thought Lisanda was joking, but her tone was accusatory. She had the same noble accent and low voice as Jessend, though it felt far less playful, as she seemed to be blaming him for something.

"I'm not sure what you mean." Cleve continued to eat,

hoping this conversation would end when he was finished.

"My sister has always been so sure of herself. But recently she questions her own desires, she weeps easily, and she's even told me she's not sure she knows what love is. So I ask again, what have you done to her?"

Cleve was starting to get the feeling that Lisanda was just being protective in that moment. At least he hoped she wasn't always like this, otherwise he'd soon find her more annoying than Captain Mmzaza.

Interestingly enough, Cleve knew exactly how Jessend was feeling, at least weeping easily and questioning her own desires. The same things had happened to Cleve since their night together.

"We've each suffered the loss of loved ones," he told Lisanda. "We're still healing, and the process of that makes us feel like we're not ourselves."

Pain seemed to strike Lisanda's previously tough face. Her tight lips loosened into a frown, and her eyes started to glisten.

"Oh." She let out a sigh. "I think I understand...I might be losing someone as well."

Might be? Her words made no sense to Cleve, but from the way she was glancing down at the table, he thought it was best not to pry.

He finished his food quickly and stood. "Is Jessend waiting for me at the stables?"

Lisanda shook her head. "Not yet. Sit back down."

Cleve didn't obey at first, hoping he could change her mind. Yet, he thought of no excuse he could give...now that he didn't have to be somewhere.

He sat, finding Lisanda's face had gone hard again as she stared at him intently.

"What do you want from us?" Lisanda had a way of sounding extraordinarily accusatory, as if she'd already assumed Cleve was guilty of something.

It made him think to ask, "What did Jessend tell you so far?"

"I want to hear you say it. I want you to tell me—if I could snap my fingers and everything you wanted could come true, what would it be?"

The answer came easily. "I'd want to be able to return to Kyrro with Rek. I'd want Kasko Lage to be gone. And I'd want Jessend to be happy." As soon as he said the three things aloud, his head felt five times heavier from guilt. He couldn't look up. "I realize how impossible it is for all three of those to come true," he muttered.

"At least you're not an idiot," Lisanda said flatly. "Jessend won't be happy if you leave, and Kasko has his eyes set on my sister like a hawk circling its prey." Lisanda tapped the table to have him look up at her. "Jessend told me she wants to help you get back to Kyrro. She believes our father will help with the ship if you can help him with something. She's planning to speak to him about this. I wanted to hear it from you. Is this what you've discussed? You're fine with allowing her to help you so that you can leave her with Kasko?"

I was before, but Lisanda's right. "I need to get back as soon as I can. There's a war in Ovira. But I won't leave Jessend until Kasko has been taken care of." Cleve felt pride lifting him from his chair. He stood with his chest out.

But the way Lisanda rolled her eyes at him made him sink back down into it, ashamed, though he didn't even know why.

"You're a skilled warrior," Lisanda said, "but the fight between you and Kasko won't be with arms. You have a lot to learn before you can even hope to scare him." Lisanda stood. "Request a meeting with Micah Vail when you can. Speak to him about it. He'll help you come up with a plan." She slipped her arm around Cleve's. "But for now, it's time to start your horseback training. Jessend is waiting for you."

"You said she wasn't."

"Would you have stayed and spoken with me as patiently if I hadn't?"

Cleve understood and let Lisanda lead him out without

argument. Gerace walked by them to clean up after Cleve.

"I'm sorry, Gerace," he said to her back.

She gave no reply, not even a look over her shoulder.

After they turned the corner onto another hall, Lisanda said, "You're saying her name wrong, you know."

Cleve sighed.

Chapter 7

The horse range, like other outdoor areas within the palace, was reached from the first floor. Cleve was starting to learn the layout of the enormous home to the Takarys and their staff and associates by then. There was actually a system, it seemed.

The entire building was symmetrical, with the nobler residents living on the top floors while the servants and chefs and other workers lived in the basement. The horse range was in the back of the palace where just one last white wall was all that remained between the palace and the northern side of the city—The Nest, a name Cleve still wasn't used to.

Lisanda took him to the glass doors that opened onto a wide field where horses ranged.

"Don't act any differently toward Jessend now that we've spoken about her," Lisanda warned him. "If you're softer on her, she'll take insult to that. She doesn't need to be coddled."

"You don't need to tell me that," Cleve said.

Lisanda nodded with a wry smile. "I'm going to go fetch Rek. I've been meaning to talk to him as well. I look forward to practicing my Elvish."

"He doesn't speak Elvish," Cleve warned her.

Lisanda's shoulders gave out. "What?"

"He doesn't know the language."

The Princess let out a long breath before turning and dragging her feet away.

There were a few horses nibbling on grass nearby with someone attending to them. Cleve figured there were many more of the massive animals in the large wooden building off against the side wall.

As he started toward it, he found Jessend talking with another young woman. They didn't seem to notice him coming, and soon Jessend was wrapping her arms under the woman's rear and hoisting her off the ground.

"Shit!—oops." The woman covered her mouth right after her accidental swearing, and Jessend burst into laughter, nearly dropping her. "Bastial hell," the woman said. "You *can* lift me!"

"I told you." Jessend's eyes found Cleve. "Finally!" She hopped over and dragged him to the woman. "This is Silvie."

Cleve held out his hand and gave his name. She shook it hard with a smile. He wondered if Silvie was a nickname, for she had hair so light it was nearly silver.

She was tall, but lean and strong. Her height might've matched Reela's, but Cleve already could tell they were nearly completely opposite. Just by the way she'd shaken his hand, he could feel a competitive edge emanating from her. She had the same physical confidence as Jessend, looking intently at Cleve as if she wanted to wrestle just to prove how strong she was.

Silvie seemed older than Jessend, though, perhaps close to twenty or even a little older.

"Now there's no way you can lift *him!*" Silvie raised her eyebrow, gesturing her head toward Cleve.

Jessend turned to study him, taking a hand to her chin and humming in thought.

Cleve shook his palm at her and stepped back. "You can't, and you're going to hurt yourself if you try."

Silvie laughed. "Don't tell her she can't do something."

"Maybe later...after some wine," Jessend said, her tone far too serious for Cleve's taste. "We have work to do. Silvie, what horse would you recommend for Cleve besides one that's strong enough to support his weight."

Silvie smiled at Jessend, taking a blade of grass out of her dark hair. "I bet you're the only princess in all of Greenedge who regularly gets grass in her hair."

With a shy grin, Jessend looked down to her feet. Silvie let the blade of grass fall and turned to Cleve. The way her eyes had lingered on Jessend made the shift of focus to him seem reluctant.

"You seem gentle for your size," she said, going into the stables and waving him in after her. "Perhaps a horse of the same type would suit you well. Come meet Nulya."

Cleve followed Silvie inside. Jessend ran past him to lock arms with her. Silvie seemed to stiffen from Jessend's touch. The Princess might've sensed it, for she unhooked her arm after just a few steps. They both seemed relieved that Nulya was right there, turning to the horse eagerly.

"She's generally a quiet horse, until someone gets on her bad side," Silvie said. "She can be quite the beast when needed."

"That's perfect for Cleve." Jessend reached out a hand to pet the side of the horse's head.

"They don't bite?" Cleve asked.

"Not usually," Silvie answered, opening the gate to let out the massive white horse. "You're not going to be riding her yet. It's best for her to learn to trust you first."

Jessend put her hand on Silvie's arm. "Unfortunately, we don't have a lot of time. Cleve has to learn how to ride as soon as possible."

Silvie's thin lips twisted. "If it must be done, then fine. But I insist he at least walk her around the range and feed her before getting on her back."

Silvie waited for Jessend to nod in agreement before handing Cleve the reins. "Lead her around while you talk to her in a friendly manner," Silvie said. "Make sure to let her know who's in charge. She might try to veer away from you or get too far into your space, pushing against you with her head. Don't let her or she might think you're weak, unfit to ride her. She usually behaves after she's gotten to know her rider. I'll get some apples ready for you to feed her when you get back. She'll trust you more quickly knowing you have access to apples."

The range was so big it took him ten minutes to get halfway across it. Most of that was from Nulya wanting to stop or change directions every few steps.

Cleve found himself talking to her as he did his best to maintain control. "Why do you let people ride you? You're huge. Do you like people...is that why?"

It seemed strange that a horse would let someone on its back unless it wanted to. Although she gave no sign of understanding him, he continued.

"Or do you just not know how to get someone off your back? How fast can you run? You must be able to throw people off you. Are you going to throw me off?" The horse whinnied, and it startled Cleve.

He laughed at himself. "You scared me."

The horse whinnied again, this time softer. Cleve laughed once more, wondering if he really was having a conversation with the animal or if it was just a coincidence.

When he turned around, Jessend was riding toward him. Her horse was going impressively fast, bouncing through the air.

She stopped it right beside Cleve and the horse reared up, letting out a loud whinny. "How's Nulya?"

"Um." Cleve couldn't tell if her question was serious or not. "She's a horse."

Jessend giggled. "Obviously. How do you like her?"

"I think I like her."

Jessend hopped off her horse to walk beside Cleve, dragging her mount along her other side. "Isn't Silvie cute?" She shot a look back at the stables.

Cleve shrugged. "I guess."

"She's really good with the horses. Her father was the stable master, but he passed away recently from an illness. She didn't take it well, but she's even better at hiding it than we are. Sometimes I wonder if she's incapable of crying."

"I thought I might have been that way," Cleve said. "But now I don't believe anyone is."

After about an hour of Silvie and Jessend coaching him, Cleve was able to trot around the range on his own, his commands to Nulya becoming well understood.

He even thought he was making quick progress until Lisanda came with Rek and the Elf was doing things with his horse that apparently neither Takary sister nor Silvie had ever seen before.

Rek chose his own horse against Silvie's wishes. It was ugly, Cleve thought, gray and white with streaks of brown down its neck and under its belly. Its mouth and knees were black, dark black, darker than Jessend's hair. From afar, the animal looked filthy.

Rek chose him because he was "the smartest," the Elf claimed.

Silvie tried to argue that the horse was wild, but Rek didn't care. He led the horse out of the stables without even holding the reins, guiding the animal with a wave of his hand. Then he pushed out his palm and told the horse to lie down. Silvie and the Takary sisters each gasped as the homely horse obeyed, folding down on all fours to let Rek climb on top.

"Up," the Elf commanded, and the horse rose.

Rek fiddled with his hands, trying to find a place to hold onto. When he grabbed the horse's mane, Silvie started to object, but Rek quickly petted the animal and took the reins instead.

"I can feel what he doesn't like," Rek explained. "I realized as soon as I did it that he didn't want me grabbing him there."

In no time, the Elf was galloping around the range, his horse leaping over low fences and whinnying in joy. Cleve couldn't help but feel somewhat discouraged, especially when he asked Silvie how long it would take for him to control his horse like Rek.

"Could be years before your horse is jumping over anything," Silvie explained.

Soon, Rek was leading his mount back into the stables.

"Done already?" Cleve asked.

"My ass hurts," Rek answered. "And I don't think I really

need practice with this sort of thing."

Now more eager than ever, after seeing what Rek could do with his horse, Cleve asked, "Can you get my horse to trust me any better?"

Rek shrugged. "I can try."

Rek followed Cleve as he trotted around and gave commands to Nulya. The Elf used psyche to help the horse understand what Cleve was commanding.

"What does Nulya think of me?" Cleve asked after the better part of an hour.

Rek walked up to place his pale hand on the top of Nulya's head. "Nothing really, at least not that I can sense."

Disappointed, Cleve let out a loud breath. He'd never been one for pets, but Nulya was no pet. She was strong and beautiful, able to carry him many more miles than he could walk in a day. He wanted to take her back to Kyrro. He wanted them to be friends.

Friends...right. The thought was silly.

Or is it? I suppose I don't know enough about horses to tell whether or not we could be friends.

A loud giggle from Jessend stole his attention, reminding him of something he needed to tell Rek. "Jessend is going to speak to her father about letting us leave," Cleve said. "She believes if we help them in a battle or some task, then the King will provide us with a ship and a crew."

Rek turned to investigate her, showing no sign of excitement. In a low voice, he asked, "Is she one to lie?"

"I don't believe so."

"Silvie has strong feelings for her," Rek mumbled.

"What?" Cleve blurted. "You mean Silvie cares for her like a good friend?"

Rek shook his head with a pressed grin. "More than that. There's a strong attraction there. I'm not going to mention it to them, but it was the first thing I noticed. It's emanating from Silvie like heat from a fire."

"What about Jessend?"

"She's a bundle of passion. Without a few direct questions, I won't know which of her emotions are associated with Silvie."

"Could it be confusion you're sensing from her? Lisanda told me her sister's been confused."

Rek nodded. "That could be it." The Elf put his hand on Cleve's shoulder. "I'm sensing a much stronger connection toward her from you. You're not losing interest in my sister, I hope?"

"No, I care for Reela just as deeply as when we left. But I worry for Jessend. I think we owe it to her to help with whatever we can, which is something I've been meaning to speak to you about."

Rek lifted an eyebrow as Cleve showed him a serious glance.

Cleve asked, "How do you feel about helping me prove someone is evil?"

Rek's long Elven eyes brightened. "I'm listening."

Chapter 8

After divulging his plan to Rek, Cleve was on his way to visit Micah Vail. Getting lost only once, he managed to find the right room through Rek's instructions.

He knocked. The door slowly opened to show Micah already walking back to his seat at a table. Cleve caught the door and shut it behind him, waiting for Micah to greet him before speaking.

Upon second sight, Cleve figured he was right that the King's adviser seemed to be in his late twenties—about Rek's age—but with black hair that hung over his forehead instead of the Elf's dark brown.

"Just a moment," he told Cleve as he finished writing.

Cleve looked around to busy his eyes. There was a set of glass doors letting in the afternoon sun, but in each corner of the room were locked chests remaining in the shadows.

"I'm glad you came to visit me, Cleve." Micah stood and held out his hand. "Thank you for keeping my secret. I understand Rek explained to you how important it is that others not know?"

Cleve nodded, shaking the man's hand and realizing that Micah's ears were covered by his hair.

"Are you an Elf as well?" Cleve asked.

"No." Micah moved his hair to show his round ears. "I understand you and Rek are trying to get back to Kyrro." Micah held out his hand to a chair against the wall. Cleve sat, feeling some soreness from the horseback riding.

"We are."

"But that's not why you're here." Micah had a knowing tone.

Cleve wondered if he was just a good guesser or he really could tell that from psyche. "No. I have a letter I'd like to reach

Kasko Lage, but I'm not sure how to get it to him." Cleve drew it from his pocket and offered it to Micah.

As the King's adviser unfolded it, the corner of his mouth twisted into a grin. "So Jessend has convinced you Kasko is *evil?*" He spoke emphatically, showing he clearly didn't believe it to be true. Cleve couldn't understand how that was possible, given that he was a psychic. *Perhaps Micah and Kasko hadn't spent much time together? Or could Kasko really be so good at disguising himself that he could keep it from a psychic?* The thought frightened him.

"Jessend didn't say anything," Cleve explained. "I could tell because he threatened to cut me and then sent me a note soaked in his blood."

Micah slowly looked up from Cleve's letter. "A note soaked in his blood, you said?"

"Jessend was there when he cut himself to make it."

Micah's face froze in a contorted look of shock. "What did the note say?"

"There was nothing written on it."

Again, Micah didn't speak, his expression frozen. "And you said he threatened you?"

Cleve nodded.

Micah Vail was no longer diverting any attention to Cleve's letter, not in that moment at least. "What were his exact words?"

"He said my skin cuts just as easily as anyone else's. He whispered it." Cleve hoped that would be enough to convince the King's adviser, but it didn't seem to be. Micah's face was relaxing now, his eyes lowering back to Cleve's letter to mumble the words on the page:

"Kasko Lage, if you wish to marry Jessend Takary, then you'll have to prove you're a better suitor than I am. Come to the Takary Palace and we'll settle this in a single day. I'll present a gift and make a final statement as to why Jessend and the

Takary family will be better off with me, and you'll do the same. Then she and her father will make a final decision."

Micah let his hand drop to his side when he finished reading. "You're sure to lose this. Jessend may choose you, but until you spend more time with the King, he's sure to pick Kasko, and his decision is more important than hers. If you want to win Danvell's favor, you're going to need more time."

"All I need is for Kasko to come. I can handle the rest." Cleve was reluctant to tell Micah how he planned to use Rek, at least while the King's adviser didn't believe Kasko to be evil. "Can you make sure this letter gets to him?"

"You might lose Jessend by doing this."

"I won't."

Micah tilted his head. "You don't even love her yet. Why are you so hasty?"

For a moment Cleve wondered if he could reveal the truth about himself and Jessend to Micah.

When he remembered the secret he held over the psychic, the decision became easy. "Jessend and I will never be together romantically. Once I remove Kasko from her life, she'll be free to marry someone else."

Micah was shaking his head. "I can tell you have good intentions, but this is the wrong way to go about this." The psychic sighed. "You remind me of another man your age, Jek Trayden, the King's Mage. Just like him, you have a kind heart, but you know nothing about nobility."

Cleve was about to demand that Micah Vail just send the letter, but Micah held up a hand and spoke before it was necessary. "I'll make sure this gets to Kasko. But I can't promise anything after that."

"That's all I need. Thank you."

"Don't thank me until you see what happens."

Cleve left to look for Jessend but found Gerace first.

"Hello," he said, not wanting to attempt her name. "Could

you tell me where Jessend is?"

"She's taking courting lessons with Lisanda right now," the young servant answered. "They should be done before dinner, and you'll be expected to join them."

"When she's done, can you tell her I'll be at the horse range?"

Gerace nodded and started to leave, stopping to look back over her shoulder. "Most people give me a note when they want a message delivered, just letting you know for next time." Her tone was a little past polite, on the verge of annoyed even. He wondered if this was just her nature or if it was him specifically who brought out her harsher side.

"Would you like me to write one for you?"

"No."

She left.

Cleve originally planned to tell his scheme involving Kasko to Jessend, but as he waited for her while riding Nulya, he figured it would be better to surprise her. She seemed like she might like surprises. And he didn't need her to be involved for the plan to work.

When she arrived, Jessend greeted him with a hug. "Gerace gave me the impression you had something to tell me?"

"I decided to leave it as a surprise."

She seemed to be holding in an excited squeal. "When will I find out what it is?"

"Hopefully within the next few days."

Jessend started to pet Nulya. "And how is he treating you?" she asked the horse. Nulya whinnied.

Cleve rode until the sun began to set. By then, Lisanda had joined Jessend as they sat and talked with Silvie by the stables.

At one point, Silvie started singing to them. Cleve was too far to hear anything besides the faint tones of a faraway melody, so he paid no attention.

But after a few circles around the range, Cleve noticed Lisanda sitting with her head in her hands. Jessend had her arm around her sister's shoulders. Silvie had stopped singing and now was leaning awkwardly over the weeping princess.

Jessend helped Lisanda up and started to lead her toward the doors of the palace. Cleve noticed the shaking of Lisanda's shoulders as the level of her weeping increased.

He rode up to Silvie, who looked ghostly, as if she'd just witnessed a catastrophe.

"What happened?" Cleve asked.

"I'm not sure. I was just singing, and halfway through the song she put her head in her hands. I didn't realize she was weeping until it got so loud that I heard it over the sound of my voice."

"What were you singing?"

"*Come Home.*" A tear rolled from Silvie's unblinking eye. "It's a song about a man making a choice to leave home to fight the desmarls. He doesn't come back when he says he will, and his wife is singing for him to return, begging for him to stop this fight for everyone else and start his fight for her, for them."

Cleve didn't understand. *But it was Jessend's first betrothed who was killed by the desmarls, not Lisanda's. Why was she the one crying?*

"Can you tell them I'm sorry?" Silvie was nearly pleading, her guilt palpable.

"I will." Cleve handed Nulya off and went inside the palace.

He tried Lisanda's room, knocking and waiting for an answer.

"Who is it?" Jessend asked.

"It's Cleve."

Jessend cracked open the door. "You should come back later." She started to shut the door.

"Silvie wanted me to apologize for her."

"He can come in," Lisanda said from inside.

Jessend pulled open the door, showing Cleve a solemn invitation by making just enough space for him to come through. She shut the door behind him and locked it.

Lisanda was hunched over her crossed legs, huddled on her massive bed. Her room was unlike Jessend's. There were no weapons on the walls, replaced instead by brightly colored paintings. In fact, everything seemed to be vividly colored in the room, making Cleve realize how dark Jessend's room really was in contrast.

"Should I say something to Silvie?" Cleve asked hesitantly. He dearly hoped they wouldn't ask him to scold her. He wouldn't even know how.

"We're not upset with her," Lisanda answered. "She didn't know what she was singing was so painful."

Cleve showed his confusion with a glance to Jessend. "Silvie told me about the song," he said. "Does she not know about your first betrothal?"

Jessend shook her head. "Silvie is still new here. She's only been the stable master for a few weeks."

A few weeks? Cleve almost blurted. He would've guessed she'd known Jessend for years from the way they interacted. Although, Jessend had treated him the same way.

I guess it isn't that strange for her.

"So she certainly didn't know about Jek." Lisanda let out a whimper. "That damn song. I don't think I can ever listen to it again. Every time I used to hear it, I would feel your pain." She spoke to Jessend. "And that was enough to make me cry. Now there's my own ache mixed into it."

Jessend sat next to Lisanda, putting her hand on her sister's back. "Jek Trayden is the King's Mage," Jessend explained to Cleve, "which is basically the top position for any mage working for our father. But there's some trust issues between him and our father. Lisanda told me all about it."

"We care for each other deeply," Lisanda said plainly, as if she were listing what she had for breakfast. "But my father doesn't believe it's genuine. When Jek was first hired, we were spending all of our free time together. My father kept claiming he was only pretending to be interested in me because he has some sort of revenge planned."

She fluttered her hand in disgust. "And Father thinks my mind is twisted from a poison I'd consumed before Jek came to the palace. It's a long story that I won't get into right now."

Jessend nodded. "It really is, but very interesting and romantic." She used her arm to scrunch Lisanda's shoulders.

"I can tell you later," Lisanda said, as if she thought Cleve was interested to hear. He decided it would be better not to tell her that he didn't care.

"Anyway," Lisanda continued, "Jek and my father got into many arguments. And then there was the worst one of all. Jek demanded to know how he could prove his loyalty to me and our family. He was sick of the accusations. My father told him to bring back ten desmarl eyes, and Jek agreed, soon leaving while consumed by rage."

Lisanda's gaze sank to her crossed legs. "He promised he would be back...and went, just like that. I couldn't change his mind." Her voice lowered to a whisper. "Men can be so stupid in their stubbornness."

"I assume it's no easy task to get desmarl eyes?" Cleve asked.

He noticed a tear fall from Lisanda's lowered face. "It would probably be easier to stop a war than to get ten desmarl eyes."

"He practically stopped a war before if Zav's army really had been planning to attack us." Jessend rubbed Lisanda's back. "He'll be back."

Is she referring to him kidnapping that boy prince?

Cleve didn't ask, figuring it wasn't the right time. Though, now he had to admit to himself he was curious about this mage.

"I'm sorry, Lisanda," Cleve said, not wanting to see her in so much pain. "Is there anything I can do?"

"Tell Silvie not to be upset with herself," Lisanda answered, a slight smile forming finally. "She didn't do anything wrong, and she has a beautiful voice."

Jessend nodded. "She does, that show-off. Did you see how

she jumped when we mentioned music?"

Lisanda let out a quick sniffle and then a giggle.

Chapter 9

Jessend didn't invite Cleve into her room that night.

He didn't realize how much harder it was to sleep on his own until he'd been with Jessend...when he'd dug up everything that had been buried for years.

He thought he'd found everything, but fragmented memories laced with a mixture of pain and happiness kept sprouting up like old skeletal remains. He'd uncover the trace of something, wanting to investigate it further, but not without Jessend there—never on his own. He wasn't ready for that.

He found himself in a storm of confusion, with memories popping into his mind, and he wasn't sure whether to fight them back or accept them along with the pain.

He found little comfort in his soft bed until his thoughts went to Reela. It hurt to realize he might be becoming the warrior he'd always despised—a weak warrior who prioritized women over training.

But it's not women, he corrected himself. *Just one woman.*

Jessend gave him comfort as well, but it was a different kind of comfort. He felt himself open up around her the same way he'd begun to do so with Reela during their last moments together. Yet, there wasn't a burning sensation coursing through his body that screamed for him to kiss Jessend.

When he closed his eyes, he could see Reela smiling, biting her lips in anticipation of his kiss. It was hard to think about anything else but her once he began.

Then his mind went to more passionate thoughts, sliding his hand down to her hip while their mouths pressed and closed around each other, peeling off her shirt as she grinned and undid his belt—

There was a knock at his door. "Are you awake?" It was

Jessend's voice.

"Come in," he called from the bed as he sat up, only then noticing the weight of his underwear and sheets against the bulge in his pants. He muttered a curse and pulled an extra blanket over himself.

"I can't sleep," Jessend said, crawling onto the bed and slipping under the covers. "I hope this is alright."

Cleve didn't want to sound too eager, not when she could discover what he was trying to hide. But he was thankful she was there. There was a lot on his mind.

"I'm glad you came. I couldn't sleep, either."

Jessend moved next to Cleve and then turned away, taking his arm and pulling it onto her stomach. Cleve turned with her, making sure to keep his lower half away, given that his manhood still was being more stubborn than he would've liked.

"There's too much to do tomorrow to talk all night," Jessend said. "But if I don't talk at all, I won't ever get to sleep. Do you mind?" With the warmth of her body, Cleve already could feel his mind beginning to relax.

"Definitely not."

She surprised him by moving her rear closer, taking away the last gap between them. Cleve pushed himself away the moment they touched, but Jessend gasped; clearly she'd felt him.

"Um." She flipped to her back and turned her head. "Have your feelings for me changed?" Her question was cautious, giving Cleve the sense she was ready to flee.

He felt his body flush with hot embarrassment. "No. I mean...I consider you a good friend, but..." *That wasn't for you.* He couldn't bring himself to say it aloud. It was too embarrassing.

"So...what were you doing before I came in here?"

"Thinking about Reela, the girl back in Kyrro."

Jessend propped herself up on her elbow to show a smirk.

"Just *thinking*?"

Cleve looked away. "Yes."

"Bastial stars, you must really like her."

"What did you want to talk about?"

"Fine, we'll change the subject. Though, I like seeing you embarrassed. It's like watching a lion run away with its tail between its legs." She gave him a quick peck on the cheek before resting her head against his shoulder. "Did Silvie understand she shouldn't blame herself?"

"I'm not sure. She seemed pretty distraught when I told her about Lisanda and Jek."

Jessend let out a breath that seemed strained, as if she was in pain. "Silvie is beautiful, don't you think?"

"You already asked me that."

"No." Jessend sat up and turned with a sly grin. "I asked if you thought she was cute."

Rek told me she has feelings for you, he almost said aloud. Cleve took his time before deciding to ask his next question, trying to figure out the most subtle way of phrasing it.

"Are you attracted to her?"

"Of course..." Jessend's voice trailed off. "Wait, do you mean, do I like her in *that* way?" Her face twisted. She looked ready to slap Cleve. "Are you asking me if I like girls?"

"No." *Yes.* Cleve turned on his side. "Never mind."

Jessend wasn't done, though. She pulled on his shoulder until he moved to his back and shifted his eyes toward her.

"Do girls date each other in Kyrro?" she asked. "Because they don't here."

"Girls are girls no matter where you go. There will be some who are attracted to each other, as there are men who like other men."

Jessend's eyes grew wide. "How can you say that so calmly?"

"Because it's the truth."

Jessend flopped onto her back, pushing her head onto

Cleve's shoulder. He could feel her hair tickling his neck until she brushed it behind her and then interlaced her fingers with his.

"The more I learn from you, the less I realize I actually know," she said. Now she was the one changing the subject, he couldn't help but realize. "What else is in that mind of yours?"

Cleve let out a long breath, squeezing Jessend's tiny hand. "You shouldn't put me on a pedestal. My mind is filled with torment, confusion, pain. Only on the surface and buried deep down am I actually strong. Everything in between is where my real emotions lie, and it's utter chaos."

"That's only because you're still young. Time will fix that. Time will close the gap between your outer and inner strength."

She sounded so confident, Cleve almost believed her.

"And how do you know that?"

Jessend shrugged, the lift of her shoulder rubbing against Cleve's arm. "Because that's what happened to my brother."

"Raymess?" Cleve vaguely remembered the name being mentioned while Rek questioned the man who'd attempted to kill Prince Harwin.

"Yes. He's been away, he and my mother. They went west to Chanren to recruit people for our army. It's very far from here."

They were silent for some time.

But then Jessend began talking about the first man she'd loved, and soon Cleve was discussing his parents.

Again, they talked until the sun peeked through the window. But no tears were shed. In fact, Cleve was smiling by the time their words ran out.

At the horse range the next day, Silvie presented two baskets filled with flowers, cheeses, and wines to both Takary sisters.

"I'm sorry about yesterday," she led with. "I—"

"Bastial stars," Lisanda interrupted. "How can you even afford this?" She hesitantly reached forward to accept her basket.

"Does our father really pay you that much?" Jessend teased, accepting her gift as well.

"No." Silvie laughed nervously. "I owe some favors now, but it's worth it."

Jessend showed a harsh glare to Cleve, stopping his heart for a breath. "Didn't you tell her it wasn't her fault?"

"I tried," Cleve began to argue.

"Please," Silvie interrupted with a hand to Jessend's shoulder. "I wanted to do this."

Lisanda moved in for a hug. "Thank you, Silvie."

Jessend was next, and they seemed to squeeze each other just a bit tighter, holding on a little longer as well. Jessend and Silvie's hands slid down each other's arms to meet for a blink, Jessend showing a flattered smile.

Rek came out later, and soon he was galloping in circles around Cleve.

Cleve's competitive nature kicked in, and he tried to keep up with the Elf and his hideous horse. But Nulya was resistant to going so fast, bucking into the air and throwing Cleve off when he kicked her too hard.

Rek's horse trotted over, and he hopped off. The Elf had a proud smile, clearly aware Cleve was competing with him.

Rek didn't bring it up. Instead, he asked, "Have you heard back from Kasko?"

"Not yet."

The Elf showed a frown. "I'm leaving for Meritar to visit the Elves in two days. If you want me to help you with your plan, it has to happen before then or when I get back. I'm trying to take this trip as quickly as possible so we can get back to Kyrro faster. The Elves may even have a ship for me and wish to join our fight."

"I'll send another letter." Cleve lowered his head to meet

Rek's eyes. "Promise you won't leave for Kyrro without me."

"If they have a ship, I'll find some way to get you on it. I promise."

For the next couple of hours, Rek assisted Cleve in his training with Nulya, using psyche to communicate with the horse for each of Cleve's commands.

When they each needed a break, Cleve went to find Micah Vail to see what he could do about Kasko not replying.

Chapter 10

"Has there been a response from Kasko?" Cleve asked, closing the door behind him. Micah Vail was just finishing writing on some scroll, putting paperweights on its edges to let the ink dry.

"No. But he has definitely received it."

"What can I do to hurry him up?"

Micah shrugged. "You can call him a coward."

It took Cleve a moment to realize the King's adviser was serious. "It's that easy?"

Micah Vail laughed. "Are you implying that wouldn't work on you either?"

Cleve realized it would and felt ashamed, making a conscious effort to remember not to be so easily manipulated in the future.

Cleve pointed to the pen. "May I draft the letter here?"

Micah gestured to it with his hand. "Please."

The beginning of the letter came easily to Cleve, though soon he ran out of things to say. After gazing at it for a few breaths, Micah busying himself at one of the other tables, Cleve decided what he'd written was enough:

Dear Kasko Lage,
You're a coward.
– Cleve Polken.

He cleared his throat to get Micah's attention, handing it to him.

Micah looked at it and smiled. "A man of few words."

"I've been told that before."

To busy his mind, Cleve went back to the horse range, glad

to find Rek still there.

The Elf helped him train with Nulya. Already, the horse was learning Cleve's commands at a rapid rate.

Silvie wasn't too fond of Rek; Cleve noticed for the first time that day.

"I have no idea what all this psyche is doing to Nulya," she commented, one hand on her hip with the other petting the horse.

"It's only helping her learn what Cleve wants her to do," Rek replied, his tone stern, showing he was ready to argue. "It's not harming her at all."

"But how can you know?" Silvie tried to hold a smile, but the tension between them was thick enough to tell it couldn't be genuine. "There are no horses in Ovira."

"I can tell," Rek said, his voice now peremptory.

Silvie gave a loud breath to show her frustration. Nulya whinnied the moment she finished stroking the horse's mane.

Cleve spent the rest of the day at the training grounds, dueling with the guards—his new favorite way of passing the time.

Enough of them joined in that no rivalries had a chance to spark. They each waited for their turn to challenge the victor, which was usually Cleve, until four or five straight victories would tire him out.

Every time he won, Cleve had to refrain from commenting how the warriors in Kyrro were far stronger. He knew it would only lead to trouble, especially when impressed whistles soon turned to mutterings of frustration.

By the time the sun was setting, Cleve left to check with Micah Vail one last time before bed, hoping he might have received a response from Kasko.

The adviser wasn't in his room, but there was a note on the door. Cleve saw his name on it.

Stepping closer for a read, he wondered how Micah knew he would come by.

"Cleve, I won't be in for the night, but there still hasn't been a reply from Kasko. We can try another letter tomorrow morning. Come by early."

Cleve pondered where Micah would be staying if it wasn't in his room, but he decided there was no point to his curiosity. The man was clearly not easy to figure out.

Jessend, on the other hand, made no effort hiding where she wanted to be at all times. When she wasn't taking dancing, singing, or other lessons, she spent even more of her time on the horse range than Cleve.

He was no expert in flirting, but that's what the interactions between her and Silvie looked like to him. He would've felt jealous if he'd had feelings for Jessend in the same way he did for Reela, but it was actually the opposite. More than anything, he just wanted the Princess to find comfort.

With the light of the sun nearly gone, Cleve knew now was his last chance to use his bow if he wanted to get some practice in before tomorrow.

While Cleve was shooting arrows at his target, Rek found him, asking, "Any luck with Kasko?"

Cleve shook his head, worried it meant he'd run out of time.

"I wish I could wait longer." Rek spoke with genuine regret. "But just getting there is going to take over a week. I want to do this soon so I can be back when we're ready to leave."

Cleve let out a defeated breath. "I understand," he said, shifting his focus back to his target as he readied an arrow.

Rek nodded apologetically. He turned toward the two guards watching Cleve by the door to the palace. "Did you know that they despise you?"

Cleve looked to find two he'd humiliated recently. "I figured."

When night made it impossible to continue training, Cleve left to retire in his room. Gerace was waiting by his door with a tray of food.

"Where have you been?"

By her menacing eyes and the way her weight was shifted to one side, she seemed to have been waiting a long time.

"I'm sorry, Ge..." Cleve stopped himself before attempting her name, figuring it would just anger her even more when he got it wrong.

"Gerace," she said it for him.

"Gerace," he tried.

Her head sank dramatically. "Just call me Gerry. It's what my father calls me."

Cleve opened his door for her and his food tray, following her inside.

"What does he do?" Cleve asked.

Gerace seemed to brighten by the question, a smile breaking across her mouth. "He's a shotmarl player, offensive swordsman. He plays for Goldram."

Cleve tried to remember what Jessend had told him about shotmarl when they were still in Kyrro. Nothing came to mind. "What is it?"

"It's a sport." Gerace's annoyance came back as she set down his tray hard. "Kyrro is missing out if there's no shotmarl there. What do you do in your stadiums, then?"

Cleve thought of Redfield. "We have our own competitions." He sat down and began eating. "Sit." He pointed at the empty seat with his knife. "Tell me about shotmarl."

She looked at the chair with one eye, as if trying to glimpse it without Cleve noticing.

"Please," Cleve added. It was much better than her waiting silently outside.

"I shouldn't."

Cleve felt physical action was better than words at this point. As Gerace started toward the door, he came up behind her, lifted her by her armpits, and maneuvered her over to the chair like a misbehaved child. She was silent as he did it, and once she was seated she seemed to be hiding a smile as best she could.

"It's that easy to pick me up?"

"Of course. You're tiny."

She folded her arms. "I'm taller than Jessend."

Cleve shrugged as he cut his meat. "She's tiny also."

"Do..." She brushed her dark hair over her ear. "Do men like women much shorter than them, usually?"

Cleve realized two things then: He'd been forgetting Gerace was much younger than him, and she didn't realize that he and Jessend weren't romantically involved.

"Every man is different," he answered, unwilling to get into his specific tastes in women, which he barely knew himself.

"What about you, then?"

Is she flirting with me? Cleve studied her face for the answer. She seemed shocked by his gaze, leaning back with startled eyes.

"I only ask because you and Jessend are together," she said with an urgent tone. "And you said she's very small. I figured..." She cleared her throat. "Well, I thought..." She shook her head. "Forgive me. It wasn't my place to ask."

Explaining his complicated relationship with Jessend was the last thing he wanted and definitely not the reason he'd invited the servant girl to his table.

"It's fine," he said. "Tell me about shotmarl."

She leaned back and finally looked relaxed for the first time since she'd entered.

"Each eastern territory has a team, well, except for the Elves. They keep to themselves. So there's four teams: Goldram, Zav, Presoren, and Waywen. Each team plays once a week, and we rotate who we play against and where we play them. When my father plays here in Goldram, I get a day off to go see him. Many people from the city watch. The tickets are expensive but worth it. The Goldram Stadium is marvelous."

She leaned forward to cup her hands on the table, forming a

circle. "It seats twenty thousand people, and it's almost always full every game." She lowered her head to show Cleve a sly look, like she was about to reveal a secret. "Most people think the most important role is the archer. But the swordsmen defending him are even more crucial to winning, and that's what my father does."

"He defends the archer from what?"

Gerace pushed three fingers onto the table. "There are three swordsmen trying to stop the archer from scoring. These swordsmen are defense." She moved two fingers in front of them with her other hand. "And offense only gets two swordsmen to stop the three swordsmen on defense from reaching the archer." She put down the thumb of her right hand behind her two fingers. "The archer has to shoot a target fifty yards behind the three swordsmen trying to stop him from doing just that."

Cleve swallowed his food to make a comment. "This whole thing sounds unnecessarily dangerous. How are people not injuring and killing each other every match?"

She let out a single innocent laugh. "Everyone wears leather armor. The swords are wooden, and the arrowhead is made from the blood of a rubber tree." She pushed out a palm. "Don't be mistaken. There are injuries, sometimes serious, because in order to stop someone on the other team, you have to either physically prevent them from getting by you or knock them off their feet. A blow from a wooden sword has to be quite strong to do that, especially since most shotmarl players are big like you. Once someone touches the ground, even with his knee, he's out for the round. There are referees to watch for that."

Nearly done with his food, Cleve slowed to make sure Gerace finished explaining the sport. He was already finding himself extremely interested, though he still barely understood it.

Competing at Redfield had always been his dream since he'd

started training with a sword. So now that he was hearing about this somewhat similar sport, he could feel himself already searching for ways to play. *Maybe once the war is over in Kyrro I could come back here, bring Reela with me.*

"How does a team win?" Cleve asked.

"Whoever scores the most points before the match is over. Only an archer can score. They get two points for hitting the target and one point for hitting the chain above the target that rings a bell when either the chain or the target is struck with an arrow. Each team gets three rounds before offense and defense are switched. Each round is over when the archer either fires an arrow or gets knocked down."

Gerace smiled and finally leaned back against her chair. "It's really exciting. And the men are so skilled it's scary, my father included. Hardly anyone can get by him without a second person helping them."

Cleve then remembered something Jessend had told him about the sport. "There's some relation between shotmarl and desmarls, right?"

"Yes. The sport originated from desmarls. The target is shaped like a desmarl eye, which is the best place to shoot a desmarl in order to kill it. And just like fighting the desmarls, the archers have to be aware of their surroundings, quick on their feet, and accurate even while moving. The swordsmen defending them are like those who protect archers from the massive tentacles the desmarls use to pick men up, crush them, and carry them to their mouths. In fact, the winning team of each season is sent to battle the desmarls."

Gerace looked at the door before leaning in and lowering her voice. "That's what happened to the first man Jessend was to marry. He was an amazing shotmarl archer, helping Goldram win the season. But he was killed when they went to battle the desmarls. They say he saved two other people in the process. Though, usually no one dies on the winning shotmarl team that is sent to fight. Someone must've made a mistake."

Cleve let down his fork, finishing his last bite. "There must be honor in going to fight the desmarls." *Honor is often the reason, when logic is lost.*

"Definitely." Gerace started cleaning up for Cleve. "And good money in being a shotmarl player as well."

And money is the other. "So why do you work here if your family has enough money?"

She stopped on the way out. "Because there's honor in my job, too."

His face must've revealed his judgment, for she looked ready to scream at him.

"You can't see the honor in my job?" Gerace asked.

"I can," Cleve lied.

She set the tray on a nearby table, in the process bumping a lamp that threatened to fall. She didn't steady it, her hands too busy making fists. Luckily, it wobbled back into place.

"Has anyone ever told you you're a bad liar?" Her arms folded.

"I'm sorry. I meant no disrespect. I just don't see the same honor in serving people as there is in fighting desmarls."

"My father explained it this way: Most people attribute honor to a job or a title, but really honor can only be found within us. It is not awarded to us, as people often believe. If you do something that makes Greenedge a better place, and you have integrity about it, then what you're doing is honorable. That's why I don't appreciate when you can't say my name right. If I were a princess or a queen, you would be inclined to practice my name until you got it right. But since I'm a servant, you haven't taken the time."

Cleve knew the young girl was right, and he felt ashamed for it. He stood and spread his palms. "I apologize. I don't want to call you anything else but your name. Will you help me practice it?"

She looked at his hands as if they had spit on them. But when her eyes rose to his face, they must've seen how serious he was, for her look of disgust faded and she nodded with a smile.

"I thought you were joking for a moment."

"I'm not usually one to joke."

She stayed to help him practice until he had it right.

Chapter 11

The warmth from the day lasted well into the night, making the sheets and even Cleve's shirt too hot for him. He'd met with Jessend briefly, just long enough for her to tell him she would be sharing his bed later.

But she hadn't come yet, and Cleve was beginning to realize he would be asleep before she did.

He awoke with the room bathed in black. Jessend was moving around his bed, doing something with his window. He couldn't even make out her silhouette, only could hear her footsteps.

He grumbled to let her know he was awake and gingerly sat up. Her sounds at the window stopped.

To Cleve's surprise, a male voice spoke out, "Don't move."

It's not Jessend...how do I know that voice?

"Who are you?" Cleve squinted, desperately trying to determine if it was friend or foe.

The man moved about the room, making a rustle as he went. Soon he'd lit a lamp and showed Cleve a sinister smile.

Foe. "What are you doing here?" Cleve started to move toward Kasko.

"I said don't move." His grin faded.

Kasko had an unusually small crossbow aimed at Cleve's chest, though Cleve knew not to doubt it still could propel an arrow through his heart.

Kasko navigated to the foot of Cleve's bed. He seemed even shorter than he had the first time they'd met, skinnier as well, like he could've slipped in through the cracks in the wall. But Cleve knew better. Kasko had come in through the door. There was a dagger in his other hand, his forearm supporting the weight of his steady crossbow.

"How did you get into the palace with weapons?" Cleve gestured at them.

"I'm welcome to come and go as I please. If I'm carrying a bag, there's no reason for them to search it." Keeping his eyes on Cleve, he let down the crossbow for a blink, knelt, and grabbed a glass vial using two fingers from the hand holding his knife. He tossed it to Cleve. "Drink that."

Cleve held it up to his eyes. It was red, and for a moment Cleve thought Kasko had bled into it. The thought sickened him, twisting his stomach.

"What's in here?"

"Your life. You drink that, you live. You don't, you die." Kasko jabbed the knife in Cleve's direction, no longer even feigning amusement at the situation. "I don't know what you have planned trying to get me here for some stupid competition, but it's not going to work. Jessend is mine. I need her. My father may be neutral still, but *my* future is with Waywen. I'm taking Jessend there after we marry, and they're going to give me my own army when they and Presoren win this war. I'll practically be a king, and you'll be nothing."

Now Cleve found genuine joy on the young man's face. He seemed deliriously happy, even, with an open-mouthed grin.

"What's Jessend going to do in Waywen?" Cleve asked.

Kasko visibly shuddered, writhing with pleasure. "So beautiful. I can't wait to see her bleed."

Cleve had heard enough. He looked around as he tried to come up with a plan.

"Keep your eyes on me, scum." Kasko's teeth were pressed together tightly, all joy gone. "Or take an arrow in the heart."

There was a knock at the door. "Cleve? Sorry I'm so late. Are you still up?" Jessend tried the doorknob, but Kasko must've locked it. "Why is this locked?" The knocking was louder. "Is something wrong, Cleve?"

"Bastial hell, why is Jessend here?" Kasko hissed. "She needs to shut up! Stay there." Kasko sidestepped toward the door, tucking the knife into his belt and keeping his crossbow aimed at Cleve.

The small man kept himself out of view of the Princess as he opened the door in front of him.

Jessend stepped in curiously. "Cleve?"

Kasko grabbed her arm, practically tossed her toward the bed, and shut the door after her, locking it hard. He had the crossbow aimed at her now.

"Either of you move or speak louder than a whisper, and I shoot." Now he was furious, practically shouting in a raspy breath. "Dammit, you whore. You little whore! Whore! Whore!" His head shook with each uttering of the word. In the low light, Cleve even saw spit fly out.

Jessend showed Cleve a fearful glance.

"You've been lying with this man?" Kasko asked, starting to growl. It grew louder, like a dog about to bark. "You damn whore, Jessend. You're supposed to be mine! I should kill you both."

Jessend was quiet, showing Cleve another fearful glance.

He didn't know what to say either.

"What do you want with us?" Jessend finally muttered.

"I'm trying to figure that out, you bitch. Shut up and let me think." His hands shook as he growled again. He grabbed the knife from his belt and waved it at Jessend. "Get over here."

Cleve grabbed her arm. "She stays right here until you tell us what's happening."

Kasko shouted into his arm to muffle it. He raised the knife to his elbow and cut himself, a thin slit. Then he pointed the bloody knife at Cleve. "Take the potion now."

Cleve noticed Jessend examining it.

She gasped. "Don't drink that, Cleve."

"What is it?"

"Mekio poison."

Kasko whistled softly. "You're smart, pretty girl. Too bad you're such a whore, and your father's on the wrong side of war."

"This is illegal." She pointed to it. "Very illegal. Where did you even get the mekio plants?"

He showed her a bored look, demonstrating he thought the question was even stupid to ask. "You're going to drink some after Cleve, and you have no one to blame but your whore self for that." He gritted his teeth and swung the knife in their direction. "Bastial hell, I can't believe you would do this to me!"

Cleve figured he'd have no better time than then. He grabbed the small bed table and jumped in front of Jessend. "Stay behind me," he told her.

Kasko shifted the crossbow into position to shoot, and Cleve moved the small table with it. Kasko raised his weapon, so Cleve did the same with the table.

"You really think you can move that in front of my arrow? Put down the table and take the potion, fool." Kasko was moving to the side now, trying to get a better angle. Cleve crept toward him, using his other hand to make sure Jessend stayed behind him.

Kasko looked like he wanted to grin but couldn't quite get his lips to twist right. His face showed nervousness, at least far more of it than Cleve felt, the table steady in his hands. He raised and lowered it with each shift of the crossbow.

"I'm going to give you until the count of three to let go of the table and take the potion," Kasko muttered angrily.

Each man continued to slowly circle the room, Jessend staying close behind Cleve.

"One..." Kasko said.

"Guards!" Jessend shouted. "Guards! Guards! Guards!"

"Bitch!" Kasko shouted back. There was a *twang* and a loud *thrum* as the arrow was fired into Cleve's table.

He rushed at Kasko, but the little man was quick, jumping to the side and slashing at Cleve with the knife. It nicked his arm, making him drop the table by accident.

Kasko dropped the crossbow and furiously rushed at him,

clearly skilled with the knife as he swung it with careful but quick motions. Cleve found himself stumbling over tables, chairs—he couldn't take his eyes off Kasko's attempts to drive the blade into his body.

Jessend tried to smash a chair over Kasko's head, only he saw it coming and jumped backward. The moment she saw she'd failed, she fled toward Cleve, positioning herself behind him again.

Guards started pounding on the door. Then Cleve heard the distinct sound of kicking at it. As quick as a rat running into a hole, Kasko scampered to the ground-floor window and dove out headfirst.

Cleve knew that just outside the window was a dirt walkway that was still within the palace walls, but there were dozens of escape routes Kasko could take.

Knowing he would be unable to fit in the tight opening that the small man had jumped through, Cleve furiously tried to open the window more. But it was stuck. Then he remembered Kasko had been doing something to it earlier.

"It's glued shut!" Cleve shouted to the guards who'd now broken in.

"It was Kasko!" Jessend shouted to them. "He went out the window."

"Kasko Lage?" They both stopped with a curious glance at the Princess, thinking she'd misspoken.

"Yes!" Jessend screamed in desperation.

"Are you sure it wasn't someone who looked like him?" The guards waited, one of them still eyeing Cleve as if he could be their enemy.

"Yes, you idiots. Hurry!"

They ran to Cleve and pushed him aside, grunting as one tried to open the window. He gave up after a breath and started using his sword to strike the glass. There were explosions of noise as the steel began to crack through. Anyone nearby who'd been sleeping surely would be up soon, if they weren't already.

When enough of the glass had shattered, the guard started to climb through, calling behind him, "Go the other way. Tell them not to let anyone through the exits!"

"Not to let *Kasko* through the exits!" Jessend shouted to correct them. But both guards already were gone by the time she'd finished.

Cleve was moving back toward the window in order to climb out when Jessend grabbed his arm, shouting, "What are you doing?"

"Going after him."

"You don't have any shoes. There's broken glass everywhere. You might not even be able to fit through that window. And you're not even wearing a shirt or pants!" She gestured at him, her face still fearful he might not be listening. "You'll probably get lost looking for Kasko, with your half-naked body ending up in some poor woman's room!" She pulled him away from the window.

Cleve sighed and began to feel his racing heart slowing back to normal. Jessend pushed herself against his chest, wrapping her arms around him.

She began to cry, so he held her tight.

"I won't let him hurt you," he told her. Cleve could feel her hot tears down his naked chest and stomach.

"I hate him so much."

"Me, too. But there's no more hiding for him. After this, everyone's going to know the truth about him."

Jessend let out a shaky breath and then a sniffle. "Will you walk me back to my room? I want to see Lisanda, make sure he didn't go that way."

"Of course. Just let me put some clothes on."

Jessend shook her head with a sniffle, letting out half a weep and a laugh. "No, don't." She showed him a smile as she wiped her eyes. "I like you like this, and I want to see what the guards think when you walk down the halls wearing nothing but your underwear." She laughed and then pressed up against him, kissing his chest.

Reflexively, he kissed the top of her head.

She looked up, putting her arms around his neck. Gazing into her dark brown eyes in the dim light did something to him. His body was still acting on its own, as if it still was ready for battle—perhaps even craving it.

No thoughts crossed his mind. So when he bent down and pressed his lips against hers, the first thing he felt was shock. They each pulled away, a loud smack of their lips parting. She looked to be just as surprised as he was.

Unsure why, his hands reached behind her thighs to hoist her up. She jumped with him, wrapping her legs around his waist. They kissed again, this time their lips moving frantically.

Cleve carried her toward the bed as their lips pressed and squeezed. There were still no thoughts, only pleasure. It felt like a cold drink of water after a long, dry day. The gulps would happen on their own without choice, just like how Cleve's mouth was moving then.

Cleve found the bed with his knees, moving himself and Jessend to its head where he slowly let her down and him with her.

She grabbed his hair, letting out a windy exhale when his hand found her breast. With her legs still around him, she pulled him lower, and soon he was pressing himself against her.

A girl cleared her throat from the doorway, and Cleve felt his body rip apart from Jessend's.

Bastial hell, what just happened?

"I heard there was an intruder in Cleve's room." Lisanda had her eyes on the window, purposefully avoiding Cleve and Jessend on the bed. "I just wanted to make sure everything was alright. Do you want me to shut the door?"

Jessend rolled off the bed and jumped to her sister. "No, silly." She whispered something and then dragged Lisanda out of the room.

Cleve waited, unsure what to think or do, even unsure if she would come back. He wanted to get up and put some clothes on, but he had to wait. Jessend had left the door open and there was nothing he could do to hide what was bulging in his underwear.

Jessend returned as he was throwing his shirt over his head. She shut the door behind her. "I don't know what happened there. Do you?"

Cleve shook his head, putting his pants on next.

"Maybe I was just so relieved by the truth of Kasko coming out." It was rare to see Jessend shy or embarrassed, but she seemed to be both at that moment as she looked at the rug between them. She kept her eyes low, her voice near a whisper. "Does this mean you like me?" She paused for a breath. "You know...I could feel you pushing against me."

"I don't know what it means, but Reela—" Cleve stopped himself, realizing he didn't know what he was even going to say. Her name had come out on its own.

"Reela?" Jessend tilted her head.

"I think I need time to think about this more." No thoughts were coming then. There was just emotion, and so much of it Cleve couldn't figure out which feeling was the strongest. He had shame for his lust, yet continued attraction toward Jessend. He felt honor for stopping Kasko, but disgust for losing control of himself with Jessend after.

Then there was a torrent of other feelings gusting around his heart that he had no hope of stopping long enough to distinguish the difference between them.

"What about you? Did this change anything for you?" Cleve asked, dearly hoping it hadn't.

Jessend pursed her lips, studying Cleve's face with a slight squint. "I'm not sure." She approached slowly. "But I think we should find out right now, right here." She stopped just before him, putting a hand on his shoulder and then sliding it up. He felt the chill when her small hands found the same position they had before—meeting at the back of his neck.

A fear passed through his skin, rattling his heart. It reminded him of Reela, when they'd first met and he was still scared of what she did to him. Jessend moved her hand to his cheek, clearly wanting a kiss, but he wouldn't lean down. Luckily, she was too short to reach him without his cooperation.

"Don't you think it's worth it to see if things have changed between us?" Jessend asked.

Cleve didn't, yet he couldn't pull away. The thought of hurting Jessend was painful, especially when he wanted the same thing as she did. But the fear that came with losing control of himself was even worse.

He felt his heart continuing to speed up. Dizziness came next. *She's making me weak, just like Reela.*

Jessend put a hand over his heart, showing a face of shock. "It's beating so hard." She rolled her eyes at him. "It's just a kiss, Cleve. How can you be fearless when a madman aims a crossbow at you, yet you quiver in terror at my approaching lips?"

He felt himself calming. It could've been her touch, maybe her mocking look, or perhaps her words alone had done it. Whatever it was, all the fear had been drained. *It's just a kiss, stupid.* Cleve could almost hear her voice in his head.

He let out a relieved smile, moved his hand behind her small head to grasp it firmly, and leaned down. She went to her toes to reach him, but she turned away and fell back to her heels with a laugh before their lips touched. He started laughing as well, unsure why.

She shook her head and tried moving her hands to a different position on his chest. She gazed into his eyes and smiled. "Sorry, I don't know why I'm so amused." He leaned down again, and they kissed just for a blink before she erupted in laughter again and stepped away. Cleve couldn't stop himself from laughing with her.

"It feels like I'm kissing my brother again!" Jessend was doubled over in hilarity, shaking her head.

Cleve suddenly felt like himself again, strong and in control. There was no yearning to lock lips with Jessend. All of the hot desire had cooled.

"Does it feel that way for you?" she asked.

"It does."

"Well, at least we know now. Come on." She started toward the door. "Let's find out what happened with Kasko."

Chapter 12

A summons from the King brought Cleve, Jessend, and Lisanda to one of the many grand dining rooms. Although it was the middle of the night, Danvell still wore his crown over a white and gold gown. Servers brought in crackers, apples, cheese, and wine.

"Kasko still hasn't been found," the King said in a solemn tone. "He's either hiding somewhere in the palace or he escaped before the exits were sealed." He turned to Cleve. "Can you describe what happened?"

Jessend folded her arms. "I already told you what happened, Father."

"I'd like to hear it from Cleve."

Jessend leaned toward Cleve and whispered loudly enough for everyone to hear, "My own father doesn't believe me."

"I do," Danvell explained. "I would just *also* like to hear it from Cleve.

"I don't make up stories anymore. I would never lie about something like this. I haven't ever lied about Kasko!"

Cleve put his hand on her arm and said, "I'm sure whatever Jessend told you is the truth. But here's what happened through my point of view."

He recounted the story, receiving emphatic nods from Jessend that he noticed in his peripheral vision.

"And you're sure it was mekio poison?" Danvell asked Jessend.

"You make me spend an inordinate amount of time studying with Chemist Guss, so I'd like to think I can recognize the most illegal poison in Greenedge."

The King put his palm flat on the table. "Curb your attitude, Jessend. I know we're tired, but I'm just making sure I have all the details. I fear for what will happen with Kasko's father when he hears about the demand for his son's arrest."

"Have Oleya look at the potion, then," Jessend said, taking a breath to calm herself. "It's still in Cleve's room."

"What does the poison do?" Cleve asked, hoping it might disrupt the burgeoning argument.

"Memory loss, anger, aggression, confusion." Jessend held up her hand as she listed each side effect. "It basically causes you to act like a madman."

"How long does it last?" Cleve asked.

"It depends on the amount," Jessend answered. "But if you drank that whole bottle, there would definitely be some permanent effects."

"So it would look like I'd just gone insane," Cleve realized. "And Kasko would leave the palace without anyone knowing he'd poisoned me."

"Then I'd be forced to marry him," Jessend said, glaring at her father.

The King ignored her, looking at Cleve instead. "We'll find another room for you. Make sure to keep your door locked when you're sleeping."

Cleve nodded, thinking that would be it. But the King took a sip of his wine and waved Cleve over to his side of the table. "Come here."

Danvell stood as Cleve approached. "Cleve Polken, I've never met a man I've been as quick to trust as you. You continue to prove yourself through honorable actions. So, I'm proud to officially grant you permission to marry my daughter, Jessend Takary."

From the King's emphatic voice and the use of Jessend's last name, Cleve figured Danvell was giving some sort of royal announcement that was customary when granting a man permission to marry his daughter.

It only made the situation more awkward, especially when a dense silence followed.

"We're not going to marry, Father," Jessend stated plainly.

Danvell looked as if he'd heard a bad joke.

"Why not?" he muttered.

"We don't think of each other in that way."

Danvell held out his hands to each of them. "You've seemed to get along nicely."

"We do," Cleve answered. "But not romantically."

"Well, that just takes time."

"Father! We're not pigs you can throw in a sty and expect to mate. We both care for someone else."

We both? Cleve wondered if she was just saying that, or if there really was another man...or woman.

"Who?" Danvell seemed to be getting ready to be upset. His eyes were slits, holding harsh judgment.

"Cleve loves someone back in Kyrro."

"And you?"

"It doesn't matter right now. Can you just agree that we'll put an end to my arranged betrothals? Look what you almost made me marry."

"I made a mistake with Kasko. But your birthday isn't too far away, and I can't have a seventeen-year-old princess unmarried. What will people think?"

"It doesn't matter—" Jessend began.

But Cleve interrupted. "May I answer?"

She nodded eagerly. Cleve met eyes with the King, who tilted his head in curiosity.

"I haven't been here long," Cleve began, keeping his voice as humble as possible, "but it seems to me that nobles will always find something to gossip about. If Jessend marries someone, they'll find something about her husband to mock. In the rare chance they're satisfied with the choice for Jessend, they'll find something else, maybe with Lisanda. And everyone else who isn't a noble will only find honor that the Princess hasn't wed yet. Marriage at her age is uncommon here for the middle and lower classes, isn't it?"

The King nodded. "It is."

"They'll find a princess is easier to relate to the more she's like them. They'll appreciate their king's wisdom for allowing his daughter to choose when she wants to wed and to whom. At least that's how I would feel."

"He's right, Father." Lisanda spoke for the first time. "The nobles will always find something to complain or gossip about. And everyone else will understand. It won't hurt the family."

"You both are forgetting something important," Danvell said, his voice tired. "We're at war. We need support where we can get it. A husband with the right family can give us the advantage we need."

At that, Cleve noticed that Jessend's shoulders had slumped.

"But..." The King had a hopeful tone, pausing so he could smile at his daughter. Jessend straightened her back. "You and Lisanda have been through so much. And I really have made a grievous error with Kasko. I'll make an agreement with you both. If Cleve and his psychic Elf fight with us, I won't force anyone upon you or Lisanda. I shouldn't need any other advantages, and we can even call back your brother and mother from recruiting early. I don't like them being in Chanren so long."

Jessend's eyes fell to her food. "I'm sorry, Father, but I can't make that agreement. I can't be responsible for Cleve and Rek staying. I already spoke to you about giving them a ship and letting them go. You told me you would think about it. This is the decision you came up with?" Jessend kept her head hovered over the table, only looking up at her father for a blink.

Lisanda put her hand on Jessend's shoulder and whispered something. Jessend nodded in a serious manner. Lisanda's brow furrowed, and she met Cleve's eyes. Again she whispered something to Jessend.

"It's true," Jessend muttered.

Cleve figured Lisanda was asking if there really was no

romantic interest between them. *She must be confused after what she saw back in the bedroom.* Even Cleve was still confused when it came to Jessend. But compared to Reela—how his whole body ached for her—he knew it would never be the same with Jessend, and that's really all he needed to know.

"I don't like it when you two whisper around me," Danvell said.

"Sorry, Father," Lisanda said, taking her hand off Jessend's shoulder and sitting up straight. "Cleve, is it true you have no interest in marrying Jessend?"

"In another life, in another time, maybe Jessend and I could've been together. But I need to get back to Kyrro."

"Even though your king is likely to throw you in prison?" Lisanda asked incredulously.

"Even with that risk, yes. My life is there. My war is there, and it's happening right now without me."

Danvell extended a hand at the empty seat. "There's something you should know, Cleve. Please sit." The monarch's soft voice made Cleve realize he was about to hear something important.

Jessend interlaced her fingers with his under the table. "I've been worried about this moment," she told him.

"What is it?" Cleve asked, feeling regretful he hadn't had more wine. He took a gulp.

"I'm not sure how familiar you are with the history of Kyrro," Danvell Takary said, leaning back to make himself comfortable. "But it was founded by Gen Takary exactly one hundred eighty-five years ago. He traveled from Goldram looking for land we could use for when the desmarls took over the continent of Greenedge completely. Gen Takary was the first of a line of Takarys who ruled for nearly a century before the rebellions started. But the last time we heard from Kyrro was twenty-eight years ago—that was, until Jessend came back from there."

He looked to his daughter with a nod. She sighed and

nodded back, as if giving him permission to continue.

"Rinn Takary was king, last we'd heard," Danvell said. "We found out that he'd managed to retake control of Kyrro after a series of rebellions. But the year after that, which we didn't know until now, Westin Kimard took over—the father to your current king. Jessend discovered this when she was sent there to recruit men and women for our upcoming war."

Cleve noticed his stomach tightening along with his hand. Jessend slid her fingers out of his with a soft grunt of pain.

"Sorry," he whispered.

Danvell continued. "There are many more Takarys than just our immediate family, and we've sent out letters to the other Takarys about this change in leadership in Kyrro." The King exhaled deeply, showing his frustration. "The majority of our family is not pleased. People in Greenedge believe that our children's children will have a safe future, not here, but across the Starving Ocean where they can live in Ovira without fear of the desmarls. However, that was under the belief we had control of Kyrro. Now there's the fear our kin won't even be welcome there. This war between Kyrro and Tenred needs to end with a Takary in charge of the winning territory. After we're done fighting our own war, we'll be sending an army to Ovira."

Cleve was surprised by the lack of pride in Danvell's voice compared to its usual tone. It was meek, like a boy admitting he'd broken a vase.

Anger stiffened Cleve's body, and he stood abruptly. "The only reason a Takary wouldn't be welcome in Kyrro would be if you sent an army there. I can't understand this idea! Why must your family control the land just to live there?"

"Cleve." The pride came back into Danvell's tone, his voice deep and loud as he rose to his feet. "Remember who you're talking to. Sit back down."

Cleve gulped down his annoyance as best he could and sat. Jessend took his hand again, and he felt some anger diminish.

Danvell's mouth moved, but no words came out. He sat back down as well, letting out another long breath.

"I actually agree with you, Cleve," he said, his voice now calm. "I don't believe we need to control Ovira. But I have other family members—many of them. And nearly all wish to send an army across the Starving Ocean once we've won this war against Waywen and Presoren. I wanted to warn you about this. If that decision remains when our war is over, I'll need to support the rest of my family and oblige."

"How many men?" Cleve resisted standing as he blurted out the words.

"Excuse me?"

"How many would you send?"

The King rubbed his cheek in thought. "Maybe twenty to thirty thousand. And many would have swords crafted from Bastial steel. We'd have horses as well. The few brought to Ovira over the years died out long ago, so we know they don't have any."

Danvell held out a palm. "Cleve, whoever controls Ovira at the time will be warned before we come. They'll realize they don't have a chance against us...as long as they're smart. Taking control should be a simple process, without any death, as long as whoever is king at the time steps down."

Cleve felt a dry swallow run down his throat as he knew it wasn't his place to say what he was about to tell the King of Goldram. But he wasn't about to let that stop him.

"Men and women should be sent to Kyrro now to stop the Krepps and end the war, not years from now just to take it over."

Danvell looked as if he wanted to stand, his palms pushing against the table. With an angry look, he uttered through his teeth, "We would, Cleve. But we need our men and women here for this war. You can help with the transition when it happens. Convince whoever is leading Ovira not to resist, and it can be done peacefully."

A warm tingle swam through him, burrowing deep in his chest and putting him at ease. "So, you'll let me go back?"

"I hadn't decided that until now," Danvell said. "But I will." He raised a finger to stop Cleve's budding excitement. "However, I want you and the psychic Elf to do something while you're here. Then I'll give you a ship and a crew."

Cleve jumped to his feet. "Anything."

"I want you to remember what I'm doing for you is a favor...a great one." Danvell raised an eyebrow. "I expect your continued cooperation in the future, even after this task. You'll help with transitioning Ovira into the hands of the Takary family when we need it."

Cleve took a breath to think. "I'll cooperate with you, as long as I'm also cooperating with Jessend and Lisanda. If you believe something is right...if all three of you believe it, then I'll go along. Only then will I follow your exact orders—when your daughters agree it's the best decision."

The sisters stood, as did Danvell, each of them sharing glances.

"My daughters don't make decisions that have to do with our military, especially overseas, which is what we're discussing here."

"They don't have to make the decision about what the Takarys' involvement will be in Ovira," Cleve elaborated. "They just have to agree with whatever you and the other Takarys decide. And then I'll do whatever is asked of me, be it tomorrow or ten years from now. As a family, I trust the three of you as I would trust my own."

"Father," Lisanda said. "I haven't spent nearly as much time with Cleve as Jessend has, but I can still tell he'll keep his word."

"Please agree, Father," Jessend added.

It seemed as if both sisters were eager to be more involved.

The King let out a breath with a subtle nod of his head. "I don't suppose it's the worst idea. I'll get Micah Vail to write up the contract if I still think it's a good idea tomorrow morning. Now, let's get some rest." He took a step away from his chair.

"Your highness?" Cleve said to stop him. "What task is it you have for me and Rek?"

"Oh." Danvell grunted out a laugh. "I'm so tired, I'd forgotten about that. Since you and Rek won't be staying with us to fight, Rek can take this opportunity of reprieve before major battles begin to travel to Meritar for a couple of weeks. When he comes back, I want you both to escort my wife and son home. They left for Chanren months ago, and the territories surrounding us have grown dangerous since then. I fear for their safety when they return. There have already been attacks. Just yesterday an enemy army of five hundred were killed trying to travel across Zav—our new allies. We don't even know where they were going or what they were doing."

Danvell paused for a sip of wine, leaning down to take it from the table without sitting. "Waywen and Presoren have been preparing for this war much longer than we have, and they've set up scouts across our lands. So, the smaller the party, the better the chances we go unnoticed. My wife and son are safe in Chanren for now. They have one more castle to visit before they return. Rek should be back by then. If not, Jek Trayden should be here. You can go with him."

Lisanda nearly jumped. "He's alive?"

Danvell grew a wide smile. "Yes. We just received a letter from him. He's on the way back with his army. I wanted to surprise you."

Lisanda collapsed to the floor, weeping with joy.

Danvell bent down, picked her up, and embraced her.

"I've been worried as well," Danvell admitted. "I let distrust get the better of me when I sent him north to fight the desmarls. The way he marched out of here so proudly, I should have known right then that I'd made a mistake. But it took me all this time to realize it. The first thing I'm going to do when he gets back is throw a feast."

Lisanda's weeping was nearly deafening.

A few servants came in to check on her.

"We're alright," Jessend told them with a smile.

Cleve thought of the relief that would overwhelm him if he got back to Kyrro to find out Reela was unharmed. It would be like a metal pipe in his throat finally had been removed.

Stay safe, Reela.

Chapter 13

Nearly a week passed without much excitement.

Cleve spent most of each day with Nulya. When Silvie and Jessend weren't flirting with each other, they helped him realize his subtle riding mistakes. The hardest problem for him to correct was his posture. He tended to either lean forward or slouch, both of which were wrong according to the giddy young women. He didn't notice a difference in the horse's behavior or the soreness in his back either way, but he trusted them to be right.

At one point, they decided he was ready to take the horse out of the palace for a ride.

Silvie and Jessend rode with him, zipping through the city. A retinue of guards came along, too.

Jessend soon took the lead. When the Princess wasn't navigating through crowded streets, smiling and waving at nearly every commoner who looked her way, she found a secluded area for some respite from all the screaming and pointing.

Eventually, Cleve asked if they could leave the city. It took some time, but Jessend convinced the guards they wouldn't stray too far from the walls of The Nest.

Once they were on the open land of Goldram, galloping across long fields of grass, Cleve made a startling realization. If Kyrro had horses, the war would be won easily.

He wondered what had been happening since he'd left. As what usually happened when his focus traveled over the Starving Ocean, he found himself muttering hopeful wishes about Reela, Terren, Effie, Alarex, and even Steffen.

He wondered what they would think when he told them of his time in Goldram with the Takary Princesses. Jessend would be easy to describe, but then he pondered what he would say of Lisanda. He still didn't know her that well, except that she was quite different from Jessend.

Lisanda had changed her hair nearly every day since her father had announced that Jek was on his way back. The whole time that Cleve was in the palace before then, she'd worn her hair like Jessend—long and wavy. It was almost identical to Reela's hair, except for the sheer darkness of it. Reela's was so light brown it was nearly blonde.

But since then, Cleve had seen Lisanda with curls, buns, a double tail, and even perfectly straight hair, which was her most recent style. She had it shortened as well, so that it only fell to her shoulders.

Each day, Jessend would spend up to an hour in Lisanda's room while she tried on different dresses, trying to find the perfect one with her new hairstyle.

Jessend was always excited at first to see her sister's new hairstyle, eagerly helping her choose an outfit as well. But that excitement would fade quicker than the surge of brightness that came with lightning. Soon, she would be making excuses to leave, complaining later to Cleve how surprising it was that Lisanda could spend so much time in front of a mirror.

Jessend also told Cleve that Lisanda claimed her reasoning behind this was to look good for Jek. But everyone knew he wouldn't care how she wore her hair or what dress she had on. The latest gossip was that Lisanda was just using it as an excuse to get excited about trying out new looks.

The day after their trip outside The Nest, Cleve received permission to ride out of the city on his own.

He spent the day on Nulya's back with a sword, a bow borrowed from Jessend, and a quiver packed with arrows. He shot at the rotten wood of fallen trees while trotting; he swiped his sword at stumps and bushes while galloping; and soon both he and Nulya were sweating.

While resting by a small lake that shimmered in the evening

sun, he wondered what would happen if he just rode north and kept going as far as he could.

He knew enough of the land to realize he would reach Waywen in a day or two. He figured no one would stop him.

There was no way they'd know he had an allegiance to the Takary family, unless Kasko had made it there somehow. Maybe he had, and now he was devising a plan for revenge.

They assumed by now he'd escaped, probably fled Goldram. Cleve didn't like to think about it, constantly going back to that night, realizing it was his fault Kasko had gotten away with his life.

Cleve decided to let it out of his mind.

If he went so far north that he made it past Waywen, Cleve could keep going all the way to the desmarls. The thought was tantalizing, though he didn't know why. There was something about the danger that made it intriguing, perhaps because only the brave would go out of their way to travel there. *Or maybe just the stupid.*

A now-renowned artist once had climbed up a cliff that overlooked much of the north and painted what he saw. The artwork became famous enough that Cleve had seen several copies around the palace.

The view the artist depicted was like standing atop the mountain in the middle of an endless sea, but instead of water in every direction, there was a thick cloud of green Sartious Energy that covered the vast flatlands as far as the eye could see.

It was eerie to think that massive man-eating creatures were hidden in the green fog, and with tentacles so strong they could break bones.

A chill tickled the top of his spine. *And Jek was there. He killed ten of those creatures, now returning with their eyes.* Cleve wondered how he'd done it and how many of his men had died.

Someone had called Jek "The Sartious Mage" in front of

Cleve. He'd heard that name more than once but couldn't figure out what it meant until he'd asked Jessend.

"I already told you," she claimed. "Because he has the most control over Sartious Energy for anyone his age, possibly anyone in Greenedge. You really should ask Lisanda the story about how they met. She's wondering why you haven't inquired yet."

Cleve did later. Lisanda smiled gleefully and began. She didn't shy away from any details, and he could tell she'd told the story at least a few times before. Her face didn't show any sense of urgency to finish. The pride in her eyes was bright throughout the tale.

It was hard for Cleve to sit and listen for so long, as doing so was never his strong suit. So they took a total of four breaks throughout the story, some as long as an hour so Cleve could spend much-needed time with a weapon or with Nulya.

When she finally finished, Cleve didn't know what to say besides, "When's the wedding?"

She laughed and blushed at the same time. "He hasn't asked me yet, but I think he will when he comes back." Her mouth straightened, and Cleve realized then that her lips were different from Jessend's. The curve in the middle of her top lip was more accentuated, making her expressions even easier to read. "But he has to get permission from my father first, who I believe has begun to trust Jek as he trusts you. Do you think?"

"It seemed that way from the last conversation we had about Jek."

Lisanda stood and straightened her arms toward Cleve. He stood as well, and they hugged.

"It's too bad you and Jessend don't feel the same way about each other that Jek and I do. I think you would make her a good husband."

Cleve stepped back and shook his head. "I really wouldn't, but thank you for that."

Later, in the shower, that phrase repeated itself in his head, and he found himself laughing.

    Good husband. He laughed some more.

Chapter 14

Jek was supposed to have arrived two days ago, but there'd been no word.

"He's coming back in through Waywen," Danvell said solemnly, leaning over the table toward Lisanda. "The stubborn idiot didn't want to take the extra time going around to Zav where his party would be much safer."

Lisanda let out an annoyed breath. "He's never been very patient."

Cleve was surprised she didn't seem more worried about the delay, so much so that he even asked her why she wasn't.

"Jek's good at getting where he needs to go," she answered. "I'm sure he can handle himself."

So can Reela, Cleve realized. He felt some of his incessant tightness loosen in his throat.

Danvell had gathered them for dinner, claiming there were several things they needed to know. Micah Vail had been brought in to eat with them as well, the man barely touching his food.

"Are you sending people out for Jek?" Jessend asked.

"Men and women were sent yesterday," Micah answered. "But we don't know his army's exact location, and our people can't ride with too much haste. There are many scouts and traps the farther north we go. It could take some time to figure out what happened."

Lisanda's mouth popped open. "It's that dangerous in Waywen?"

"I'm afraid so," Micah answered.

A look of guilt crossed Lisanda's face. Worry came soon after. "I didn't realize." She seemed to be speaking mostly to herself.

Cleve felt the same guilt for believing Reela would be fine on her own. He should be there with her.

"Unfortunately, that's not the worst news," the King said, showing tightened eyes full of pain.

His daughters must've sensed it like Cleve had, for they leaned forward, widening their already large eyes.

Jessend spoke first. "What happened?"

"We haven't heard from your brother." Cleve could feel the pride in Danvell's voice when he uttered the words "your brother." But the King's face showed nothing but concern, with his twisted mouth and furrowed brow.

"Raymess was supposed to send a letter when he reached the last castle he was to visit in Chanren—Castle Stamuth," Danvell continued. "Not only haven't we received a letter from him, King Stamuth wrote to us upset because Raymess never arrived."

"What about the rest of those with him?" Jessend asked. "What about Mother?"

"No one arrived at Castle Stamuth," Micah answered for Danvell, who seemed too distraught to say the words.

Lisanda gasped.

"So what does that mean?" Jessend asked, jumping off her seat.

"We don't know yet," Micah Vail answered. "We're waiting to hear back from scouts we have around that area and in Zav. But based on the movements we've seen, we think it's likely they've been taken by men in Waywen."

"There were hundreds with them!" Jessend was shouting now. "How could they be taken so easily?"

"They might not have been taken at all," Lisanda muttered to the table.

Jessend turned to her sister. "What do you mean?"

Lisanda looked up at Danvell. "Isn't that right, Father? You don't know for sure they were taken?"

Danvell let out a slow breath as his gaze fell. "We don't."

"I don't understand!" Jessend was frantically looking back and forth at them, clearly sensing something was even worse than she'd realized. "What are you saying?"

"They could've been killed already, slain in battle," Lisanda answered meekly. Her eyes were fixed on the table. She seemed emotionless.

Micah stood, speaking as he made his way toward the sisters. "I'm sure they're still alive. It's best to stay calm. Our worst thoughts are produced when we panic."

He put a hand on each princess' shoulder. Cleve assumed he was using psyche to comfort them.

Jessend sank back into her chair, and soon each sister was nodding.

"What about the psychic Elf?" Jessend met eyes with Cleve. "Can he find people who're missing?"

Cleve shook his head. "Psyche doesn't work like that." He made a conscious effort not to gaze at Micah. "Rek can't find anyone unless they're already close and he's familiar with them."

"How close?" Lisanda asked.

"Less than fifty yards," Cleve answered.

Jessend pounded her fist on the table. "Then what can we do?"

Danvell tilted his head, showing a sad smile. "Jessend, this is not up to you to solve. Don't you trust I'm doing everything I can?"

Defeated, Jessend's shoulders slumped. "Yes. I'm sorry, Father."

Cleve stood. "What about me? Is there anything I can do to help?"

"As soon as we have a better idea where they might be, then yes," Danvell answered. "That's why you're in here. If it's a rescue mission we need, then the less people we send, the better. And as you and Jessend have described, your psychic friend is the most powerful person we have. We've sent a message to the Elves in Meritar, but we can't even be certain he'll receive it. If he's not back in time, I'll have to figure out something else."

Jessend stood, shouldering her way in front of Cleve. "Isn't that too dangerous for Cleve?"

Danvell spread his palms as if confused by her question. "Cleve wants to help, he's just as skilled as the best warriors among our army, and I trust him. Is there something I'm missing?"

His question sounded rhetorical. But Jessend answered it as if it wasn't.

"He doesn't know the land!"

"Jessend, no one knows the land these days," Danvell said. "It's filled with enemy armies in friendly territories, along with allied men hiding among our enemies. This is what happens when four bordered territories go to war with each other. It's happened before, but at least this time we have Zav on our side."

"You must at least send someone who knows the terrain of Greenedge!" Jessend shouted.

"Of course, dear. Please." His face showed annoyance, matching his voice. "I know you care about Cleve, but it's not your place to question my decisions."

She spun around, looking up to meet Cleve's eyes. "Are you certain you're alright with this?"

He put his hand on her shoulder, looking over her head to meet Danvell's gaze. "After this, you'll help me and Rek get back to Kyrro?"

"I will. I promise it."

Cleve swallowed hard, still reluctant to agree. *Why am I so nervous about this?*

Something didn't feel right. He trusted Danvell, so what was it? If Rek was with him, they should be able to handle anything as long as they were cautious.

That was it—Rek might not be back in time before they

caught a lead on Raymess' location.

"Without Rek, I don't feel confident about retrieving a man and a woman from an enemy territory I've never been in before," Cleve admitted.

"But we can't wait for Rek," Micah Vail answered. "As soon as we know where they are, we have to go."

Searching for ideas, Cleve's eyes found Micah. "Will you come with me if Rek isn't here in time?"

Danvell laughed. "Micah Vail? He has no weapons training. Why him?"

Micah glared at Cleve. "My place is inside the palace."

"Cleve." Jessend pulled on his arm. "Are you feeling alright? It's strange of you to suggest Micah Vail go with you. And you seem pale as well." She touched his cheek. The coolness of her palm made him realize how flushed he felt. He sat down.

"Here." Micah Vail brought over a glass of water, touching his shoulder in the process. Cleve felt steadiness return to his mind that he was sure was from psyche. He thanked Micah.

"I know it needs to be done," Cleve said. "And I *do* want to be the one to do it. I guess I'm just nervous." It was so unlike him to feel this way, he couldn't help but wonder why it was happening.

Is this because my barrier has been down? Every feeling he'd had in the last few weeks had been like a needle pricking his skin. He'd laughed, cried, and even smiled more in this palace than he'd done in the past year.

He closed his eyes to meditate, pulling in Bastial Energy. There was chatter around him, but it quickly faded away, leaving just the sound of a river flowing past him, calming him as it brushed by rocks. Trees appeared, and the sun brightened everything, melting the black to leave a blue sky.

He opened his eyes and let the warm Bastial Energy seep out of him.

Taking a breath, he stood. "When you know where they are, tell me. I'll be ready."

He found everyone to be smiling at him. Danvell waved at a servant, who brought forward a sword in its sheath. Just by the handle, Cleve could tell it was no mediocre weapon.

"I have a gift for you," the King told him. The servant gave the sword to Danvell and left. "I'm sure Jessend has told you all about Bastial steel."

Cleve felt chills down his arms as he reached out to take Danvell's offering.

"This weapon, along with Nulya, are yours, even when you leave."

Cleve slowly drew the sword from its sheath. Its sunset color caught the light, and for a moment Cleve thought it was glowing.

He expected it to be hot, as that's how it appeared—like a burning ember—but the steel was cold just like any other sword.

Though it didn't feel like any other sword.

"It's so light," Cleve marveled.

"It's about half the weight of iron," Danvell said. "This is how we won the Bastial Steel War ten years ago." He pointed at the weapon and then folded his arms. "And with it, you'll get back my son and wife."

Chapter 15

After receiving the dreadful news about Queen Vala and Prince Raymess, Lisanda was first out of the room. Suddenly, she let out a shriek that pulled everyone's gaze.

She must've seen something, Cleve figured. But instead of running away from it, she was darting farther into the hall.

Cleve walked up to see what it was. Lisanda's lips were locked with some young man's. *Must be that Sartious mage. Looks like he's made it back safely.*

Lisanda separated from him, a wide smile giving sight to her teeth. "You're filthy. You need a shower."

"So, let's go." He started pulling her down the hall. Around his shoulder was a giant sack making sloppy squishing sounds with each step. *The desmarl eyes.*

She tugged on his arm to stop him. "What do you mean?"

"You can get in with me."

She laughed and squeezed his cheeks with one hand. "With the amount of dirt on your body, I'm more likely to come out dirtier than I am now."

"Oh, I can guarantee you will." He leaned down, and they kissed again.

Danvell cleared his throat.

They stopped, looking up with guilt.

"I apologize, my king," Jek said, now with a flat line across his mouth. "I didn't see you there." Jek took a step forward and then kneeled, bowing his head and presenting the sack to Danvell.

"Please, stand up straight." The King's eyebrows arched, and a smile formed. "There's no need for that. I have an apology as well. I should've trusted you more. Instead, I sent you to the desmarls." The King let the sack rest in front of him without looking inside.

"I understand. You didn't think my feelings for Lisanda were genuine, and you were worried hers weren't, either."

"You've proven your allegiance. You proved it before you even left. I just failed to realize it. There will be no more tests. I promise this."

Jek seemed to be holding in a laugh.

"Is something funny?" Danvell asked, now deciding to open the sack for a glance, anger forming in his tone.

Cleve peered into it for a look at the monstrous eyes. They were easy to see, as the sack was nearly filled to the brim with them. They had an oval shape, like a head turned on its side. In fact, they were about the same size as a Human head as well. They were mostly white with a tall black pupil, each one ruptured and somewhat disfigured.

Jessend had told him that chemists used desmarl eyes in mixtures with different plants for several potions, the most valuable heightening eyesight for a brief time.

"No, my king. Nothing's funny." Jek answered. "It's just that your mention of a promise brought back memories." He looked to Lisanda. "Fond ones."

"I see." The King's smile returned. "You must be hungry for a decent meal. I'll have someone prepare something for you. But first, you must bathe. I can smell you from here."

"You do stink," Lisanda added with a giggle.

"One last thing," Danvell said. "The party that was sent with you—in your letter they were all uninjured. Where are they now?"

"They made it back with me. We got held up in Waywen, but everyone survived. I dismissed them once we were in the palace."

"We sent an army to retrieve you."

"Yes, they found us when we were already in Goldram. They're back as well."

"Very well. You can tell me the rest after you bathe." The

King walked by Jek, placing a hand on his shoulder for a squeeze.

Micah took that as his cue to approach Jek. "I'm very glad you're back." They shook hands.

Lisanda clung to Jek's other arm, using her feet to fiddle with the marble floor.

Jessend approached next, and Cleve felt as if he should go with her. "I'm sorry about what happened last time we met," she told Jek, though Cleve didn't know what she was referring to.

Jek bowed. "I understand, Jessend. I'm just relieved you're not upset with me anymore. You can be quite scary, especially with a knife in your hand."

Lisanda laughed, and Jek smiled wide. Jessend poked him in the chest. "That's right," she said facetiously. She gestured toward Cleve. "This is Cleve Polken. Cleve, this is Jek Trayden."

Cleve didn't know if he should bow or what, so he waited to see what the Sartious mage would do. Jek extended his hand with a warm smile, and Cleve shook it.

Jessend continued, "Cleve came back with me from Kyrro. He saved not only my life, but Lisanda's and our father's as well."

Surprise struck Jek's face. He looked to Lisanda, and she nodded to him.

"It's true," Lisanda said. "He's quite the warrior, and he's going to help retrieve our mother and brother."

The surprise deepened. "What happened?"

"I'll tell you everything," Lisanda said. "But you must shower first. I'm starting to feel faint."

Jek laughed. "Alright. And I like your hair."

Lisanda ran a hand through it. She was glowing with glee. "Thank you."

Later that night, Cleve couldn't get to sleep. The dread of being sent after the Takary Prince and Queen when he knew so little about the land had started to creep back into his body. It was a physical feeling, this dread, like his muscles were in constant use.

He tried to relax, but he was hungry as well. He hadn't eaten much during dinner. He figured no one had, not with the conversation that had taken place.

Getting up, Cleve decided he needed to eat something before he would ever fall asleep. *And it will get my mind off these incessant worries as well.*

Reluctant to disturb Gerace, he made his way to the pantry on his own, using a lamp to light the dark hallways. Moving about in low light always reminded him of Effie. The white glow from her wand as she paced around the dark house they shared would dance around the hallway in what seemed to be an aimless route. Many nights Cleve had fallen asleep listening to the soft patter of her feet traveling back and forth outside his closed door, her light brightening and dimming as she went.

A few times, he'd gotten up himself, and they'd shared a conversation. She had a lot on her mind during those nights— maybe she always had, he realized now.

Usually it was easy for Cleve to bury his worries, but as he came close to the pantry, he felt more similar to Effie than to his old self. *If this is what her mind is like every night, I feel sorry for her.*

The pantry was well lit, he saw as he approached the door. He blew out his lamp but stopped in the doorway when he heard voices.

Lisanda was seated on the counter, her bare legs wrapped around Jek as he stood before her. She wore a man's buttoned shirt. Cleve figured it was Jek's, as he had no shirt on himself.

The mage was average height, maybe a little taller. His body was muscular but lean, with scars and even fresh cuts that Cleve figured were from the desmarls.

Cleve hadn't noticed his eyes before. But now, among the

light of several lamps around the pantry, he could see how blue they were—distractingly blue.

The two of them didn't seem to notice Cleve yet.

He froze, reluctant to enter but too hungry to leave. Jek was feeding Lisanda a strawberry, each giggling. He leaned in for a kiss, but she playfully pushed him away. "You have strawberry all over your mouth."

"You love it," he joked, puckering his lips and looming toward her.

She let out a squeak and leaned back. "I do not."

"How is it not all over your mouth as well?" he asked, looking for something to use to wipe his mouth.

"Because I know how to eat without making a mess, unlike you." She handed him a cloth.

He used it. "Clean enough for you, Princess?"

"Much better."

Her light giggling died down as they leaned in to kiss each other. Soon the motion became fierce, their lips wrestling, their mouths opening wider. They separated, and Jek urgently started unbuttoning the shirt covering Lisanda.

The moment Cleve realized she had nothing on underneath it, he turned and left.

He took a different route back to his room, still trying to figure out how to fill his stomach without bothering a servant.

He passed by a room with two guards stationed outside. It was strange because they weren't there during the day. A quick peek inside gave insight as to why they were there. Cleve found Danvell Takary scribbling away, hunched over a table with a lowly lamp beside him. The King looked up and then pushed himself to his feet.

"Cleve." He motioned for Cleve to come in, then sat back down and returned to his writing before Cleve could even reply.

He entered, sat, and waited, deciding not to speak until Danvell said something first. But his stomach wasn't as obedient, grumbling loudly as the King wrote.

Danvell looked up. "I didn't eat much, either. Let's have a small meal, shall we?" From the way Danvell was smiling, it was clear he already knew Cleve's answer.

"That would be wonderful."

Danvell turned to his guards and barked some orders. One of them walked off.

"I'll be done soon," the King told Cleve, switching his gaze back to the scroll and murmuring words. Soon, his pen was dancing again, the scratch it produced echoing off the walls.

The monarch whistled, and the other guard approached with a hand extended. Danvell handed him the scroll, took a culminating breath, and turned his focus to Cleve. "Were you wondering why I write in here?"

Cleve glanced around the room for the first time. There were no windows on the stone walls. The room was a rare dead end unless there was some hidden passage behind the hearth where the fire crackled.

"I do now," Cleve admitted.

"Dank, isn't it?" The King wafted his hand as if he could feel the wetness in the air. "I get my best writing done in here. I'm not sure why. You'd think I'd hate it in here, but I like how bare the walls are. I like the sound the fire makes bouncing off them." The crackle was dull, like someone tapping fingernails on a table.

Cleve nodded. "We can't help what we like, only embrace it or suppress it." He thought of Reela, wondering if she'd smile if she'd heard him just now. *Of course she would. She's always smiling.*

"You're very wise. Anyone tell you that?"

Cleve shook his head. "It must be a recent development."

The King laughed, thinking Cleve was joking. Both guards had returned to their post. The one who had been sent off first leaned in and announced, "They're cooking now, my king."

"Thank you."

Cleve's stomach rumbled again.

"What's going on between you and Jessend?" Danvell asked. "Did she tell you to claim you love someone else back in Kyrro, or is that the truth?"

"That's the truth—well, I'm not sure about love. But I care for her deeply."

"Don't you care for Jessend *deeply*?"

Cleve's mouth opened before he knew what he was going to say. Then it just hung there, waiting for his mind to catch up. "I do," he finally uttered. "But more as a friend."

"What did she do for you to feel this way? She can be quite crude. Is that it? She needs to learn some better manners."

"Her behavior has nothing to do with it. And I actually like the way she's straightforward. I don't think she should change anything about herself."

"Then what is it? Do you not think she's beautiful?"

What kind of question is that from a father about his own daughter? There is ever only one answer. "Of course she's beautiful."

"Too short for you?"

Cleve let out a frustrated laugh. "She's quite short, but it has nothing to do with that."

The King leaned back in his chair. "So, everything you said before is really true? In another life, you and Jessend could've been together, but not now—not with...what's her name? The one back in Kyrro."

"Reela."

"Not with Reela waiting for you?"

"Yes. All of that's true." Cleve was beginning to feel frustrated for Jessend's sake...to not have her own father believe her.

"I understand. Please don't tell Jessend I asked. She used to make up stories about other people when she was younger, and she still tends to exaggerate the truth. But I think you bring out her best side. Can we really ask for anything more than that?"

"That's the finest reason I've heard to be with someone," Cleve admitted.

"Well, I hope Reela does that for you, and you do that for Reela. I know my wife only makes me stronger. I feel like half of me has been missing since she left. I'm sure I would've made better decisions with her here, especially involving Jek."

"She'll be back, along with your son." Cleve let his tone reflect his responsibility. He would make sure of it.

"Thank you, Cleve. I hope we hear from them and the Elf soon."

Two servants stood in the doorway with trays of food. "My king," one said, lowering her head.

"Come in."

As they ate, Danvell told Cleve more about his wife and son. At first Cleve thought the information he was sharing would be helpful for their retrieval. But soon it became clear that Danvell just wanted to speak of them. The way his eyes looked when he gazed up from his food was as if he was picturing them as he spoke.

By the time they were finished, Cleve felt that sleep might take him before he made it back to his room.

He thanked the King and left.

Back in his room, he was surprised to find someone was already in his bed. Jessend sat up and covered her mouth as she yawned.

"How'd you get in?" Cleve was sure he'd locked the door.

"I have a key, silly. Do you not want me in here?"

He removed his pants and slid his feet under the covers. "You're always welcome to share my bed."

"Always?" She put her arm across his stomach. "Even if Reela's there with you?"

"If she's fine with it, then I am."

Jessend giggled. "She definitely wouldn't be."

"I realize that."

"So you're not worried about what she's going to think

about all the nights we've spent together? You told me she's a psychic. Won't she know?"

"She can't read direct thoughts. No psychic can—though she might be able to pick up on some guilt if I feel it strongly enough."

"But there won't be any, right?"

"No." Cleve knew many people suffered from guilt over the smallest things, but not him. *If things had gone further with Jessend that night Kasko came, then I would.*

"Good. Because I don't want to leave this warm bed."

They were silent for some time. Cleve was phasing in and out of sleep when Jessend blurted something that woke him up fully.

"I think I'm going to kiss Silvie tomorrow. When is a good time to kiss a girl?"

Cleve would've been surprised if it weren't for all the hours atop Nulya's back that he'd spent noticing their flirtation.

"I'm sure you know better than me. I've only ever kissed you and Reela. And both times I practically had to be begged."

Jessend scoffed. "I wish Silvie would beg me to kiss her, or she would just do it herself." She sat up suddenly. "Don't tell anyone about this." Her tone couldn't have been more serious. "My father would force me to marry the next man he saw."

"Does Lisanda know you feel this way about Silvie?"

"Of course. She's seen me out there almost as much as you have, and she's not stupid."

"Does this mean you aren't interested in men anymore?" The moment Cleve asked his question, he wondered if he should have. He'd never had any conversation like this before, and he didn't know how she would take it.

Jessend was silent, her hand tracing Cleve's abs.

"I still like men," she said. "I don't really know what this means, to be honest. All I know is that I can be who I am around Silvie—I like who I am around her. She makes me feel safe, but also weak, like how you've talked about Reela. But this isn't a real weakness. I think you're mistaken about that, Cleve. It's more of a yearning. Sometimes we desire things that we shouldn't, and that makes us feel weak, but *this* desire is healthy. I can feel it. It's like craving food when we're hungry, and I'm always hungry around her. Do you know what I mean?"

Cleve hadn't thought about it in that way. *I've always been hungry for Reela as well, since the moment I saw her.*

More out of curiosity than anything else, Cleve thought to give Jessend the same compliment that her father had given him, just to see how she would react.

"You're very wise. Has anyone ever told you that?"

She scoffed once more. "Don't be stupid." She twisted up to peck his cheek. "Now let's get some rest. In the morning, you'll help me think of some way to get Silvie into the back of the stables. That's where I'll kiss her. Out of view."

Chapter 16

That morning, Gerace delivered their food along with a note for each of them from Danvell. The King still didn't know Cleve and Jessend had been sharing a bed, and Gerace knew better than to tell him. The note said they were to meet in the throne room after breakfast.

"I hate meeting him in there," Jessend stated, swallowing completely first. She never spoke with food in her mouth. Cleve figured it was one of the many lessons taught to her. "When he's sitting on the throne, I never feel like he's my father, only my king."

They were the last to arrive, Micah told them as he waited in the doorway. Then he left to retrieve Danvell Takary, who usually waited until everyone was there before entering his own meeting.

Cleve caught the middle of a conversation between Jek and Lisanda.

"...I did," Lisanda said. "I visited a few days ago."

"How are they?" Jek asked.

Jessend stepped up to them, dragging Cleve over. "How are who?" she asked.

"My father and sister," Jek answered, shifting back to Lisanda for the answer. He had a look about him as if he wanted to be touching her, the way he leaned forward, his eyes darting over her body.

"Kalli met a man she likes," Lisanda said. "He lives in Facian like her and Sannil, so they see each other a lot."

Jek's eyes squinted in concern. "What's he like?"

Lisanda blew out hot air. "Please." Her arms folded. "You're going to pretend you know who would be good for Kalli? She knows better than you do."

The corner of Jek's mouth scrunched, and his eyes relaxed. "I suppose you're right."

"He's a good man, anyway. At least she thinks so. Sannil's thrilled, but both of them have been worried about you."

"You told them I was sent north to the desmarls?" A mix of frustration and urgency crossed his face.

Lisanda's hands flew to her hips. "I was supposed to lie?"

Micah returned with Danvell just then.

"No," Jek whispered. He leaned over and kissed Lisanda's forehead. "Thank you for visiting them."

"I wanted to." She threw her arm around his and leaned against his shoulder.

"I have some bad news," Danvell announced, seating himself on the throne, looking mostly at Jessend and Lisanda. "We've received a demand from King Belwoll in Waywen. They have our family, and they want five thousand Bastial steel swords in exchange for their lives."

The fact that Waywen was at least making demands would've sounded like good news to Cleve, but the King's tone was as if he was already announcing their deaths.

The Takary sisters each gasped at the news. Jessend grabbed Cleve's hand and squeezed hard.

What am I missing?

"Why am I getting the sense you won't be agreeing?" Cleve decided to ask, disrupting the silence.

"We can't give them five thousand Bastial steel swords," Micah Vail answered. "Or the war is lost."

"The only reason we won last time is because of the advantage the weapons gave us. There's only been about ten thousand made, and the Bastial steel in the crater is running out. Now it takes weeks just to find enough to make one."

Cleve realized what this meant. "So how do I retrieve your family?"

"You?" Jek blurted. It seemed to have come out by accident, for his hand shot to his mouth. "Sorry. I was just surprised by your statement. How are you so confident you'll be going?"

"He is, Jek," Danvell answered calmly. "We've already discussed this."

Cleve found himself being studied by Jek's deep blue eyes. They ran around his face, his mouth growing tighter and tighter with each breath. He turned to Lisanda and whispered something. She stood on her toes and cupped her hands around his ear to whisper back.

"What's your concern, Jek?" Micah asked.

The mage answered without looking at Cleve. "I'm just not sure why someone from Kyrro is the best one to be sent to Waywen to retrieve Takary royalty."

"He's not going to Waywen," Danvell answered. "That would be suicide."

"Then where?" Jek asked.

"Our scouts found the bodies from the battle that took place in Chanren. All of our men were killed except our family. Our scouts tracked those who took them to an uncontrolled territory—Karri Forest. They're being held in a small encampment there. We believe the reason they didn't take them back to Waywen was a fear that when they crossed through Zav, they would be discovered. Our allies are well aware of the situation and always on the lookout for suspicious activity."

"Have we heard from Rek?" Cleve asked.

"Unfortunately, no," Micah answered. "And you need to leave today. We don't have time to wait."

No Rek? Cleve had found comfort with this mission only when he'd convinced himself that Rek would return in time. Now he could feel his body stiffening, the familiar tightness of worry returning to his stomach.

"The note from King Belwoll of Waywen told us we have ten days before they give the order to kill," Danvell said. "They also wrote that Raymess and Vala will die if anyone attempts to break them out. They've probably assumed we know where they're being held. Luckily, it's not too heavily guarded. They weren't able to send too many men through Zav without being seen. Our scouts have reported somewhere between one hundred and fifty to two hundred enemies in the encampment."

"But look at him!" Jek gestured at Cleve. "How can someone of his size not be seen?"

"That's why you're going with him," Danvell said firmly.

"What!" Lisanda shouted. "No." She stepped between Jek and the throne. "He just got back."

Jessend stepped forward. "Send me, Father."

He stood from his throne. "Absolutely not."

"Don't make Jek go, please!" Lisanda pleaded, grabbing her father's arm.

But Jek turned her away from him with a hand to her shoulder, pulling her in for an embrace. "I was going to demand to go even if he didn't request it." Jek's tone was soft, nearly a whisper.

"I'm sending another as well," the King said, sitting back down. "Lysha. She's on her way here now."

Cleve heard an audible slap and turned to find Lisanda had struck her own forehead. "Her?" she mumbled with her hand still over her face. "She's never had less than two boyfriends at once, always younger men, and it seems to even be a matter of pride for her! She should be ashamed of that, not proud! I don't want her going." With a scrunched face, Lisanda folded her arms tightly.

Jek laughed and squeezed her shoulders into him. "You're worried?"

"She's very beautiful." Lisanda's tone was so low and rough that her words grumbled out like a river of rocks rolling downhill. Cleve couldn't tell whether the Princess was trying to be comical, but her voice was.

Jek laughed even harder. "We're being sent to save your mother and brother against two hundred men, and this is what you worry about?"

"I've seen you get out of nearly every situation," Lisanda said. "But none of those have involved another woman who's going to be trying to seduce you."

"If you two are done, we have more to discuss," Danvell stated plainly, his arms now folded.

"Sorry, Father," Lisanda said.

"Lysha knows Karri Forest well. She'll be in command," Danvell said. "Time is going to be the biggest issue because it's probably going to take nine days just to get to the encampment in the middle of Karri Forest. That leaves only one day to get Raymess and Vala out. Then you'll send back a pigeon to let us know it's done. Cleve, I'll have Gerace help you pack for the trip. She's been given instructions what you'll need to bring. We'll supply the clothing."

Danvell's gaze sank to Cleve's hip, where he wore the Bastial steel sword on his belt. "I would've reminded you to bring that weapon, but it looks like it won't be leaving your side anytime soon."

"Only when I sleep and bathe," Cleve admitted.

A few people laughed, making him realize it sounded like he was joking.

He wondered why the mood wasn't more solemn. Even he himself felt no dread, no terror. Cleve searched within and was surprised to realize he was eager.

Was it Lisanda's humorous response to all this that had done it? Maybe the confidence he could feel from Jek? Something during the recent conversation had prevented him from worrying. Or maybe it was from knowing this was the last task he needed to do before he could go home.

Whatever it was, he was ready.

Gerace stepped in and bowed her head.

The King stood. "It's time."

Chapter 17

Gerace was unnervingly silent as she thumbed through the wardrobe in Cleve's room, tossing some clothes onto the bed. She folded a shirt and coat and placed them neatly in the backpack. His undergarments were tossed in after.

She hadn't given him much, but he didn't mind. He wouldn't be changing often anyway.

The young servant brought another bag to his bed, taking out pouches of food and telling him what each of them contained. Only when she handed over his water pouch did she look him in the eye. For a heartbeat, she just stared.

"Gerace." Cleve spoke slowly to make sure he got it right. "Thank you."

She lowered her head, then left without a word.

Jessend came in soon after, shutting the door behind her. "This is going to sound strange, but I want you to hear it anyway." She walked up and patted his stomach. "I love you like I love Lisanda."

"You're right. That is strange."

A faint giggle came out as she said, "Shut up. You love me, too."

They hugged.

"Bring back my family, but be careful," Jessend said, jabbing a finger at him. "Don't do anything stupid."

"I can't guarantee that."

She laughed.

Again, my words are taken facetiously. Cleve had made more statements that were taken as jokes than actual jokes since entering the palace. He thought this time he should clarify.

"I'm serious. You should expect me to do something stupid with such a risky task."

She leaned back to look at his face, tilting her head as she studied his eyes. "You *are* serious."

"I am."

"Well then, if you're going to be stupid, at least make sure you have support from Jek and Lysha. Cover each other."

"I will."

She leaned back in for another tight squeeze.

Lisanda appeared in the doorway. "Lysha's outside the palace."

"Then I should go," Cleve said, releasing his grip around Jessend.

After throwing on his backpack, he extended his hand to Lisanda. But she ignored it and moved in for a hug.

"Make sure Jek doesn't do anything stupid," Lisanda said, her tone completely serious.

"I can't promise that," Cleve admitted. Jek seemed like a brash man, not easily controlled.

"Well then, promise you'll try!" Her voice squeaked.

"Alright, I promise."

The King was already at the bottom of the steps, discussing something with a woman Cleve assumed to be Lysha. Her skin was a darker tint than the golden brown hue of the King's, a mix between black and brown. She was tall and muscular, matching the King's height, though he wasn't very tall himself.

A bow was over her shoulder, a quiver on her hip. Cleve thought to ask why he wasn't given a bow and quiver, but then he realized he'd have too much too carry. Lysha had less bags than he did.

There was a knife on her other hip. Like Cleve's sword, it was made from Bastial steel. When she turned to greet Cleve, it reflected the sun like a mirror and exploded with light.

"Lysha," she said, squeezing his hand hard, competitively hard.

So he squeezed back. "Cleve."

Instead of the grimace he expected to find from his firm

grasp, she formed a wry smile.

"I'm going to have fun with you," she said.

Cleve tried to hide his feelings of discouragement. Another confident woman...and he'd figured he'd already reached his lifetime quota. Reela, Effie, Jessend...the shyness of Gerace was a relief at first, but it didn't last.

Lysha didn't seem likely to keep to herself. In another situation, he wouldn't have minded. But the last thing he wanted in this mission was any other distractions.

"So, this is the famous Lysha," Jek announced, walking down the steps with a speculative glare.

"You the Sartious mage?" Lysha asked.

They shook hands.

"Jek," he introduced himself.

Lysha whistled. "Two young men. A pretty boy...and a handsome brute." She brushed her thick locks over her shoulder. The weight of them against her skin made a sound like fingers drumming.

"Keep your pants on, Lysha," Danvell warned her. "This is serious."

"Sorry, my king. You know me. I can't help but make jokes. My boyfriends would be upset with me anyway." She smiled wide. Her teeth looked almost blindingly white.

"Are you sure you don't need a map?" Danvell tried to hand it to her for what seemed like the second or third time.

"I'm sure." She held her palm out as if to block it. "I've been through Karri Forest enough to know how to navigate around safely."

Safely?

"What's in the forest?" Cleve asked.

Lysha's eyes went wide and her mouth dropped open. She turned to Danvell. "You didn't tell him about the mookers?"

"Tell him on the way. It'll take many days to cross through Zav before you even reach the forest. You'll have plenty of time to go over the rules."

Rules? Cleve wished he had the mind to ask earlier if there was anything he should know. The mention of rules was unnerving.

Their horses were brought to them by guards. Nulya approached Cleve and rested her head on his shoulder. He stroked her mane.

"Extra food and water are strapped to the horses," Danvell said. "Travel fast, but don't push them too hard. A twisted ankle could mean the lives of my son and wife."

Nulya spluttered out air, her lips flapping with the sound.

"Sounds like Cleve's horse is saying not to worry," Lysha teased, getting on her mount.

She turned her horse and sped off without a look back, expecting Cleve and Jek to follow.

They tore through the city like a knife through stretched cloth, everyone jumping out of the way and cursing at them. Cleve wondered why he didn't receive the same reaction when he was with Jessend and her guards. Then the obvious answer came—*because I was with a Takary princess.*

By the time they were through the western wall, Cleve started to wonder how old Lysha was. He was having a tough time figuring it out. She was clearly older than him and Jek, but it could've been by five years or fifteen.

They rode without rest until the sun began to set. Then Lysha's horse slowed to a halt and she jumped off, leading the animal to a small stream for water.

Cleve and Jek followed suit.

"Hungry yet?" Lysha asked.

"Yes," Cleve admitted, only now realizing his mission had begun. In a little more than a week's time, he'd be breaking into an encampment to rescue a Prince and a Queen.

They let their horses drink, and then tied them to trees, breaking out the food next.

"What's in Karri Forest that's dangerous besides men from Waywen?" Cleve asked.

"Aren't you cute, already worrying about that when we're not even out of Goldram yet." Lysha reached over to pat Cleve's cheek. He whipped his head back reflexively. "Ever been with an older woman?" Lysha blurted.

"Bastial hell," Jek said. "What's wrong with you?"

"Just having some fun, trying to get a sense of what kind of men you are. The only way this is going to work is if we know each other very well. Want to guess how old I am?"

Cleve turned to find a disgruntled expression on Jek's face. Because no one was speaking, Cleve decided to break the awkward silence. "I've been told not to guess a lady's age."

Lysha laughed, some crumbs flying from her mouth. "I'm no lady. I'm a damn woman." She pointed at Jek. "You...Pretty Eyes. How old do you think I am?"

Jek shrugged and answered plainly. "I don't know, twenty-five."

Put off by Jek's disinterest, Lysha ignored his answer and turned to Cleve. An excited grin returned.

"What about you, Muscles?"

Cleve decided to give an age years older than he really thought, just to see how she would react. "Thirty," he answered as indifferently as he could.

Her eyes squinted, looking deep into Cleve's. He felt a tickle within his mind, the touch of an outside source. It was so subtle it felt like a drop of warm water had splashed on his brain. It still created a disruption, though, as if his thoughts were a massive lake and Lysha had dipped her toe into it.

All his training with Rek had paid off. It was psyche.

"You don't really think that," Lysha answered, confidently gesturing at him with her bread. "Give me your real answer."

"You're a psychic."

Shock filled her eyes, and she nearly fell backward. Jek started coughing from his food. "She is?" he sputtered.

"Not a very strong one, but yes," Cleve said.

The shock was gone now, Lysha staring coldly at Cleve. "I'm

no psychic. Why would you say that?"

Cleve sighed, remembering how psychics in Greenedge were treated. "Fine," he muttered, unwilling to deal with it. He was confident she couldn't do anything to him anyway. She didn't even have a tenth of Rek's power.

"Wait," Jek said. "What do you mean, 'fine'?"

"I mean I don't care to argue."

"But she is a psychic?" Jek asked, his pitch rising.

"Yes."

"I'm not." Lysha stood and pointed. "I don't know why you're lying, but I'm getting sick of it."

Cleve waved his hand petulantly to show his frustration. "Fine. I don't care."

"No." Jek stood. "I see what's going on here." He opened his palms, turning to face Lysha. "You said we need to get to know each other for this to work. But how can we trust you when you won't tell us the truth about yourself? How could we ever tell you the truth about ourselves?"

Jek waited, but Lysha seemed reluctant to reply.

"We won't tell anyone," Jek added. "So be honest. Are you a psychic?"

Lysha bit down on her lip, let out a grunt, and whipped her head to show Cleve a gut-punching glare. "I have some psychic ability. But how did you know?" She was near shouting, but not there yet.

"I've trained with the most powerful psychic in the world. I can feel when you use it on me."

"Bastial stars," Jek muttered to himself.

"No one else will hear of this." Lysha's tone was peremptory. She sat and stuffed some food in her mouth.

"That's it?" Jek blurted, now in a high-pitched voice. "Nothing more to say...either of you?"

Cleve shrugged.

"Sit down and eat," Lysha demanded. "We have to get back to riding."

They didn't speak again until it became too dark to ride.

When the horses were tied and a fire was crackling, Jek sat by it and told them, "There's something I need to warn you both about."

Something about his ominous tone made Cleve want to keep standing, but Lysha had sat, and Jek was waiting for Cleve to join them.

There were patches of grass throughout the soft dirt. Cleve positioned himself onto one.

"A few hours after I fall asleep, Sartious Energy is going to burst out of my body, and there's a good chance I'll involuntarily make enough noise to wake you up."

"That rumor's true?" Lysha asked.

"Who told you?" Jek seemed more embarrassed than curious.

"Guards who were flirting with me. You know how they love to gossip."

Jek rubbed the back of his neck, letting out a breath. "Too much Sartious Energy in my body makes it happen. So, if either of you knows of a plant or animal that absorbs SE, tell me now. It's likely the cure to this."

Cleve thought of Steffen. *He'd probably know.*

"You're a mage," Lysha said. "Why don't you just push the SE out of your body?"

"My body reabsorbs it after I fall asleep."

"I don't know of a plant or animal," Cleve said. "But I know someone who probably does. He's in Kyrro, though."

Jek looked toward the fire, his shoulders slumping. "I wouldn't leave Goldram."

Besides the soft crackle of the fire, all was silent. Jek then turned to show Cleve one eye. "When you go to Kyrro and ask your friend, will you come back and let me know the answer?" Jek smiled to show he was facetious, though his tone sounded serious to Cleve.

"I can't promise that. I'm sorry."

Jek nodded solemnly. "Of course, I understand."

"Let's rest so we can be up at sunrise," Lysha suggested.

"No flirtatious comments?" Jek teased. "Did Cleve's discovery of your psychic ability manage to finally kill your legendary hubris?"

Lysha grumbled as she lay flat, soon uttering, "Prideful little runt. Just wait until I find out a secret about you."

Cleve woke during the night to a burst of light and the sound of Jek painfully groaning. He watched as Jek twisted with each explosion. Watching the poor mage's skin being ripped open was enough to give Cleve nightmares of his own.

Soon, Jek was awake, sitting up and checking his body for wounds. Blood trickled down from his chest.

"Bastial hell," Lysha complained. "That's going to happen every night?"

"Yes," Jek stated angrily. "And I'd better not hear you complain about it. It's much worse for me than it is for you."

"Fine, but tomorrow you're sleeping father from us, at least while we're in Goldram or Zav where it's safe. Once we get to the forest, it's better to stick close while we remain hidden."

Jek seemed to be looking for his bag. Cleve found it a few yards from the fire and retrieved it for him, asking, "How long has this been happening?"

"Years." Jek opened his bag to remove a cloth and his water pouch. "If you want, I'll tell you more about it tomorrow."

Cleve nodded, letting his thoughts go to Reela as he eased back into slumber.

Chapter 18

They rode hard, giving them no chance to talk until they stopped to give their horses a rest.

The long days of riding might've felt dull if the constant urge to hurry wasn't tugging on Cleve's shoulders. It felt like a nagging boy wanting him to kneel so he could jump on his back.

Ten days they had until Jessend's brother and mother were to be killed—though Cleve suspected the King would send the five thousand Bastial steel swords in exchange for their lives if the rescue party didn't make it in time, not that he ever would let that lessen his eagerness to save them.

Jek talked about his "darkness," as he called it, describing the nightmares that terrorized him with each attack. Cleve had never known himself to be especially empathetic, but Jek's affliction seemed truly awful. He wondered how Jek could even get to sleep knowing what was about to happen.

When Jek was done, all the talk about magic had made Cleve think of an important question.

"Jek, if my sword is made from Bastial steel, what's to stop mages from shattering it with a stroke of their wand?"

"I'm not sure," Jek said, reaching his free hand toward Cleve for the weapon, his other stuffing food in his mouth. "May I?"

Cleve reluctantly handed it to him. If a mage could break it, he'd rather know now than later.

Jek studied the weapon with his fingers, tracing the swirls of red and orange on its flat side.

"I don't even know if this is pure Bastial Energy," he said. "I can feel some familiarity, but there's nothing I can do to manipulate it." Jek handed the sword back to Cleve.

He eagerly put it in its sheath. "What does it feel like...this familiarity?"

Jek scratched his chin, his eyes looking at the cased weapon. "It's like how we can know that food is a fruit or a meat even if we've never had it before. I can tell there's magic there, something close to BE, but I also know there's nothing I can do to manipulate it. It would be like asking you to move a mountain using nothing but your breath. You know it would be impossible, even without trying."

"I see."

A silence followed. Cleve rubbed his eyes, trying to ignore the drowsiness he was beginning to feel. The thought that they wouldn't be sleeping much in the following days only made it worse. Lysha stood and started walking toward some trees.

"Going to piss," she called over her shoulder.

The moment she was out of earshot, Jek said, "I almost wish we'd been sent on this mission before I came back to see Lisanda." With his lowered voice, it seemed as if he didn't want Lysha to overhear.

"Why is that?" Cleve asked.

"Because the little time I had with her made it even harder to leave."

Cleve wondered if he should tell Jek that he'd seen them in the pantry, but he quickly decided against it.

"You don't care for Jessend?" Jek asked.

"I care, but not in the same way you and Lisanda do for each other."

"I've heard there's someone else in Kyrro, Reela is it?"

Cleve felt his stomach tightening defensively, as if his body was putting up walls internally. He hated people knowing his emotions, always had. Even though he'd gotten to know Jek better in the last few days, he felt nowhere near as comfortable with him as he did with Jessend.

"I'd rather not talk about it," Cleve said.

Lysha surprised them by coming up from behind. "It's too bad you both have ladies already. We could've had some fun."

She folded her legs to sit between them, extending an arm around their shoulders. "There's no one around here. We're right in between Goldram and Zav with only the trees watching."

A gust of wind picked up, causing branches to look like they were waving.

"The trees keep all secrets." She leaned in and kissed Cleve on the cheek.

He could feel her using psyche again, trying to twist his affection toward her.

He simply thought of Reela, and Lysha's unbidden touch was thrown from his heart. Lysha sucked in air as if she'd been struck.

"You can try all the psyche you want," Cleve said, taking her arm off his shoulder. "It's not going to work."

Jek jumped up. "Keep your lips to yourself, psychic."

With both arms now in her lap, Lysha's head lowered. Even without psyche, she was a beautiful woman. She had dark eyes, oval and mysterious. Cleve had never seen her wear something with sleeves, so her toned shoulders and arms were always exposed. She was tall yet compact, without a trace of fat throughout her muscular body.

"Is this how you use psyche?" Jek asked, his tone accusatory. "Seducing men?"

Lysha stood and offered a sly grin. "I've never needed psyche before."

"You know what people say about you, right?" Jek asked. "The names they call you? You must."

"Whore, man-thief, heartless bitch, yeah I've heard them. It's for that reason I make even more of an effort to do what I want. Why should *men* be the only ones to have all the fun?" Her head stretched forward. She looked ready for an argument.

"I didn't mean..." Jek sighed. "I would never call you those names. It just strikes me as strange that you don't seem to care."

"Of course I care." She made a fist. "I care enough to try to make a difference. Women didn't make the rules, so why are we the only ones who have to follow them? Don't we deserve the same freedom as you?"

"Yes, but a woman who comes between two people in love is just as bad as a man doing it," Jek said softly, speaking each word quite carefully, as if lecturing a child.

"I don't do that," Lysha said, frustration building in her tone. "I'm just having fun with you both to lighten our mood. It's been working...at least until now when you made me get serious." She stood and held out her hand to be shaken. "I won't do it anymore if that's what you really want."

Jek hesitantly walked toward her, reaching out his hand

She grabbed it and smiled. "If you can beat me in wrestling."

"What?" Jek muttered. Lysha grabbed his arm with both hands and zipped around him, taking his arm with her so that his whole body flipped and he landed on his back with a loud grunt.

Feeling competitive, Cleve stepped toward her. "Me next."

She looked him over with a wide smile, showing her teeth. "You can wrestle that tree over there, big guy." Lysha pointed. "It's closer to your size."

"One hand, then."

Lysha rubbed her chin in thought, holding her smile.

"One minute, Cleve." Jek got to his feet with a grin of his own. "Try that again, Lysha, now that I'm ready."

Lysha folded her arms and pointed at his belt. "Throw your wand away first."

Jek shrugged. "Fine."

Lysha moved toward him, feigning in and out with wild speed.

Jek simply stood with a straight back, his arms resting at his sides. "Whenever you're ready." He faked a yawn.

Lysha laughed. "You're going to regret that."

She came at him. He pushed both palms out at her before she reached him, and the massive gust of hot Bastial wind nearly took Cleve off his feet even though he was well behind her.

Lysha tumbled backward, letting out a guttural scream.

After coming to a stop, she casually got to her knees and fixed her long fall of hair, putting it behind her shoulders. "Without a wand? Really?" She laughed bitterly. "I can't say I expected that."

She stood and walked toward the horses, Cleve and Jek following. "I think they've rested long enough," Lysha said. "Let's get back to riding. I'll beat you both next time they need a break. And no magic!"

"Fine," Jek said. "But I'm not stupid enough to wrestle Cleve without it."

Nulya whinnied, nudging Cleve with her head. Jek and Lysha burst into laughter.

"Look, Nulya says she could beat you, Cleve," Lysha teased.

Cleve petted her. "I'm sure she could."

The land in Zav wasn't too different from that in Goldram. The hills were sparse, grass came in either small patches or vast fields, and sightings of other people were limited to about one or two a day.

Lysha had explained that there weren't any small towns along the route she'd chosen. Because their group was more than two, they were likely to be met with aggression.

With war starting up again, spies were on the move. When their identities were revealed, they would relocate, meaning trouble often would follow them. People knew this, so they didn't treat strangers too kindly.

"That's what happens when four territories have touching borders," Cleve remembered Danvell saying. He'd recently learned more about the history of Greenedge from Lysha and Jek. He'd already heard that desmarls had taken over both the

north and south, pushing everyone to the center of the continent, but he never would've guessed it was the fault of Humans that it had happened.

Back when people slept in huts, insects were a big annoyance and an even bigger issue for their crops. But there was a simple solution: desmarls. Back then, desmarls were small, not growing bigger than a hand. Just like now, they produced Sartious Energy clouds, and they ate only meat, meaning they didn't kill the plants around them.

Most people either lived in the north or the south, and they bred and traded desmarls, making them a form of currency. Over hundreds of years, the desmarls thrived with Human assistance, growing much larger and more quickly, and producing many offspring. But by the time it became clear that Humans were being attacked, it was already too late.

There were too many of the creatures to fight against then, so the Humans battled their way through the less dense clusters of desmarls to the middle of the continent, leaving the north and south to the beasts. It was how the term "common tongue" came to be. There were several languages before then. But when everyone came together, common tongue took over as the main language.

"Why didn't people fight back against the desmarls and clear them out while they were still small?" Cleve had asked after Lysha and Jek finished telling the story.

"People weren't powerful enough," Lysha answered. "They couldn't fight what they couldn't see."

"How do you fight against desmarls now, then?"

Cleve looked to Jek, hoping he wasn't eliciting any traumatizing memories for the mage. Cleve couldn't tell by Jek's calm expression.

"Mages can blow the Sartious Energy out of the way with Bastial wind. Or if they're Sartious mages like me, there's plenty we can do. The desmarls produce it, but they can't manipulate it once it's in the air. With enough time and caution, we can slowly make our way toward their bodies, which is when the archers finish them with arrows."

"That's how you killed each of them?" Cleve asked.

Jek seemed lost in thought for a moment. "There was too much chaos for me to really know what we did to kill the first desmarl. I'm still surprised that no one died. But I'll tell you how we killed our tenth one. By then our strategy was sound. When we reached the edge of the SE cloud, the mages with me used Bastial wind to blow the SE farther ahead until a tentacle was revealed. They tend to sway back and forth, so we had to stay out of range until we saw one."

"Why don't you just shoot the tentacle at that point...or cut it with a sword?" Lysha asked.

"It's not so easy. They're so large, an arrow won't do much, neither will a fireball. And if a warrior doesn't cut deep enough with his sword, he's dead. Even if he does sever the limb, another tentacle could come from somewhere out of the cloud of SE to defend itself, lashing wildly through the air until it feels something to wrap around."

"My Bastial stars," Lysha murmured.

"It gets worse," Jek warned her. "Finding the tentacle is the easy part. But in order to kill each beast, we had to expose its body so our team of archers could shoot it. An arrow to the eye is the best way, as their brain is right behind it. We'd find a gap between tentacles where we could move in. By then, the mages could no longer use Bastial wind because the desmarls would feel it on their tentacles. So I had to keep the SE out of the way while we continued forward by manipulating the heavy energy. A desmarl can only reach one spot with three of its eight tentacles at once, so the end of the bout always involved archers shooting at the body while everyone else defended against the three tentacles trying to crush or grab us."

"That's a sound strategy?" Lysha blurted.

"There were a few close incidents," Jek admitted. "The worst was when we'd misjudge our distance to the tentacles and one would surprise us before we could find the beast's body. Luckily, a good team of swordsmen, archers, and mages can fend off three tentacles fairly well. And that's what we were."

"How many desmarls are out there?" Cleve asked.

"In the north?" Jek asked.

"In all of Greenedge, north and south."

Lysha and Jek both shook their heads at him. "No one knows," Jek answered. "But it's estimated to be between thirty and fifty thousand."

Cleve felt his mouth drop open. "And how long did it take to kill ten of them?"

"Most days we killed two. Other days, only one."

"No one has come up with an efficient way of killing them yet," Lysha said.

"There probably isn't a way," Jek added. "It's just a slow process. But if everyone came together to fight them, we could win in a matter of months."

But instead, everyone fights for the middle of the continent or wants to leave. Cleve felt guilt gnawing at him. *And I'm one of those who wants to leave.*

An idea came to him. "What about psychics? They should be efficient at helping kill desmarls."

Jek looked to Lysha. She waved her palms at them. "My Bastial stars, I'm not getting anywhere near those things."

"I wasn't thinking of her," Cleve said. "I know other psychics who are strong enough to kill one on their own."

This time Jek and Lysha's mouths came open. "Are you serious?" Jek asked.

Cleve nodded. "How long did you say their tentacles are from their body?"

"Somewhere around fifty yards. We don't know for sure."

"Fifty yards would be tough," Cleve said. "But with a team of mages helping psychics get closer to the body, they could."

Jek's eyes shifted to Lysha. "Are you getting chills as well?"

"Yes...how would a psychic kill a desmarl?" Lysha asked.

"Through pain?"

"I suppose," Cleve said. "Or they wouldn't deliver the killing blow, just stop the desmarl from attacking so archers could shoot it."

"Psychics can stop the limbs of the desmarl on their own?"

"At least one psychic can," Cleve said, thinking of Rek. "He single-handedly stopped a ship-eater that attacked our boat on the way over here."

"A ship-eater?" Lysha asked.

"I think some call them giant squids," Cleve said. *Though, Mmzaza said they weren't that.*

Jek practically jumped. "He did?" the mage screamed. "How?"

"It was grabbing the boat, so he pained it until it stopped. It didn't follow us after that." Cleve shook as he remembered how it had felt when he'd first met Rek. "I've felt the spell of pain he can produce. It's completely debilitating."

"Enough of this," Lysha demanded. "These wild stories are why people with even a slight psychic ability like me are considered dangerous."

"Can't you tell I'm speaking the truth?" Cleve asked, dumbfounded that again his words might not be taken seriously.

"I can," Lysha answered to his relief. "And that's what makes me so angry. It's psychics like that who make it so the rest of us are forced to keep it a secret, even though I can't do anything like that." She turned. "It's time to ride. We have some Takarys to save, and our horses have rested enough by now."

Their next few conversations were all about Rek.

Jek made it clear that he hoped Rek could help with Greenedge's desmarl problem, but Cleve couldn't give him what he wanted—a promise that Cleve and Rek would return.

"At least come back to tell me what can cure my darkness when you find that out," Jek pleaded.

"I'm sorry," Cleve said. "I just can't make that promise."

Jek looked away and shook his head. "You're right. I should be the one to come to Kyrro, if anything. It's not your responsibility."

Perhaps it was because they'd been speaking about Rek so much recently, but Cleve decided to put his hand on Jek's shoulder just as the Elf often did with him. "I understand," he said.

Lysha came over and put her hands on both of their shoulders. "Are we done having a moment, boys?"

Jek rolled his eyes and walked toward a tree, unzipping his fly on the way there. "We are now."

It left Cleve alone with Lysha as they waited.

"How long have you known you're a psychic?" he asked to break the silence that came with her awkward stare.

"Since I was twenty, maybe." She pointed, her tone suddenly scolding. "And don't try and guess how long ago that was."

"Or you'll try to wrestle me again?" Cleve joked. "Should I beat you with no arms this time?"

They'd wrestled three times by then, Cleve winning each time with one arm held behind his back. At one point he'd teased that Jessend could beat Lysha, and he actually wondered if it was true.

"Hold your tongue, Muscles," Lysha said. "Or I won't tell you all the mooker rules."

"Mooker?" Cleve asked, the name sounding familiar.

Jek came back to join them. "I'll need a reminder of the mooker rules before we get into Karri Forest. I'm sure there's some I've forgotten."

Cleve held his puzzled look, planning to do so until he was answered.

"When we met, I mentioned mookers living in Karri Forest," Lysha said. "They're short little creatures that come up to our knees, though their bite and claws are deadly when they attack in numbers—which they always do. In fact, they're always in numbers in general. If you see one that looks to be alone, there are really others around that are hidden."

"Do not underestimate a mooker." Jek grabbed Cleve's shoulder, somewhat fiercely. "Or you could get us all killed."

"I'll explain the rules before we get to the forest," Lysha said. "For now, we ride."

Chapter 19

When darkness had taken over the land, the three of them settled near a fire for a late meal.

"We'll reach the forest tomorrow," Lysha said. "It will be our eighth day, which gives us only that day and the next to get Raymess and Vala out and send the pigeon back. Do you have a good memory, Cleve?"

"It depends what I need to remember."

"How about information that's necessary for you to stay alive?"

"I can remember that."

"Good, because I'm about to tell you everything you need to know about mookers." Lysha cleared her throat, brushing her hair over her shoulder. "First, think of someone who has done things so strange and risky that you couldn't understand them no matter how hard you tried."

Steffen.

"Done."

"Now, imagine he or she is a creature with claws and teeth that abides by rules instead of logic, has no sense of fear, and lives with thousands of others just like itself. That's the best description I can give of a mooker."

Jek was nodding. "Sounds about right."

"Stand up," Lysha told Cleve. "We'll start with the dances. They're the most important."

"Dances?" Cleve wasn't happy about this already.

"Yes, and you'd better learn to smile while you do them. They don't like it when you don't."

Bastial hell. He tried forcing a smile.

Laughter erupted from Jek and Lysha, both of them doubling over. Cleve felt himself immediately frowning.

"Forget the dancing," Lysha managed to get out as her laughter quieted. "You'd better practice your smile first."

Jek was still laughing. "No, maybe they'll like a giant man who looks like he's shat his pants."

Lysha's laughter came back.

When they both were done, Lysha told Cleve to try again.

"I'd better not look," Jek teased. "Or I might die from laughter."

"I can't just do it," Cleve admitted, not even wanting to try again.

"You make it sound like you're performing some difficult stunt," Lysha said. "My Bastial stars, it's just a smile. Just think of something that'll make you smile."

Cleve imagined returning to Kyrro and opening the door to his home. Steffen and Effie were there, greeting him with happy grins. He hugged Effie and shook Steffen's hand. Then Reela burst out of her room and ran toward him.

"There we go," Lysha said. "Now we can get to the dancing."

Cleve felt his grin fade.

Lysha grunted. "But you'd better practice keeping that smile while we do it."

He pushed it back onto his face...and again, they were overcome with laughter.

Luckily, picking up the dances was much easier for Cleve than learning the false smile. It seemed that he had far more control over his body than his face.

The *polite introduction* dance was the simplest, involving only two outstretched arms shifting left and right with a lift of both shoulders each time.

Lysha explained that once a dance is initiated by a Human, the mooker will start dancing along, chanting, "mook, mook, mook, mook" usually four times, and the Human must move with the rhythm of the chant. If the mooker keeps chanting after four, the Human has to keep moving, otherwise it's considered an insult and the mookers are likely to attack.

The other dances were a bit more complicated.

We have a gift involved a fancy twirl, but luckily only the gift giver needed to do the dance, so Cleve didn't have to learn that one.

Lysha showed him her many "mooker flowers" that she'd been given by Danvell Takary. The round, gray plant was quite ugly and apparently the same color as a mooker's skin. No bigger than Cleve's palm, the mooker flower was riddled with holes of all sizes.

"Isn't a mooker going to be insulted by that?" Cleve pointed at it.

"No, they love this hideous plant," Lysha said. "They use it for a mating ritual. I don't know how that custom started because the mooker flower doesn't even grow in Karri Forest, and that's the only place they've ever lived. I assume it used to grow there until it went extinct from all the mookers picking it."

"Why don't they leave the forest?" Cleve asked.

Lysha shrugged. "It's their home, always has been." She leaned forward. "And they're very protective of it."

The most important dance was *we are peaceful*. At any point, doing this dance should alleviate any aggression other mistakes might've caused. Humans performed it by tucking their elbows against their sides and gyrating their hips in a quick motion, creating a full circle for every "mook" a mooker chanted.

"If at any point the mooker doesn't start 'mooking' along with you—chanting 'mook' and matching your dance—then you're not doing the dance right," Lysha explained.

"Is it better to stop at that point or keep trying?" Cleve asked.

"It's better to run," Lysha answered. "Oh, and you should know that turning your back on a mooker is the worst insult. You need to show them the *goodbye* dance if you're going to leave before them."

"This one, I remember," Jek said with a smile. "It's my favorite." He broke into dance by thrusting his pelvis, lifting and dropping one leg at a time in rhythm. Although only one leg was moved with each forward thrust of his pelvis, both hands were balled, and both elbows swung behind him to emphasize the thrusting motion.

"You're not leaning back far enough," Lysha said.

Jek bent backward, making his thrusting pelvis his forward-most body part besides his knees.

"That's it," Lysha said, her face deathly serious, as if teaching Jek how to dodge the slash of a sword.

It didn't feel right to Cleve when he tried, but apparently he got it on his first attempt.

"How long do we have to do it?" Cleve asked.

"Until they stop mooking and leave," she answered.

"Please tell me that's the last dance," Cleve said, beginning to worry he would forget at least one of them.

"It is the last one you need to know, but there's something just as important you should remember."

"Oh, yes," Jek added. "I'd forgotten."

They both spoke at the same time, each pointing at Cleve. "No talking."

Lysha added, "At least not loud enough to be heard while a mooker's around."

"They take grave offense to it...for whatever reason," Jek said.

"It's like when we whisper to each other in the presence of others," Lysha explained. "To a mooker, talking seems like we're keeping a secret from them."

"I can manage that far easier than the smile," Cleve said.

"We'll practice again in the morning," Lysha said. "Jek, you should keep closer to us tonight. We're on the western edge of Zav, not nearly as safe as the rest of the territory. Who knows, maybe this will be the night you actually kill your darkness and you won't wake us up," she teased.

"Yeah, and maybe we'll get to the center of Karri Forest without running into a mooker," Jek said sarcastically.

A silence followed. It was solemn, tightening Cleve's previously relaxed muscles, for he knew what it meant. Everyone did.

That will be the last joke we hear until this is done.

Chapter 20

"The trees look blue," Cleve commented.

"I'd say turquoise," Lysha said.

The rising sun was pouring in from the west—the opposite side from which they were entering Karri Forest. The trees along the outer rim were narrow, with few branches covered in small leaves. But many layers of thick green shrubbery hid the rest of the forest ahead, so much so that there was no clear path to take.

"How will we ride through?" Cleve asked.

"We may have to walk for a mile," Lysha said. "There's more space farther in."

She turned out to be right. They led their horses through thick clusters of plants and trees, eventually making it past what Lysha called "the barrier."

Just after they remounted, Jek held out a hand. "Wait, listen." A light breeze was gliding through the trees, giving the branches a spirited shake. Nulya whinnied. Cleve pet her mane and shushed her.

Then he heard it, a dull roar of voices, like a distant crowd. It came from deeper within the forest, growing louder and more thunderous with each breath Cleve took. A group of elk darted past them, running away from the sound.

"Shit." Lysha nearly spat out the word. "A mooker gathering." She turned to Cleve. "Hundreds of them have chosen a place to meet, so groups of them will be headed there from all directions."

Then Cleve noticed the same noise coming from the opposite side.

"Where's their meeting point?" he asked.

"There's no way to know." Lysha spoke with a pressing tone.

"But we don't want to run into them."

"We have to go back!" Jek said urgently.

"No, we don't have time to go through the barrier again if we're going to make it to the center before sunset, especially when they could be meeting here for hours. Follow me." Her horse galloped forward.

Cleve and Jek followed. The strange dialogue of the mookers was on either side of them but not ahead.

The horses' speed soon proved to be too fast when Cleve nearly had his head taken off by a low branch. Lysha's horse stumbled, slowing too suddenly, and Jek's nearly rammed into hers.

"We have to slow our pace!" Lysha shouted to be heard.

"They're ahead of us now!" Jek yelled.

Cleve heard it as well—the noise of a thousand creatures grumbling, like a dozen boulders rolling down hills.

Then a line of mookers pushed through the plants, stopping at the sight of the three of them.

Each mooker stood on two stumpy legs, but some leaned forward to rest the knuckles of their long arms on the ground as well, putting them on all fours. Their faces looked like a mix between an Elf and a dog, with a small round nose, two gray eyes with dark circles around them, a massive mouth that basically split their head in two, and a square chin. Their ears were even longer than Rek's, pointed just like his.

Behind their ears were horns that were the length of Cleve's hand. A few of them sat, plopping down on their rears in a motion so quick it looked painful. They leaned forward so that their elbows rested near their short legs, their long outstretched arms with black claws resting on the forest floor as well.

While they were gray overall, a dark hue covered the top of their heads down to their tails. Each had a massive chin and a pronounced underbite, with two large teeth coming out to point up toward their eyes.

"Dismount slowly, tie your horse, smile, and don't talk," Lysha whispered.

They did, and when they were done, three mookers had come forward, each speaking loudly.

"Mook kakamook," one said, waving a claw at Cleve. It seemed to be talking to the two mookers next to it.

"Bra kuka mooka," another said, pointing at Jek.

The last one pointed at Lysha. "Guba yarka mook."

Lysha started the *polite introduction* dance, swaying her arms left and right with a lift to her shoulders. Cleve joined in, noticing Jek doing the same.

Cleve tried to think of Reela to make his smile genuine, but it was hard to picture her with all the little mookers watching him. He could feel his grin wasn't sitting right on his face, so he tried to make some adjustments.

The two mookers in front of Lysha and Jek each started dancing...no, *mooking* with them, chanting "mook, mook, mook, mook."

But Cleve's mooker wasn't joining the other two.

It approached Cleve, stopping at his knees where it twisted its head up to study his face. He tried to smile wider, but it only felt more disingenuous.

Lysha and Jek continued to dance, so Cleve figured he should do the same instead of stop. Though it instantly became harder when the creature jumped up and grabbed onto Cleve's thigh. With the agility of a monkey, it swung around Cleve to grab his shoulders, placing its feet on his back.

He almost asked Lysha what he should do. He knew he shouldn't talk, but fear was gripping his heart, making it harder to follow the rules. He shot her a glance. Her smile was still there as she danced, but her teeth were gritted. She seemed panicked.

Lysha lifted a thumb to her mouth, only for a blink, quickly bringing it back so as not to disrupt her dance. *Is she telling me it's my smile?*

The mooker balanced its plump belly on Cleve's shoulder to lean around in front of his face. It took its black claws and patted his cheek, muttering, "Mook zuka nook. Mook zuka zuke."

Cleve tried to fix his smile again, but it was becoming even more difficult just to keep his lips bent. The mooker bit the air in front of him threateningly. Cleve was feeling himself coming close to tossing the mooker off his shoulder. Then he remembered the *we are peaceful* dance.

He tucked in his elbows and twirled his hips in a circle. Lysha and Jek joined him.

The creature leapt off his shoulder, gaining some distance before turning back with a tilt to its head, studying Cleve. With the newfound respite, Cleve felt it easier to smile.

The mooker in front of him shifted its elbows against its body and twirled its waist, chanting, "mook, mook, mook, mook."

It stopped chanting after four, and the other two stopped with it.

Immense relief flowed into Cleve's body with his next breath, as he let his dancing come to a halt.

Lysha immediately started her *I have a gift* dance, twirling in a circle with her arms over her head.

Her mooker came forward and joined her, chanting along.

When they were finished, she opened her bag and placed a mooker flower on the ground and stepped away from it. The mooker ran to its gift with startling speed, tumbling over the flower and grabbing it, as if the ugly plant could've gotten away if left for another second.

A roaring chatter rang out from all the mookers. Cleve thought the rest of them were upset that they weren't given a gift, but then he saw the smile on Jek and Lysha's faces and realized the mookers must be happy.

It was a good thing he'd figured that out. For he surely would've drawn his weapon when, soon after, all the mookers ran at them, galloping on their little legs and long arms like lopsided horses.

But then Cleve noticed that one of the mookers hadn't moved yet—the one that had danced with him and climbed on his shoulder. It sauntered right up to Cleve and tapped his shoe with a claw, scooping up some dirt to toss on it.

Cleve still didn't know if he should speak, so he remained quiet. A few of the mookers running by had stopped, investigating the exchange between Cleve and the mooker, which was now slapping his shoe with both hands.

Two other mookers joined it, and soon they had pulled his shoe off without even undoing the laces. They gave it to the first mooker, who lifted it above its head, waddled a few awkward steps, and hurled Cleve's shoe into a sea of bushes.

Then the three mookers began what seemed to be cheering, jumping up and down with their arms in the air.

Soon they were done, zipping right by Cleve, brushing his leg they were so close.

The three original mookers were last to go, and a deafening quiet followed that begged to be broken.

"What the Bastial hell was that with my shoe?" Cleve asked.

"Your punishment," Lysha answered. "They didn't like your smile, but everything else was fine. You did well for your first time. I've seen men get stripped completely naked, their undergarments eaten right before their eyes."

"I guess I should be thankful," Cleve said. "As long as I can find my shoe."

The little mooker had surprising strength. Cleve's shoe was found about thirty yards from their original spot. It took them the better part of an hour.

"That wasn't too bad," Jek said. "But we don't have a lot of time, so try to smile better next time."

Cleve felt the air rush out of his lungs in despair. "There's going to be a next time?"

"Most likely," Jek said. "The entire forest is inhabited by

them."

They got back on their horses and rode west, toward the heart of the forest where the encampment was supposed to be. Every time Cleve heard a noise he didn't recognize, he felt his body stiffening nervously. The thought of having his undergarments eaten was beginning to frustrate him, making him feel he'd have even more trouble smiling next time the little bastards came around.

Why do they need me to smile? Why do we have to dance? He thought to ask Lysha and Jek but soon realized that the answers wouldn't matter. A better question came to mind when they stopped to eat and give the horses a much-needed rest.

"What's the plan, Lysha? How are we going to get Raymess and Vala out without being seen?"

"I have to see the encampment first and figure out where they have guards posted."

"How much longer until we get there?" Jek asked.

Lysha pursed her lips, turning to the west with a hand over her eyes. "Can't say for sure...sometime tomorrow, though."

Jek grumbled. "I'm not looking forward to spending the night in here."

"I know," Lysha muttered under her breath. "No one would."

"What happens at night?" Cleve asked.

"The mookers don't like Humans sleeping in their forest." Lysha's tone was ominous.

"They'll attack us?"

"Yes, which is why we'll need cover," Lysha said. "They're dumb creatures, unable to figure out what is man-made and what is natural. They would walk by a wooden cabin without even thinking to look inside. But if they happened to see a Human, they would either initiate an introduction and expect the Human to comply, or attack if the Human was doing something offensive like sleeping."

"So the encampment holding Raymess and Vala must be

designed in some special way so that mookers can't see anyone," Cleve figured.

"Correct," Lysha answered. "Which should make it easier for us to sneak in. They won't have guards positioned right outside the encampment."

She stood, gesturing that it was time to ride again.

The sun was at eye level when Lysha stopped and dismounted. It came through the trees like a fireball, blasting Cleve with warmth whenever it found his cold skin between pillars of shadow.

"We'd better figure out where we're going to be sleeping," Lysha said.

They searched until they found a fallen tree lying between two others still standing. "This should work," Lysha said, tying her horse and kneeling over her bag.

She took out her blanket and a long stretch of rope. "Looks like you and I are going to be snuggled close tonight," Lysha said with a surprisingly plain tone that made Cleve believe she wasn't joking.

He checked her face as she wrapped the rope around the two standing trees. She wore no smile.

"Why is that?" Cleve asked.

"You'd rather sleep beside Jek and get hit with his SE and blood?" Noticing how the rope was tied around the two standing trees, Cleve realized what she meant. They would be hanging their blankets along the two lines of rope to keep themselves hidden. The fallen tree would separate Jek from Cleve and Lysha.

"Trust me, Cleve," Jek said. "You'd rather sleep beside her."

"Don't worry," Lysha added, balancing the blankets over the ropes. "Times are too serious to have fun. We have a prince and a queen to save tomorrow, and I'm sure I don't need to tell either of you how difficult it's going to be."

Lysha went out hunting while there was still some light

filtering in through the trees. It left Cleve alone with Jek, who leaned against the fallen tree and looked at Cleve curiously.

"You don't talk much about yourself, do you?"

"No."

"Why is that?" Jek asked.

Cleve shrugged, beginning to feel uneasiness holding down his tongue.

"But you listen well."

"It's important to listen," Cleve said.

"It's important to talk as well."

"Most people talk more than they listen."

Jek had a wry smile as he shook his finger at Cleve. "You should talk more, and maybe more people will shut up and listen."

Their little debate was becoming circular, starting to give Cleve a headache. He decided to bring up something else that had been on his mind.

"I might come back here after I'm done in Kyrro." Cleve held his palms out to stop Jek's budding excitement. "I might. There's a good chance I won't."

"You want to help us with the desmarl problem, is that it?"

"I do. If there are no more desmarls to worry about, maybe the Takarys will be content without taking over Ovira and bringing more war to us."

"But you and your Elven psychic friend are already here." Jek seemed to be more curious than argumentative. "Why not just stay and fight if that's the only reason to come back?"

"You want me to find out if there's a plant or animal that will end your nightmares, don't you?"

Jek's blue eyes widened. "You plan to do that for me?"

"If I'm coming back, I'll find that out first, of course."

Jek looked surprised, not that Cleve knew why.

"You think I wouldn't?" Cleve asked.

"I didn't imagine you actually cared. It's hard to tell with you."

"How could I not? I may be quiet, but I still have a heart."

Jek nodded. "Thank you."

"Don't thank me yet. First we have to rescue some Takarys." Cleve suddenly remembered the Princess' warning. "Lisanda told me not to let you do anything stupid. Are you planning on that?"

Jek laughed. "Jessend told me the same thing about you. Are you planning on doing something stupid?"

"If I need to," Cleve said.

"Me as well."

Each of them went silent.

"So, what do we do, then?"

"Isn't it simple?" Jek's palms lifted. "We need to support each other's stupidity. I'm sure Lysha will give her cooperation as well."

"She does seem the type to be brash."

"Funny, I've heard that same thing about myself."

"I guess I can be as well," Cleve realized aloud.

"Well, that guarantees at least one thing." Jek hopped off the fallen tree and started toward a sound that turned out to be Lysha. She was carrying two dead rabbits. "Tomorrow will hold surprises for both us and the bastards in Waywen who killed our men and took our prince and queen."

Night came quickly. The forest grew dark before they were done eating.

Cleve and Lysha squeezed into their spot between the trees and hanging blankets. Cleve pressed himself into the nook created by the fallen tree, while she was curled up against the standing tree on the other side.

Supine, and constantly bumping his arm against Lysha with every subtle movement, Cleve began to feel like flipping on his side and putting his arm over her stomach just like he'd done with Jessend sometimes. There was nothing intimate about the thought. Although the act itself held certain intimacy, it was just a way to get comfortable.

"I can't sleep like this," he warned her before touching.

"I'm not comfortable, either," she admitted.

"Like it's so great over here," Jek said from his side of the fallen tree.

Cleve turned to his side and stretched his arm over Lysha's stomach.

"You'd better take your arm off me," she threatened.

Cleve left it there. "This is the only way I can be comfortable in this tight space."

"How do you expect me to fall asleep with your gigantic arm pressing down on me?"

"What's going on over there?" Jek asked.

"Keep quiet," Lysha whispered loudly. "We don't want a mooker to hear us." She took Cleve's arm and laid it on his hip so that it ran parallel to his body. "Keep it there."

Knowing he couldn't fall asleep like that, he turned to his back again. Lysha must've moved over a little when he was on his side because now his arm was pushed against hers. He lifted his over her head and shoulders, letting it down on the other side of her. But in order for his arm to fit between her and the tree, he had to pull her toward him.

"There's no other place for my arm," he said. "If you're going to sleep on your back, then put your head on my shoulder."

"Why are you being like this all of a sudden?" she asked, unwilling to move. "I would've welcomed flirtation the first few nights, but not now. I'm trying to sleep and focus on tomorrow."

"I'm not doing anything but trying to sleep," Cleve told her.

"And how do you expect me to sleep feeling coddled like a helpless woman?"

"Just forget your pride for one night. We might as well sleep while we can't walk in the dark forest."

She let out air loudly and slid over to rest her head on Cleve's shoulder. Cleve remembered she was a psychic then.

"Can you use psyche to help me fall asleep?"

"Your friend can do that?" Lysha whispered in disbelief.

"Yes."

"Well, I can't."

"Fine." A few breaths later, Cleve decided to add, "You should really practice your psychic ability. It's an amazing weapon."

"And you should practice smiling. It's a far better tool than psyche."

Cleve refrained himself from scoffing.

Chapter 21

At first light, Cleve climbed onto the fallen tree to look for any mookers before emerging. Sleep had been sporadic, and his body felt as if it were moving through water.

He saw no mookers, so he woke Jek and Lysha, and soon they were riding west.

"Are we meeting the scouts who followed Raymess and Vala to this place?" Cleve asked.

"They left already," Lysha said. "Didn't want to risk being caught. I know where the encampment is. Don't fret."

After riding half the day, they stopped for a quick meal.

"We should be there soon," Lysha said with a hopeful tone. "Raymess and Vala are to be executed tomorrow. After I get a look at the place, I'll decide if we should strike right when we arrive...or tonight instead."

"But..." Jek objected, waiting for Lysha to turn to him before continuing. "We'll be seen if we don't wait until night. Then they'll kill Raymess and Vala before we can even get to them."

Lysha was shaking her head, her heavy locks bouncing along her shoulders. "If there's a chance we can make it before night, we'll take it. I don't want to risk waiting. I'm sure Danvell Takary wouldn't allow it, either."

"But how will we ever break them out without the cover of darkness?" With an aggressive tone, Jek seemed ready to argue.

"I'm sure even at night they'll have the place lit with lamps. We can be stealthy in other ways." A rush of anger seemed to strike her face. She shook her palm out at Jek. "Enough with the questions. Just let me take a look at the encampment first."

The sun was just starting to set when the encampment finally came into view. Lysha dismounted, tied her horse to a tree, and had a strange smile as she hummed in thought.

"Those idiots," she muttered. "They've built this place near a hill." She pointed south of the encampment where the peak of a long hill rested in the sky.

The encampment itself was a simple design...surprisingly simple. All they'd done was take a bunch of black cloth and wrapped it around about a hundred trees to make an uneven circle.

"Is there nothing else in this forest besides mookers?" Cleve asked. He figured a bear might smell something within the cloth fortress and simply swipe its way in.

"Nothing that can break through cloth," Lysha said. "Mookers have scared most animals with claws away to other forests over the years. They've been in Greenedge as long as Humans, as far as we can tell, but have stuck to Karri Forest all of their existence."

She pointed at the cloth walls. "Mookers can break through this, but they never would unless they'd already seen what was on the other side. It just looks like a wall to them."

Lysha gestured for them to follow her as she walked toward the hill. "Let's get a look inside to see what we're dealing with."

Atop the mountainside, Lysha lay flat and crawled to the edge where she parted tall grass for a look. Then she waved Jek and Cleve forward to join her.

There were makeshift shelters within the encampment, but Cleve found only one wooden building with four walls.

"That has to be where they're holding them," Lysha said, not needing to even point. There was nothing else she could've been referring to.

Many of the trees within the encampment had been cut down. Cleve figured their wood had been used for fire when needed, for the cabin containing the Takary Prince and Queen, and for the many shelters that were composed of nothing more than two walls and a roof.

There were a few dozen hammocks set up between two thick rods of wood as well. Some were being used at the moment. From the way men's limbs dangled off them, they looked to be asleep.

"Definitely over a hundred of them." Lysha's discouraged tone was revealing—she still didn't have any idea how they would get Raymess and Vala out without being seen. "Anything you can do with Sartious magic?" Lysha asked, each of them still lying flat.

"Not really," Jek said. "We could set fire to the cloth barrier and try to get in through the other side during the panic, but there's a risk they would realize what was happening and kill the Takarys before we made it to the cabin. I wouldn't want to try it."

"Neither would I," Lysha said. She let out a loud breath as she pushed herself to her knees. "Looks like we're going to need to wait until night." She turned to start down the hill. "At least then—" Lysha stopped abruptly.

Cleve looked over his shoulder to find that a mooker had come up the hill behind them. It had an angry look. A growl rumbled out of its throat.

It didn't like us talking, Cleve realized.

Lysha started the *we are peaceful* dance.

The mooker's growl stopped and he mooked with her, chanting "mook" with his movements.

Jek whispered, "Stay low and behind Lysha to make it clear she's the one who represents us."

The mooker stopped chanting. Then Lysha switched her dance to one that Cleve hadn't seen before. She turned sideways. With her hands on her thighs, she bent her knees up and down as her whole body moved to and fro in a wavelike motion. It was slow and careful, strangely sexual, even.

"What's that dance?" Cleve whispered.

"I think it's the *come here* dance," Jek whispered back. "There's usually not a good reason to call over a mooker, so most people don't even take the time to learn it."

The mooker smiled at the sight of Lysha's movements. With

his egregious underbite, the shape of his mouth didn't change much, only the corners lifted. He turned sideways and joined Lysha with his own wavelike motion. Being such a small creature with a large belly, Cleve was impressed how well it could mimic Lysha, such a slender woman. It sidestepped toward her as it mooked.

The moment the creature was close, it jumped onto her shoulder in one leap and sat with its legs dangling. Jek stood and moved out of the way, pulling Cleve with him.

Lysha brought the mooker to the edge and pointed down at the encampment. Cleve followed her finger with his eyes. It seemed like she was directing the mooker's attention at the sleeping men in the hammocks.

"Mook?" The creature hopped up onto its feet, still on Lysha's shoulder and using one hand on her head for balance. It pointed with its other. "Mook! Dura maba!"

It leapt off her shoulder and started back down the hill, continuing to yell words Cleve couldn't hope to understand. The next sight caused his hand to draw his Bastial steel sword without even a thought. His chest squeezed around his heart with a surge of panic.

Hundreds of mookers were jumping out of the bushes, from behind trees, from out of nooks, from between rocks. They were swarming like bees, rushing toward the encampment in a mad scramble. Their shouts had become high-pitched, sounding akin to a war cry.

Lysha started down the hill. "Come on!" she screamed.

Cleve and Jek followed. "Will they attack us?" Jek asked.

"Maybe after we get inside, if they confuse us with being associated with the sleepers," Lysha answered. "But not until then."

Lysha stopped at the bottom of the hill, waiting for all the hidden mookers to emerge and join the stampede of little monsters. There must've been a thousand of them. The sound of their grumbly shouts piqued someone's interest, for a man within the encampment lifted up one of the black pieces of cloth between two trees for a look.

He didn't glance over at Cleve and the others to the side of the stampede. He didn't give himself enough time for that. The moment he saw the mookers a few seconds from him, he screamed and ran farther into the encampment.

Lysha broke into a sprint, keeping close to the mookers. "Jek, keep us as hidden as you can with SE clouds once we get inside." She was holding her bow now. Cleve already had his sword in hand, and he noticed Jek drawing the wand from his belt.

The mookers were so fast, Cleve would barely be able to catch up to them if he wanted to. It was a frightening thought to think that his party might not be able to outrun them. They kept to the side of the stampede of mookers, making sure they weren't easily seen by those within the encampment.

Already there were screams of both man and mooker. Cleve stopped next to Lysha behind a tree that used to have black cloth stretched around it. But now the cloth had fallen, trampled to shreds by mookers.

Jek peaked around the tree, poking out his wand and beginning to produce a green cloud of Sartious Energy.

Lysha looked around the other side of the tree. "The cabin is about seventy yards ahead of us," she said. "We're going to fight our way there. Keep moving at all times. We need to get inside of the cabin and shut the door behind us to keep out the mookers."

"Alright, ready?" Jek asked, his tone cool and collected.

"Yes," Cleve and Lysha answered.

By then, the Sartious cloud around them was too thick to see through. "I'm going to use Bastial wind to blow this cloud ahead of us," Jek said. "It won't stretch too far, maybe ten yards. But I'll try to drag it with us."

Lysha grabbed Cleve's wrist. "Careful swinging that sword around me. It'll open up my flesh as if I were made of butter."

"It won't touch you," Cleve said. He realized he was sounding arrogant, but he just meant it as the truth. He knew how to control a weapon.

"Good." Lysha nodded. "Go, Jek."

Cleve leaned out behind Jek to watch. The mage pushed his wand forward and a windy sound followed. The green cloud flowed forward at about the speed of a jog. The three of them followed behind it.

On either side of the SE were battles all throughout the encampment. For every man, there were ten mookers. And each time, Cleve saw mookers jumping onto the man's face and shoulders, taking him down. In a matter of seconds they'd move on to the next.

They continued forward, and Cleve found someone who'd backed against a tree and found some success simply screaming and thrashing his sword about to keep the little monsters at bay. They edged in and out, looking for a safe way to attack. One jumped at him, only to be hit by the man's weapon, letting out a shriek and flying through the air like a ball.

Two more jumped at once. One of them was struck like the first, but the other latched onto the man's face. He tried to pry off the mooker, only to be taken down by the rest waiting for their opportunity.

"Can we go any faster?" Lysha asked, her tone somewhat panicked. "This might've been a bad idea."

"I can't!" Jek yelled. "And it was definitely a bad idea." His frantic tone was the exact opposite of what it was before.

Cleve couldn't help but realize this was the stupid decision the Takary sisters had been worried Jek and Cleve would make. He found it almost comical that it was Lysha's choice, though, not theirs...*almost* comical.

A mooker jumped onto his leg and opened its mouth to bite Cleve, but he kicked the creature off before it could. Lysha shot it with an arrow before Cleve had a chance to drive his sword into it. Another one jumped at Jek. Cleve saw it coming and slashed his sword downward, slicing the creature in half.

If a mooker had never been on his shoulder, he would've thought they had soft skin given how easy it was to cut the little monster with his Bastial steel sword. But he'd felt one enough to know that their skin was even tougher than his.

"We should be close," Lysha said from the front. "Let the cloud fizzle out so we can see."

Jek let his arm drop, giving out an exhausted breath. Lysha was right, the cabin was just ahead.

With immense fury, Lysha pushed on the door, but it wouldn't budge. "Cleve!"

"I got it." He kicked the door with all his strength.

It flew open, and the three of them jumped in, shutting the door behind them. The cabin was small enough to see everything the moment Cleve stepped inside.

"Kasko," Cleve muttered, taking a step toward the small man.

"Stop," Kasko said calmly...too calmly for Cleve's taste. "Throw down your weapons or she dies." He had a knife pressing into the throat of a woman who had to be Vala Takary, the Queen of Goldram.

Her hands and feet were bound with rope. Kasko stood against the wall, holding her in front of him. Vala's eyes were wide in fear, her mouth twisted and uttering little gasps with each subtle movement Kasko made.

Beside Vala was a man in his twenties with the same golden brown skin as his mother and the other Takarys.

Raymess...not moving.

"Is Raymess alive?" Lysha asked, keeping her bow aimed at Kasko. The Prince was slumped in the corner, cuts covering his face and arms.

Outside, screams of death were becoming less frequent. It was only a matter of time before the mookers had killed everyone. Cleve still didn't know if they would force their way into the cabin or not, but he did know he needed to hurry.

Cleve decided to toss down his sword as Kasko had demanded. Jek threw down his wand next. Lysha kept her bow aimed high, though, even taking a step forward.

"Don't test me," Kasko warned her.

"Is Raymess alive?" Lysha repeated, this time louder.

"Yes," Kasko said. "I know how much I can bleed a man before he dies. Now throw down your bow or I'll kill Vala Takary."

The Queen whimpered.

Lysha tossed her weapon, taking her Bastial steel knife from her belt and throwing it on the ground as well.

"Now what?" Cleve asked. He had no idea what Kasko had planned, but whatever it was, it needed to happen soon. The mookers could find them at any moment.

"Someone is going to die," Kasko said. "It can either be you, Cleve, or Vala Takary here."

"The moment you kill her, you're dead as well," Cleve said.

"I'm fine with that," Kasko said with startling confidence. "Once the Takarys hear how you let her die instead of yourself, your life will be over anyway. And there's nothing more I want right now than for you to suffer."

Kasko grabbed the whimpering queen by the hair. Gritting his teeth, he muttered, "Stop struggling or I'll kill you now." He pressed the knife into the underside of her chin, and a trickle of blood ran down it. She stiffened, closing her eyes and shedding a tear.

Kasko let go of her hair to jab his finger at Cleve. "You've ruined everything I've been working toward with Jessend. I was going to use her to take power in Waywen and win this war. Capturing Raymess and Vala was done under my command. And now you're about to ruin that as well!" Kasko screamed. A silence followed that allowed Cleve to hear the grunt-filled dialogue of a group of mookers walking around outside.

"Keep your voice down," Lysha urged through a whisper.

"Or we're all dead."

"I'll shut up once you run a knife across Cleve's neck!" Kasko screamed.

The mookers outside grew louder. Jek seemed to be using Sartious Energy to do something with the door.

Lysha moved away from the one window, refusing to look at Cleve. "I will not kill Cleve, and you will not kill Vala or Raymess," she threatened. "The only way you're getting out of this alive is if you let her go and we bind your wrists with SE. We'll take you out of here safely."

A smile formed on Kasko's lips—one that sent a chill down Cleve's back. "I'd rather be killed here after watching Cleve die than spend my life in the Takary prison. But if that's not going to happen, I'll settle for killing Vala. First, Raymess needs to know what's happening."

Kasko kicked the Prince in the side. Raymess groaned but did not wake. Kasko kicked him harder, and the Prince's face came to life, scrunching with pain. When he found Cleve and the others, his eyes widened.

"You're getting out of here," Kasko told him. "But your mother might die first. It's up to this man, Cleve Polken." Kasko pointed at Cleve. "It's his choice as to who lives and who dies. If he lets Lysha cut open his throat, I'll let your mother go. But if he doesn't, then I'll cut hers open...and with great pleasure. You'll tell your father what happened here. Understand?"

Raymess looked back and forth between Cleve and Vala. He tried to mouth words, but only a murmur came out.

"Louder," Kasko told him, shoving him with the sole of his boot.

Raymess tried to stand, only to receive a kick from Kasko.

"Stay down!"

Cleve started toward Kasko, but he squeezed his grip harder on Vala. She let out a scream.

"Get back, fool. Get back! This is your last chance or I will cut her."

The mookers were right outside their window now—Cleve could hear them.

Lysha held out her palms. "Calm yourself, Kasko."

Kasko ignored her, switching his focus back to Raymess. "Answer me. Do you understand that if Cleve doesn't die, he's allowing your mother to be killed?"

Raymess licked his parched lips with the very tip of his tongue, as if the effort alone was too much to bear. He nodded at Kasko.

"Good." Kasko smiled again, changing his focus to Cleve.

Jek was at the window now, barring it with Sartious Energy. "Lysha's not going to do it." He spoke softly as he worked. "Even if Cleve tells her to."

"It's true," Lysha said. "No one's going to go along with this plan. If Vala dies, then it's purely your fault."

Cleve felt even more dread when Kasko's grin only widened. "You really think Danvell Takary will forgive you three when he hears what happened? Think about it. Bastial hell, you're idiots if you don't realize all of your lives are over if you allow me to kill Vala instead of Cleve."

Cleve glanced at Lysha, finding a disquieting lack of confidence in her eyes as she stared at Kasko. Next he turned to Jek. The mage had finished with the window, his glance now fallen to the ground. Neither of them would look at Cleve.

Is this what my life has come to? He tried to find some solace in the idea that Kasko would be killed shortly after he was, but it didn't make his despair any more bearable.

"Lysha," Cleve said, waiting for her to look at him before continuing. He put his hand on her shoulder. "He's right. There will be no life after this for the three of us if I don't agree to his terms."

Cleve slowly started toward the knife she'd thrown down. Keeping his gaze on Kasko, he said, "I'm going to pick up this weapon and give it to her."

"Keep moving slowly or I kill Vala."

"Cleve, don't do this." Jek's tone was pleading. "This is a stupid decision, and there's no way for me to support it. We told each other we wouldn't do something like this without support from each other."

"I'm sorry, Jek. And tell Jessend I'm sorry as well."

Cleve handed the knife to Lysha, but she wouldn't take it. He stepped closer to her, leaning in to whisper, "Take it by the blade and hold it steady."

She did.

Keeping his voice low so no one else could hear, he said, "When I say 'go,' use psyche to tell Vala to get out of the way as best she can."

Lysha's eyes opened wider. Her neck stiffened with a nod. Cleve stepped back and lifted his chin, exposing his neck.

"Do it!" Kasko screamed.

Again, the mookers' dialogue started up. There was even some tapping on the walls.

"Go," Cleve told Lysha.

She shot her palm forward at Vala behind him. Meanwhile, Cleve grabbed the knife by the handle, spun around, and threw it where he remembered Kasko to be.

It all happened in a blink—Vala fell to her knees, Kasko lunged downward after her, and Cleve's Bastial steel knife struck the small man in the shoulder.

It caused Kasko to stop for a heartbeat, staggering back with a scream. Jek let loose a fireball. It was small, the size of a fist. But it did strike Kasko in the chest.

Vala was on her hands and knees shrieking, crawling away as quickly as possible. Kasko was yelling as well, scrabbling forward after her, nearly tripping in his dazed state. Though, he was on target, his knife held in the air.

Cleve jumped forward, grabbed his sword off the ground, and sliced off Kasko's head in one smooth motion.

It only caused Vala's shrieking to grow louder, mixed now

with manic crying.

Raymess was unconscious again. Vala crawled over to hold his head in her hands for a breath, then maneuvered herself around his back to rest him upright against her.

The mookers outside seemed to have figured out there were Humans in the cabin. They were shouting and pounding on the walls. One broke the window and was trying to smash its way through Jek's Sartious barrier of two crossed planks. Another jumped up to join it.

Lysha loosed an arrow and hit one in the shoulder. It fell back with a shout. The other one snarled and jumped off before she could shoot it.

Pounding picked up at the door. Cleve saw that Jek had filled the gap between the door and its frame with Sartious Energy, but green flakes were flying from it as the shaking became more violent. Jek pointed his wand to repair the unending damage.

Cleve's attention shot to the ceiling as the scraping of claws threatened to break through the wood above them.

Vala Takary was helping Raymess up. Cleve ran over to help, throwing the Prince's arm over his shoulder and using one arm to hold on to him while the other held his sword firm and ready for any mookers that broke through.

"Will the *we are peaceful* dance work?" Cleve asked.

"Not at this point," Lysha answered, keeping her bow aimed at the window. Two more mookers jumped up, grabbing onto the Sartious bars and trying to pry them off. Lysha let down her bow and ran to them with her dagger out, jabbing each one in the finger to make them let go and drop. Three more jumped up in their place.

"Jek!" Lysha shouted as she swiped at them with her Bastial dagger.

He waved his wand to repair the bars that were barely managing to keep the mookers from coming in through the window.

"We'd better come up with something soon," Jek said through heavy breaths. "I can't keep this up too much longer."

"We can't fight through hundreds of mookers." Lysha's tone was urgent, desperate. Cleary, she had no ideas. Hearing her made Cleve's mind work twice as fast.

"I'm quicker than they are," he said. "Make an opening in the roof with your strongest fireball, Jek. I'll pull myself through and distract them."

"Now *that* is the stupid decision we were talking about!" Jek yelled.

"You can't run from mookers," Lysha added. "They're everywhere. They'll close off every route."

"Jek, just do it before we all die!" Cleve screamed.

"Do it," Vala said. "Let him distract them."

Cleve went to the corner to drag one of two chairs over to the center of the small cabin.

"Fine!" Jek's tone was exasperated, his anger startling Cleve. "But I'm telling Jessend that I tried to stop you."

"Hurry up." Cleve was in no mood. "It sounds like some are already on the roof," he added. "So they might come in after you make an opening, but I need time to pull myself out, so I can't stay to help. Otherwise, more will—"

Lysha interrupted him. "We know, Cleve!" she said, now just as angered as Jek. "We can take care of the mookers that come in on your way out. Don't stick around to fight them—Bastial stars, this is stupid."

"Ready?" Jek asked, his wand pointed at the thin wooden ceiling above Cleve.

Taking a breath, Cleve nodded.

There was a flash of light and then the sound of wood cracking. Something fell—two of them. Mookers.

Lysha kicked one and stabbed the other. That's all Cleve could see before he jumped up from the chair, using his forearms to propel himself onto the roof in one fluid motion.

He drew his Bastial steel sword and gave a quick look to

each direction. There were no other mookers on the roof...at least not yet. Many were jumping on top of each other, scrambling up the sides of the wall for a look.

One of them grabbed hold of the edge and poked its snarling face over. Cleve kicked it and jumped after, soaring behind its body that squeaked and tumbled into the smallest patch of mookers he'd found so far—maybe five of them within clawing range.

In the moment he needed to regain his footing from the landing, he swiped his sword at them to create enough distance. They jumped back, teeth bared, and then Cleve was off.

He ran west, the opposite direction of their horses. He knew Nulya was his best hope for survival, but he didn't know what the mookers would do to Jek and Lysha's horse near Nulya if he made it there in time, nor did he know what they would do to the caged pigeon that needed to be released to inform the King of the status of the rescue mission.

Bastial hell, I hope nothing happened to the bird. If the King didn't hear soon enough that the rescue was complete, it may as well never have happened, for he'd send the requested five thousand Bastial steel swords to his enemy.

Cleve was weaving between clumps of mookers. Fortunately, many of them seemed surprised to see Cleve running in their direction, almost as if they were afraid he would attack. But the moment he passed by, they would join the hundreds behind him, galloping on all fours like a stampede of tiny horses.

He didn't have time to see if all he'd passed were still following him. It took too much focus to see where he was going.

Soon, Cleve was out of the encampment, but there were many more trees blocking his path.

Lysha was right—there were mookers everywhere. Many were even jumping from the branches of trees.

One landed on his back and bit into his shoulder just as he

twisted to get it off him.

Their teeth were unimaginably sharp, or maybe the strength behind the bite was just extremely powerful. Either way, he'd felt the fangs go deep into his body. Tendrils of hot pain twisted through him.

He kept a closer eye to the sky from that point forward, though it was tough with all the plants and roots seemingly rising to trip him every few steps.

I need more distance to lose them, but too many keep popping out and joining the stampede.

Cleve didn't know what needed to be done, and he was only beginning to realize he didn't have the ability to figure it out while running at full speed.

A terrible fear began—that he'd run into another group of mookers, and then he'd be cut off.

And soon, it happened.

Cleve came to a hillside that forced him to turn left or right. Choosing left, he encountered a group of six or seven mookers strolling toward him in a lively fashion. At the sight of him being chased by the others, their mouths opened to show the rest of their teeth, and they galloped toward him.

Knowing he couldn't slow down, he ran at them in hopes of scaring them as he'd done to others. But this group was far more courageous, picking up speed as they were about to clash.

Cleve slowed so he could slice his sword at the diving mookers, cutting two in half. The other three were already in the air. The force of them slamming into Cleve nearly halted his movement.

He jumped and spun to get them off him. Two of the three were flung before they could sink their teeth in, but one remained around his leg and bit down hard.

He heard himself scream just before stabbing the little bastard with his sword.

It felt like hot coals were in his thigh while he continued to run, a meager attempt to escape the hundreds more behind him. Soon, Cleve felt something else latch onto his leg—another mooker.

It bit him before he could do anything. Then he cut it away with a quick downward swing.

Cleve was slowing, he could feel it. The other mookers were loud behind him, a roaring entourage of "mooks" said with such anger that the fright of being their target sent another surge of energy into his legs.

He had gained back his speed, both legs screaming at him to stop, however.

I can't go on much longer, he realized. A quick look over his shoulder showed there were too many mookers to consider fighting. *Is there a dance I could do?*

He thought back to asking Lysha about the *we are peaceful* dance. If that wouldn't work, why would any other? Now his exhaustion was catching up to him. *Push!* Cleve yelled at himself.

He had to find his second wind. *Without it, I'm dead.* He searched deep for strength but couldn't find it. Again he was slowing, and the mookers grew louder.

Then he thought he heard his name. But it was difficult to tell through the roaring "mooks" behind him.

"Cleve!" This time he knew he'd heard it for sure. He looked over his shoulder. Coming from the distance were three horses. *Jek and Lysha?*

They were riding toward him, continuing to shout. "Hold on! We're almost there!"

Just the glance over his shoulder was enough to allow two more mookers to catch up. He could feel them jumping at him, nicking his heels with their claws. But they didn't grab on, weren't close enough yet.

More were jumping at him, and he felt scratches on the backs of his thighs now. One nearly grabbed on but slipped down in the process and fell off.

Cleve felt himself stumble. He couldn't recover in time and fell, rolling twice. He pointed his weapon behind him, anticipating being crushed by a river of mookers.

There was an explosion, the force of it sending him in a backward somersault. A green cloud covered everything. *Sartious Energy?*

With great confusion, Cleve tried to get to his feet. He fell once, but quickly tried again and was successful.

"Hurry! Get on." It was Lysha. She was grabbing Cleve and moving him through the cloud.

Cleve was absolutely bewildered as to what was happening. Then he remembered not to leave his sword. He stopped. It felt so wonderful to cease movement, he wasn't sure he wanted to start up again.

"What are you doing?" Lysha screamed. "Let's go!"

"I need my sword. Can you get it?"

"It's on your belt, you idiot!" Lysha grunted and pulled him hard. Cleve stumbled and fell into her. "What's wrong with you? Jek can't hold them off much longer. Get on my horse!" Then she was helping him up, lifting him onto the horse, and they were riding in some direction.

Cleve couldn't keep his head up. It felt numb. In fact, everything was beginning to feel numb. This wasn't just exhaustion. Something was wrong. But for some reason, he didn't care. He felt at ease, leaning forward to rest his chin on Lysha's shoulder.

She was saying something to him. She sounded upset. But her voice, along with all the other sounds of the forest, had become a running river of noise, high-pitched like the squeal of a teapot over a fire. *Like Lisanda when she saw Jek.*

As the pitch increased, bubbles formed at the bottom of Cleve's vision. He couldn't even tell if his eyes were open. The world around him had become like the noise, just a stream of white. The bubbles rose, and the moment they reached the top, he couldn't even tell if he was on the horse any longer.

Whatever was happening took over his body.

The white slowly began to dim, until all was black.

Chapter 22

When Cleve's vision came back, everything was distorted as if he were in an oven looking out through the waves of heat. His body was burning. He needed to cool down fast or it felt as if his skin soon would catch fire.

"He's awake!" It was Lysha's voice. She was touching his forehead now. He barely could make out her face. "He has a fever. Help me drag him away from the fire."

"How could he have a fever?" Jek spoke next.

Cleve felt himself being lifted off the ground. His rear dragged against dirt as they moved him out of the oven.

"Take my clothes off," Cleve said.

No one replied.

"Take my clothes off," he repeated, desperation growing. He was so fatigued and hot, the last thing he cared about was how others perceived him. He had the realization that his request was strange, but he didn't care. It felt like all inhibitions had left his body, replaced by burning coals. Nothing mattered except that his clothes be removed.

"Wait, he's talking." Lysha moved her face, or maybe her ear, over him.

"Take my clothes off," he said a third time, the strain of repeating it making his heavy eyes want to shut.

"He says to take his clothes off," Lysha said.

"Why?" Jek asked.

"He's out of his mind," Lysha said too indifferently for Cleve's taste, as if it were a fact.

"I'm not." Cleve wasn't sure he was even speaking aloud anymore. He couldn't hear his own voice. Only then did he start to notice the foreign feeling within him. This wasn't just exhaustion, but some sort of sickness, possibly even a poison.

He tried to speak once more, but this time he couldn't even feel his mouth move.

Next thing he knew, he was falling back into a fitful slumber.

Cleve awoke many times. He could tell time was passing, but he never knew whether he was back in reality or the images and sounds invading his senses were of dreams. He constantly tried to sit up to ensure he was awake, but he never could.

At one point, his whole body felt wet, like he'd been doused with water. Later, he was as dry as a desert, the dirt beneath him prickly on his skin. Cold and then hot, touched by wind, rain, and then sun, it was as if Cleve were sleeping through the seasons.

There was a frightful moment when darkness completely took him and he felt nothing, saw nothing, heard nothing. He couldn't move, but he knew himself to be awake. He tried to open his eyes, but they wouldn't obey.

Am I dead? Is this what death is? The thought of spending eternity like this started a fright in his chest that quickly spread throughout his body until he was shaking. At least then he felt it, the shaking.

He could feel himself breathing next.

I'm still alive. What's happening to me?

It was like his body was a soup, full of unknown ingredients. Hot and messy, Cleve spooned around trying to figure out what was within him. He found the fear again. It seemed to be the easiest to find: the broth of the soup.

Where's my strength? Reela and Rek both have found it before. I need it now more than ever. He felt his stomach churning as he shifted through himself: the rest of the soup. There were too many clumps of vegetables and meats he didn't recognize. He had to stop—nausea was taking over.

But he couldn't. He tried desperately, but the broth was

mixing on its own now, his spoon taken out of his hand and fallen into the spiraling soup. He could taste the metal.

His eyes were open, finally. Everything was blurred still, but at least he knew he was back in reality. He pushed himself to his hands and knees and let the vomit come.

There was a hand on his back. He only noticed it after he was done.

Now the hand was patting him. "It looks like you're going to make it." Jek's voice again, his tone overjoyed. "You've been in and out for about two days now."

"Two days?" Cleve heard his voice, meek, but he didn't care. He almost cried from the feeling of relief that came with hearing it.

"How do you feel now?" Jek asked.

Cleve tried to sit up, but fatigue overtook him. He was starting to fall forward when he felt Jek's hands grab his shoulders.

"I'm tired." Cleve laughed. "I feel good otherwise now." He laughed again, just for the fun of it.

"Is something funny?" Jek asked.

"No. It just feels good to laugh." Cleve could tell he wasn't himself, but he didn't care. Nothing mattered to him except that moment.

He was lying down again, this time on his back. He felt as if everything in the world was right. He was where he needed to be. Nothing was going to move him. But the thought of food and water suddenly made him eager to sit up again. He tried but couldn't even move.

With his eyes shut, at least he had enough energy to speak. "Feed me, please."

"What's with you?" Jek asked. "You sound drunk."

Cleve remembered the mookers then. All of it came back in such a rush he almost slipped into unconsciousness again. But he fought it. He felt his teeth grit together with resolve.

"You and Lysha saved me." Cleve was whispering now. He

couldn't go any louder. "Was that Raymess and Vala I saw with you two when you were riding toward me?"

"Yes. Are you able to eat something?"

"So, they're safe?"

"Yes, and the bird we released should've reached Danvell by now," Jek said. "Raymess was in bad shape. We cleaned his wounds and fed him, and he's gotten better. But Lysha and Vala still wanted him to be treated by a chemist before the long trip back. They couldn't wait for you to be able to ride. We had no idea how long it would take. They left." Jek took a breath. "I'm staying here with you."

"Will they be alright?"

"We rode all night while you were unconscious, Cleve. We're out of Karri Forest, back in Zav. They should be fine. You need to eat something. I've only been able to give you a little bit of water. Do you feel hungry?"

"Food..." Cleve couldn't even express how badly he wanted something in his stomach. "Nothing in the world would be better," he muttered.

"Can you get up? Lysha went hunting for us before she left, so we have plenty of meat."

"Meat..." Cleve's voice rumbled on even after he tried to make it stop. He felt drool slipping from his mouth.

"Yes, meat. Sit up and get some."

Cleve tried to push himself up, but he couldn't even move his arms. Bastial hell, he couldn't even open his eyes.

"I can't," he admitted. "Feed me."

"Is this a joke?"

"No. I need meat, but I can't get it."

There was a pause. It was only the length of a breath, but Cleve was too impatient to let it go longer.

"Feed me," he said again.

"Are you sure your stomach can handle it if you're in this kind of state?" Cleve heard Jek moving around him. "You probably can't even chew it."

"Chew it for me," Cleve said, completely serious. Though, he realized Jek probably would need some convincing.

"I've never seen anything like this." Jek seemed intrigued, but Cleve didn't know why. "Lysha and I noticed you were bitten by mookers. From your body's reaction, we figured they must've poisoned you. I'm thinking the way you're acting now is a side effect of that poison."

"That's what this is?" Cleve could tell he was far from his usual self, but still, he didn't care.

"It has to be. We've never heard of someone being bitten by a mooker and living to feel the effects of the poison. Every time a mooker bites someone, there's ten more mookers there to finish the job. We can't even say how long this will last."

"I don't mind it as long as you feed me."

Jek sighed. "I'll try, but I'm not going to chew your food for you."

Cleve managed to adjust his hand, moving it just slightly. He noticed then that he wasn't lying on dirt, but grass. It felt wondrous against his palm.

He twitched his fingers—it was the most he could do. The grass tickled him as if it were alive. He laughed.

"I'm going to need to sit you up so you don't choke." He felt Jek grab his hands and pull. "You're so heavy!" Jek's voice was strained. "You need to help me."

"I can't." Cleve laughed, now enjoying the situation more than he knew he should.

Jek let him back down, giving out an exasperated breath. "Bastial hell, I'll just flip you on your side and put food in your mouth. We're starting with bread, though."

"No, give me meat."

Jek sighed. "You're acting like a child right now. I really hope this doesn't last long."

Cleve tried to feel sympathetic, but it was too hard when all he cared about was tasting meat as soon as possible.

Jek eventually convinced him to try a bite of bread.

At first, it was the most delicious food he'd ever tasted. But then, before he even could swallow it, his stomach already was trying to expel it.

He spat out the bread. "I'm going to vomit again."

"I had a feeling."

Luckily, the nausea passed, and Jek gave him some water, bringing the flask to his lips.

"Where is Nulya?" Cleve couldn't open his eyes to check.

"She's not far, same with my horse." Jek pressed the flask against Cleve's lips again. "We're in the middle of an open field of grass, just outside Karri Forest. It's not the safest place, so we should be moving as soon as you can. Any idea how long that will be?"

"I have no idea."

"Then, go back to sleep." Cleve felt Jek's hand squeeze his shoulder. "I'm going to rest as well. I've gone too long without it."

Next thing Cleve knew, his blanket was draping him, covering him with warmth that made him feel even more at ease. He wanted to thank Jek, but sleep was taking him, and he didn't have the strength for even the words.

Chapter 23

Cleve awoke to voices he didn't recognize.

In his groggy state, he still couldn't open his eyes, nor could he understand the words he was hearing. It felt like being underwater.

Someone stepped between him and Jek. A voice farther away spoke out. "Don't do that," she whispered. There was something about her voice and tone that gave Cleve the impression she was young, perhaps eleven or twelve.

"Quiet," a boy—the stranger between Cleve and Jek— whispered back. Cleve almost asked what he was doing. But being unable to move made it seem like a bad idea to give away that he was actually awake.

He heard the boy step over him, joining the girl near his feet.

"Are they dead?" she asked.

"No. I saw one of them breathing."

"Why are they sleeping in the middle of the field?"

"Maybe they're hurt," the boy answered.

Cleve heard Jek grumbling and sitting up. "Who are you?" Jek asked.

"We live around here," the girl answered.

"Who are you?" the boy asked in return.

"We're from Goldram, trying to get home. My friend is sick." Cleve felt Jek shaking his shoulder. "You awake?"

Now that it was clear Jek didn't see these kids as a threat, Cleve decided to try moving. His eyes opened easily, at least far easier than earlier.

Words came out of his mouth with no effort at all. "I'm awake."

"Can you get up now?" Jek asked.

Cleve pushed. Expecting it to be impossible, Cleve was delighted to find his strength had returned. His appetite was back as well.

Sitting up straight, he said, "I'm starving."

Jek stood and helped Cleve to his feet. "It looks like my friend is feeling better," Jek said. "We'll be leaving soon."

He handed Cleve some bread and water. Although it didn't taste as delicious as earlier, it still made his mouth water.

"What happened to him?" the girl asked.

The boy shushed her, trying to drag her away. But she held steady, waiting for an answer.

Cleve glimpsed them for the first time and realized his earlier assumption was right. They were young. He didn't get a good look at the boy, who was turned around with his hand shielding the sun, as if looking at something. But the girl's face was frightened, as if the wrong word would send her fleeing. Her whole body was leaned back except for her neck, which was stretched forward.

There were hills ahead, but nothing else. Grass was everywhere.

"I was bit by mookers," Cleve admitted. He didn't see the harm in telling them. If they lived around here, that meant they were part of Zav—part of the territory allied with Goldram.

The boy turned around with wide eyes. "And you lived?"

"So far," Cleve joked, letting out the first words that came to mind.

"I didn't know there was a town around here," Jek said, looking past the boy at the hills behind him.

"It's just a small group of us," the girl answered. "A village. We hardly get any visitors."

The boy cleared his throat and took the girl by the wrist. He shook his head at her, and she let her gaze fall to her feet.

"What's wrong?" Cleve asked.

"Nothing," the boy answered for her. "We'd better be

leaving. The only reason we came over was because we saw you and your horses, and we were curious." He turned and pulled the girl with him.

She looked back over her shoulder at Cleve, and then the boy did as well.

Then they straightened up and started jogging. Something about it was on the verge of being suspicious.

Cleve checked Jek's face. He seemed to have the same thoughts. His eyes were squinted, the corner of his mouth twisted with concern.

"What do you think that was?" Cleve asked.

"It certainly wasn't nothing," Jek said, a hand pressing into his cheek. "I'm hoping they just weren't allowed to be out here and that's the reason for their behavior."

Jek let his eyes fall to the food. He knelt. "I'll heat some of this meat for you while you start with bread." He took out his wand and pointed it. "Then we should be leaving. We have a long road ahead, and I don't want to stick around to find out what the deal was with those kids."

"I feel the same way. Is Lysha going to be okay with Raymess and Vala?"

"She should be. She knows the land better than anyone—the towns as well." Jek's head turned to follow the boy and girl. "She'd probably know this area enough to realize what those kids were up to."

Jek and Cleve ate quickly. They were running low on both food and water.

"We'll need to find a town on the way back to buy more food," Jek said. "Lysha took Raymess and Vala to Gajiri. It's about a day's ride northeast and is known to be controlled by the kingdom of Zav. They'll help the Takarys, and they'll definitely sell us food and water when we get there. We might even find some men from Goldram stationed there to help escort us back. I doubt we'll run into any trouble crossing through Zav, but it's better to be safe."

"I'm more concerned about the kids anyway."

When they finished eating, Cleve threw on his backpack, checked his Bastial steel sword, and then whistled to Nulya.

She galloped over, resting her head on his shoulder as he pet her.

"I can't find my bandana," Jek said, looking around him. He took off his bag to look within it. "I took it off before I went to sleep."

"Could the wind have picked it up?" Cleve asked.

"It was under my backpack," Jek answered in a doubtful tone. "At least I thought so."

Then Cleve remembered the boy stepping near them, the girl telling him not to do something.

"The boy took it," Cleve realized.

A mixture of confusion and worry creased Jek's brow. "How do you know?"

"I heard him rustling around you when I was waking up," Cleve said. "If you can't find it, he certainly took it."

"But why would he do that?"

Cleve shrugged. "To impress the girl, to show he's courageous, because he's a dumb kid? I don't know." He paused for a breath, wondering if he should continue to speculate. He decided not to. "Let's hope it's one of those reasons and not something else."

Jek seemed to be struck by sadness. He let out a long sigh. "I really liked that bandana. It meant something to me."

"Should we go after them?" Cleve dearly hoped Jek would say no. Though sympathetic, Cleve was eager to get back so he finally could go home to Kyrro, and there was something about the kids that made it seem dangerous to follow them.

"We shouldn't," Jek answered to Cleve's relief. "Lisanda's not going to be happy. But she'll understand."

Oh, it's that bandana. Cleve remembered Lisanda's story about her and Jek—the bandana played a big role early on. *That's why it's so important to him.* If there was something like that between him and Reela, it would be difficult for him to leave it as well.

He was beginning to change his mind. "You sure you don't want to go after them?"

"I want to. But something's telling me we shouldn't."

Cleve nodded. He had the same feeling.

They rode at a trot. The hills kept most of the wind from reaching them while the hanging sun gave the sky an orange glow.

"What happened after I left you and Lysha with the Takarys in the cabin?" Cleve asked, realizing there were many details he couldn't figure out.

"All of the mookers chased you. We thought you were going to be dead for sure." Jek had a wry smile. "You'll never know the shock I felt when we found you."

"How did you find me?"

"We saw the direction you went. It was the opposite way from the horses. Lysha and I carried Raymess, who was barely conscious. We put him with Vala on your horse and then went after you. It wasn't too hard to find you. We just followed the sounds of the mookers, and then eventually we saw them." Jek let out a laugh. "You attracted even more than there were in the encampment."

"They kept coming out of hiding to join the pack."

"I imagined so," Jek said. "Who knows how many are really in the forest. Hundreds of thousands, I'm sure."

"Now that I've had time to think about it, I was beginning to feel the effects of the poison from being bitten by the time I saw you and Lysha. But that memory is jumbled, fragmented like broken glass. What exactly happened?"

The answer didn't seem to come easy to Jek, as he took a slow breath and let his eyes lift to the clouds. "It's hard to remember. So much was happening at once."

He turned his head to look at Cleve, the bouncing of their trotting mounts making it difficult to maintain eye contact.

"Lysha was yelling at me to do this and do that. I remember focusing as hard as I could to produce the biggest cloud of SE that I could manage. Then I shot fireballs at the mookers near you, continuing to shoot more to keep them from following. I helped Lysha get you on her horse. You were still cooperating somewhat at that point. I don't know how I found my horse again." Jek leaned forward to stroke his horse's mane. "Nor do I know how Vala kept your horse with us through that, while a nearly unconscious Raymess was holding on to her. But somehow we rode out of there together and got far enough from the mookers that they lost track of us."

Hearing Jek describe it made the memories clearer. Cleve could see himself being put on the horse now. But he certainly didn't remember anything after that.

"You said I was unconscious for two days?"

"Pretty much," Jek said. "You were on Lysha's horse with her the entire first day, definitely unconscious then. We rode until we were out of the forest and then practically passed out where we could sleep without being attacked by mookers. You were still asleep when we woke. That's when you came down with a fever. You were in and out of consciousness after that, and soon Vala and Lysha decided they needed to leave to make sure Raymess got the attention he needed for his wounds."

"You should've left me," Cleve said, guilt pushing out his words before he really could consider them. "If anything happens to Raymess and Vala, then everything we did will be for nothing."

"Cleve, even Vala wouldn't have let me leave you. She saw what you did in the cabin. You killed Kasko, and then you risked your life to save the rest of us. Without you..." Jek shook his head. "I don't even want to think about what would've happened." The mage had a disgustingly humble tone.

"It sounds like you're calling me a hero." Cleve was feeling annoyed for reasons he didn't quite understand. He figured it was because he didn't feel like a hero. He'd just done what needed to be done. But the way Jek was looking at him—like he deserved to be crowned—made him painfully uncomfortable.

Jek slowed his horse, and Cleve did as well...reluctantly.

"I couldn't have done what you did," Jek said.

"Yes, you could've," Cleve said, refraining from rolling his eyes.

"No." Jek was firm. "I mean, I physically couldn't have outrun all those mookers. I'm not fast enough. Lysha couldn't have, either. That's why we were sure you were going to be dead when we found you. If you don't want to be a hero, fine. But at least accept our gratitude. There's no way we were going to leave you sick and alone."

Cleve felt the anger drain from him. He was even embarrassed he'd let it show. Jek was right. Cleve wouldn't have left another person in his place. He felt as if he should say something.

"Thank you for staying," he grumbled.

Jek extended his hand for Cleve to shake. "We're not parting until we make it back to the palace, no matter what happens."

Cleve shook the mage's hand. "Jek, why are you being so dramatic?" He smiled to show he meant no harm with the question. "We're in Zav already, the territory of Goldram's ally. You make it sound like it's inevitable that something will happen."

Jek didn't smile back. "That's because it always does, at least to me."

Cleve felt his grin fade. As he stared at Jek, he felt his decision changing. His mind was working like the wind in that moment, ebbing and flowing.

Just then, a big gust of it struck him from the side, turning his face north, toward the hills where the children had gone. With it, his mind changed as well, this time for good.

He looked at Jek and realized they were thinking the same thing.

"If we don't go after them and figure out what they were really up to, trouble will find us," Cleve said.

"I was about to say the same thing to you."

They turned their horses.

Chapter 24

In hopes of catching up before the young teenagers reached whatever town they'd come from, Cleve and Jek pushed their horses to gallop, slowing only once they reached the hills that blocked whatever was behind them.

The sun no longer could be found in the sky by then, but it comforted Cleve to know that Jek could make light if they needed it.

Cleve still wasn't feeling completely himself. It seemed as if sleep was waiting to strike every time his mind was at rest, sending his eyes shut and his head falling forward. Then in an instant, he was back.

He figured there was still poison running through his blood from the mooker bites. But by the rate he'd recovered in the last few hours, he knew it couldn't continue to affect him too much longer.

Reaching the peak of the hill gave sight to a mountain about five miles in the distance. Halfway between the mountain and the hill they were on was a small village that must be where the boy and girl came from.

"Do you see them?" Jek asked.

"It's too dark to tell."

"And soon there will be no light left." Jek's tone was urgent, but he kept his horse slow as he started down the hill. Cleve figured it was dangerous to make the animals gallop down a slope, so he kept Nulya at the same pace.

"If we don't see them by the time we're close to the village, we should stop before going in," Jek said. "There are some villages in every territory that do not abide by the rules of the kingdom."

"They don't pay taxes?" Cleve asked, amazed by the concept.

"They usually don't even have money. Most of the time they don't use currency—or at least the same currency as everyone else. These are usually barbaric people living among each other, most of them on the outskirts of Zav, Presoren, and Waywen, not so much in Goldram anymore since it's surrounded by the other three territories with the Elves in Meritar behind it."

"Those kids didn't seem barbaric."

"No, but there are plenty of dangerous people who act just as civilized as you and me."

Cleve thought of Kasko. "You're right about that."

When they reached the base of the hill, they sent their horses into a gallop, the village barely able to be seen by then. It had a wooden fence around it about the height of the Academy's walls: ten feet tall. Though, it seemed to be intended more for protection against animals than men. It looked thin, as if Cleve could push it over with his shoulder if he was feeling completely himself.

It certainly could be burned by fire.

Cleve startled himself with the thought, unsure why it even came. Perhaps, some part of him figured it might be necessary.

The wind picked up, displacing his hair and giving him a chill.

"See the boy and girl yet?" Jek asked.

"Maybe. Or it could just be my eyes seeing what they want to see."

"I'm going to use my wand to aim light in that direction. It'll make us more obvious than a virgin in a brothel, though." Jek's tone was as if he was asking a question.

"I think it's worth the risk."

Jek drew his wand and held it steady for two breaths before grunting and snapping it in front of him.

Almost as bright as a flash of lightning, everything in front of them was lit...and then back to black.

Cleve and Jek both stopped their horses, startled by what

they saw.

"Was that—" Jek started.

"A bunch of men on horseback with dogs?" Cleve guessed. It was difficult to tell. "And they're coming toward us?"

"I was going to say men with wolves," Jek said.

"Oh, you're right. It was wolves." Then Cleve heard the howls.

Neither of them moved nor said anything.

Though he thought about turning his horse, curiosity was holding Cleve in place. He figured it was the same for Jek.

"What could they want with us?" Cleve asked.

"I don't know, but since they have my bandana and the wolves obviously know my scent, they could easily track us." Jek dismounted.

"I take it you don't want to run." Cleve got off his horse as well.

"I try to avoid running when I can these days. I've had enough of it for a lifetime when I took Lisanda from the palace."

"Fine with me." Cleve drew his sword. "I've never been one to run."

The men were close enough for Cleve and Jek to see they were carrying lamps.

"At least they aren't mages," Jek commented. Cleve could hear it in his tone—Jek's body was tense, his mind focused.

Cleve felt himself harden in the same way. There could be a battle soon—one heavily not in their favor. At least no sleep attacks from the mooker poison were striking...yet.

When the men were even closer, Jek raised his wand and yelled, "Stop right there."

They formed a line, their two wolves snarling. They were almost the size of the horses the men dismounted from.

Cleve started to count how many there were. But before he could finish, his knees gave out and he fell.

Somehow he'd managed to hold onto his sword, but

everything had gone numb. He could hear Jek muttering, "Not again."

"What's wrong with him?" Cleve heard one man ask.

But Cleve was already on his way back up, his strength returning. "Nothing," he answered.

He finished counting the men. There were six of them. The one in front had graying hair, long at the back, balding on top. But while his face showed old age, his body was muscular, and he stood with a straight back. In his hand was a sword, the other holding Jek's bandana.

Cleve already knew he didn't like this man, something about his wind-burned face and his beady eyes.

"What do you want with us?" Jek asked, his tone between curious and aggressive.

"That depends," the old man answered. "My name is Enri. What are your names, and where are you from?"

"Just give me my bandana and let us go." Jek took a brave step toward Enri, one Cleve would've waited to take.

An archer behind Enri drew an arrow and pulled back his string. Jek stopped, raising his hands. To Cleve's surprise, Jek slowly turned around and shook his head as he walked back to Cleve's side. The motion was so calm, it was as if the mage felt no danger from the arrow now aimed at his back. Jek sighed in frustration, mumbled something under his breath about archers, found his place next to Cleve, and turned around again to face them.

"It's rude to show your rear," Enri said, looking as if he wanted to spit.

"It can't be worse than stealing and then aiming bows at people," Jek retorted, a dangerously pompous smile forming.

"What do you want?" Cleve said, before Enri decided to give his archer the order to shoot.

Then Cleve felt rain touch his arms. The wind was picking up as well.

"It's going to be a stormy night, boys," Enri said. "And we

don't want to stay out here any longer than we need to, so help us out and answer my questions." He shrugged. "Or we might just kill you here." With his plain tone, Enri did a fine job demonstrating how little their lives meant to him. "What are your names? Tell me."

Jek turned to whisper to Cleve, "Are any of them psychics?"

"I can't tell unless they use psyche on me. No one has—" An arrow flew between their faces, interrupting Cleve.

"You do anything but answer my question again, and you're both dead," Enri said. He sounded enraged, perhaps even embarrassed he wasn't doing well at frightening Cleve and Jek.

Proud and impatient, Cleve realized. *Those can be the most dangerous kinds of men.*

"I'm Jek Trayden. This is Cleve Polken. We're from Goldram, allies of Zav—"

"We know nothing about allies," Enri interrupted. "We may live in Zav, but this here is *our* land." He thumped his chest. "Now what are you doing out here?"

"Just headed back to Goldram," Jek answered. Cleve could hear some nervousness slipping out. It was becoming clear a conversation wasn't going to be the last thing they shared with these men.

"Do you work for the King?" Enri asked, taking a step forward.

"We do," Jek answered, turning to show Cleve a concerned glance.

Cleve tightened his grip on his sword.

"You stay honest like that and you'll live." Enri tilted his head at Jek, as if giving advice. "How many Bastial steel swords are both of you worth? I'm thinking five. That sound about right?"

"Maybe a dagger between the two of us," Jek answered. "We mean very little to the King of Goldram, just low-level scouts who can be replaced. It's better if you let us go."

Enri took another step forward, now with a smile. "Want to

know how I know you're lying?"

Jek folded his arms. "It's the truth."

"First, you're not a very good liar. Second, you're an idiot. Your friend here has a Bastial steel sword on him right now." Enri gestured with a hand.

Cleve felt like an idiot himself for having the sword out of its sheath, but then again he didn't know Jek was going to try lying.

Jek looked over and slapped his forehead reflexively. "Bastial hell, Cleve."

Before he could retort, Enri pointed his sword at Cleve. The wolves started snarling again. "One more lie and he dies right now." Enri held Cleve in his gaze, continuing to point his sword at him. It was several breaths before he finally looked back at Jek. "I'm asking you again: How many are you worth?"

"Maybe four between the two of us, could be five."

Everything always boils down to Bastial steel.

Cleve was certain now that this continent would've been better off without the precious metal, especially given how few Bastial steel weapons were used to kill desmarls compared to fellow Humans.

Jek seemed to have the same thought, for Cleve noticed him rolling his eyes when he answered Enri.

"Now, you're going to come with us and wait in our village while we send a message to your king," Enri instructed, his confident tone really beginning to irritate Cleve. "If you cooperate, you won't be harmed."

"You can't possibly expect that to work?" Jek said, seemingly perplexed. If he wasn't legitimately confused, then he sure acted it well.

In return, Enri seemed puzzled by Jek's question. But he didn't let his confusion show for long. Soon, anger had taken back over his face. "It'll work fine, and if you resist, you'll die."

"Yes, you can take us back and hold us captive. Of course, you can get a message to Danvell Takary. And yes, they'll even come over here with Bastial swords...but not to give them to you. They'll be in the hands of a few hundred men sent here to kill you." Jek leaned back and folded his arms assertively. "Your plan won't work."

"It will when you write the note yourself, pleading for the King of Goldram to oblige," Enri replied, a cool smile stuck to his face. "You'll tell him that we'll kill you if he sends an army. Someone within the palace can verify your handwriting, I'm sure."

"Yes, but why would I do that?" Jek asked.

"Because we're also sending them one of your fingers...and if you resist, we'll send your whole hand instead."

Jek stared at Enri as silence fell back upon them. Cleve tried to read what Jek was thinking, but his face told none of his thoughts in that moment. He held no expression, as if he was simply waiting for Enri to act.

Finally, Jek turned to Cleve, showing the same face as he had to Enri. It was as if he was asking, *what do you want to do?*

Cleve knew what he wanted to do, but he didn't know how to tell Jek without making it clear to the others.

Then he realized it didn't matter. It wasn't as if they'd have the element of surprise anyway.

"You picked the wrong two people," Cleve muttered, running toward the old man.

Complete shock made Enri's eyes double in size. "Shoot them!" He fell backward as he said it, quickly scrambling back to his feet to retreat.

Cleve rolled to the side to dodge the arrow he knew had to be coming. Amid the battle cries of his enemies, he still noticed the sound of an arrow pass by his ear.

"Get the archer!" Cleve yelled to Jek, popping back to his feet to chase down the old man.

There was a flash of light—a fireball. A man screamed.

"He's down," Jek yelled back.

Just before Cleve was in range to take off Enri's leg, he

noticed a blur of gray leaping toward him. *The damn wolves.*

He turned and slashed, feeling his sword drive into the poor beast's skull.

There were two. Where's the other?

Lightning flashed through the sky, rain pouring down. Cleve saw the other wolf then, rushing toward Jek. The mage held his wand steady and released another fireball. It sent the animal spiraling backward.

Two men were on Cleve next, each one cursing at him. One had on a helmet, and Cleve kicked him away after ducking under a wild swing.

The other one jabbed his weapon forward. The motion was sloppy, leaving him undefended. Cleve put his sword through the man's chest after dodging his attack.

The first man was back, along with another wearing a steel helmet. Cleve thought to check on Enri, but he didn't have time to look around. Who knew what the old man was doing? *Did Jek take care of him already?* Cleve had to jump backward to dodge the two men furiously trying to drive their weapons into him.

There was another flash, but this one sent Cleve soaring for what felt like seconds before he hit the ground. Thunder came with it, so loud it shook his heart. On reflex, he let go of his sword before somersaulting three times when he hit the ground. He didn't want his weapon to end up in one of his limbs.

His ears were ringing. He didn't see anyone for a moment— or really anything, for that matter, he soon came to realize.

He tried to yell, "Jek? Jek!" But he couldn't even hear his own voice over the loud ringing stuck in his ears.

Cleve pushed himself to his feet, only to trip and fall. The second time had the same result.

He shouted again, and he could hear his voice this time. It was muffled, as if he heard himself in the distance. *What was that?* Stumbling, he found his sword and looked to where he thought everyone should be.

Three men were picking themselves up off the ground. Jek was there too, shaking his head while doubled over.

"Was that you?" Cleve yelled to Jek, running over to help him stand up.

Jek was even more dazed than Cleve, shutting his eyes and opening them as if he couldn't see and thought blinking would help.

Rain and wind were terrorizing Cleve's senses as they started sharpening back to normal.

"Jek! Can you hear me?" Cleve grabbed his face and patted his cheek. Jek finally looked over and seemed to recognize Cleve. "Jek—"

"What was that?" Jek interrupted. He pointed his wand and let out some light.

There was a circle of charred dirt around the bodies of two men, all the grass in that area disintegrated.

"Lightning." Cleve realized.

The three men who were left seemed to have realized it as well. Two of them threw off their helmets. The other was the old man, pointing and shouting orders that Cleve couldn't hear over the wind and rain.

Whatever was to happen needed to be soon. The storm was raging. Lightning could strike again, and maybe this time it wanted a taste of Cleve's sword. Jek was holding his wand out, steadily moving toward the three men.

Then Cleve noticed two more were coming from behind the three men in front of them. They were smaller, and one was a girl hollering at the top of her lungs, chasing after a boy.

The kids who we met earlier, Cleve realized. The boy had a sword now.

"Enri stop him!" the girl was shouting.

The boy ran by the three men, who were just turning around as he passed them. To Cleve's amazement, the boy ran right at Jek.

"Stop," Jek tried to tell him, beginning to back up but keeping his wand steady. "Stop right now!"

Cleve ran to intercept the boy, slamming a shoulder into him to knock him off his feet. From the corner of his eye he noticed the three men coming at him now.

"That's my grandson!" Enri screamed. One of them was struck by Jek's fireball before he reached Cleve. A second one turned to chase after Jek before he could shoot another.

Cleve knew he only had a brief moment to deal with Enri if he was to protect Jek from the man running toward him and the boy, who was now back on his feet. So Cleve ran at Enri and slammed his Bastial sword into the old man's weapon as hard as he could, knocking it from his hand. With a quick spin, he brought his sword down across Enri's chest, opening up his flesh.

There was another flash of lightning somewhere nearby. The boom of thunder almost took Cleve off his feet. But he kept his balance and ran after the man going at Jek. There were only two attackers left now, and one was the boy.

The girl was still screaming, "Stop! Stop! You have to stop!"

But no one listened, so Cleve certainly wasn't going to, either. He didn't even know who she was referring to, him or the boy.

Luckily, Jek was quick, ducking under the man's swing and coming back toward Cleve for protection.

The boy then engaged Cleve with the man close behind him.

Unwilling to kill someone so young, Cleve blocked the blow of his sword and hit him in the face to knock him backward, hopefully dazing him.

The other man took out a knife and threw it at Cleve. He had to duck to avoid it. The man followed his knife attack by running at Cleve and jumping through the air before Cleve could get back upright.

Barely getting his weapon up in time, Cleve did manage to block the assault.

"You've lost!" Jek shouted. "Put down your weapons!"

"Do it!" the girl screamed in agreement. "Please stop." She was crying so hard it was louder than the violent wind.

But the man and the boy didn't stop.

"You killed them," the boy said, clearly not dazed and gritting his teeth as he stepped overconfidently toward Cleve. The boy screamed as he swung his weapon through the rain and wind. Cleve rolled forward to go between the boy and the man coming from his other side.

He heard the boy scream and the man curse. Turning, Cleve saw the boy fall to his knees, grabbing his chest. Cleve had seen no burst of light, though. He didn't know what Jek had done to them. But then he noticed the man dropping his weapon and crouching over the boy, cursing even more now.

"You stabbed him!" the girl yelled.

"It was an accident," the man replied.

By then, the boy had fallen on his back. Jek and Cleve cautiously approached.

The girl was there first, weeping.

Cleve couldn't find Nulya. He figured she'd run off when she heard the lightning. He whistled before he took the time to lean over the boy and check his wound. His little chest had been pierced deeply.

"It missed his heart," Cleve said. "He may live with the help of a chemist."

The boy was gasping in fright. "I don't want to die! Please! Help me! Help me!"

The man shot up to look around. "Where are the horses?"

"Scared by the lightning," Cleve answered. He stood and whistled again for Nulya.

"Please...please..." The boy sputtered out between gasps. "Don't let me die."

The girl fell to her knees and wept over him.

"Jek, can we get some light to look for our horses?" Cleve asked.

Jek had just come back with his bandana and backpack. "I found them already," he said, leaning over the boy for a look. "They're coming now." He took a shirt from his backpack and tied it around the boy's chest to put pressure on his wound. "Our horses will be here soon. We'll take you back to the village."

Cleve and Jek's mounts came then. Cleve positioned himself to lift the boy, but the one man left jumped to his feet and grabbed his sword from where he'd let it fall.

He pointed the weapon at Cleve. "You will not take him anywhere. Give me your horse, and I'll bring him to the village."

Cleve considered killing the man right then. There was no time to argue, and his anger made the idea tempting.

Luckily, Jek spoke first. "Shut up. Put down your weapon and shut your damn mouth. You will not take our horses, and you will die if you threaten us again."

The man lowered his sword. His shoulders slumped.

"Hurry!" the girl screamed.

The boy was shaking now, gasping wildly. Tears were rolling down his cheeks.

"Put him on my horse," Jek said, climbing on and then reaching out his hand.

Cleve picked up the boy and carefully put him on Jek's saddle.

They rode off while Cleve jumped on Nulya.

"I'm coming with you," the man stated.

"You're walking back." Cleve was about to give Nulya a kick, but the girl grabbed his leg.

"Please," she pleaded, still weeping. "Take me back with you."

Cleve pulled her up by the arm. She grabbed his stomach to hold on as Nulya started galloping after Jek's mount.

There was another strike of lightning, and this one Cleve actually saw. It hit a tree on the mountain behind the village, catching it on fire. Thunder followed, building and building until Cleve felt it rumbling within him. Jek's horse and Nulya both stopped, rearing up and whinnying in fear.

Cleve felt the girl's grip come loose as she fell.

When Nulya was under control again, Cleve saw Jek had fallen, along with the boy, who'd been in front of Jek on his saddle. Cleve yelled at the girl to get up, practically throwing her on the saddle behind him when she offered her hand, and then galloped over to Jek.

He dismounted and knelt to pick up the boy again while Jek got back on his horse. But Cleve was struck with numbness.

No, not now!

Instead of falling on the boy, he did manage to turn enough to avoid him. He tried to fight the paralysis, but he couldn't even speak. All he could do was utter a whimper.

The boy was either silent or unconscious by then. Cleve couldn't lift his head to see for himself.

He felt someone kicking him, at least he thought he did. "Get up and help him! What are you doing?" It was the girl. She pulled his hair now—*that* he could feel.

Strength was returning, and he popped back up. Taking a breath, he scooped his arms under the boy and put him on the saddle in front of Jek. They were off again.

For some reason, the girl was still kicking and punching him. So he turned and grabbed her wrist, dragged her to Nulya, got on himself, and then pulled her up next.

She was still pounding his back and crying as they started catching up to Jek's horse. It seemed as if she was yelling at him, but no words were clear enough to understand through her weeping.

"Stop," he told her. "Or I'll throw you off this horse."

She didn't let up. "You want him to die! You're playing games, and he's bleeding to death. I should throw *you* from this horse." He felt her hands grab his sides and start to push, pull...frantically she was swaying his body in all directions at once.

Cleve couldn't turn behind him while Nulya was galloping. He barely could look at the girl over his shoulder without falling off.

"Stop right now!" Cleve screamed.

She was using all her strength by then. He could feel it. And he was going to fall soon.

He managed to slow Nulya to a halt before the girl was successful. He jumped to the ground in preparation of removing her safely from his saddle, but then the girl tried to grab the reins and speed off.

Fortunately, he quickly was able to get her little wrists under control. He moved them both to one hand so he could use his other to scoop her legs, putting her stomach on his shoulder.

She screamed and thrashed, nearly making him lose his grip on her. But he managed to get her on the ground without throwing her down and jumped back onto Nulya, leaving the girl there.

With her screams dying out from the noise of the wind, Cleve could hear himself breathing heavily. Guilt came next, twisting inside of him hard. He thought about going back for her but decided against it.

He had other things to worry about, like what the villagers were going to think when he and Jek brought in the dying grandson of their apparent leader.

Chapter 25

If it wasn't for the light from Jek's wand, they no longer would've been able to find the wooden fence of the village. The darkness was too thick, the rain so hard it was as if Cleve were standing beneath a waterfall.

Jek was stopped at the wall of the village. Cleve could hear him screaming, but not what about until he got closer.

"How do I know he isn't dead already?" someone shouted from the other side of the wall.

"He'll be dead soon if you don't let us in!" Jek screamed back. "He needs a chemist. He's bleeding out."

Cleve let out a hand to catch the rain. As he'd expected, it had started to hail. Lightning struck somewhere. Thunder scared the horses once again, but not enough to make them throw Cleve or Jek from their backs.

"Where is everyone else who went out looking for you two?" a different man shouted from behind the wooden gate.

"They attacked us," Jek replied. "Most are dead. And if you don't let us in now, this boy will die with them."

Cleve wished he hadn't removed the girl from his saddle. She could've convinced these men with her incessant weeping to open the gate.

"Throw your weapons over and we'll let you in."

"My sword doesn't leave my hand," Cleve said firmly.

The hail was giving him a beating. Nulya stirred, and he worried for her.

"I'm about to put this dying boy here and leave," Jek threatened. "Or I can bring him inside and take him to your closest chemist."

There was muttering between the two men behind the gate.

"Hurry," Jek said.

Cleve heard the sweet sound of a bolt being undone. The gate was pulled open.

"Give him here," one of the men said, lifting his arms toward Jek. Cleve barely could make out his silhouette as Jek let the light from his wand go out to hand over the boy. The man ran off with the dying child, disappearing into the night within seconds.

Cleve looked around within the walls but soon found it to be hopeless. He couldn't see anything.

"You tell me what happened," someone said from Jek's far side. "Or I'll kill your horse right now."

"You do that, you die," Cleve said, moving over for a glimpse of the man. He had a knife held to Jek's horse.

Jek reached out and grabbed Cleve's shoulder in a firm embrace. "It's alright." He looked down at the man holding the knife and took a slow breath. "We told you already, we were attacked by your people. We defended ourselves, and now most of them are dead."

A flash—lightning somewhere. Thunder roared. Cleve barely could keep Nulya under control. She wanted to turn and run away from the village, but he kept her steady by pulling tight on her reins and telling her to stay calm.

A familiar voice yelled from behind, "Don't let them leave! They have unpunished crimes." Cleve found the last surviving man to be the one shouting. The crying girl was with him as well, holding onto his arm.

Cleve wasn't sure how he wanted to handle this, so he looked to Jek.

"Where is he?" the girl asked, tugging on Jek's leg to get his attention.

"I handed your boyfriend to some man who ran off with him," Jek answered. He pulled his leg away from her grasp petulantly. Cleve figured Jek was just as angry as he was about this whole thing.

Cleve thought it best to try leaving one more time. "We have committed no crimes," he said. "We defended ourselves and that's it. The boy was cut by one of his own, not by me nor my friend."

"Who?" the man with a knife to Jek's horse asked. "Who cut the boy?"

Cleve looked to the guilty man behind him to find his eyes low, avoiding. "Someone who later died to my sword," Cleve lied for him. He found no reason why an accident should haunt this man's life.

"That's not true!" It was the stupid girl shouting now. Cleve had never wanted to strike a girl before, but it took all his strength not to kick her in her mouth, which was so conveniently right by his foot.

"Who then?" the man with the knife asked her. "Was it one of these two?" Lightning struck as he gestured the weapon at Cleve and Jek.

"No," the girl answered.

"It was Enri," the guilty man blurted. The girl gasped and spun to face him. He put his hand up to stop her. "We can discuss this more later, but these men are right. All they did was defend themselves. You know what the plan was," the guilty man told the remaining sentry. "They didn't want to come with us, and a battle ensued. They've broken none of our rules."

"You can speak to Azaylee on their behalf?"

"I can."

"I can as well," the girl chimed in.

"No need for that," the guard told her. "Now let's get out of this weather before we all freeze." He closed the gate and bolted it shut after Cleve and Jek dismounted and led their horses through.

The girl ran ahead, probably to check on the boy, wherever he was.

The sentry put away his knife. "Follow me," he told Cleve and Jek.

They shared a glance first, Cleve wondering if it would be better to stay or leave this village and look for shelter.

"What do you want to do?" Jek asked him.

"You still can't leave," the guilty man said. "Not until the trial is done."

"Then, I guess we'll stay," Cleve said. He figured they could fight their way out, but the thought of spilling more blood, along with the hours it would take searching for cover from the hail, made the decision easy.

Jek seemed curious about the village, shining his wand in every direction as they pulled their horses along and followed the man who'd accidentally stabbed the boy.

"My name is Jaffo," he told them.

"Jek, and that's Cleve," Jek said, needing to shout to be heard. "Fight a lot of people before you learn their name, Jaffo?" The mage seemed exasperated.

Jaffo didn't answer.

Jek went back to looking at the various houses they passed. It was hard to ignore the heavy awkwardness that was growing worse in the silence. Just a short while ago, the man leading them through this village was trying to kill them. Even worse, Cleve and Jek had killed his comrades.

What does he think of us? But Cleve couldn't even figure out what he thought of Jaffo or the people in this village. *Perhaps once this hail stops beating down on me, I can think straight.*

"Where are you taking us?" Cleve asked.

"To my house," Jaffo said. "I have a barn for your horses."

"Then what?" Cleve asked.

"Then we talk."

They were silent until they reached their destination.

Inside the barn, Jek investigated each wall carefully using the light from his wand. He looked in every crevice as if expecting to find someone hiding. He was mumbling something to himself about being forced to kill people, his tone still infuriated.

Cleve told Nulya he would be back in the morning and reluctantly left, eager to learn more about this trial they seemed destined to be part of.

Jaffo locked the barn door and led them to his house.

Jek kept pushing Bastial Energy through his wand to make it glow white until Jaffo lit a lamp.

"I need to find out if Olmi is alive," Jaffo said, taking his sword from its sheath and setting it on a nearby table.

"Olmi is the boy?" Jek asked.

"The one I stabbed, yes." Jaffo rubbed the back of his neck and bent to look out the window.

In the light, Cleve could see that Jaffo was not nearly as old as Enri, the man who'd led the attempted kidnapping on Cleve and Jek. Jaffo seemed to be in his mid-twenties, with hair that hung down to his shoulders like Rek, except Jaffo's was black instead of brown.

He was about Jek's size, average build and height. Though his features were so rough in comparison to the mage they made Cleve feel his eyes were running down sandpaper when he glimpsed the man. Thick stubble lined his cheeks and neck. He had wide lips, a wide nose, even wide eyes.

"Thank you for lying for me," Jaffo told Cleve. "Although I'm not sure I can contain the truth during the trial."

"People always need someone to blame," Cleve said. "I thought it would be better for it to be a dead man."

"It would," Jaffo agreed. "But I can't pass my own guilt off as easily as blame, especially if the boy dies." Jaffo took a slow breath, then lifted his gaze. "I would offer a towel, but we're going back out there to visit Olmi. Leave your weapons here."

Jek put his wand on the table, but Cleve didn't move. He met Jaffo's eyes.

"My sword stays with me."

Hail slamming against the windows grew louder with a gust of wind. Then it faded back to its usual drumming, making the silence between Cleve and Jaffo noticeably heavy, like a weight pressed down.

"I won't leave you in my house alone," Jaffo said. "And the chemist won't let you bring it in with you."

"Then I'll wait outside."

"You're a stubborn one...but fine. Let's go."

Each man lifted his coat over his head, meager protection against the unrelenting frozen pebbles falling from the sky. The light from lamps within the houses did little to break through the darkness of the storm. Without the Bastial light from Jek's hand, they wouldn't even have been able to see their feet.

When they reached the building of the chemist, Cleve could hear crying from within. *It's the girl,* he realized. *The one who wouldn't stop weeping.*

Jaffo opened the door first, letting himself in. Jek followed, while Cleve waited at the window, watching the conversation ensue.

The chemist was in a long gray coat, not unlike the chemists Cleve had seen in Welson Kimard's castle in Kyrro. On a bedded table was the boy, lying lifelessly. His shirt had been removed. Cleve found it on the floor, soaking up a puddle of blood.

There was an older woman there as well. The boy's mother, Cleve figured. She and the girl were embracing each other. Jaffo and the chemist were sharing words, each of their expressions solemn.

Images of the wounded boy jumped into Cleve's mind. *"Please, I don't want to die!"* He'd been so desperate for help, gasping, pleading.

He died scared, Cleve said to himself. *The worst way to go.* He felt gripping sadness take hold of his stomach. More thoughts sprouted up from wherever they dwelled—the other men he'd killed, gone, dead. He'd taken their lives.

Surprisingly, he didn't feel the same remorse for them as he did when thinking of the gasping boy.

Those were grown man who made a choice to attack—the wrong choice. But the boy was just stupid, acting without thought as boys often do. He doesn't deserve to die for one mistake.

Cleve had made many mistakes himself. He could've been killed or imprisoned just for continuing to use the bow, but he'd gotten lucky.

Not this boy. There was no luck for him.

Jek tried to say something to the girl and the boy's mother. He lowered his head. *An apology,* Cleve realized.

The sadness within Cleve began spreading, tugging on his heart. *Why must death always remind me of my parents?* But then he thought of Jessend beside him. He thought of her touch, of holding her tightly against his body as they drifted in and out of sleep and spoke of feelings and memories he'd thought had been lost over the years.

A warmth—strength—started fighting the sadness. He took a breath. Although he was shaky from oncoming shivers, he could feel his resolve coming back.

Life goes on. Death either makes us weaker or stronger, and I'm not going to let it weaken me any longer. It had taken so long for Cleve to realize that grief was only a temporary weakness, but he was relieved it finally had happened.

Suddenly, old conversations about his parents with his uncle, Terren, began to make sense.

After Cleve's parents had died, Cleve had caught his uncle crying when the tough warrior thought he was alone. But moments later, Terren had come into Cleve's room, and there were no signs of his recent sadness, of his recent weakness. He'd knelt down and reassured Cleve that everything would be fine, his expression strong and confident.

Cleve had never been able to change the way he felt about his parents' passing, and it made him believe Terren was simply a good actor. But he realized now that Terren wasn't acting at all. The death of Terren's brother—Cleve's father—

really didn't mean the end of life for the rest of them, as Terren would insist when Cleve was unwilling to eat.

Yes, it hurt. Certainly, it had made Terren feel like curling up in bed all day and weeping like Cleve had done. But with strength, this stark grief was accepted.

Cleve never had accepted the grief before. *I'd always buried it. I couldn't live with it, so I tried to ignore it. But it's possible to live with grief. In fact, that's the only way to deal with it. We must accept it and go on.*

He looked at the young girl and the boy's mother for what he knew would be the last time.

And now they'll have to live with it as well. It might take some time, but they'll learn how to do it.

Cleve sank down to sit against the exterior wall of the building as he waited. He let his eyelids close and tried to think of the brilliant green of Reela's eyes that always made a surge of heat swarm through his body from his heart.

He wondered what she was doing in this moment.

He tried to imagine what it was, but without a single clue to go on, he found it to be impossible. Too much could've happened since he'd left to even guess.

Cleve refrained from wondering if it was possible that she could be dead already...too late. The thought was there, and a dry swallow forced its way down his throat.

I need to get home. I just need to get home. Terren, Reela, even Steffen. That's where he belonged.

A few minutes later, Jek came out. Cleve stood to face him, each of them shielding their scalps with coats.

"Probably better that you didn't come in," Jek said. "Not a good scene in there."

"I got the general idea," Cleve said. "Is the lie going to keep up—that his grandfather was the one to stab him by accident?"

"It seems so. Definitely easier that way." Jek peered in through the window. "Though, the girl might bring out the truth later. She was unusually mute just now."

The door opened, and Jaffo came out. He said nothing, but his expression was clear: He was done.

As they walked back to his house, Jaffo stood between Cleve and Jek, his pace slower than Cleve would've liked, as if Jaffo wanted to torture himself by staying out in the weather longer than necessary.

"Is the trial tomorrow?" Cleve asked.

"Yes. You'll see the village leader, Azaylee. She'll ask you some questions and then decide your punishment."

"What kind of punishments are usually given?" Cleve asked.

"She takes fingers, sometimes more. But you shouldn't worry."

Cleve remembered a conversation he'd had with Effie, how she'd told him how much she hated it when people told her not to worry. He'd never understood her issue with it until now—with his fingers at stake.

Cleve felt as though he would've been better off without Jaffo's advice. *Or if I'd never asked,* he realized.

So he remained silent until they reached Jaffo's home, unwilling to learn anymore about the trial except for when it was scheduled.

"It'll be first thing in the morning," Jaffo said. "And don't try to leave before it. Azaylee won't like that."

Cleve had been out in the rain so long, the frustration of the day was starting to get to him. *Azaylee won't like that.* He was imitating Jaffo in his mind with a contemptuous cadence, his inner child lashing out. He took a breath to relax and looked to Jek to see how this fared with him.

The mage already had his eyes on Cleve, his head lowered with his eyebrows raised. Clearly, he was just as annoyed.

Inside, Jaffo kicked off his boots, hung his jacket over a chair, and retrieved three towels from the next room. "We don't have an inn or anything like that here. Though, most of us have an extra bed for the occasional visitor from other parts of the village. You can share it."

"I'll just take the floor near the fire," Jek muttered, kneeling down in front of the hearth. "I would just get the sheets bloody."

"Are you injured?" Jaffo asked.

"No. Never mind," Jek pointed his wand toward the logs to start them ablaze. Jaffo stood there with his arms folded. Cleve wasn't sure what he wanted, but it was surely something.

"Aren't you going to sleep?" Cleve asked him.

"I'm waiting for you," Jaffo said, annoyed.

"I wanted to speak to Jek for a moment." *We have a lot to discuss.*

"That's why I'm waiting." Jaffo gestured at the two of them. "I don't want you scheming something. You're my responsibility while you're in this village. I vouched for you. You're going to stay in this house tonight and see Azaylee tomorrow at sunrise, or it's my fingers that will be taken."

Jek stood. "We're not planning to leave, Jaffo. We just need to talk."

"Then do it now or in there." Jaffo pointed at the bedroom where Jaffo and Cleve's beds were side by side. "Or wait until after your trial."

Cleve decided just to say what needed to be said. "No matter what happens tomorrow, we won't leave without each other," he told Jek.

The mage nodded. "Of course. Keep that sword close."

"You don't need to tell me that." Cleve patted his belt, showing no signs of removing it like he had his coat.

"After this, we'll see if Lysha is still in the town where she took..." Jek stopped himself to eye Jaffo, reluctant to say the Takary Prince's name. "We'll talk tomorrow," Jek concluded.

Cleve bent his head for a brief nod and then turned, leaving Jek by the crackling fire.

Chapter 26

Besides being awakened a few times when the wind picked up, which caused the hail to bang against the window, Cleve mostly slept throughout the night.

Being in the same room as Jaffo was strange at first, but Jaffo seemed so relaxed about it, making it easy for Cleve to ignore that they were battling just recently.

He and Jaffo didn't say one word until the storm had cleared and the sun had begun to brighten the now cloudless sky.

"I'll make us some breakfast before we go," Jaffo said as he clothed himself, leaving the room shortly after.

It just then came to Cleve that Jaffo hadn't been afraid he and Jek would attack him during the night, or even now. There must be something about them that Jaffo didn't find threatening, but Cleve didn't know what it was.

So he figured he would ask as he followed Jaffo out of the bedroom. "Why do you trust us not to fight you after your attempt on our lives?"

Jaffo's head snapped around his shoulder to eye Cleve, his gaze looking down to Cleve's sheathed Bastial steel sword. After a breath, he turned the rest of his body around and said, "After the effort you both put in to try to save Olmi's life, I knew you were good people. I will tell this to Azaylee."

"You'll speak for us?" Cleve asked.

"Not for you, each person meets with her alone. But I can speak of you during my own trial. I'll most likely be going first, being the oldest."

"I didn't know there would be a trial for you as well," Cleve said, beginning to wonder if the lie he'd created was the best idea. "Will they take a finger?"

"I can't say." Jaffo nearly whispered it as he glimpsed his

hand. "Never been on trial before."

Jek was still sleeping, the fire beside him dead cold. His chest was bare with a fresh bandage over his stomach.

Cleve knelt to wake him with a low voice. "Jek, it's morning."

The light coming in through the window hit his widening eyes to give them a shine. *Just like Reela's,* Cleve couldn't help but think. *Except such a blue instead of green.*

After some porridge, they were on their way to the center of the village where Azaylee's tower could be seen shadowing the buildings in front of it.

On the way there, puddles scattered throughout the road were the only sign of last night's storm. Families of birds took residence on the roofs of surprisingly large houses—they were bigger than most in Kyrro City, at least.

Cleve noticed that most people walking by him were in their second half of life, usually older than forty. Most of them weren't shy about staring. Cleve was always first to draw their glance, and then Jek and Jaffo were next. Cleve figured it was his size. It had constantly been a source of unwanted attention, but he wouldn't trade his body for any other.

An old man stopped Jaffo to ask him about Cleve and Jek.

"I'll tell you later," Jaffo said, not stopping longer than a breath to lower his head in respect before continuing.

When they reached the tower, Cleve was shocked to learn from Jaffo that Azaylee was its only inhabitant. The structure was big enough to house fifty people.

What a waste, Cleve thought as he stopped at the door to strain his neck for a glimpse at the top of it.

"No guards outside the door?" Jek asked.

Cleve realized he was right. Why were there no guards for their leader?

"None inside either—no need," Jaffo answered. "Azaylee can protect herself better than any man with a sword. At least that's what they say. I've never met her." His tone was soft, growing weaker the more he spoke of her. "And I'd hoped I never would." His last words were whispered.

Jaffo raised his knuckles as if to knock on the door, but he stopped. "The bell..." he muttered, looking around. "There's supposed to be a bell."

Jek seemed to find it, reaching up to unhook a thin chain blending into the wall beside the door. He tugged on it. Cleve listened but heard nothing. Jek pulled down harder, and Jaffo's hand snatched his wrist.

"Stop," he whispered. "Wait to see if she comes." His fearful tone made it clear he was afraid of this woman—this leader he'd never met.

They waited in silence, Cleve unsure if he should be nervous, though he wasn't.

"She should really have some guards outside the door to move things along," Jek said, his voice annoyed. Cleve couldn't help but notice how easily frustrated the mage had become since the villagers had attacked, as if taking the lives of those men had stirred an insatiable frustration.

At least he's not taking it out on himself.

Jaffo pretended not to hear, stepping toward the door while his hands fidgeted with his belt.

"I'm going to ring it again," Jek said. But just then, Cleve heard a latch being undone. The door swung open, and a middle-aged blonde woman had a prepared smile for them.

"You're early," she said sweetly, her red lips the color of thick blood. "State your names before entering."

Jaffo introduced himself first, his voice eager. Cleve figured he just wanted to finish this as quickly as possible.

After Cleve and Jek told Azaylee their names, she nodded, making sure to keep her smile in place. Her hair had a unique hue to it, almost as if it were made of gold. Her eyes were somewhere between green and blue, complementing the shine of her lips that Cleve thought must've had some sort of substance added to color them.

It made him wonder if her hair was dyed as well. The way it

glimmered didn't seem natural, like Reela's hair...*could she be an Elf?*

Her ears were covered...no way to be certain. Her creamy skin could be Elvish, the same with her soft features, her dainty nose, her rounded chin.

"Follow me," Azaylee said, her cheerful tone on the verge of excited.

Cleve expected there to be stairs, only to find out that the massive tower was built without them. Its entrance led them into an enormous room that was nearly the entire building. All along its walls were stained-glass windows, coloring the piercing sunlight into rainbows.

A stone walkway led them between two pools of water. Walking behind Azaylee, Cleve still had little idea what to think of her. She was pretty—clearly more so in her youth than now, but she still had the confidence of a woman in her prime.

Passing by a table with a bowl of fruit, she picked up a peach and bit into it.

As Jek started to reach toward the bowl, she spoke without turning. "No food for those on trial." Her tone was indifferent, as if she wouldn't mind if the rule was broken just this once.

Jek's hand froze. Slowly it slid into his pants pocket. But then, as if testing the temperature of water, he brought his other hand toward the bowl.

"No food!" Azaylee shouted this time, only now turning to face Jek, folding her arms with a glare.

"How did you know?" Jek asked.

Her smile was back, seemingly genuine, to Cleve's surprise.

"Keep up." She turned again, quickening her pace.

Jek looked at the fruit once more, scratching his head.

"Just leave it," Cleve whispered, putting his hand on Jek's arm.

Nodding, the mage continued forward.

Azaylee led them to a boxed room within the tower.

"This is the trial chamber." She opened the door but turned

and stood in the doorway, pointing at Jaffo. "You first," she demanded. "Cleve and Jek, wait out here and don't try to come in no matter what you hear." She waited for them to agree.

"Fine," Jek said, while Cleve nodded.

She gestured for Jaffo to enter, following him and then shutting and bolting the door behind them.

Cleve had brought his sword, Jek his wand, but Azaylee had asked neither of them to remove their weapons. Normally, it would've made Cleve more comfortable for his sword to remain with him. But in this case, he took it as a sign to be even more uneasy.

"How confident she must be not to care about our weapons," Cleve said, leaning against an outer wall of the boxed room.

"I don't like this," Jek said. "There's something about her that's familiar. Is it the same for you?"

"Not at all," Cleve admitted.

Jek let out a hum, stroking his chin. "I'm not sure what it could be."

"How long do you suppose Lysha would wait for us before leaving?"

Jek shrugged. "A day, maybe. She's probably already gone. Raymess didn't need to be in the care of a chemist for too long, and I'm sure Vala was eager to get back to the palace."

"Do you know the way back?" Cleve asked, hopeful Jek did. He'd had enough adventures already without getting lost in the middle of Zav.

"I do," Jek said confidently.

During their silence, Cleve pressed his ear against the door to listen. He could hear murmurs, but nothing above that.

Then a scream startled him. It was a man's voice—had to be Jaffo's.

The screaming grew louder. Cleve could hear words: "No, no! Please, no!"

For a blink, Cleve thought to kick down the door, but he

wisely remembered Azaylee's warning not to disturb them. He reminded himself that Jaffo was part of the group that had wanted to hold them hostage for Bastial steel swords.

Still, he couldn't ignore the empathy that clawed within him, begging him to make the screams stop by any means necessary.

"No, don't do it!" Jaffo continued to yell. A guttural howl of pain followed.

Jek pounded on the door. "Bastial hell, what's happening?" he yelled. But the screams within continued, overpowering Jek's voice.

And then there were none, no sounds at all.

Jek pounded again. "Jaffo!"

The door's latch slid undone with a crash, and the door was pulled open. "Do not touch my door!" Azaylee warned Jek with such malice in her eyes that Cleve felt the chill just for thinking of breaking it down.

She moved aside to let Jaffo hobble out from behind her, holding a bloody hand. He looked pale, his knees buckling under the weight of each step.

Azaylee caught up to him, sliding something into his shirt pocket. "Don't forget this." She patted his chest, and then Cleve saw it was his finger.

Azaylee calmly walked back to the doorway. "You," she pointed at Cleve. "You're next."

Cleve kept his hand near the handle of his sword as he entered. He could hear Jek gulp down a dry swallow behind him.

Cleve didn't know who this woman was, but she was in for a surprise if she tried to take his finger. This thought was the only thing keeping him calm for the moment, though he could feel panic beginning to stir when she bolted the door behind him.

"Sit or stand?" she asked, walking past him toward a garish seat lined with gold and studded with diamonds.

He waited for her to seat herself before answering.

"Stand."

"Very well," she said, her tone morose as if she'd expected his answer and didn't like it.

The room was square and large, with nothing to take the attention of his eye except for one other person sitting at a table against a side wall. He held a knife with one hand, his expression numb, as if he didn't know or care that Cleve was even there.

Walking forward, Cleve got a glimpse under the table and noticed the man had no legs.

"Don't worry about him," Azaylee said. "It's me you should be thinking about."

Cleve noticed the familiar interruption of psyche then. She was stirring in his thoughts like a spider crawling around in his hair. She was far more powerful than Lysha. He wondered if she might even be close to the same ability as Rek.

He felt a bead of sweat slide down his temple. "Are you an Elf?" Cleve decided to ask, preparing a mental wall.

Her face held shock, her head snapping back and her eyes widening. Before answering, she leaned forward again, using a finger to gesture for Cleve to come closer. He took one step and waited.

"Come on," she urged.

He continued, giving another glance to the legless man to his side. He seemed to be looking right through Cleve.

Azaylee continued to motion for Cleve to come toward her until he was close enough to touch. She stood, and his heart shook. With both hands, she grabbed his head.

Paralyzed with fear, no thoughts came. He was hers in that moment; he could feel it. All his strength was gone. Not ready for this, his diminutive wall had crumbled. He was an empty shell, and she'd already cracked him open.

"And why would you ask if I'm an Elf?" Azaylee said in a threatening tone, not even pretending to hide the importance of the question. "Have you heard anything about me before?"

"No. But I know Elves who are very powerful psychics."

She parted her hair to show her round Human ears. "I'm no Elf, but I do respect them greatly."

She released her grasp on him. Cleve nearly fell stepping away from her, tripping over nothing. He felt his thoughts returning, filling him back with strength in the same way a meal does to satisfy a famished body.

"Most people don't even believe in psyche, and here you've figured out I'm a psychic within the first moment of your trial."

So the trial has started?

Azaylee was waiting for his reply, tilting her head as if expecting him to answer a specific question.

But he had one of his own for her. "Why did you take Jaffo's finger?"

"Why do you think you can ask the questions here?"

Cleve decided to be honest, figuring perhaps that was the reason Jaffo had lost his finger—lying.

"Because you haven't told me not to ask a question, and I'm not familiar with the rules."

She didn't find any entertainment in his answer, her mouth twisting in disapproval. "There are no rules, just decisions—my decisions. And now I have decided that you will not ask any more questions." She leaned forward, waiting.

"Fine," Cleve said.

Leaning back, she continued. "Jaffo lost his finger because he tried to hide the truth, something you will not do, correct?"

"There's no truth I'd wish to hide."

"Not about what happened last night, but I have some other questions that need answering now...after your 'Elf' comment."

Cleve sighed, figuring he could've been out of here already if he'd kept his mouth shut like he usually did. *It's Jessend's fault,* he told himself. *My barrier's been down for so long, I tend to let out thoughts and curiosities I never used to.*

He wanted to put all the blame on her, but really he knew

he should be thanking the Princess. Life had only gotten easier since their talks. He'd never realized how much of a burden holding back his emotions had been until he was able to let them out.

"Tell me everything you know about me," Azaylee said. She gestured at the seat next to Cleve, inviting him with her hand to sit. He did, taking out his sword to rest on his lap as he spoke.

"You're the leader of this village, and no one seems to oppose you. You take people's fingers if you decide to, so it seems to me you can really do anything you want, probably through the use of psyche." Cleve couldn't think of anything else, so he stopped.

"Do you sing?" Her tone made Cleve exceedingly curious. Her question was asked with a rising pitch, as if the answer to it wasn't important. But clearly it was, for it had nothing to do with what they were just talking about.

"Or," she continued, "do you know a lot of songs?"

"I don't," Cleve admitted. "The only song I've heard that you would know is *Come Home*, but I don't even know the words."

Her eyes squinted in disbelief. "I can tell you're being honest, but I don't understand how it's possible? Even a child knows more than one song."

"I'm not from here. I came across the Starving Ocean from Kyrro."

She licked her lips as she leaned back, her genuine smile returning. "Then that's all I need to know about that."

Cleve couldn't figure out why songs would be important to Azaylee, but clearly they were. She even seemed relieved to change the subject.

"Jaffo already told me what happened yesterday. You won't be punished for defending yourself, but there's something I want to know. You've chosen Goldram's side in this war even though you're from the continent of Ovira. What's your reasoning for this?"

Cleve remembered this village had no association with Zav or any other kingdom. So why was she curious? He almost asked, but he didn't feel it wise to go against her rule of no questions.

"I've seen what Waywen and Presoren tried to do. They used spies in an attempt to kill the Kings of Zav and Goldram, along with a young child. It would've worked too, if I hadn't stopped them. It was then that I knew my side had been chosen...at least while I'm here."

"You're leaving?"

"I'm going back to Kyrro as soon as possible. My home is there, and a war is being fought."

Someone knocked on the door. Jek's voice followed it. "Cleve, everything alright in there?"

Azaylee jumped to her feet, nearly growling with anger.

"Everything's fine!" Cleve called, before Azaylee could erupt. "Stay away from the door."

With her hands wrapped around the armrests of her chair, she stood and looked like she was undecided about what she wanted to do.

Cleve was relieved when only silence followed, and she slowly sat back down.

"You make it seem as if Presoren and Waywen are the only territories to use spies and kill children," she said with some disdain. "But every kingdom is the same. We've had attackers from Zav, Presoren, even a group from Waywen years ago. Considering how far north they are, we were dumbfounded they had any interest in this village until we found out later about their alliance with Presoren just south of us." She flipped some of her curly golden hair over her shoulder. "We defended ourselves each time, but many lives were lost."

"What do Presoren and Waywen want in this war?" The moment his question escaped his lips, Cleve cursed himself aloud. "I apologize. I momentarily forgot your rule."

She stood again, her grip tightening on the armrests of her

chair. Cleve stood as well, taking a step back.

His old fear of psychics returned in that moment, making him feel like a child at the mercy of a full-grown man. Although, this was no man before him, but a woman more than twice his age and half his weight.

It didn't matter. He could feel her ready to strike, a snake coiling back before a lunge. She lifted her hand, pointing, her sharp nails stained red by some substance Cleve wasn't familiar with.

"Let it be the last time you *forget* my rules if you want to leave with all your fingers. Now sit."

With a surge of psyche like a gust of wind, his body screamed at him to be seated. His knees gave out and he fell back into the chair, utter satisfaction for following the order rippling through his body.

Then it passed, and the fear returned. His nerves were back on edge, ready to protect him from an unknown force that could attack at any moment.

Unable to relax, he sat forward, gripping the handle of his weapon firmly.

"Everyone wants the same thing," Azaylee said. "Bastial steel. Nothing is more valuable in this world than a rare and deadly weapon."

"So you think psychics would be treated differently," Cleve couldn't help but comment.

"There's a major difference between a Bastial steel sword and a psychic," Azaylee said. "My kind is not understood. People fear what they cannot see, what they cannot touch, what they cannot feel, and what they cannot hear. Psyche is all four of these things combined. Bastial steel is none of them."

Cleve understood, for it was that exact reason he had feared psyche so much. He used to think of it like an invisible tidal wave, a force of power crashing down on him so strong and quick, there was no hope of defending against it. But instead of his body being crushed, it would reach into the depths of his mind, pushing out all his secrets and fears until he was empty.

"Bastial steel should've been used to fight the desmarls." Azaylee looked as if she wanted to spit. "Instead, Danvell Takary used it to further his wealth and power. Greed..." She shook her head. "Greed doesn't go well with Bastial steel, and ten years later, Greenedge is still driven to war by the combination of both."

She pointed at Cleve's lap. "You've felt the power in your own hands. Yet, you sit there and judge others for going to war over it—I can feel these thoughts steaming off you."

"I agree with you," Cleve said. "The weapons should be used against the desmarls, not against each other."

"But would you give your weapon to someone else to use against the desmarls?"

Cleve wanted to tell her he would, but he knew he'd be lying. "I need the weapon to protect myself and my home. The use I make of it is just as important as fighting the desmarls."

"Just as important *to you*," Azaylee corrected. "Everyone shares this same thought. Don't you see? You're just like us and everyone else involved in this war. My villagers want the weapons for their own reasons, but I can assure you they believe their reasons to be just as important as your reasons."

She stood, walking toward Cleve. "There's a common belief shared among many in Greenedge. People say that good deeds will bring forth rewards and bad deeds will be punished. It's such a popular belief, there's even a phrase for it: 'the cycle'. But what people who believe this don't realize is that, if 'the cycle' really existed, it would have to follow some sort of universal law of morality controlled by some higher force than man. It would mean there were definitive rights and wrongs in the world, each deed categorized as one or the other and punished appropriately."

Azaylee continued to approach Cleve as she spoke. "But everyone knows there's no universal law of morality. Justice is decided by people—the punishments and rewards we invoke on one another. When I ask if someone believes in a universal law of morality, meaning every action is either right or wrong and will be punished or rewarded appropriately by a force outside the control of man, they always say they do not. But then, if I ask them if they believe in 'the cycle,' many will say they do!" She was nearly shouting. "That's because people often haven't taken the time to actually consider what they're really saying they believe in. To say 'the cycle' exists is to say there is a universal law of morality."

She scoffed. "People are fools, and you are as well if you think you can use that sword for *good*." She practically spat the word. "There's no good! There's just *is*."

She was nearly to Cleve by then, and he jumped from his seat when he saw she wasn't stopping. He backed up to keep his distance. But Azaylee followed, even picking up her pace.

"You're an honest man," she said. "Strong in your beliefs. But you still have a lot to learn about right and wrong. I think you've either forgotten how young you are or you haven't truly realized it. What's your age?"

"Seventeen," Cleve answered, nearly pushed to the door now.

"Take my advice, Cleve. Run home to Kyrro and don't come back. The worst years of Greenedge are yet to come."

Cleve had his back against the door. With his sword in hand, he contemplated raising it to fend her off but knew it would be little use against her psyche.

She reached out her hand, pressing her palm against his cheek. Pain swelled into his body, causing his grip to loosen and his sword to fall. He refrained from screaming, not wanting to startle Jek into making the situation worse.

Instead, he whimpered like a sniveling child, falling to his knees. "Stop," he managed to get out.

He didn't fight the psyche, not then. He wasn't prepared for this and couldn't ignore the pain enough to get his mental wall up.

"Tell one person a single detail about me, and this pain you feel will be bliss compared to what I have prepared for you. Understand?"

"Yes!" Cleve would've said anything to make it stop.

She let go of him, his whole body puddled to the floor.

"Get up," she said, unlatching the door and nudging him with her foot. "And get out."

By the time Cleve was up, the door was open and Jek was staring in with wide eyes. "Cleve—"

"I'm fine," Cleve interrupted, sheathing his weapon and putting up his hands to show he still had all his fingers.

Jek let out a breath of relief.

But then Azaylee told Jek it was his turn, and Cleve saw him stiffening once again.

Chapter 27

Cleve paced in front of the door until he no longer felt the rapid heartbeats against his chest, then he sat.

Jaffo was gone, the trail of blood he'd left already joining the other stains along the stone walkway to the exit. *She puts no effort into cleaning up their blood, probably enjoys seeing it as she busies herself in this tower during the day...doing who knows what.*

Though he'd just sat, Cleve couldn't sit any longer.

Getting up to walk about the tower, his first decision was to investigate the bowl of fruit. Cleve wondered if Jek had decided to take something during Cleve's trial.

He hadn't.

The fruit was tempting, even now after witnessing Azaylee's power firsthand. *She ate right in front of us,* he realized, *as if daring us to take it.*

He ran his finger down a banana, testing its firmness. His mouth started to water as he wondered how he could hide the peel.

There was a shout.

Jek! Cleve ran to the door, pressing his ear against it.

The shouting stopped, replaced by Azaylee's infuriated voice. Her words were muffled by the wall between them, but her exasperated tone came through as clear as the pristine pools of water within the tower.

Jek screamed again, this time louder and lasting an entire breath.

"Jek, what's happening?" Cleve yelled. "Are you alright?"

Just kick it in! a voice screamed.

No, I shouldn't.

Cleve tried to resist the urge, but he was receiving no reply to his previous question about Jek's well-being.

Jek's scream worsened. It sounded now as if he was being tortured. That was enough for Cleve.

The span of a heartbeat was all he needed to gather the necessary Bastial Energy into his right leg. He leaned back and began to kick with the heel of his boot, putting all his weight into it.

He didn't count how many times he kicked before the door burst open.

Storming into the room with his sword in hand, the first thing Cleve saw was Jek on the floor, his head against his knees and his hands over his temples. His screaming stopped momentarily when Azaylee no longer held her palm out at Jek, but at Cleve instead.

She yelled, "Stop right there!"

Cleve was content to listen so long as Jek was no longer being harmed. But just after he obeyed, Jek said something that jolted Cleve back into motion.

"She's going to kill me..." His tone was strained. With heavy breaths, it seemed as if it took all his strength to utter the words.

Jek tried to pick himself up, only to fall back down with another scream, Azaylee's outstretched arm pointed back at him.

Cleve ran at Azaylee. She lifted her other palm at him and pain took his feet out, as if a sword had slashed across his knees and shins. After he hit the ground, it started to feel like she was twisting his muscles together.

But the worst of it was in his head, a tearing sensation. He was ready for it this time, though.

Before his wall crumbled completely, he focused to rebuild it.

She was strong. It felt like her whole hand was in his mind, squeezing, clawing, tearing out pieces of him like a madwoman.

He imagined grabbing her wrist to try tugging her out. She needed to be gone before he could get his wall up again. The focus it took made him scream, his body on the verge of convulsing from pain.

Then it dulled as he fought, just barely, but enough for him to get back on his feet. He trudged forward, feeling as if he were walking against a windstorm. He felt a stinging sensation throughout his whole body, as if a thousand bees had covered his skin and pricked him at once.

This was her changing her spell, he could feel it. This was her ultimate power being unleashed.

Cleve collapsed once more, unable to bear his own weight. He knew he was losing, his strength quickly fading.

Searching through past lessons with Rek, his mind was desperate to find something to fight this. *"Go someplace else,"* he remembered Rek telling him after hours of failing. *"If you can't get me out, then bring yourself out. Imagine you're somewhere else, move your mind and body with it, and replace your sense of pain with love. It's far stronger."*

Cleve had never done it successfully before, but it was his only hope now. He tried to imagine Reela, being somewhere with her that was safe. He wanted to feel her in his arms, but he couldn't do it. It wasn't working.

With a chill of relief down his neck, his next thoughts were of him and Jessend in bed, cuddled close together, holding each other tight. Never had he felt safer than then, with her small body clutching him with such surprising strength.

He felt a wave of relaxation come over him, but it only lasted until he got back on his feet. The sting came again, shattering his thoughts like a hammer to glass.

He wanted to ask why Azaylee was doing this. Why kill them?

What did Jek say to make you this way? But he barely could see straight from the pain.

He needed something else to escape the agony, to comfort

him. Luckily, a thought came to him—Kasko. Cleve saw himself throwing a dagger at the evil little man, then slicing his head off. He was dead. Cleve had killed him, and Cleve could see himself there in the cabin, doing it over and over as he pushed himself a step forward and then another.

Burning came next to replace the stinging, as if he were walking into an oven.

He felt as if he should see his arms and legs on fire...if he looked down. But he chose not to.

Instead, he squinted to see his target—a now grunting Azaylee. He'd gotten farther than he thought. She was just a few more steps in front of him. Her teeth were clenched, her brow creased in worry.

Lysha was next in Cleve's mind, her silly annoyance at his attempts to get more comfortable sleeping beside her. It wasn't enough to distract him, to comfort him by bringing him out of this painful moment, and so it too was broken apart easily.

The closer he got to Azaylee, the more powerful her spell.

Cleve could feel himself about to fall again, his body giving out. His heart would be next.

Psyche really can kill, he realized.

It was too much for his body to endure, too much at once, at least.

Pain, he told himself. He knew pain well, had dealt with it nearly his whole life. *That's all this is,* he told himself. *Pain.*

Then Cleve saw his parents. Dizziness nearly overcame him with the image of them. He hadn't pictured them in years, but there they were, bright and full of life. He felt unrestricted tears flowing from his eyes.

His father, Dex...they were in the forest together. Cleve was just a little boy. His mother, Lena, was there as well. It wasn't even a memory, or it didn't feel like one. He was *there.*

"This is for you," Dex said, kneeling down to present a short sword to Cleve. His father's blond hair was rustled by the wind, but his wide smile remained steady.

Lena gasped dramatically. "Look at what Father has gotten you for your birthday!"

Cleve was old enough to know that his mother wasn't really as enthusiastic as she pretended to be, but he was too excited to care. Reaching out toward the weapon, he waited for his father's permission to touch it.

"Go ahead," Dex said. "It's yours."

But his mother knelt down and put her arm around Cleve's shoulders before he could. "Remember what we talked about, Cleve. What is the point of the weapon?"

It was hard to take his gaze off of it, but he looked to his mother for a sign of the answer. The wind made her hair dance, brown like the trees around them. She didn't have the same smile as his father, at least not in that moment. She looked intensely into his eyes, waiting for him to answer.

But he didn't know what she wanted to hear. What was the point of the weapon to a child like him?

"I know you know," Lena said. "Just think about it."

Only wrong answers came to mind: to hurt, to kill, to defend myself, to learn to fight.

He could recall the respect his father made him learn later, when he gave Cleve his first bow. But Cleve couldn't remember the point of a weapon in the first place. Was there one? Of course. But it was different for every person, so what did his mother have in mind?

"Tell me," she said, pointing to it. "What does this sword mean to you?"

He remembered the answer then. It came back to him as she squeezed his shoulder and parted the hair that had fallen in front of his eyes.

"A weapon is nothing but a way for us to express ourselves," he said. To his ears, his childlike voice was like the squeak of a mouse. But it didn't stop him from remembering what he was taught. "It's never a reason to do anything we wouldn't normally do with our bare hands. It is *us* who make the decision of how and when to use it, not the weapon."

She nodded, encouraging him to continue. "And?" She wiggled her wand in front of him. "When would I use this on another person?"

Cleve swallowed hard as the words came to him. "Never."

"That's right." She smiled and stood.

"Never?" Dex blurted, standing to match her. "Why are you teaching him that? What if his life is in danger—can he use the weapon then?"

"His life won't be in danger until he's old enough to know that answer for himself. Isn't that right?" Lena retorted.

Dex let out a defeated laugh. Kneeling back down, he said, "Your mother's very wise. It's best you listen to her."

"I know," Cleve muttered, grasping the sword carefully by the handle.

The moment he touched it, he was back in the tower with his own sword in hand. He could see the fear in Azaylee's eyes, for he just needed one more step to reach her.

Sweat made her hair stick to her cheeks and forehead. She was against the wall, nowhere to go. Her psyche couldn't stop him. It was clear to the both of them now.

Knowing his mother would approve of his choice to use his weapon, all his strength returned, and he drove his blade into Azaylee's stomach.

She collapsed, gasping in pain.

He raised his sword to end her suffering, but Jek painfully grunted out, "Wait!" and knelt down in front of her. "Why kill me just because I found out who you are?" Jek asked her. "Why is it so important to you?"

"Because *she's* a failure," Azaylee muttered, sliding down against the wall and holding her stomach. "I'd rather die than be haunted by her mistakes as I have been for so many years." A wave of coughing interrupted her. She wiped blood from her mouth. "I control this land, this village. This is who I really am. And I have plans for more. Golden Girl is dead. There will be a new song once Azaylee is known across the world."

Jek looked up at Cleve from his knees, his expression perplexed. Cleve could tell they were thinking the same thing. *She doesn't realize she's going to die?*

Was it right to tell her? Cleve didn't know. Though, he felt even worse about the idea of leaving her like that—to die alone.

Well, she's not completely alone if we leave. Cleve looked at the legless man once more, still at the table with his knife. He was disinterested, somehow even then. *Yeah...alone,* Cleve concluded.

Then he thought of something she might want, perhaps a dying wish. "What would you like us to tell the villagers?" Cleve asked.

Azaylee lost her breath for a moment, swallowing a gulp of blood that had climbed to her mouth through her previous coughing. Her strength was gone, her eyes no longer seeing him or Jek.

Her breath did not come back. Her head sank to her chest.

"She's dead," Jek said, getting to his feet.

"Let's get out of here," Cleve said, feeling an urgency to flee.

"One moment." Something about Azaylee seemed to draw Jek's interest. He leaned down and removed her golden necklace. It matched her hair.

"Lisanda might like this," Jek said.

Cleve reached out to stop him, grabbing his wrist. "Have you no respect for the dead?" Cleve glanced over his shoulder to make sure no one had come into the tower.

"Not when she tried to kill me just moments ago."

Cleve sighed. He couldn't argue with that. "Fine."

"Since you're so decisive about the rules of the dead, what do you want to do with her?" Jek didn't take his eyes off Azaylee's body as he spoke, as if waiting for her to come back to life. Leaving as soon as possible didn't seem nearly as vital to the mage as it did to Cleve.

"I don't know," Cleve admitted, having an easier time looking away from her body than Jek. His eyes found the legless man seated at the table with a knife. It piqued Cleve's curiosity.

"You have no words for what just happened?" Cleve asked him.

But the man's gaze did not shift. It remained steady, fixed in their general direction.

Cleve waved. "Can you hear me?"

"Go put your finger on his table and see what happens," Jek said jokingly.

Cleve didn't find it humorous. "I think we should forget about her and leave as quickly as we can."

"That's good with me." Jek knelt once more, this time to stick his hands in Azaylee's pockets.

Cleve couldn't help but sigh.

"Judge me all you want," Jek said. "I'm curious what she has on her." He pulled out a folded paper and opened it for a read.

Cleve waited for Jek to tell him what was on it. But the mage simply put it in his pocket, then started toward the exit at a lively pace. "She can rot in this tower for all I care," he muttered. "She would've killed me."

Cleve followed after him. "Not going to tell me what it says?"

"Now look who's curious," Jek teased. "I couldn't if I wanted to. It's in Elvish. Lisanda can read it, though."

Elvish? Suddenly everything came back—Azaylee's insecurities of what Cleve had heard about her, her reason for wanting to kill Jek.

"You said you found out who she was, and that's why she wanted to kill you," Cleve said, now out of the boxed room and shutting the door behind him. "Who was she?"

"Have you heard the song *Golden Girl*?"

"No."

"It was the first song I sang with Lisanda," Jek said, letting his eyes drift to a memory for a moment. "Apparently, it's a true story about Azaylee and her family. She was the youngest of four gifted sisters." Jek opened the door of the tower to leave, keeping it open for Cleve and shutting it the moment he passed through. "She was the only blonde girl in the family, and her parents had great expectations for her, hence the 'Golden Girl' name that—"

Jek stopped when he turned and saw the two men in front of them. Cleve didn't recognize either of them. They were clad in armor, each with a sword on his hip.

"That was a short trial," one of them commented, lifting his head for a glimpse over Cleve's shoulder. "Where's Azaylee?"

Cleve could think of no answer he wished to give. Jek couldn't seem to, either.

"Where is she..." the man asked again, his curiosity completely gone now. He held on to the hilt of his sword, not drawing it yet.

"She's sleeping," Jek said. "It would be wise not to disturb her."

"Sleeping, at this time?" The men shared a glance. "We heard Jaffo had a finger taken. Is it true?"

"Yes," Jek answered.

Cleve was content letting Jek handle this. Trying to lie his way out of a situation had always resulted in failure, so Cleve usually just stuck with the truth and dealt with the consequences. But he was thankful that Jek was there to fib. He knew there was no way they could reveal the truth and still leave this village peacefully.

"So, she let you both go without punishment, it seems." Though it wasn't a question, the way the man phrased it was as if it could be.

"She did, and if you men don't mind, we'd like to be leaving now." Jek started walking around them, Cleve following close behind with his eyes ready to detect movement.

The men said nothing as Cleve passed them, just watched with silent stares.

There had been enough death recently. Cleve dearly hoped these men would suppress their suspicions.

He and Jek didn't look back, not at first. Doing so would've been too obvious. But the moment Cleve was far enough that the tension had dissolved, he shot a look over his shoulder.

The two men were still there, standing by the door and conversing with each other. One man's eyes found Cleve's, so he quickly turned back to face forward.

It soon became difficult to maintain a slow pace. So when they turned and put a house between them and the men, Cleve and Jek started into a sprint.

"Our horses still better be there," Jek said.

Chapter 28

Jek tried the door to Jaffo's house without a knock. He nearly fell inside when it opened, clearly expecting the door to be locked.

Jaffo was seated at a table with his hand bandaged, a chemist standing beside him—the same one they'd brought the boy to last night.

"We need our horses," Jek said, making no effort to hide his urgency. "Can you unlock the barn?"

"Already have," Jaffo answered in a meek voice. "What did she—?"

"Thank you," Jek interrupted, turning so quickly he nearly ran into Cleve on his way out the door.

Cleve turned to follow, only to stop and glimpse Jaffo over his shoulder. "I'm sorry about your finger." He didn't wait for a response.

Jek was already in the barn when Cleve stepped outside.

"You!" someone shouted.

Cleve's heart jumped when he turned to see five armed men rushing toward him.

"Don't you run," one of them warned him.

But it was too late for that. Into the barn he went, untying Nulya in such a hurry he didn't know his hands could move so fast.

He could hear the boots of the men behind him, then the scared whinnying of Jaffo's horses by the door as the men stormed into the barn.

By the time Cleve was on his horse, Jek was beside him on his, and the five men stood between them and the doorway. One of them had enough presence of mind to close the door, *or maybe it was stupidity,* Cleve corrected himself. Luckily, there was no lock on the inside.

They drew their swords, Cleve and Jek drawing their weapons as well.

"I don't know how you killed her," one man said as he stepped forward, "but you'll die for this."

"She was going to kill me," Jek argued. "It was the only way to stop her."

"If she'd decided to take your life, then she must've had good reason."

"Murderers!" another man shouted from the back.

"And they took her necklace as well," someone else joined in.

Cleve could've spit if he'd had the time. *More death.*

Was there any way out of this? What would his mother say right now if she were here? He looked to Jek, hoping the mage had thought of something.

But his wand was out, pointed at the lot of them. He'd clearly given up on words. So it was up to Cleve.

With a frightening lack of confidence, he sheathed his sword, and pushed out his palms. "Listen to me," he started. At least it got their attention. Though, none of them put away their weapons. "This doesn't need to end with the loss of more lives." He gestured at Jek. "My friend is right. She would've killed him, and it definitely wasn't for a good reason. She's Golden Girl...from the song." Cleve dearly hoped they knew what this meant, for Jek still hadn't explained enough for Cleve to know himself.

Cleve continued, "Jek figured that out, and Azaylee would've killed him to keep that information secret."

He noticed a few of them lowering their swords, most sharing looks of confusion.

"That's just a song," the man in front said, speaking as if he was prepared to be proven wrong. "She can't be Golden Girl...Golden Girl doesn't exist."

"She does," Jek answered. "Or she did. Your leader was the

powerful psychic from the song—the one who lived with the Elves for years, and when she returned, she was cast out by her own family. You must've already known she was a powerful psychic?"

An eerie silence followed. *Why aren't they responding? Could it be none of them knew?* "Have any of you met her?" Cleve asked.

"I have." The man in front answered proudly, too proudly for Cleve's taste, for he knew what was coming next. "And she was no psychic!"

"Ask Jaffo!" Jek yelled. "She must've used psyche to convince him to allow his finger to be cut off."

"No," the man in front answered, shaking his head. "Jaffo knows she's our leader and to go against her is the same as forfeiting his life."

The men raised their swords again, a hardened look in each of their squinted eyes.

Cleve had spent enough time around men who wanted to fight to know there was no way out of this now.

He dismounted, stepping in front of Nulya to make sure she wouldn't be injured. Jek jumped off his mount as well.

"Finally decided to give up?" the man in front asked, his tone more disappointed than hopeful.

"No," Cleve answered for them. "We're ready to fight if you don't move."

"It would be a good idea to move," Jek added. "My friend here is—"

A dagger was thrown at Jek. He ducked. The startled horses cried out as the men came.

Jek sent a fireball. It exploded within the group of them, sending two to the ground. Cleve jumped in front of the other three storming toward Jek.

They slashed wildly. It was clear they figured he wouldn't be able to defend himself against all of them at once. And it was true. Cleve had to jump back. But with little room behind him, he needed to make something happen now.

He swung in a wide forward thrust, surprising the overconfident men with the speed of his attack. He opened the stomach of one of them, catching another on the arm.

Jek sent a fireball at the third.

When the burst of light faded, only one man was still standing, holding his injured arm, his sword on the ground.

Realizing it was over, he raised his good arm outward. "Fine, leave. But word of your actions is already spreading, so don't think the rest of the village will let you out of here."

Jek sighed loudly. "Of course not. That would be too easy."

Cleve leapt past the fallen men to open the door. Jek followed with the reins of their horses in hand.

Cleve took one look back at the last man standing. He was crouching over his wounded comrades, despair beginning to strike his face.

Cleve was surprised to find he had no remorse for them. *There's only so much compassion I can give, and it's all been used up,* he figured.

His patience was gone as well—anyone else who stood in their way would fall.

With looks over their shoulders, Jek and Cleve swung up onto their horses and began riding at a trot. The winding pathways between houses didn't allow them to go much faster.

They made a turn and found the path to be crowded by people conversing, trading, and exchanging goods. Unaware of another route, they slowed and continued forward, dismounting to walk their horses by.

Someone tugged on Cleve's shirt. "What happened with Azaylee?" It was a girl's voice.

Turning, he saw it was the same girl as before, the one who'd nearly thrown him from his mount. Her eyes were red, her long hair unkempt.

Cleve continued forward, hoping she would let go of him if he ignored her.

She didn't. Instead, she used her other hand to grab his wrist, pulling him back even harder.

"I need to leave," he told her, unwilling to snatch his arm away with the sight it would create.

A few dozen people had encircled him and Nulya by then. Jek had stopped ahead, looking back to see why Cleve wasn't following.

"Did they really take Jaffo's finger?" The girl didn't let go of Cleve.

"Yes, but not mine or Jek's. You can go see Jaffo. I need to leave now." Cleve continued forward, dragging her behind him, as she didn't let go.

"I don't want to stay here any longer," the girl said, moving her hands up and clinging tighter to his bicep than a wet shirt.

Cleve looked around for the girl's mother, but he found no one with her. "Where are your parents? Go to them."

"I hate them. They pretend to be sad that Olmi's dead, but I know they're actually happy. They didn't like me with him. I can't stand their faces or their fake feelings." She lowered her voice, leaning in. "Take me with you."

Jek had dragged his horse back into the crowd by then. "What's going on?"

"I want to come with you!" the girl shouted now. A few heads turned. Murmurs began. Cleve heard two people realizing aloud that he and Jek were the ones responsible for Enri's death.

"That's them," someone else said, pointing.

Alarmed chatter broke out, and Cleve felt more than just the girl's hands on him.

"Did they have their trial?"

"We haven't heard from Azaylee."

"Stop them!" a man's voice boomed louder than everyone else's. "They killed Azaylee!"

Then ten people were shouting at once.

Someone jumped on Cleve's back. He thrashed to create

some space. It scared Nulya enough to rear up.

He managed to get on her back before she could gallop off. Jek was on his mount also, riding beside him.

People were shouting for their heads now, chasing after them. Those in front, within earshot of the hostile crowd, turned, but they didn't seem to know what to do. With palms out, they stood their ground for a moment before jumping out of the way when Nulya didn't slow.

The gate wasn't far ahead, which Cleve realized was actually a problem. They couldn't distance themselves far enough from the mob before they got there, and anyone guarding the exit would hear the angry shouts to stop Cleve and Jek.

They took a turn and saw another group of people who acted as if they would stop the horses, only to jump out of the way when they realized it would be impossible.

The houses became sparse. The ten-foot-high wooden wall could be seen just ahead. Cleve unsheathed his sword when he saw the three men there.

One turned to put some sort of lock across the opening of the wooden gate, the other two pointing their weapons and yelling at Cleve and Jek to stop.

"Move or die!" Jek shouted, now just in front of Cleve.

The man who'd locked the gate decided to run, but the other two cursed him and remained steady.

Cleve felt nothing but urgency. He didn't worry for these men's lives. He couldn't in that moment. If they slowed their exit, then Cleve and Jek would just have to deal with more people—possibly more lives he would need to take. Anger surged through Cleve at the thought of it. He blamed the two in front of him for the possibility of needing to kill more.

He jumped off his mount, charging at them with one last warning: "Move!"

They didn't, attacking instead.

He easily dodged one man's thrust and finished him with a clean slice across his neck. The other was taken by Jek's fireball.

Done with them, Cleve turned his focus to the lock holding the gate shut. To Cleve's dismay, he found it wasn't a simple lock but a thick bar of steel held in place by several smaller locks.

He searched the fallen guards for keys for a breath before giving up.

Jek blasted the gate with fire to no avail.

"Use your sword!" Jek shouted

"It'll ruin it." The moment Cleve spoke, he realized how absurd he sounded. Yes, he was right—the sword would be ruined being bashed against metal and wood until it broke through, but the alternative of not escaping was much worse.

The mob of angry villagers had grown. He could hear them coming, their shouts so loud it was like an oncoming tidal wave.

Jek sent another fireball against the gate. No result. Breathing heavy, he moved back to give Cleve room.

"Do it. I'll hold them off," Jek said.

In a blink, Cleve focused all the Bastial Energy within him into his arms. They were burning hot and couldn't be held still any longer.

With the strength of two men, he slammed his weapon down against the steel bar holding the gate shut. A sting of pain just as torturous as Azaylee's spells shot from his fingers to his shoulders. But he didn't stop.

Letting out the agony through screams, he focused on nothing but hitting the same spot over and over. He could hear the horses being frightened, Jek yelling something to the crowd.

They're almost here. He didn't waste a moment turning around to check. He was making progress, a dent at first and then cracks soon after. His sword was chipping away, though. It might not last long enough before it cracked.

A final blow and the bar came apart with a loud snap. He

shoved the gate open and looked behind him. Jek was getting on his mount, keeping the reins of Cleve's in hand as well.

Cleve jumped on Nulya just as arrows started passing by his ears.

Out of all the shouts, one stood out—the girl's. "Wait, please!" Cleve and Jek were out of the gate, the mob slowing to a halt except for her.

She ran out after them onto the open land. No one came after her. Not one person stopped her.

As hopeless as it was, she didn't stop. She kept running and running.

The distance between them became insurmountable. Didn't she realize it? Was she that dumb? *Or maybe just that stubborn.*

Even when Cleve and Jek eventually got to the top of the hill miles out, she was still puttering after them, looking even more like a desperate child than ever as she struggled to stay on her feet.

Jek dismounted, looking down the hill with his hand over his eyes to block the high sun. "Girl's like a mooker," he said. "Won't stop chasing us."

With the villagers no longer a threat, Cleve's emotions re-emerged from wherever they'd been. Pity stuck him hard, making frustration twist within.

Why must I care what happens to this girl?

He despised her, yet couldn't bring himself to ignore her. He couldn't even look away, wondering when she would stop, figuring she couldn't possibly keep running all the way to Goldram.

But then where will she run to instead? Will she go back to her village?

"How far is the town Lysha took the Takarys to?" Cleve asked.

"About a day's ride northeast. You don't think she'll follow us there, do you?"

Cleve was so distracted by this incessant child, he'd momentarily forgotten to check his weapon. Looking at it now, he felt his heart shatter. Chunks of Bastial steel had been chipped out of it, leaving the blade grotesquely uneven and even dull in some places along one edge.

Jek noticed him looking. Putting his hand on Cleve's shoulder, he said, "It was worth it."

Cleve let out a breath, nodding to show he agreed.

"But it still won't make me feel any better about ruining it," he said.

"You probably shouldn't let Danvell Takary see how his gift turned out," Jek advised. "He might think of it as an act of disrespect."

Again, Cleve nodded.

He was so frustrated he wanted to throw the weapon off the hill, but it was a childish thought. The disfigured weapon was still more useful than a sword of regular steel, at least on one of its sides.

Nulya let out a sputter of air, her lips flapping loudly.

"Let's go," Jek calmly stated. "I want to learn what's written on this paper of Azaylee's."

Jek was right. As hard as it was for Cleve to turn his back on the desperate girl still running toward them, it was time to leave.

Chapter 29

By the time the sun was setting, they'd reached the city of Gajiri—where Lysha had taken Raymess and Vala. Guards belonging to Zav's kingdom protected the entrance.

They informed Cleve and Jek that Lysha already had left. One of them even had a note from her:

My handsome young men,

We got all the support we needed from the people in this town. Prince Raymess has made a full recovery, so I am taking him and Queen Vala back to the palace. I'll tell the Takarys that you should be close behind. Don't come into Goldram too far in the north. There have been battles around the southern edges of Waywen.

I'm coming in around Lake Mercy. I recommend doing the same. Let's celebrate when you get back.

Liquor. Lots of it.

"You know where Lake Mercy is?" Cleve asked, shortly after they thanked the guards and entered in hopes of purchasing some food.

"Yes. I've crossed from Zav to Goldram through there before, when I took Prince Harwin." Jek's eyes went unfocused as he said the boy's name. "I can't believe how close he came to being murdered. It would've been my fault for bringing him there."

"Those spies would've come up with some plan to kill him at another time," Cleve said. "And who knows who would've been there to save him...probably no one. I'm glad it occurred when it did. You were part of making that happen."

"You tease," Jek replied with a smile. "Or you're the most

modest person I've ever met."

Cleve supposed he was modest, for he certainly wasn't joking, and he'd heard something along those lines before. "Just don't call me a hero," he muttered. There was something about the word that made him cringe.

Then he realized what it was. Looking at the hills ahead, poking out from behind the city...the many miles left to travel, he felt insignificant.

Cleve had done nothing for the war in Ovira. He'd almost killed Rek, and that was it. Before he ever could be a hero, he needed to go home and fight for Kyrro. He was nothing until then.

It seemed as if Gajiri had been ravaged by a recent battle. Old fires had left their mark on the roofs and walls of many houses. People had uneasy stares for Cleve and Jek—strangers on horses. Many hobbled on a wounded leg or nursed a bandaged arm.

Before asking what happened, Cleve and Jek decided it would be wise to ask for food.

A saleswoman with a cart of fruits, dried meats, and bread wanted to see their money first, eyeing Cleve's sheathed sword for a long while before speaking.

Eating right there, Jek asked the woman, "Who attacked this village?"

"Presoren bastards," she spat out. "They were our allies ten years ago, many of their kin still living here until recently. A lot of us even have some Presoren in our blood." The way her eyes tightened made it clear she was speaking for herself, her self-disdain palpable. "Used to be a wonderful thing when I was young—when people mixed together knowing their true enemy was the desmarls. Now a group of Elves are the only ones with enough honor to fight those monsters while the rest of us fight each other."

Cleve studied Jek's face to see if this was news to the mage. His head was tilted, his blue eyes squinted skeptically.

"What is this you speak of?" Jek asked.

"You're from Goldram, right?" the saleswoman assumed, leaning forward as if ready to reveal a secret.

Jek didn't reply, not before studying her expression to see if the wrong answer might be dangerous.

But the saleswoman continued without waiting, seemingly content that her assumption was correct. "News must not have reached there yet. Everyone's heard about it in southern Zav." She leaned back with a smug grin, saying no more.

"Heard about what?" Jek asked.

"Why don't you ask the Elves yourself? You're the only people who can reach them, being in Goldram."

Cleve thought of the note in Jek's pocket, wondering if it might have to do with this rumor. But then he reminded himself that that's all this was, some rumor. In fact, it had nothing to do with Kyrro.

Still...he had to admit to himself that he was interested.

The woman seemed to enjoy knowing something they didn't, so Cleve didn't want to waste his time playing her game any longer.

"Thank you for the food," Cleve told her, putting his hand on Jek's back. "Let's go."

The mage was reluctant at first, his body turning while his head remained on the saleswoman. But with a little added force, he joined Cleve in stride.

Soon they were back to riding, their horses just as eager to get back as they were, it seemed. Nulya's rhythmic hooves didn't slow, even when they came to shallow streams.

They rode until night came, and then they continued by the light from Jek's wand.

When the mage grew weary of keeping up the white glow, they finally stopped to rest.

While sleeping, Jek had light burst from his body, waking Cleve.

"It even happens when you don't use any SE during the

day?" Cleve asked.

"Yes, because I can't stop my body from absorbing too much of it." Jek wiped the blood from the fresh wound across his chest.

Cleve despised the idea that Jek's only cure was waiting somewhere in Ovira, making Cleve responsible for bringing it back. Jek didn't deserve these nightly terrors, but Cleve couldn't bring himself to promise to return.

"There must be something in Greenedge that absorbs SE," Cleve said.

"I'm thinking the same thing, but no one I've talked to knows of anything. There's no reason anyone else might find use in a plant or animal that absorbs SE. So it's unlikely someone has the answer for me." Jek took his eyes off his wound to look up at Cleve. "How confident are you that your chemist friend would know of such a thing?"

Cleve started to yawn. He let it come out slow and long to give himself time to think of how he should answer.

He was confident Steffen would know of such a plant or animal, but only because the young chemist seemed to find interest in everything. His mind was filled with what Cleve would call useless information.

But what was the point behind giving Jek this false hope? It felt better not to. There was a chance Cleve would never see him again, even if Steffen had the answer.

Maybe Steffen would want to visit Greenedge.

Cleve tried to imagine what Steffen was doing during the war in Ovira. He'd never asked Terren what chemists' roles were.

The thought was dumb, he realized right away. Chemists had medical training as well as skill in potion creation and usage. They were responsible for injured soldiers during war, of course.

His yawn finished. An answer still hadn't come.

"I'm not sure," Cleve decided to say, lying down and

shutting his eyes in hopes Jek wouldn't continue the conversation.

I'll do everything I can, Cleve wanted to say. *When the war ends, I'll come back if I'm able to.*

Cleve didn't see any reason to say it aloud, though. As long as it was true, that's all that mattered. If Cleve never came back, yet he gave Jek the hope he would, it only would make things worse.

Days later, when they crossed around Lake Mercy, Cleve finally got the sense his adventure was coming to an end. The reality that he would be going home to Kyrro soon started to sink in.

He'd never taken the time to think about all the fighting ahead of him until then.

Just his experiences in Karri Forest and at the village in southern Zav had resulted in enough death for a lifetime. But it was really only the beginning—a daunting realization.

He'd had dreams of riding into battle on Nulya's back, wielding his red-orange Bastial steel sword, killing Krepps on either side of him. But he knew battle was far more complicated than that.

It always is.

And his sword was chipped now, so dull in some places it wouldn't even cut the skin of a Human, let alone a lizard-like Krepp.

Cleve sighed at the thought of it.

He and Jek had stopped for a quick meal, Jek looking up at the sound of Cleve's loud exhale.

"What's wrong?"

Cleve shook his head. "It's nothing."

Frustration twisted the corner of Jek's mouth. He swallowed his food, then spoke. "I don't know why you think people aren't interested in what you have to say. It's not true, you know?"

"I'm not worried about boring you," Cleve answered. "I just

don't see the reason my thoughts need to be shared when there's nothing you can do to help."

"Haven't you learned anything from Jessend? Just letting it out is helpful, even if I have no wisdom of my own to share on the topic." As if channeling the diminutive princess, Jek folded his arms in a proud fashion. "Now what's bothering you?"

Cleve let out another sigh, knowing it was easier to just tell the mage. "I've spent all this time in Greenedge, meanwhile my friends and family are fighting in Kyrro. I finally feel confident I'll return, but what difference will it really make...and what if I'm too late?" He picked up his sword, twisting it to catch the sunlight. "I'm not sure I'll even want to use this weapon anymore with one side being useless. And Nulya could be killed the first moment I take her into battle. I have no training in battle-riding."

Cleve let down his sword, beginning to feel that he was rambling...whining, even. "I'm just coming to realize that it's silly to be so eager to return. I'm just one man—a man who's wasted so much time on another continent, only to return to be part of an army that already has thousands of men just like me."

He really felt it now...sniveling like a child. That was all he was going to say.

Jek looked as if he had no reply, taking a swig from his water pouch and glancing out over the land of Goldram to the east.

"You can't honestly believe your time here was wasted." It wasn't even a question, not the way Jek's judgmental tone carried his words. "Think about all you've done for us...what could've happened if you'd never come. Think about who you were stepping off that ship and who you are now."

The two men's eyes met, and Cleve tilted his head to show skepticism.

"If you still believe it was a waste, you're either lying to me or lying to yourself," Jek said.

An itch came to Cleve's forehead. He looked away as he

scratched it.

"You're right," he admitted. "But how could you even know how I've changed?"

Jek shrugged. "We all change, especially around our age. It was a pretty safe assumption."

Cleve couldn't believe he'd had to cross the Starving Ocean just to find himself—his inner strength that Reela had discovered during their *first* conversation. He always assumed it would be her who brought it out of him. *But it was a tiny princess,* he said to himself.

Suddenly, he felt as if he hadn't done enough for the Takary family. Jessend had saved him from imprisonment in Kyrro, helped him heal old wounds he thought would just continue to fester, and even given him a means to return home with kingly gifts.

So what if his sword was chipped and dull on one side. He could get used to that. And having the only horse in Ovira would be a major advantage in times of war. Then there was Rek—Rek! How could he forget? Rek had a horse as well and should be returning with him.

I hope he's back at the palace by the time we return. Cleve couldn't even guess what had happened with him and the Elves.

Cleve's eagerness was bubbling up from his stomach once again, making it hard to sit still. He finished the rest of his meal quickly, hopping on Nulya's back and waiting for Jek. The mage rushed to stuff his mouth, standing and wiping his hands together. He mumbled something, his full mouth preventing any hope of Cleve being able to understand his words.

With that, they were off.

Chapter 30

A few days later, the walls surrounding The Nest crept into view between low hills, and a tingling sensation washed over Cleve's body. The evening sun bounced off the city, giving it a golden glow so bright Cleve couldn't look directly at it.

"Is this why it's called Goldram?" Jek wondered aloud. "I've never seen the land look like this before. Perhaps I've just never had the time to pay attention."

It made Cleve wonder something himself. "The continent is called Greenedge—is that because of the green Sartious Energy of the desmarls that have taken over the edges?"

"Yes," Jek answered. "This continent used to go by a different name until the northern and southern edges were covered by their SE mist. 'Greenedge' was just a nickname at first, from what I've heard. I don't even know the original name. I doubt many do anymore."

They kept their horses at a trot, both unwilling to risk injury to their mounts when they would be at the palace by sunset at a slower pace anyway. It also gave them time to speak, for it was painfully obvious this might be the last time they had the chance.

"Are there any competitions that award titles to the victors?" Cleve asked, thinking of Redfield.

"Competitions?" Jek questioned. "Do you mean like shotmarl?"

"I suppose," Cleve said, "if titles are awarded in that."

"Only nobles have titles, and you're asking the wrong person if you want to know what each of them means. Royalty has titles as well, prince, queen, like that. But the men who are part of the winning shotmarl team don't receive a title. Their honor comes mostly in praise, salary from their king to play in the next season, and of course fame. Did you know they're required to go fight the desmarls for a week, and Jessend's first betrothed died doing so?"

"I know," Cleve said. "I was more curious about the titles, specifically. There are a few traditions in Kyrro—competitions that result in titles for the victors. Though, with war going on, I doubt any will happen this year."

Winning the Redfield competition at the Academy and earning the champion title was always Cleve's dream before he was a student. But ever since his first day at the Academy, when he met Reela and his other roommates, that dream was lost in a sea of trouble.

He wondered why it suddenly had come back to him now. Could he be that calm about the war in Ovira to be thinking of earning himself a title?

It's strange how easy it is to remember old desires. But how rare is it for them to come back just as strong as they were when they were lost?

Cleve actually had an "adept" title granted to him from winning the weapons demonstration. *Cleve The Adept.* He'd never really liked the sound of it, even now as he said it in his head.

But to Cleve, the champion title was immeasurably better, and it lasted forever as well. The adept title was gone after a year—when the next weapons demonstration took place, it would transfer to the winner. Luckily for Cleve, he'd won each year he'd competed since the age of fourteen.

But to have a title that could be gone in an instant seemed worthless to him. He'd never entered the weapons demonstration competition for the sake of the title anyway.

He almost laughed at how much his mind had wandered during the brief pause in his conversation with Jek. There was something about titles that he could get lost in, as if the moment he started thinking about them he drifted out to sea without realizing where he was going. Next thing he knew, he didn't know which direction he'd come from.

"Cleve the Superficial," Jek said in a teasing cadence. "That's what I should call you...caring about silly titles." He let out a laugh. "I never would've figured you would."

"Everyone has a guilty pleasure."

"Is that true?"

"Of course."

"Then what's mine?" Jek asked, genuinely curious.

"You're overconfident and take pleasure in getting out of tricky situations, so you push boundaries until you've meddled your way into something you shouldn't have."

Cleve thought it might've been humorous to tease Jek about his rash decision-making. But the moment he finished speaking, it felt as if he'd been too accurate for it to be taken as a joke. He really did mean everything he'd said...which was a mistake.

Before he thought to apologize, Jek retorted with a smile, "Says the man who attacked his own castle with an army of rats."

"So you've heard about that."

"Jessend loves to share."

Cleve felt his heart jumping in his chest. Did she tell others of their private conversations about loss...about deep sorrow...about true weakness? He couldn't stand the thought of someone knowing how weak he'd been—how weak he could be in any given moment when the sting of death came back to his thoughts, wrapping around his body like chains, squeezing all the strength out of him.

The question of whether or not she'd told someone was burning in his brain, stealing all his focus.

So he gave up trying to ignore it, letting it dwell in his mind and falling silent until they reached the walls of the city.

The guards recognized Jek, letting him and Cleve through without question. At a slow pace, they rode their horses side by side down the King's Road.

"Cleve, I know I shouldn't ask, but I can't stop wondering something." Jek paused, allowing Cleve to decide whether or not he was willing to hear the question.

"What is it?"

"How likely is it that you'll be coming back?"

Cleve tried to glance to his side as subtly as possible, not wanting Jek to know he was examining his expression.

Jek kept his head straight ahead, though his eyes shifted to Cleve for a blink. Then Jek wiped his nose, as if suddenly self-conscious, and looked back ahead.

"I honestly don't know," Cleve said. "I don't want to tell you it's likely unless I know that for sure. I don't even know what the chances are that the chemist I told you about will know of a cure to your darkness. Then there's the war...it could last years, we could lose...I could die."

"Stop." Jek let out a defeated laugh. He started to say something, but no words came. Finally, he uttered, "I don't want to get back to the palace depressed from such a bleak conversation. I appreciate your honesty, always have."

Again, Jek started to say something but coughed instead, as if the words got caught on the way out. He cleared his throat and tried again.

"You saved my life...more than once. I would've suffered a terrible death from both the mookers and from Azaylee if it wasn't for you. You've already done more than I could ask for. And I don't know what would've happened to Harwin and Lisanda in that room if you weren't there."

Cleve was about to tell him to stop. It was too strange to be complemented so generously, especially with the crowded streets filled with listening ears. But Jek seemed to be finished. He was awkwardly quiet.

Then he cleared his throat again, following with, "I just wanted to say thank you and wish you the best of luck."

Cleve felt as if it was his turn to compliment Jek, but he was just as bad at giving them as he was at receiving them. Nothing came to mind. He knew the mage had done just as much to ensure that their mission was a success and that everyone came back alive, probably even more than Cleve had. But in that moment, with the bursting noise from the activity on the street, Cleve had no words for Jek.

It hit him how exhausted he truly was, how little sleep he'd been getting in the last few weeks. Having no idea what would come out, Cleve decided he just needed to start speaking.

"You have my thanks as well."

Discouraged, Cleve let that be it.

Or at least he thought so, until something else came to mind. "I have a feeling we'll meet again, whether it be if I come back here or I see you in Kyrro when the Takarys decide they want to take control of Ovira."

Cleve still didn't know how he would fix that dilemma. But there was too much else to worry about first for him to be concerned at that moment.

"I have the same feeling," Jek agreed with an embarrassed grin.

"So let us stop this sentimental talk," Cleve said.

Jek laughed. "So be it."

Chapter 31

Cleve and Jek both went around to the back of the palace to drop off their horses at the stables.

It was no surprise for Cleve to find Jessend there with Silvie. The Princess ran and jumped at him with such startling speed it scared Nulya into rearing up.

Trying to control the horse and deal with Jessend's flying body at the same time made Cleve fall hard on his back from her impact. He could see Nulya running off out of the corner of his eye, Silvie chasing after her and hollering for her to stop.

"It's gotten too easy to knock you off your feet," Jessend teased, climbing off Cleve and attempting to pull him up by wrapping her small hands around his right wrist and tugging with all her might.

Once he was upright, she went to her toes, and he leaned down to let her give him a kiss on the cheek.

"Lysha told us everything," Jessend said. "But we expected you back sooner. Did something happen after she left, or did it really just take that long for you to recover from the mooker bites?"

Cleve checked to make sure Silvie had Nulya under control. She did, walking his horse into the stables.

Lisanda came running then. Jek smartly stepped away from his mount before she jumped up into his arms and matched her lips with his.

"What took you so long?" Lisanda asked when the kiss was done.

"I was just asking the same thing," Jessend added.

"Is Rek back?" Cleve needed to know before getting into anything else.

"Yes," Jessend answered. "Just got to the palace yesterday.

He's been in quite a mood, doesn't want to tell anyone what happened with the Elves. Not that anyone really wants to be in the same room with him. His power is too scary."

Jek took the note from his pocket. "Lisanda, can you read this?"

She squinted curiously as she took it. Then her eyes widened excitedly. Her mouth gaped as her gaze traveled up and down the page in disbelief.

"Elvish?" Lisanda looked up at Jek. "Where did you get this?"

Jessend came around to peer over her sister's shoulder. Then she looked up as well, both of their large brown eyes waiting eagerly.

"Can you just read it first?" Jek asked. "Then I'll tell you the whole story."

Lisanda studied Jek for a moment, tilting her head as she did so. After her mouth scrunched, she looked down at the note again.

During their silence, Cleve watched the door to the palace. Just then, Rek came out to the horse range. Cleve couldn't help but smile, even if he'd wanted to hide it. There'd been a small fear he'd never see the Elf again, and he was only now able to admit that to himself.

As Rek came closer, Cleve noticed a line on his face. *A scar,* Cleve realized. It couldn't have been that new, a gash down his cheek, already completely closed up.

Jessend seemed to shy away from him when she noticed his presence, taking a noticeable step back. Lisanda looked up from the note for a moment and then did the same.

But Rek didn't look threatening at all, besides the scar. He had a wide smile. His hand was out, ready to be shaken. Cleve grabbed it firmly and didn't hold back his own grin.

"Glad to see you again," Rek said.

"Same here," Cleve agreed.

Just then Lisanda covered her mouth as she read, muffling a gasp.

"What is that?" Rek asked Cleve, pointing to the paper.

"A note in Elvish that we..." Cleve wasn't sure how to introduce it. "That we found...I guess."

Lisanda now had the note pressed against her bosom, a confused glare on her face. "Who wrote this note?" she asked Jek.

"A woman," Jek said. "A powerful psychic woman."

"She's writing to someone by the name of Fatholl."

"Fatholl?" Rek nearly shouted the name. He reached out for the note, and Lisanda nervously handed it over.

"It's in Elvish," she reminded him.

"Bastial hell!" Rek screamed, handing it back to her. "What does it say about Fatholl?"

Cleve hadn't seen Rek so flustered before. He grew nervous at the sight of it.

Lisanda's eyes found Rek's scar. They tried to avoid it but kept bouncing back. In an uneasy tone, she told him, "Whoever wrote this note seems to know him well. She discusses how many men she has, her riches in gold and weapons. She's inquiring about how much his army has grown since the last time they spoke. She asks specifically..." Lisanda glanced down at the note again, reading: "What is our first target, and when will you be ready?"

Lisanda took a moment to skim the note in silence. "That's it," she concluded, looking to Rek for answers.

He leaned forward. "Are you sure?"

The question somehow seemed dangerous to answer, the way he looked down at her, with his almond eyes shaped as slits.

Jek must've felt the same uneasiness that Cleve did. He stepped in front of Lisanda. "If she says that's it, then that's it."

Rek straightened his back, giving out a discouraged sigh. "I apologize for frightening you all. Ever since arriving in Meritar, I've grown a feeling I can't seem to get rid of—that everyone wants me either gone or dead. It's made me quite..." His hands went to his chin as he thought of the right word. "Easily annoyed...perhaps insensitive."

"The Elves gave you that scar?" Jessend bravely asked.

Rek's hand went to it unconsciously. "One Elf did when he tried to stop me from leaving." Rek passed a glance by each of their faces. "While all of you Humans are frightened of psyche and don't seem to understand it, the Elves just simply condemn it." Cleve noticed that Rek was now looking at him as he spoke, as if he didn't care who else heard as long as Cleve did. "They talk of psyche as a weapon they wish they'd never discovered."

A disgusted look came about Rek's face. "It's madness. At sword point, they demanded I offer some of my blood and swear an oath to never use psyche again."

"Did you..." Cleve let his voice trail off. A desperate tone came out that he'd wished to hide better. The thought of his strongest ally losing his psychic ability made panic and despair start swelling in his chest.

"Even if I did comply with their ridiculous blood oath, I wouldn't follow it. I have no plans of going back to Meritar. It's Fatholl I want to find." He pointed at the note, tapping his finger in the air with the corner of his mouth scrunched. "He and the Elves with him are the ones I really wish to speak to. I only found that out too late once I arrived in Meritar."

"Who are they?" Jek asked.

Rek made a fist to gesture with, grim determination in his tone. "With psyche being illegal in Meritar, a group of Elves had secret meetings to train out of sight. Their numbers grew, and rumors say they had plans to not only change the laws of Meritar when they had enough people on their side, but to free Greenedge from the desmarls—that was their ultimate goal."

Shock hit Cleve hard, buckling his knees for a breath. *Did I kill a woman who was intent on saving the continent from desmarls?*

Jek muttered something to himself that Cleve didn't catch.

He had his hand on his forehead.

"What's wrong with you two?" Rek asked.

Lisanda put her hand on Jek's back. "What happened?"

"It's just..." Jek went silent.

"We might've done something we're about to regret," Cleve said. It was too early, though. Cleve needed to hear the rest of what Rek had to say before passing judgment upon himself. "Please continue," Cleve asked him.

Rek took a breath to examine Cleve's hard eyes before speaking again. "The majority of Elves know their homeland is at no risk of being taken over by the desmarls. An active volcano sits north of Meritar, while miles of mountains cover the southern edge. Then there's Goldram and then Zav and Waywen even farther northwest. The Elves have walls thirty feet high around the city. No desmarls will be harassing anyone in Meritar, but at the same time the Elves are leaving the rest of the continent to fend for itself. Two hundred years from now, the Elves expect all of Greenedge to be covered by desmarls except for Meritar, and they plan to allow this to happen."

"I think most people already have assumed that," Jek said.

"They have," Lisanda agreed.

Rek raised a finger, his eyebrows arching as well. "Except there has been a small group of Elves who've always disagreed with this thought. In fact, my direct ancestors are those who left Meritar by ship to make a home in Ovira."

"Merejic," Cleve said aloud before thinking. When heads turned to him, he felt the need to continue. "There was a territory on the northwestern edge of Ovira where Elves lived. Rek was born there."

Rek nodded, continuing for Cleve. "But many were killed by an army of a different type, Krepps led by Doe and Haemon— there's no reason to get into that now. The surviving Elves fled on ship, back to Greenedge. But they weren't welcomed back into Meritar. They'd broken two rules: practicing psyche and leaving. They've taken up residence somewhere else."

Again, Rek made a fist. "Though I don't know where. The rest of the Elves who practiced psyche left to join them. Fatholl is known to be their leader. But there are some rumors that give insight to a controversial plan. Many in Meritar say this group of Elves wants to first take over the warring Human territories: Goldram, Zav, Waywen, and Presoren. Once they have control, then they can focus on building the army they need to sweep through the land, ridding it of desmarls for good." Rek was looking right at Cleve, as if ready to judge his actions.

Cleve felt chills coursing down his spine, for he knew it was his turn next, time to explain what he'd done.

"That's all I know." The Elf's voice was nearly a whisper.

Jek spoke for Cleve. "She was going to kill me." He held out his palms. "We had to do it."

"Who?" Lisanda took his cheek in her palm to turn him toward her.

"Golden girl...she exists," Jek said, taking her hand to hold. "Well, she did."

The Takary sisters each gasped.

"From the song?" Lisanda asked incredulously.

"No," Jessend uttered in a grunt. "Can't be."

"It was her," Jek said, enclosing his other hand around Lisanda's. "She was the leader of some village in southern Zav. She was probably somewhere in her fifties but still such a powerful psychic."

"What's this song that she's part of it?" Rek asked.

The mage let go of Lisanda's hand as he told the story of the four sisters—the youngest being "Golden Girl," named for the color of her hair. Unable to meet her family's expectations, she traveled to Meritar to live with the Elves, eventually learning the secrets of psyche. When she returned, she was feared and outcast, never to be seen again.

"She ended up in that village somehow," Jek said. "But based on that note, I'd wager she'd lived with Fatholl and the other psychic Elves at some point. She clearly was involved with them. She even admitted how her name would be famous again, her new name: Azaylee. She wanted to hide her old self so much she was willing to kill me for discovering it. But Cleve saved me."

Jessend seemed to figure out what Jek was saying. She covered her mouth, her wide eyes looking up at Cleve.

Then she let her hand drop to whisper, "You killed her."

Cleve couldn't answer with words, not at that moment. He took in a slow breath instead, then nodded.

"I didn't realize she wished to fight the desmarls," Cleve said, guilt making his words feel too much like an excuse for his liking.

"But that doesn't matter!" Jek grabbed his shoulder. "Don't ever regret what you did. She brought this on herself. She was going to kill me!"

Lisanda gestured with the note. "And it sounds like she and Fatholl had plans to take over the Human territories before they fight the desmarls. Remember, this note is about finding their first target. They're probably referring to a city."

"You're right," Rek said. "It goes along with everything I heard in Meritar before I made it out of there." Rek's mouth twisted as if he needed to spit. "My own kind in Meritar tried to kill me, and those who've separated themselves from Meritar—many of whom are my kin from Ovira—have plans to fight against the Humans. I don't know what to think of my fellow Elves. It's too much to consider at once."

"Rek," Cleve said to take his friend's attention before thoughts of despair continued to confuse him. "I know what you're feeling. I've felt much of the same conflict myself recently from being here. But I've come to realize that we can't fight two wars at once. Let's worry about Kyrro first. Then we can discuss other matters."

Cleve turned to face the others, Jessend specifically. "I

apologize that there isn't more we can do to help. But the war in Ovira is our priority—"

Jessend took his hand to interrupt him. "We understand. You don't need to explain." She went to her toes to kiss his check. "But I have a feeling this isn't the last we'll see of each other," she said with a sly grin.

Cleve knew then that it was wrong of him not to trust Jessend to keep their talks to herself. She wouldn't tell others of his moments of weakness. It was silly to even worry.

"Go home, Cleve," Jek said with cheery smile. "We can take care of things here."

"The King has already prepared a ship and a crew," Rek stated. "We just need a captain because no one would volunteer to sail a ship across the Starving Ocean and back, and the King isn't going to force anyone on his staff to do it. He'll agree to pay, if we find someone."

"What about Captain Mmzaza?" Cleve asked.

"I thought of him, but I don't know where he is." Rek's tone was sad, as if he were telling Cleve the old madman had died.

"Have you checked the prison?" Cleve asked.

Some spirit came back into Rek's face, his grin forming once again. "Prison, of course." He looked to the Takary sisters. "Has anyone checked?"

"No," Jessend answered first. "I suppose we found him in prison in Kyrro. It wouldn't be too surprising for him to be locked up again."

"I'm sure he's there," Cleve said.

Chapter 32

Sure enough, the prison guard in the depths of the palace knew exactly who Captain Mmzaza was.

"The man's been in here for weeks," the guard answered, opening the metal grille to the prison so the jailer could take them the rest of the way.

"Weeks?" Jessend said with a laugh, taking Cleve's hand on the way down the stairs. "He must've been imprisoned soon after we got here."

The air was cool but stale, reminding Cleve of his short time in a cell below King Welson Kimard's castle. He wondered what the chances were he would end up back there.

Surely the King of Kyrro hadn't changed his mind about Cleve and Rek. Cleve would need to prove himself first, and he would have to figure out a way to do so before the King knew he was back.

"He's over there," the jailer told them, pointing with his lantern to one of the cells.

"Who's 'der?" The old captain's voice echoed against the walls, his strange manner of speaking more prevalent than ever. "These bars are too thin for Captain Mmzaza to put his head through."

Cleve showed himself, Jessend at his side.

"What did you do now?" Cleve asked, not sure he wanted to know, as the captain was coming with them no matter what.

Captain Mmzaza slapped his knee, giving off a shaky laugh. "Hohoho, if it isn't the giant boy who wouldn't know a joke if it bedded his mother."

Not even understanding the analogy, Cleve instantly remembered how easily Captain Mmzaza could get on his nerves.

"And his beauty's here as well!" Captain Mmzaza reached through the bars as if to take Jessend's hand for a kiss.

Shockingly to Cleve, she let him have it with a smile. He puckered his lips and kissed her loudly three times. She pulled back before he was ready to let go.

"Aren't you delicious!" Captain Mmzaza said. "Though, I must complain. This prison of your father's will make a man mad, even one already as mad as me. The light is low, the food grim, the shitter too small, and the meals—oh, the meals! We only get two per day. Two meals for Captain Mmzaza is one too few, especially when all there is to do is eat and shit."

The old man snapped his head back as if suddenly realizing something. "Are you here to get Captain Mmzaza out?"

"Perhaps." Jessend turned to the jailer. "Why is he in here?"

"He smashed some street merchant's melons, made a terrible mess."

"He was trying to sell me rancid fruit!" Captain Mmzaza interjected.

The jailer ignored him and continued. "Then he refused to pay and got in a scuffle with a few guards."

"They put their hands on me!" Captain Mmzaza yelled.

"That's when he started to spit."

"No one puts their hands on Captain Mmzaza!"

"I see," Jessend said. "Well, I'll come back with my father's papers for his release."

"Thank you, me pretty. Thank you!"

"And then you're steering the ship back to Gendock," Cleve added. "That's the only reason you're being released."

"Good. Captain Mmzaza doesn't like this place anyway." Cleve was curious how much of it he'd actually seen before being imprisoned...but not curious enough to ask.

He went with Jessend to meet with her father one last time, his fingertips grazing the handle of his chipped sword several times on the way there.

They were informed by guards that Danvell Takary was already in the throne room.

Jek was just leaving by the time Cleve got there, Lisanda hooked around his arm as they walked down the hall, unaware Cleve and Jessend were behind them.

The guards let him inside. Jessend came in with him.

Danvell stood to smile at her. "Do you mind if I speak to Cleve alone?"

"Alright." She patted Cleve's stomach before leaving.

With the door shut behind him, Cleve noticed there weren't even any guards left. It was just him and the King of Goldram.

"Can I see your sword?" Danvell asked, not yet sitting back down on his throne, but stepping forward instead.

Cleve felt some nervousness sparking within his chest as he pulled it from its sheath. The King let out a breath. It wasn't quite a gasp, but close.

"Lysha told me everything that happened before leaving you and Jek...and Jek has just finished telling me the rest."

"So he told you what happened to this weapon?" Cleve asked.

"No. But the young mage isn't as good as you at keeping information hidden," Danvell said. "I asked him how you both got out of the village with everyone chasing you, and he told me he held everyone back while you broke through the gate. But then his face froze. I could tell he'd already said more than he wanted to. I had a feeling you had to use the sword to get through the gate and had damaged my gift to you. I listen to a lot of tales, Cleve. I know when people are keeping things from me. Were you not going to tell me?"

"I wasn't," Cleve admitted. "I didn't want you to believe I would mistreat the weapon if I had a choice."

Danvell laughed as if Cleve had said something amusing. "I realize we haven't met too long ago, but I do feel as if I know you, Cleve Polken, son of Dex Polken," he said. "I know your father also, at least the story of him. And I know your mother was a mage, Lena Polken. I know they were both killed when you were still a boy, their bodies found impaled by arrows with the shooter undiscovered."

He looked from the sides of his eyes, sly and cunning for the first time, reminding Cleve of Jessend. "You might think my daughters and I don't speak much, but we do. Jessend's told me a lot about you, yet none of it has surprised me. I saw your true self the first day we met, and nothing you've done has diminished the impression you gave me. I know you would never mistreat a gift, you would never mistreat Jessend, and you will always do what you think to be right, as hard as it might be. This is obvious to anyone who meets you, Cleve."

The King paced behind his throne and leaned down to get something. "I was going to give this to you anyway, even if you hadn't chipped my first gift." He came back with an extremely long sword in a leather sheath dyed black. It shone in the light dancing from the lamps—now the only light of the palace with the sun completely set.

Danvell handed it to Cleve without drawing the sword. "Go ahead, take a look," he said with a knowing grin.

The bright Bastial steel seemed to flicker as Cleve pulled it from its case. The weapon was the longest sword he'd ever wielded, but it was still lighter than any short sword he'd felt. There was a slight bend to it, like the curve from a woman's hip to her ankle.

He gave it a slash, then another. It seemed to cut the air, it was so sharp. It even made a different noise than normal steel, a lighter sound, like a quiet breeze whispering.

Cleve even noticed an aroma.

As awkward as it was, he sniffed the weapon. It smelled like a mixture of soap and blood, beauty and gore—for that's what it was, he realized. The most stunning weapon he'd ever seen, yet the destruction he could deal with it was startling.

"I don't deserve such a kingly gift," he admitted. "Why are you giving it to me?"

The King lowered his hand for Cleve's old, chipped weapon. "Think of it as an upgrade, not a gift," Danvell said as he accepted the other sword. "I want you to think of me whenever you use it. Think of our agreement."

Danvell started toward a table a few steps away. "You'll do everything in your power to make the transition peaceful when my army comes to Ovira...both you and Rek will do this as long as Jessend and Lisanda agree to the plan I propose." Danvell waved Cleve over, pointing at a contract and handing him a quill. "You'll sign this agreement, and you'll follow it, correct?"

Cleve nodded. "I'm in your debt," he said. "I just hope you won't assist Tenred and the Krepps in this war against my people in Kyrro."

"No, of course not," Danvell answered. "And there's too much to do here for that to even be a worry. Our war is of a far greater scale than yours. There's no way we'll be done first."

Especially not with an army of psychic Elves yet to introduce themselves. "Did Jek tell you about the Elvish note?"

"Yes, I heard about the Elves." Danvell's steady eyes were solemn. "Jek's on his way to discuss it further with Micah Vail. I'll be joining them once we're finished here." The King looked at the dark sky out the window. "They say there's a storm coming tomorrow morning. You should leave before then or you might be stuck here until it passes. Are you ready?"

Cleve was about to say that he'd been ready to leave since the first day he'd arrived, but not only would it be an insult, it wasn't true. He was a different man now. It felt as if his former self was a child—eager to fight when he hadn't even killed a man, when he hadn't even figured out how to overcome the torment that his parents' death caused him.

His weakness was ignored before...that was his way of staying strong. But now, he actually could feel his strength, the same strength Reela found within him. It was there, burning to be used like a live flame daring to be put out.

"I am," he answered.

"Then this is goodbye."

They shook hands.

"For now," Cleve added.

Danvell gave a chuckle. "For now," he agreed.

Cleve's final goodbyes with Jessend, Lisanda, Jek, and Micah were simple hugs and handshakes, along with promises they would see each other again.

Jessend's servant, Gerace, escorted him out.

Not knowing what to say to her, Cleve simply stated, "Thank you for your help."

"I'm proud to be of service," she answered confidently, her subtle smile holding great honor. "You remember how to say my name?" Gerace teased, though Cleve could tell there was a seriousness to her question he didn't quite understand, as if she actually was worried he'd forgotten.

"Gerace, Gerace, Gerace," he answered, saying it three times just to show how confident he was.

She applauded excitedly.

At the door, they shared an awkward hug, then she ran off at full speed, nearly colliding with two guards patrolling toward them.

I'll never understand women, was all Cleve could take from it.

Outside, the storm was preparing to strike, the air already wet with oncoming rain.

Silvie and Rek were at the base of the stone steps. Rek got on his mount at the sight of Cleve. Silvie shook Cleve's hand before passing off Nulya's reins.

"How have you and Jessend been?" Cleve asked.

Silvie's lips twisted into a wry smile. "Very good."

"Let's go, Cleve," Rek said. "We don't have much time, and they've already taken Captain Mmzaza and a small crew of sailors to the docks. I don't feel comfortable leaving him alone."

"You're right." Cleve climbed on Nulya's back, allowing

Silvie to help him up even though he didn't need it.

"Take care of Jessend," Cleve told her.

"We'll take care of each other," Silvie answered.

Leaving the palace grounds, Cleve realized he was sad to go. But then thoughts of his house in the Academy sprouted up, and he felt himself smiling. He had no idea where he would put Nulya, but he didn't care. He would figure it out.

He was going home.

Chapter 33

The boat Danvell Takary had given them was no great ship, especially not to Captain Mmzaza. Once everyone was aboard and the horses safely stowed in the cabin, the gnarled old seaman claimed, "I've dropped vessels mightier than this one into a chamber pot."

Cleve was about to tell him that he should just be happy he was free, but then Cleve remembered Jessend doing the same to him when she'd put him on a boat in Gendock.

"I'll be back. The rowers need a good shouting," Captain Mmzaza said, making his way over to them. "If we're going to beat this storm, they'd better be rowing all night!" he yelled over his shoulder.

Cleve decided to make himself comfortable in his shared cabin with Rek. There was a lot of sleep that needed catching up on.

The Elf was already inside, removing his belt. "You're going to have to tell me everything that happened after I left," Rek said. "Apparently I missed a lot."

"I suppose that's true."

Rek put his hand on Cleve's shoulder, showing a brotherly smile. "We did it. We're going back, and I have you to thank. The Elves were no help at all."

Cleve felt a spark in his mind, the familiar touch of psyche. Rek's hand came off quickly, as if the spark had reached him as well.

"You've grown even stronger than when we were last on a ship together," Rek said. "I think you're finally ready for the truth."

Sleep could wait—what was Rek talking about? Cleve knew he didn't even need to ask. His face was already showing his confusion.

"How is it you don't know what I'm referring to?" Rek asked genuinely.

Then it struck Cleve...*my parents. He knows about their deaths.* He and Rek had discussed it briefly when they'd first met. *When he looked into my mind on the hill outside his cabin.* There was something the King of Kyrro had told Rek that he didn't wish to let slip.

"I'm ready," Cleve answered confidently. *I was ready weeks ago.*

But Rek's expression made Cleve already begin to question his confidence. The Elf looked to be on the verge of crying.

What's this? It made Cleve so uneasy, he couldn't stand still. He had to pace the small cabin as he waited for Rek to gather his thoughts.

"I never thought how hard it would be to tell you." Rek sat on his bed, giving a loud exhale. "I was so worried for *you*, I didn't realize how difficult it was going to be for me just to say it."

"Say it." Cleve felt his fists clenching, suddenly having an idea what must be so hard to tell him. "Did Welson Kimard kill my parents?" His voice was becoming angry, louder as well. He could hear it, but he couldn't stop. "Did the King of Kyrro order the deaths of my mother and father?"

When Rek was unable to look up from the floor, Cleve knew the answer.

But why?

Cleve waited as patiently as he could, but it was impossibly difficult when he had no clue as to when Rek would answer him.

Soon he was shouting. "Why, Rek? Tell me!"

Rek reached out toward Cleve's arm. "I think it would be wise if I calmed you before continuing."

Cleve stepped back, snapping his arm away. "I don't want to be calm. Just tell me what you know and leave the rest up to me."

Rek was nodding sullenly. "That's a good plan, at least to begin." He took a breath and then stood, still unable to meet Cleve's eyes. "When Welson summoned me, it was because of the worries he'd received from students and teachers at the Academy. Gossip spread throughout Kyrro City as well, that I was dangerously powerful. As I've told you, people are scared of what they don't understand, and everyone has secrets and even more doubts."

The Elf gave another sigh, so long and slow Cleve felt the urge to interrupt it by demanding that Rek continue. Though, he was able to contain himself and remain silent, tapping his foot impatiently as he waited.

Rek continued. "Welson had a few secrets he was so worried I would discover, they were bubbling at the surface of each thought. I could barely focus on anything else, they were so strong. It was as if I could feel them."

Rek finally met Cleve's eyes. "Remember, during my time in the castle, Welson was always frightened of me—of his *younger brother*." Rek laughed bitterly. "But there was something different about this fear I was sensing. I hadn't seen him in years. What had he done that he was so worried I would discover? My curiosity got the better of me, and I started fishing, working to get the information out of him. I was certain it had to do with me, or at least with the reason behind summoning me. There had to be something else behind my visit besides mere worries and complaints from his citizens. But I was wrong. There were *other* secrets he was trying to hide."

Rek eyes were glistening. He closed them for a breath as he continued. "That was the first and last time I've ever prodded the truth out of someone based on my own selfish curiosity, and I shouldn't have even done it that once. As much as I despise Welson for the unfairness in the way he's treated me, I do care for him. I feel his pain, his guilt, and his worries, especially after that meeting."

"What happened?" Cleve asked.

Rek unconsciously rubbed the scar on his cheek. "Welson blames himself for the war of Ovira. There was an incident at his doing that could be looked at as the reason peace could never be reached between Kyrro and Tenred. But remember, Welson came into his kingship with a shaky relationship already existing between Kyrro and Tenred due to some issues his father had with them." Rek shook his head. "He takes far too much of the blame upon himself."

Cleve still hadn't decided how much blame he would attribute to Welson Kimard. First he needed to hear of his parents.

"With the only ironbark trees being in southern Kyrro, Tenred offered a tremendous amount of iron to trade for them," Rek continued. "These trades went well until Welson Kimard's father, Westin, traded boats to Tenred, and then two of the boats ended up sinking from what was theorized to be rotten wood, killing the crews aboard. Without proof, and with neither territory being unable to win a war against the other, Tenred had no choice but to forgive Kyrro. Only a few could say if it was really sincere or not, just as only a few knew of the incident between Kyrro and Tenred that happened years later...after Westin was killed and Welson took over as king.

"Welson's father was never interested in the small islands around Ovira, but Welson was, especially when Tegry—the King of Tenred—was sending out ship after ship to explore them. There were a few minor problems that ensued first, some near crashes and arguments, but nothing major. That is, until one of Welson's ships arrived at an undiscovered island with Tegry's ship already there.

"Welson's men had orders to kill only if they were attacked or if they believed a battle was likely to occur over the discovery of rich resources. And there was a battle on this island, with Welson's men of Kyrro winning. Only...there was nothing on the island to show for it, and there was no proof that Tegry's men had shown any aggression. Assassinations and poisoning attempts increased greatly after that incident."

Rek cleared his throat. "From then on, Welson knew war was coming. He just didn't know when."

"What does that have to do with my parents?" Cleve couldn't wait any longer. Although all of this information was new to him, there were other answers he needed.

Rek shook his head. His hair had gotten longer in the time he'd spent in Greenedge, with it now hanging to his shoulder blades.

"That was Welson's first guilty incident that I discovered...that I practically pulled out of him while searching for something about myself. His next secret was about your parents." Rek paused to look at Cleve, as if to judge if he was ready.

Then the Elf continued. "He was a young king, Cleve. He admitted to me in that room that he'd made mistakes and that his deepest regret was what happened with your parents, for he let his emotions take control when he made the decision to...ki—" The word got stuck.

Rek plopped back onto the bed. "I'm sorry, Cleve. This is going to be hard to hear. Perhaps this wasn't the best time—with us on the way back to defend the kingdom of the man who I'm talking about."

Just say it, Cleve almost shouted. "I don't need to care about him to defend the people in Kyrro."

"I want you to promise me something," Rek said, "because the need for revenge is what caused the initial separation between Tenred and Kyrro, even what caused the war that we're now fighting. And revenge is the reason for the death of your parents. Promise me you won't take it out on our king. You can wish it. You can dream about it. But you will not act upon it. Promise me, Cleve."

Cleve tried to imagine being in the same room as his

parents' killer, wondering how it would feel. It wasn't easy, especially when he'd never thought about it before.

When just the thought of his parents had caused such misery, he couldn't bring himself to consider the one who'd killed them alive and breathing in the same room as him.

But now he could; he had the strength to do so without the deep pain of loss crippling him for hours after. It was Welson's face he saw, wide and thin-nosed. But to his surprise, the King of Kyrro wasn't snickering or smiling balefully. He was filled with sorrow, regret, suffering from the same despair that Cleve often had felt when thoughts of his parents resurfaced from wherever he'd buried them.

He could let the monarch live...so long as he repented. "If I discover that the man responsible for my parents' death already suffers from remorse, then I can make this promise." Cleve was careful to say no more.

"That's fine. I don't know who actually committed the murders, only the one who set them up. And I know the King does regret it. Even when I saw him again, with you beside me, after all his practice resisting psyche, his worries and guilt were still there. Welson Kimard ordered the death of your father, and he'll never forgive himself for it."

Cleve already had assumed this, but there was something Rek said that surprised him. "You only mentioned my father just now. What of my mother?"

"He didn't order the death of your mother. That was an accident."

Cleve was shocked to find himself more curious than angry. "What happened?"

"When Welson Kimard became king, he was only fifteen years old, and his father had just been murdered. He couldn't focus on anything but finding the man who shot the arrow that struck his father in the heart. He told me that your father did it, Cleve. Dex Polken was the one to kill Welson's father."

"That can't be!" Cleve knew his father was no murderer,

certainly not someone to commit treason.

Rek held out his palms. "I can't say whether or not it's the truth, just that Welson was not lying when he said he was certain."

Overwhelmed by confusion, Cleve felt as if the room was doing more than just swaying from the waves below them. It was spinning.

He decided it might be a good idea to sit.

Rubbing his eyes, he tried to focus on what he was feeling, but nausea had taken over, the same question repeating over and over: *What could've happened for Welson to believe that Dex had killed his father?*

Cleve couldn't even consider the concept that his father really had assassinated a king. The father he knew never would've done such a thing. Chills nearly stopped his heart as he remembered his conversation with the King of Kyrro the first time he met him—when his bow was leaning against the throne as he was questioned.

The King had told him that his father had shot at a man. *He really does believe Dex killed his father, and he wanted to see what I knew of it.*

"If Welson believes my father killed his father, then why would he have my parents honored with a burial in Kyrro City instead of in their hometown of Trentyre?" Cleve asked.

Rek shrugged slowly, as if apologizing for not knowing. "Maybe he wanted to see their bodies for himself? Or maybe he already felt remorseful and wished to pay them respect? Who knows?"

"How did my mother end up being killed?"

"I didn't ask," Rek said. "We were too busy yelling at each other. Remember, this was just before he exiled me. All I know about your mother is that she was with your father when he was killed, and I know that Welson didn't expect her to be there. Welson had sent your father out of Kyrro on some sort of task, and assassins were waiting for him to be out of the territory before they struck so that it could look like Tenred might've been responsible. Your mother and father either went together, or she followed him on her own and he didn't know it. Whatever it was, they were both shot down."

Cleve stood back up, feeling himself again. "Who is the man who did it?"

"I didn't ask that, either. I didn't know you and I would ever meet, Cleve. The only reason this came out was because I thought Welson's secrets were about me. But they weren't. The guilt of his decision has aged him twice what the years alone have done. He doesn't think he's fit to be king. He'd never admit it aloud, but he hates the task that was given to him. I think the part of the job he despises the most is that every decision he makes is part of history."

Rek's finger traced his scar, and soon he began to scratch. "When Welson was younger, he was always fond of the history of kings and their mark on the world. But being suddenly thrown into that role before he was ready...and with the death of his father being the catalyst..."

Rek took his time, breathing slowly and then letting the air out in a sigh. "Anyone would've made mistakes under that pressure. I'm just sorry it had to be at the expense of you and your parents."

Cleve was suddenly aware of his exhaustion. His anger was gone for now, replaced by a weighty sadness that made his eyelids heavy. He let himself down on his back, putting his forearm over his eyes to help comfort him.

His other hand went to his stomach in the same way Jessend had placed her hand there. "Is that all you know?" Cleve asked, still unsure of what he thought.

"It is," Rek answered, blowing out the lamp.

In the darkness, Cleve felt alone. He was caught between worlds. On the outside, he was between Ovira and Greenedge, on the inside, between resentment and sorrow.

"I would ask what you're feeling right now," Rek said. "But

the better question is to wonder what you'll be feeling five days from now when we reach Kyrro."

"If I had the answer to that, I would tell you."

"Because we need the King as much as he needs us. He isn't a bad ruler."

"I know that," Cleve said.

"I realize my prodding is frustrating you, but I want you to remember the lack of anger you have at this moment for Welson Kimard. Because when you see him again, you won't feel the same. He's smart enough to know I will have told you the truth, so he'll be watching you closely, making it easy for something to spark an argument. It might be a gesture or a look, maybe even something one of you says, but there will be something."

Rek paused to take a breath. "There is anger within you, Cleve—anger for him specifically. I can't sense it with psyche, it's too deep, but I know it must be there. And that kind of anger doesn't fade on its own. It'll come out when you see him again...and you will see him again."

By the time the Elf had finished, Cleve knew he was right. There was anger deep down, and it was solely for the King of Kyrro.

"It's best if we avoid him as long as possible," Rek added. "We need time to prove ourselves so that he won't throw us in prison again. We might have to take up arms against Tenred or the Krepps on our own. If we're found in the Academy or one of the cities in Kyrro, we might be detained."

Cleve hadn't considered himself and Rek marching into enemy territory on their own. But again, the Elf was right. They couldn't risk being seen until their loyalty had been proven...and that was one way to go about doing it.

"We'll take all the time we need," Cleve agreed. "But no matter how long it takes, I'm not sure it will ever change the way I think about Welson Kimard."

Cleve must've been asleep when Rek finally responded, for he woke to the Elf calling his name.

"Cleve, Cleve? Did you hear me?"

"Can't you tell if I'm awake or asleep with psyche?" Rek grunted. "I'm tired. Psyche takes effort."

"What was your question?"

"You said you're not sure time will change how you feel about our king. But you promised you won't kill him."

But Cleve had been careful in his responses to Rek throughout their conversation. There were a few simple words he'd made sure to avoid...it was a bad idea to reveal this to Rek, he knew, but he was too tired to think of something better.

"I never actually promised I wouldn't kill him," Cleve said.

Rek began to say something, but his breath just came out as the start of a surprised whisper, nothing intelligible.

The sound of the ship rocking was all that could be heard as Cleve started drifting back to sleep. Then Rek muttered something that was barely loud enough for him to understand.

"Oh, Bastial hell."

End of Book 2

The Series Continues

The next novel in the series follows the same perspectives as in Book 1, *Bastial Energy*: Effie, Steffen, Zoke, and Zeti (and possibly Cleve...). The timeline of the novel begins around the same time as Cleve's journey did in *Bastial Steel*.

Jek and the Takarys will be back later in the series.

Author Information

I would love to hear from you. All feedback is welcome.
Please email me at btnarro@gmail.com

Visit btnarro.com to view maps and other info on the Rhythm of Rivalry series.

Acknowledgements

Getting into the minds of Cleve and Jessend involved exploring many feelings and affairs that I myself have had little to no experience with. Therefore, I want to thank my friends who so patiently helped answer my interminable questions, as personal as they were.

To my editor: I didn't think I would get even more stubborn and demanding by the third novel, but I have. Thank you for your unending patience and hard work.

To KMM: for your enthusiasm and vigor. Thank you for your continued support and feedback, and for your wonderfully helpful comments on this novel.

To MJV: I strongly believe everyone needs a friend like you. Your support toward my writing and your all-around life advice has been invaluable...and at least comical when it hasn't.

To anyone who has recommended one of my novels to a friend, written me an email with their feedback, or written a review, thank you. Having my novels read, shared, discussed, and, of course, enjoyed is a dream come true.

Made in the USA
Middletown, DE
06 September 2023